THE Gypsy Crown

The spellbinding adventures of two daring
children, a monkey, a dog and a dancing bear

THE GYPSY CROWN

KATE FORSYTH

■SCHOLASTIC

First published in 2008 by Scholastic Children's Books
An imprint of Scholastic Ltd
Euston House, 24 Eversholt Street
London, NW1 1DB, UK
Registered office: Westfield Road, Southam, Warwickshire, CV47 0RA
SCHOLASTIC and associated logos are trademarks and/or registered trademarks
of Scholastic Inc.

10 digit ISBN 1 407 10239 7
13 digit ISBN 978 1407 10239 9

Printed by GGP Media GmbH, Poessneck
Papers used by Scholastic Children's Books are made from wood
grown in sustainable forests.

1 3 5 7 9 10 8 6 4 2

www.scholastic.co.uk/zone

For Emily and Ben, the original cheeky monkeys.
May your names live forever.

PART ONE

The Gypsy Crown

The Owl Cried

Thornton Heath, Surrey, England
12 August 1658

"I heard the owl cry last night," Maggie Finch said, her gnarled hands clenched on her shawl. "That means a death to come."

Stooped, black-eyed, with a high-bridged nose and wild grizzled hair, Maggie was often called the Queen of the Gypsies, for her fame as a fortune-teller had spread wide. "I don't think you should go to the fair today," she said. "Stay safe in the woods."

All her grandchildren cried out in disappointment. "No, Baba! Let us go to the fair! We've never been before. Let us go!"

Only Emilia did not protest. A thin, brown girl with tangled black curls, she was crouched at the foot of an oak tree, trying to coax a squirrel to come and take an acorn from her hand. Emilia was a wheedler, a charmer, a whistler of animals, what the gypsies called a *gule romni*. She could cozen a halfpenny from the meanest

3

fishwife, a smile from farmers, and birds from the tree into her hand. It was a gift much prized by the Rom.

Much as Emilia longed to go to the fair, she believed absolutely in her grandmother's premonitions. "You heard what Baba said. The cry of the owl means death. . ."

". . .for mice and voles," her cousin Luka said, grinning.

Emilia rolled her eyes. Of all of her family, Luka was the one who paid the least heed to their baba, often forgetting the respect she was due as *shuvani* of the tribe. He was as curious and cheeky as his monkey, Zizi, who crouched on his shoulder as always, pushing his hat to a rakish angle so she could hold on to his ear with her paw.

"But we need to raise the bride money for Beatrice somehow," Luka's father, Jacob, said, the worry-lines on his weather-beaten face deeper than ever. "How else are we to raise the money if we don't go to the fair?"

Emilia's sister, Beatrice, blushed pink as a peony. Jacob gave her a reassuring smile. "You're worth every penny, darling girl," he said. "Don't you fret."

"I'd feel safer if we just went back to Norwood," Maggie said. "The squire will give us work."

"Aye, digging ditches for a few pennies a day," Jacob said. "It'll take us a year to raise the gold for Beatrice. Yet if we go into Kingston on fair day, we could earn ten times as much, twenty times as much, if we're lucky. It's the only market for miles around, you know that.

Sweetheart can dance, and Luka can play his fiddle, and you can tell the *gorgios'* fortunes. . ."

"I will not go to town today," Maggie said. "I tell you, death lies ahead."

Jacob was silent. "For us?" he asked at last.

Maggie looked slowly round at them all. "Nay. I don't see the shadow on any of you. But still I think you shouldn't go. The Rom should keep to the Rom."

"Except none of the Rom have gold in their pockets," Jacob pointed out. "We won't go for long. Just a little wander through to test the temper of the town."

"It's market day," Luka cried. "Everyone's happy on market day, aren't they?"

"There are some people in this world who are never happy," Maggie replied.

"Then we need to go to the fair to cheer them up," Luka declared. He seized his fiddle from the ground and played an infectious tune. At once Zizi leapt off his shoulder and began to turn rapid cartwheels all around the camp. A huge brown bear that lay sleeping in the shade sat up, then got ponderously to her feet, her eyes brightening in anticipation. For Sweetheart the bear, music meant dancing, and dancing meant applause and praise and nice things to eat.

The joyful music lifted everyone's spirits.

"There'd be fish from the river," Jacob said. "Happen we could barter with the fishmongers."

"Sweets," Luka's little sister, Mimi, cried, clasping her hands together.

5

"I need some new clothes for Emilia," Luka's mother, Silvia, said. "I do wish you'd not run wild in the woods, Milly! You're not a boy; you shouldn't go climbing trees and galloping that horse of yours around as if you were."

Emilia and Luka grinned at each other. They were only three weeks apart in age and had been brought up together as brother and sister, since both Emilia's parents were dead. Luka's parents were sorry for Emilia and her family, and so were always kind and indulgent towards them. Two years older than Emilia, Beatrice was a sweet, biddable girl, quite content to stay near the campfire with her Aunt Silvia, while Emilia's younger brother, Noah, liked to stay where the sounds and smells were familiar, since he had lost his sight when he was four, from the smallpox that had killed the children's mother.

Emilia was quite as adventurous as Luka, however. The two of them spent their days roaming the forest, tickling for trout in the streams, making bows and arrows out of bits of old sticks and practising their handstands and cartwheels, Emilia hitching her skirts up in her sash.

"But is it safe?" Beatrice asked. "I don't want you all to risk yourselves for me. I don't need to get married right away. Sebastien and I can wait." She hesitated a little over the name of her betrothed, who belonged to another gypsy clan, the Hearnes. Sebastien and Beatrice had met only the night before.

"You're fifteen already," Silvia scolded. "High time you were married."

"The Major-General is gone," Jacob said. "Surely the people of Kingston will be glad for a bit of song and dance after all the gloom of these last few years? It used to be a merry town, I remember."

"It's not as if it's a Roundhead town," Luka said, "with a name like *King*ston."

Everyone snorted with laughter. So many inns and villages had changed their names after the civil war that a great deal of confusion had been caused all over the country. No one wanted to be considered Royalist, though, with Cromwell and his army rounding up and beheading anyone who expressed sympathy for the dead king.

"Daya, you've got all those baskets you made this summer," Mimi said to her mother. "You could maybe sell the lot."

"If we leave now, we'll be home by sunset," Silvia said, untying her apron from about her waist. Everyone knew that she was the true power in the family, despite her soft figure and sweet face. All the children began to shout with joy and Luka turned cartwheels all round the camp, Zizi tumbling head over heels behind him. She did not know why Luka was so excited, but she shared in all his emotions as always.

Emilia had never been to a market fair. She had been only four years old when the old king had had his head cut off, and they had not travelled away from the Great North Wood since. She had never even seen a big town. She ran smiling to change her skirt. She had only two; a patched brown one for everyday wear, and a pink flounced skirt of many colours, for feast days and special occasions.

A year ago the Finch family would not have risked leaving the safety of the wood. Life had always been hard for the gypsies, who lived to their own rhythm and their own rules, but since Oliver Cromwell had seized control, life had been drabber, and more dangerous, than ever. Under his rule, it was not safe or seemly to love bright colours, nor music, nor dancing, nor magic, nor any of the things that the gypsies most loved, and which made them who they were.

Under Lord Protector Cromwell, the land was controlled by twelve Major-Generals. It had been their job to arrest anyone found singing or swearing or drinking or dancing. Christmas had been banned, and the smell of roast goose on Christmas Day would bring the Major-Generals to break down the door and arrest all those feasting within. Maypoles had been cut down all over the country, theatres had been closed, and horse-racing and football were banned. It was said the Major-Generals even patrolled the streets, making women scrub their faces free of make-up. In Suffolk, thirteen gypsies had been hanged simply for being gypsies.

Yet the Major-Generals were gone now. Cromwell had been forced to dismiss them or lose the support of the common people. The Finch family had heard accounts of maypoles being put up in spring. If people dared to dance about a maypole, which the Puritans thought a most ungodly thing to do, surely it could do no harm for the Rom to mingle with the crowds at the fair, and maybe sing a song or two?

So Beatrice and Mimi chattered and giggled as they plaited their hair, and Emilia groomed her mare, Alida, until she shone. Luka combed his hair for the first time in quite a long while, and then combed Zizi's hair too, much to her delight. Jacob oiled his moustache and polished the ring through Sweetheart's snout, while Silvia busied herself gathering together all the goods she had made to barter.

"Bye, Baba!" Emilia cried, and gave her grandmother a fierce hug.

"I don't like this plan of going to the fair. Who put the idea into Luka's head?"

"Sebastien's cousin, Nadine," Emilia said. "You know, the one that kept on commenting how shabby our caravans were. I didn't like her much at all."

"Jealous of our Beatrice's beauty, no doubt," Maggie replied. "Oh well, keep yourself safe, darling girl. Make sure Sweetheart is kept on a tight chain. She's not used to crowds, and if she lashes out at anyone, there'll be trouble for sure."

"You worry too much, Baba!" Luka said with a grin, coming up with Zizi swinging from his hand.

"That goes for your monkey too. Make sure she doesn't go stealing any fruit or sweets; the merchants don't like thieves, no matter how small. And you, Luka, keep your sticky fingers in your pocket!"

Luka's grin faded. "I'm not going to steal anything," he said indignantly. "I won't need to. We're going to make a fortune! Nadine said they love travelling performers at these fairs."

"That may have been true once, but not any more," Maggie said. "Nowadays they'll whip you just for kicking a ball around on a Sunday. . ."

"Well, today's Thursday, so no problem there," Luka replied with a wide grin.

"Cheeky monkey," Maggie said. He bowed theatrically, sweeping off his hat.

"We'll be fine, Baba, don't you worry," Emilia said. "Don't we have Rollo to guard us?"

"One dog is not much good against a whole marketplace of angry merchants," Maggie replied dourly.

"We won't stay long," Emilia promised.

"Just long enough to fill our pockets with gold!" Luka exulted. "Come on, Milly! The day's a-wasting!" He bounded away towards the road, his monkey gripping his neck and shrieking with joy.

Emilia vaulted on to Alida's back, and raced after him. The mare was dapple-grey, with an arched neck and a silky tail that she carried high so it rippled behind her like a white banner. Emilia's mother had always said that the horses of Arabia were made by God from the fierce desert wind because He wanted to make a creature that could fly without wings. Since her mare ran so lightly and fluidly it seemed as if she flew, Emilia had named her Alida, which meant "winged".

The rest of the Finch family followed eagerly, leading the bear by a chain attached to the ring in her nose. After more than an hour of walking, they came to a stream crossing the road. Luka felt the squelching of the mud between his toes and grinned. He jumped into the stream, spraying water everywhere.

"Nay, don't, I'll be drenched!" Beatrice cried. "I don't want to turn up at the fair all wet and muddy!"

"Here, allow me, my fine lady." Luka bowed mockingly, sweeping his hand through the water so it sprayed all over her. Beatrice shrieked with indignation.

A black carriage, pulled by four black horses, galloped round the bend in the road. At once the children pressed back into the hedgerow, Rollo growling deep in his throat.

The coach raced through the stream, a great gush of muddy water rising up and wetting the children from head to foot. Luka saw a black heron of a man lean forward, frowning in disapproval at the sight of their vivid clothes and wild hair. As the carriage rattled on, the black-clad man leant out of the window to stare back at them.

Emilia stood gazing after the coach. All the hairs on her arms stood erect and quivering. She trembled as if a bitter-cold wind had blown over her.

"A devil of a man, a devil," she whispered. "I wish he had not seen us."

"It's nothing." Beatrice tried to smile. "A pastor anxious for his supper, no more. Come on! Let's hurry.

I'm hungry too. We can get something to eat at the fair."

"Pork pies, jam tarts, honey cakes," Luka chanted.

"Really?" Noah said. "I've never had a pork pie."

"Neither have I," Luka admitted. "But I bet they taste good."

They all smiled, and walked on. Except Emilia. She stood still, her hands clenched, Alida standing quietly beside her.

Emilia had felt this dark shadow before, several times. Usually it was vague, a blotting out of warmth and colour like a cloud passing before the sun. Once, though, it had been bitter and icy like this, as if a bough had bent and dumped its load of snow upon her.

It had been a few months ago. The Finches had been haymaking at Whitehorse Manor. It had been a warm, soft, burnished day, yet suddenly Emilia had felt a cold that struck to the very marrow. She had cried out, and stopped still where she stood, seeing a shadow falling through the air, hearing a thump, feeling the impact reverberating through the soles of her feet. Only an instant; then it was gone. Emilia had glanced wildly about her. Ahead was the cart, a young farmhand riding high on the hay. Suddenly the cart lurched. The farmhand lost his balance, tumbled sideways, slid down the precarious mountain of hay, and fell heavily just in front of the great iron wheel. It rolled inexorably over him, the crack of his bones as loud as a firing shot.

Her grandmother had said it was a sign that she was to

be a true *drabardi*, someone who saw genuine visions of the future, rather than most fortune-tellers, who told only what their listener most wanted to hear. Maggie had the gift herself, and thought it more an affliction then a blessing. It was a rare person who truly wanted to know what lay ahead of them, Maggie said.

Feeling that dreadful creeping chill again, Emilia could only agree.

Crow-Fair

"Come on, Milly!" Beatrice turned to call to her sister.

"Are you all right?" Luka fell back and waited for her.

"I felt the shadow again," she whispered. "Something bad's going to happen."

Luka looked uncomfortable. He did not like to hear such talk. "Baba's just got you spooked with all her talk of owls crying. Nothing bad's going to happen!"

"I hope not," Emilia muttered. She did not know what to think about these strange feelings that sometimes came upon her. Maggie said it took years for a *drabardi* to learn what was true, and what was merely a trick of the mind. Emilia pushed the sense of doom away firmly, determined to enjoy the road unrolling beneath her feet, the prospect of fun ahead.

It was late morning by the time the Finch family came into Kingston-upon-Thames, a large town made prosperous by the building of Hampton Court Palace just across the river. The streets were crowded with wagons and carts, and people pushed and shoved all around. There was a girl herding along a flock of geese, a long switch in her hand, and several boys carried big baskets of vegetables. A man dragged along a cart filled with crates of baby goats. The air rang with shouts, honks, cackles, bleats and barks.

Luka and Emilia were wide-eyed, fascinated by the hustle and bustle. Zizi clung to Luka's neck, her tail wrapped about his throat, while Emilia kept a tight hold on Alida's lead rein.

"Why don't we all split up?" Jacob suggested. "We can make four times as much money then! We'll meet at the clock tower at noon, all right?"

He headed off down a side street towards a busy-looking inn, Sweetheart lumbering along behind him, her snout lifted to sniff the air. Mimi went with them, a beribboned tambourine in her hand. A large crowd soon gathered to watch Sweetheart dance, rising high on her hind paws.

Beatrice and Noah found a cool spot near the church, at the far end of the market square. It was a dour, grey church, built of flint and stone, with a tall square tower topped with a wooden roof, and a narrow avenue of gloomy yew trees that led through a few crooked gravestones. Quite a few people had gathered there, out of the sun. Rollo lay down at Noah's feet, panting, as the little boy lifted his violin to his chin. As Luka and Emilia went deeper into the market, they could hear Beatrice's clear voice raised in an old ballad.

Luka found a stall where a wood-carver was selling puppets and dolls and rocking-horses. A mob of small children were hanging around, playing with all the toys. It seemed a good place to begin, and so Luka played his fiddle and Emilia danced and clapped her hands and snapped her fingers and stamped her feet, her skirts belling out. Zizi danced too, shrieking with excitement, and Alida delighted the crowd by lifting high her forelegs in time to the music. When the song came to an end, Alida bowed deeply, sliding her cheek down her foreleg. Everyone clapped, and quite a few people dropped coins into the hat that Zizi carried, bounding around. Emilia scooped them out and put them away in her hidden pocket.

By the time the sun was nearing the midpoint, they had more coins than Emilia had ever seen before. Flushed with success, they bought themselves a hot pie each, and went wandering through the fair.

"Look, there's Tom Whitehorse!" Emilia cried.

Luka made a face. "Stuck-up snob."

"You're just jealous," Emilia said. "You'd be stuck-up too if your father was the local squire and you had servants waiting on you hand and foot all the time. I like him."

"Well, you only like him because he admires Alida," Luka shot back.

She grinned. "He has very good taste."

The boy hurrying towards them through the crowd

was tall and fair, with long curls hanging past his shoulder, a velvet coat trimmed with lace, and a large feathered hat. He kept looking behind him as if worried he was being followed. Suspecting he had come to the fair without his father's permission, Luka grinned and stepped forward, crying in a loud voice, "Master Whitehorse! Fancy seeing you here! Where are your footmen? I'm surprised you don't have one holding a parasol over you today, it's so hot."

Tom Whitehorse flushed angrily. "Don't be silly. I don't need a parasol."

"But surely you need someone to carry your handkerchief for you? And a little basket of sweetmeats in case you get peckish?"

"I don't have time for this," Tom answered and went to brush past them.

"Don't mind Luka. You know he likes to tease. We're just surprised to see you here at the fair, since your father normally likes to keep you so close. Has he given you leave for the day?"

"Sort of," Tom answered. He glanced round anxiously and went to hurry past them.

Luka, however, gave a crow of laughter. "You've given him the slip, haven't you? Good on you!"

"Not at all," Tom replied coolly. "I'm here on my father's business."

"What a shame," Emilia said. "It's fair day! You should be having some fun."

"Fun!" Tom said scornfully. "There's not much fun to

be had in England these days, is there? Can't raise a toast to an absent friend, or choose the way you wear your hair."

Luka looked at Tom's long curls critically and said, "Well, the Lord Protector's got it right about the unloveliness of lovelocks!"

Tom glared at him. "I'm not going to cut my hair just because Cromwell tells us to! Why should I? My father says the whole world is coming to ruin, and he's right! We should never have let them kill the king."

Emilia bit back a little gasp, and glanced about them quickly. It was not wise to say such things. She noticed a soldier squinting suspiciously at them from under the shadow of a canopy. He was big and burly, with a grey-bristled chin and a nose that looked like it had been spread flat by being pressed against too many windows. He wore a buff coat and a steel gauntlet on his left hand, and had a pistol and a dagger thrust through his broad leather belt.

"Sssh!" she hissed. "Do you want your tongue nailed to the pillory?"

Tom looked round himself too, and stiffened when he saw the soldier watching. "I have to go," he said at once and, without a word of farewell, went hurrying away into the crowd.

"Well," Luka said. "Our fine young cock was rather ruffled today, wasn't he? Probably scared someone would tell on him to his father." He let one hand flop over at the wrist and minced forward, saying in a high, affected voice, "Oh, my goodness gracious, I would so hate my dear old daddy to hear I've been hobnobbing with those dreadful dirty gypsy children. I might spoil my velvet coat!"

"Well, his father is very protective of him," Emilia said. "Remember how much trouble he got in that time we convinced him to come out one night and look for badgers?"

As they moved into the crowd, Emilia looked round for any sign of the watching soldier, but he had disappeared, and she felt herself relax. "We should be more careful," she said to Luka. "You know Baba says Cromwell has spies everywhere."

"It wasn't me flapping my tongue about," Luka said. He clasped his hands under his chin, flapped his eyelashes and said in a high, girlish voice, "Oh! It's fair day! You should be having some fun!"

Zizi shrieked with laughter and copied him, her wizened paws tucked under her chin, her head tilted girlishly to one side.

Emilia punched him.

"Ow! Do you have to hit so hard?"

"I can hit harder," Emilia threatened.

"Only if you catch me!" Luka cried, and broke into a run, weaving in and out of the barrows. Emilia raced after him, Alida cantering behind her. People looked after them, wondering if they should call a hue and cry, but the children's laughter reassured them and they went back to their work.

"Let's go get Beatrice and show her all the money we've raised!" Emilia cried. "She'll be so pleased."

Beatrice and Noah were still performing before the church, Rollo lying at their feet. In her green ruffled skirts, with a rose tucked behind her ear, Beatrice looked prettier than ever amongst the farmers' wives in their drab blacks. Noah was exciting a lot of attention too, a small blind boy playing the fiddle with such fierce skill. Emilia could see the cap at his feet was filled with coins.

Beatrice was singing a favourite song of hers:

"If I were a blackbird I would whistle and sing,
I would follow the vessel my true love sailed in
All on the top rigging I would build my nest
And I'd sleep the long night on his lily-white breast."

It was a lovely song with a lovely tune, and a large crowd had gathered to listen.

The two children joined the throng, then clapped loudly as the song finished. Beatrice smiled and glanced their way. Suddenly her expression changed. She shrank back, pale and frightened.

A shadow had fallen over the square, pointing like an accusing finger at Beatrice. Noah lowered his violin, wondering why she had stopped singing. Emilia turned to look, and felt her heart sink.

The pastor stood frowning in the square. He was tall and thin and very pale, and dressed all in black, except for his collar and cuffs, which were white as frost. His tall steeple hat was set very straight on his head, and it was the shadow of this which had fallen upon Beatrice. Two deep lines were driven from the sides of his high-bridged nose to the corners of his narrow mouth. He looked at Beatrice and Noah with loathing. Behind him was the soldier with the bristly chin who had been staring at them in the square.

"Singing for coins, right before our blessed church!" The pastor's eyes blazed with righteousness. "Surely such brazen-faced sin must offend us all?"

"It's gypsies, sir," the soldier said in a harsh voice. "Filthy, thieving hedge-birds. Should be hanged, they should. Only cure for them."

"Indeed, Coldham, they are an ungodly people," the pastor said, and folded his long, pale hands. "And if you are right in your suspicions, dabbling in treason too. Very well. Let us have them to prison. I will not have gypsies singing and fiddling at the very door of my church. Seize them!"

"Criminy!" Luka exclaimed. "It's a crow-fair!"

"Quick!" Emilia cried. "Find your dado! We've got to get out of here!"

Luka nodded and went running back towards the inn. Coldham strode forward and gripped Beatrice and Noah firmly. Beatrice was weeping and trying to reach her brother, who was struggling as well as he could with a fiddle and bow clutched to his skinny chest. Rollo snarled and lunged at Coldham, who kicked him hard in the side, knocking him head over heels, yelping.

21

Noah turned his face from side to side anxiously. "Rollo?"

Coldham drew his knife.

"No!" Beatrice and Emilia screamed together. Emilia whistled urgently, and Beatrice cried, "Go, Rollo! Go to Milly!"

"Go!" Noah called, his voice high with fear. "Rollo, go!"

The big dog reluctantly obeyed, head down and tail sunk between his legs, turning to look back at Noah. Beatrice reached out and grabbed her brother, drawing him to her side, and he hid his sightless eyes against her skirt.

Just then Luka and Jacob came running towards them, Sweetheart loping behind. Silvia and Mimi hurried after them, looking scared.

"A whole tribe of the infidels!" the pastor exclaimed. "Arrest them all!"

Jacob pushed Sweetheart's chain into Luka's hand and came forward, both hands raised. "Come now, we're not doing any harm."

"Call the constables!" the pastor cried. "I will not have thieves and vagrants causing trouble in my town."

"Nay, no need for that," Jacob said. "We're just here for the fair, like all these other good people. We've done our business, we'll be on our way; no need for any bother."

The pastor looked at him in contempt. "Get the constables," he said to a bystander, who went running away through the square, shouting. Within moments three constables were in the square, cudgels in their hands. Jacob began to look about him for some way out. "Get the girls out of here," he hissed at Luka.

Luka nodded and jerked his head at Emilia, who began to retreat, her hand tight on Alida's bridle. Mimi and Silvia began to back away too, looking for some way through the crowd. One of the constables seized Mimi by the wrist, dragging her back towards the pastor.

"Stop it, you're hurting me," Mimi wept.

"How dare you! She's naught but a babe!" Silvia cried. She swung her basket and hit the constable hard across the head. "Take that, you big bully!" she yelled. "And that!"

The constable let go of Mimi's wrist and raised his arm to protect his head, as Silvia rained blows upon him. She was a tall, strong woman, and her basket was laden with all she had bought or bartered for at the fair. The constable retreated, cursing, and Silvia charged after him, her basket swinging. Then he tripped and fell back over a stall of ironware. The whole thing came crashing down upon him, pots and pans and ladles and skillets raining everywhere. They banged and clattered, rolling away over the cobblestones, and at last lay silent around the ruin of the stall. All that could be seen of the constable were his big boots, sticking out from underneath. They did not move.

The ironmonger struggled to raise the heavy stall. At last he managed it, but still the constable did not move.

His head lolled sideways. A shrill scream rose high into the air. "He's dead, he's dead," the ironmonger's wife shrieked.

Silvia went white as whey and dropped her basket. She did not struggle or protest as the other constables seized her, but stared in horror at the dead man lying amidst all the iron cooking ware.

Emilia could not move. It was as if the world had suddenly been disconnected from her, spinning on without her. *That's the death*, she thought. *Baba heard right.*

One of the constables seized hold of Emilia. The hard grip snapped her back to reality. She kicked him in the stomach, dodged round a fat lady, ducked behind a thin man, and dived through the constable's legs, tripping him over. Coldham tried to grab her, but Beatrice hung on to his arm with both her hands, so that Emilia was able to slip through his fingers like a will-of-the-wisp. She leapt up on to Alida's bare back. The mare whinnied and reared, the constable staggered and fell over again, and then Emilia wheeled Alida about, her eyes flashing towards her sister and brother.

"Go! Go!" Beatrice cried frantically. "Get out of here!"

Glancing about, Emilia saw all her family had now been caught. Her Uncle Jacob had been seized, and Silvia huddled next to him, Mimi shrinking into her skirt. Luka was kicking and squirming in the grasp of one of the constables, while Sweetheart, frightened by his yells, rose up on to her haunches and snarled.

"Performing bears are against the law!" the pastor shouted. "Shoot the beast!"

"No!" Jacob struggled to get to his beloved old bear.

Luka jerked Sweetheart's chain so she reared up on to her hind legs. The constable, terrified, scrambled away. Luka turned and ran, Zizi shrieking and gibbering on his shoulder, Sweetheart lumbering beside him.

Emilia held down her hand for Luka, and he strained to reach her and Alida. But Coldham lashed out at him. Luka jerked away, letting go of the bear's chain. In an instant the constable was upon him, while Sweetheart – finding herself free – roamed over to a market stall that sold honey and helped herself. One of the constables raised his pistol and pointed it at her, but people were running, screaming, everywhere and he dared not shoot.

Noah stumbled forward, his violin clutched to his chest, trying to escape.

"Here, Noah, here!" Emilia screamed. He turned towards her, hand groping out in entreaty. She kicked Alida forward, thinking for one glad moment that she could reach him and swing him up behind her. Then the pastor stepped forward and grabbed Noah, dragging him back. Noah cried out in fear, and hit out with his violin. The pastor wrested the violin from him and flung it down on the cobblestones, stamping upon it until it was smashed to smithereens.

"You devil!" Emilia cried, wild with fury and grief as Noah sobbed in despair. "How could you!"

The pastor glanced up at her, his thin mouth twisted with loathing. He strode forward and seized Alida's halter. Emilia kicked him square in the chest with her bare foot. One of his boots slipped on the filthy cobbles and he lost his balance and fell back, straight into a huge, green, sloppy cowpat.

Emilia laughed. She could not help it. The pastor glared up at her and rose slowly to his feet, his face white and rigid. Emilia knew she had made an enemy. She wheeled Alida about, and brought the mare up on to her hind hooves so that the constable trying to grab her reins stumbled back.

"Go, Milly, go!" Luka shouted. "Get yourself out of here!"

"Take Sweetheart!" Jacob shouted.

"Please, Milly, go!" Beatrice cried.

Emilia gasped a sobbing breath, then whistled to the bear and the dog. Obediently Sweetheart and Rollo turned and followed as Emilia galloped out of the market square, knocking over a cage of chickens and a barrow of apples on the way.

Behind her she could hear the pastor screaming, "Catch her and bring her back! We'll see her burn in hell for this!"

The Mace and Hand Inn

Luka rubbed his aching head. Zizi was crouched on an awning a few feet away, gibbering with fear. Luka looked up and saw the pastor staring down at him. He clutched his fiddle close under his arm, afraid the pastor might seize it and stamp it to pieces too.

"Godless heathens," the pastor hissed. He glanced at Coldham. "Lock them up. We'll have them before the magistrates at the beginning of next month. Murder, vagrancy, and begging in the marketplace without a licence."

Luka was hauled to his feet and marched along the market square with the rest of his family. Zizi leapt down on to his shoulder and cowered against his neck, her tail wrapped tight enough to half strangle him. Afraid they might drag the little monkey away from him if they noticed her, Luka tucked her away inside his coat and she lay quietly, her head pressed against his fast-beating heart.

They were hustled down a side street to a small crooked inn with a steep thatched roof and tiny mullioned windows. A poorly painted sign hung over the door, depicting a hand holding up a mace. The sour smell of beer gusted out of the front door. Inside, an innkeeper was serving beer to a handful of morose-looking customers. He looked up as the Finch family was pushed inside, and sighed. "What, more?"

"The pastor's determined to clean up this town," the constable said.

"I haven't the room for them, and what's more important, I haven't the funds. This new pastor of yours has scared away all my customers with his hellfire talk."

"Thank your lucky stars he hasn't had you closed down altogether, *Warden* Riley," one of the constables growled, jerking Luka towards a set of narrow, dark stairs.

"Where would he lock up all his prisoners if he did?" Riley cried, opening a drawer and taking out a ring of jangling keys. "I'm offering a community service, I am, and for precious little reward too. Doesn't he have anything better to do than arrest half the town?"

As he grumbled, he led the way up the stairs and the Finch family was pushed along after him, one constable at their head and another at their heels. Both were very large, burly men with rough manners, and the only difference between them that Luka could see was that one had a misshapen, red nose, rather like a squashed tomato, and the other had a hook like an eagle's beak.

"It's on the orders of the Lord Protector," said The Beak. "Haven't you heard the young king Charles Stuart has set a price on Cromwell's head? They say he dare not sleep without his armour on, in fear of secret assassins."

"One of Charles Stuart's men has been seen here in England, in disguise," said Tomato-Nose excitedly, giving Luka a rough push from behind to make him quicken his step.

"The Marquis of Ormonde!" The Beak said.

"No! Really?" the innkeeper said, fumbling with his keys at the lock of a thick wooden door. "Dangerous job, spying for the young king . . . I mean, tyrant. I wouldn't want to be in his shoes if Cromwell's spymaster gets hold of him."

"That thief-taker Coldham is here in Kingston to search for him. Apparently the Marquis managed to slip the net in London, despite all of Cromwell's soldiers being on the lookout for him," Tomato-Nose continued.

"It'd be a feather in our caps if we helped capture him!" The Beak said.

"But surely the pastor does not think this raggedy lot has anything to do with a marquis in disguise, does he?" The innkeeper cast a scornful look over the small group of gypsies waiting apprehensively on the stairs, their festive clothes dishevelled after the scuffle.

"We don't know anything about marquises," Jacob said. "It's obviously a mistake! Let us go!"

The constables just jerked their thumbs at the doorway. Apprehensively the Finch family stumbled through. Beyond was a long, roughly furnished room, where a guard sat cleaning his fingernails with a knife. He got up at the sight of all the prisoners, and exclaimed loudly, "What, more prisoners? This pastor's a Devil-chaser for sure! He's arrested just about every tramp in town."

"He's trying to impress the Lord Protector, but it won't do him any good. They say Cromwell's taken to his bed ever since his daughter died. He's sick as a dog, they say," The Beak said.

"Old Ironsides?" Riley cried. "I thought he'd rust before he ever got old and sick like the rest of us."

Luka could not help a little grin, and filed the joke away to use one day himself.

The prison guard passed Jacob his quill, and told him to make his mark in his ledger. Since Luka's father could not write his name, he made a shaky-looking *X*. Silvia, Beatrice and the children were not required to record their presence, having no legal status, and so the guard scattered sand over the page to dry the ink, then ordered them all to hand over all their possessions. It upset everyone to see the money they had earned at the fair disappearing into the guard's strongbox.

"I've heard the Lord Protector suspects his daughter was poisoned," The Beak said.

"Or that it was witchcraft," Tomato-Nose muttered.

"So Cromwell thinks it was some kind of Royalist plot?" Riley said. "But what would be gained by murdering little Betty Cromwell, let alone her baby son?"

The guard looked troubled. "Beats me. Revenge? Charles Stuart must hate all the Cromwells after they killed his father and took his throne."

Tomato-Nose scowled. "His father was a tyrant, and was put on trial and found guilty for it. That boy should be grateful he was not executed too."

The guard held up both hands. "Of course, of course!"

"It's not just the Royalists who want the Lord Protector dead," The Beak said. "Just think of that mad Leveller who died in the Tower earlier this year. How many times did he try and kill His Highness before he was caught?"

"Did you know we have a Leveller in here now? The pastor had him brought in this morning, charged with conspiracy," the innkeeper said. "Yet he's lived round here for years, quiet as a mouse."

"It's that thief-taker Coldham," The Beak said. "He's got the pastor convinced this marquis is being hidden round here somewhere. The pastor's determined to be the one to catch him!"

"The pastor will be here soon to gloat over his prisoners," the guard said, a large bunch of keys in his hand. "I'd best be getting them settled."

"Time for a quick ale?" Riley suggested to the two constables. "Hot and thirsty work, rounding up rebels and spies."

"That it is," the constables agreed. Together the three men went out of the door, slamming it and locking it behind them.

31

"We're not rebels or spies," Jacob said desperately to the guard. "Really we're not. We've just come to the fair to raise a little money."

The guard shrugged. "This way, now."

He ushered them through another door, and Luka saw that one whole side of the inn was divided into two big cells, with heavy iron-barred doors. Silvia, Beatrice and Mimi were pushed into one cell, and Luka, Noah and Jacob into the other.

The cell was crowded with men. Two looked as though they had been in a fight, with black eyes and bloodied noses. There was a one-armed soldier in a tattered uniform, one sleeve pinned across his breast, and several filthy tramps, their beards matted with leaves, their rags stinking of sour ale. Lying on the floor was a young man, very thin and pale, who coughed and coughed and coughed into a bloodstained rag.

There was also a thin man of about fifty, who was seated at the table scribbling away at a scroll of paper with a tattered quill. Every now and again he spat in his inkwell to thin the ink, for it had almost run out.

Luka rubbed his arms, which felt bruised where the constables had gripped him. His eyes lit up when he saw a narrow window set high into the wall. Luka gently touched his father's sleeve, and jerked his thumb at it.

"Luka! Can you get out, do you think?"

Luka shrugged, trying not to show his pride in his agility. "Think so."

"Get Baba away! She'll die if they lock her up in this foul place. You'll need to get us help, if you can. Go in search of the Hearnes; they've gone to Epsom Downs for the races. They may be able to do something."

"What?" Luka demanded. "I doubt greasing the pastor's palm will work."

"Nay, I doubt it too. But surely they can do *something*!"

"All right, Dado, I'll do my best," Luka said.

"Don't let them get Sweetheart. They'll kill her, for sure."

"I'll try," Luka said, rather dubiously, for he had no idea how to keep *himself* safe, let alone a six-hundred-pound brown bear.

He let Zizi out of his coat and she leapt about, gibbering loudly, much to the surprise and amusement of the other prisoners. In the other cell he could hear sobbing, and he pressed his face against the wall and whispered, "Mimi! Don't cry! I'll be out of here in a trice, and I'll come back to get you when I can."

"Luka, be careful, darling boy!" Silvia cried.

"Keep Milly safe, Luka, please!" Beatrice called, her voice breaking.

"I don't like this place," Mimi wept. "Will you come and get us soon?"

"Aye, I will, I will," Luka promised, unable to do anything else. He bent to put his hand on Noah's shoulder, whispering, "Don't fret, boyo, I'll have you back in your woods before you know it." Noah smiled tremulously, and Luka gave him an encouraging pat, then turned to throw his arms about his father. Jacob ruffled his hair. "Be careful, my boy!"

"I will. See you soon." Luka felt a hot, dense tightness in his throat. He took a deep breath and shook it away, determined no one should see. He passed his father his violin, broke into a swift run and flung his body over into a high backflip that took him up to the window, where he clung to the bars for dear life.

The man with the quill looked up at him in surprise, then smiled. "Good luck to thee, friend!" he said. "I wish that I too could leap free of this foul place."

Luka grinned. "Thanks," he said, reached down to take his fiddle from his father, who had to stand on tip-toe to pass it to him, then wriggled through the window and was gone.

It was a steep drop down to the street, so he clambered up the gutter and on to the steep thatched roof, his fiddle slung over his shoulder, Zizi leaping nimbly ahead of him. Keeping low, he climbed over the pitch and hid behind the chimneys so he could peer around. Below was a stable-yard, and Luka was pleased to see a large black stallion was being readied to ride by two grooms.

Keeping as quiet as he could, he slipped over the edge of the pediment and rested his feet on the window ledge below, then, when he felt secure, slipped down to crouch there. Zizi dropped on to his shoulder, chattering in curiosity. He heard voices and pressed closer to the window, hoping no one would look out and see him.

"I want you to get that girl, Coldham, and I want you to bring her back to me," the pastor was saying. "I shall have her whipped for insolence before she hangs! Go and raid that camp of theirs. They'll be about the Devil's work for sure. Look for any sign of witchcraft, any spells, curses, charms, or other sign of Devil worship."

"Yes, sir," a man replied. Luka recognized Coldham's harsh voice. "I'll look for any signs they've been in contact with the Royalists too, sir. These gypsies travel all round the country, sir; they could easily be carrying treasonous messages around."

"Very good, Coldham!" the pastor said. Coins clinked as money changed hands. "The Lord Protector would be most pleased with us if we've managed to capture a nest of spies and traitors!"

There was a knock on the door. The pastor called out impatiently. The door opened, and another voice said, "Your horse is ready, Pastor Spurgeon."

"Very good," Pastor Spurgeon replied, while Luka, clinging with hands and feet to the window frame outside, thought to himself, *Spurgeon sturgeon! It's a good name for you, Fish-Face. And as for you, Coldham, you're a squealer if I ever heard one!*

"I must ride now to see Colonel Pride," the pastor said. "He will be most anxious to know all that I have been doing. I will be back tomorrow. Make sure that wild, malicious girl-child is under lock and key, Coldham."

"Yes, sir!" Coldham said.

"The court will sit on the first of September," the pastor mused. Through the window, Luka could see him putting on his tall steeple hat, and he ducked down, not wanting to be seen. "The prison is already packed to the hilt, unfortunately. The magistrates will have their hands full. It will be worth it to send a message to the people, though, that God's work will be done."

"Yes, sir," Coldham said again. Luka imitated him silently to Zizi, who gave a wide monkey grin.

Then the voices died away. With his violin banging awkwardly on his back, Luka shinned down to the ground and grabbed a pitchfork from a pile of manure.

"Stand and deliver, laddies!" he cried.

The grooms swung around in surprise. Luka did not waste any time. He shoved the pitchfork at them, so that they scrambled backwards, then seized the horse's reins and swung himself up into the saddle. Zizi leapt up lightly and settled on the pommel before him, her tail wrapped about his wrist. The horse snorted and pranced, and Luka tightened his hold on the reins, bringing the stallion's head around and urging him forward.

"Stop him!" a voice shouted.

The pastor stood in the doorway like a pillar of black marble. Only his face and hands and collar were white. His pale eyes were blazing. Coldham came running out of the door, his face set in a grimace of hatred, his pistol in his hand. Luka wheeled the stallion about and pulled off his cap, making a low, sweeping bow.

"Thanks for the horse, Fish-Face!" he cried; then he was off, out of the gateway and through the town at a mad gallop.

A Rom Can Never Rest

Emilia galloped along the dusty road, Sweetheart and the dog loping behind her.

What are we to do? she kept asking herself. *We should never have left Norwood! Baba was right. . .*

Alida, swift as she was, could not run all day. Soon Emilia had to slow the mare and let her rest. She glanced back over her shoulder. A great plume of dust rose into the air some miles back, showing someone was riding hard behind her. She kicked Alida with her bare feet, and the mare valiantly quickened into a canter again, even though her dappled flanks were scudded with sweat.

Emilia was filled with terror so acute it was like ice in her blood. What would they do to her family, to gentle Beatrice, to brave, blind little Noah, to kind Uncle Jacob, and cuddly Aunt Silvia, and her cousin, little Mimi, not yet ten? Surely they could not truly mean to hang them just for singing and dancing in the marketplace?

She hardly knew how she made it back to the campsite at Thornton Heath. The miles blurred past, and only clever Alida got her home safely. Emilia was shivering as if she had a fever.

The camp was very quiet. The dogs slept under the caravans, occasionally scratching at their fleas. Maggie sat on the steps of her caravan, her shawl drawn up about her face, a soft bag at her feet. Emilia slid off Alida's back and fell into her lap, sobbing.

"You knew?" she said when at last she could speak.

Maggie shrugged. "I heard the owl's cry, and then, today, the cards showed me death."

"He says they'll hang," Emilia sobbed.

Maggie took a deep breath. She looked over Emilia's shoulder at the white cloud of dust rising from the road. Rollo was drinking from the water bucket, his thin sides heaving, while Sweetheart had flopped down in the shade, grumbling to herself.

"Well, my wean, let me tell you a story," she said.

Emilia looked at her in bewilderment. These were the words she heard at night, as she was snuggled in her bunk with Beatrice and Noah, all of them warm and sleepy, tired out after the day. It was not what she expected her baba to say now, with the constables only minutes away and the whole family in gaol.

But she laid her hot, weary head on her grandmother's knee, and listened, half in a dream, to Maggie's soft voice. In a way, it was a relief, not to run or fight any more.

"A long time ago there was a travelling man who travelled as far as he could and found before him only sea. He stopped and tarried for a while, but a Rom can never rest, you know that, and so after a while he packed up his wife and his horses and his children, and he found himself a boat, and he came here to this country. It pleased him, the land he found himself in, and so he wandered this way and he wandered that way, and he found himself his roads.

"Now this man, this Traveller, had five children, and in time they all grew up, and wanted to find roads of their own. So he gave them all some money, enough to buy a wagon of their own, or to drink it all, if that was what they wanted, and he told them again the three laws of the Rom, and blessed them, and sent them on their way."

Emilia nodded her head, and Maggie smoothed the unruly curls away from her damp forehead.

"Now his wife was a woman with her own powers, what would be called a witch nowadays, no doubt," Maggie went on in her soft, singsong voice. "She wore about her wrist a chain of charms which had been passed down to her by her mother, who had had it from her mother, and so on for many years. There were five charms on this chain, and so she broke the chain and gave one to each of her five children. She thought she could protect them all this way, but from the day she broke the chain, things went from bad to worse."

"Now I haven't time today to tell you all that happened to the five children, and where they went, and what they did. That's a tale for another telling. But you should know, my wean, that this was the year that young King Harry first came to the throne. He was not much older than our Beatrice, poor Harry the Eighth, and he was mad in love for his dead brother's wife, Catherine she was called."

Emilia nodded her head again but did not speak.

"Now years passed, enough years that the Big Man's children all married and had children of their own. You must remember King Harry loved music and dancing, and he had heard of our Traveller man, who could play the fiddle so fish rose from the streams and leapt into his hands, and birds flew down from the trees and perched on his bow. His fame had spread far and wide, as had the fortune-telling fame of his wife. So the king had them brought to court, and the Traveller man played for him and then, laughing, the king asked his wife what she foresaw for him."

Emilia moved restlessly, even the comfort of her grandmother's stroking hand and soft voice unable to rid her completely of her dreadful anxiety. Maggie's voice quickened.

"No one knows what she told him but the stories say he went white as a ghost first, then red, then he fell into a fury. He threw his cup, and smashed his hand into the table, and he roared and shouted until all the servants ran and hid, and then he had the Traveller man and his wife whipped from the palace. And that very night he called for his ministers and his quill and his seal, and he wrote up a law against the Rom. And so the bad time began, and the Rom were chased from town to town with stones and whips, and some were hanged, and some were drowned, and many were branded like cattle. And now we tell our children, be careful who you tell the truth to."

"What did she see? What did she tell him?" Emilia was interested despite herself.

"Who knows? I was not there to hear it. But three years later he had put aside his wife and his baby daughter and married another, the one they call the Witch Boleyn, and in another three years he'd cut off her head and married again, and by the time another three years had passed, there'd been another three wives, and he was sick and foul and feared, where once he had been golden and loved. So what did she tell him? What she saw, no doubt, and more fool her."

"And?" Emilia knew there must be some reason Maggie was telling her this tale.

"Kings have come and kings have gone since then, and queens too," Maggie said. "But all that time the Rom have suffered because that old witch could not keep a still tongue between her teeth, and, my daya told me, because she broke the chain of charms. It's a chain of blood as well as gold, so the old tale tells, and if the charms could only be brought together again, better days will come for all of us."

Emilia struggled to understand. "You think these charms, they can help us, help Beatrice and Noah?"

Maggie nodded. "If not they themselves, at least those who carry them," she said. "We are all blood, the Rom. You must go, you must ask them for help, you must bring help back and free us. Else we will hang, I am sure of it."

All Emilia could grasp amongst this was her grandmother's use of *you* and *we*.

"But . . . but you are free . . . they have not got you. . ." she stammered.

"Not yet," Maggie said. "But they come."

Emilia became aware of the sound of galloping hooves. She had thought it was her heart.

"Baba, Baba," she wept.

"Emilia, listen well. There are five charms. There is the crown, given to the eldest son of that old Travelling man. I have it now, I have worn it all my life. Take it."

Emilia found her hand being prised open and something pressed into it. It was warm and round and worn about the edges. Maggie closed Emilia's fingers about it.

"The crown is for light and luck and magic. It's why they call me the Queen of the Gypsies."

Emilia nodded. She opened her hand and saw cupped within an old gold coin, with a hole drilled through so it could hang from a golden chain. The coin was so old it was no longer round but misshapen like a moon two days from full. Just visible on one side was a picture of a queen with stars about her. On the other side there were letters, almost all rubbed away, and the crowned woman again, with one hand raised, the other holding some kind of sceptre.

While Emilia examined the golden coin, Maggie was talking still, half to herself. "Then there is the charm of the running horse. It is silver, the moon metal, and has the power to charm all the beasts of field and forest, the charm to wheedle that you have, my darling girl. Old Janka Hearne, she has it still, I know. Go and find them, beg them for their help, wheedle them if you can. They have horses, they have money, and they have the ear of the Lord Protector, who likes them for their horses."

"What of the other charms?" Emilia asked desperately as the thunder of horses' hooves grew ever closer.

"Lost, lost, so many are lost!" For the first time Emilia heard fear in her grandmother's voice.

"But you must know what they are?" Emilia asked, slipping the golden bracelet over her hand, so it hung on her wrist, the coin dangling down.

"There was the butterfly in amber," Maggie said. "The butterfly means change and transformation, that is its power. Last I heard that family, the Graylings, went to London Town. We were all angry. Rom, living in the city! It shows how much times have changed."

"What else?"

"There was the lightning bolt charm, which I heard was made from the heart of a falling star. That belongs to the Smiths, the iron-forgers. They live and prosper in the

44

Weald, I've heard. They're strong men and fierce, they'll be able to help, I'm sure."

"Butterfly, lightning bolt," Emilia repeated, staring into her grandmother's face and trying to commit her words to memory.

"Gold crown. Silver horse. Butterfly in amber. Iron bolt of lightning. What else, what else?" Maggie was trying not to weep.

Emilia was terribly frightened. Maggie never wept. She gripped her grandmother's hands. "One more, Baba. What? What is it?"

"The herb of grace," Maggie said. "A very old and powerful charm, made of silver, and forged in the shape of a sprig of rue. You don't know it? A most useful herb. It's meant to protect you from devils and witches. They used to sprinkle rue-water in churches on Sundays, which is why it's called the herb of repentance as well as the herb of grace."

"Where can I find it? Who has it?"

"The Wood family. They used to live in the New Forest. Their charm has the power of all growing things, the plants that heal and those that kill," Maggie said. "Last I heard the Woods had all died, or been sold as slaves. One was hanged as a witch, I know."

"So how am I to find them?" Emilia asked in despair.

"I don't know, my darling girl, I don't know. Perhaps it is impossible. Perhaps it's just a story." Maggie's voice broke.

"I'll find them, Baba, don't you worry," Emilia promised. The dogs began to bark a warning, leaping to their feet and hurling themselves to the end of their chains. Sweetheart sat up, scratched her flank and yawned, peering to see who was coming towards them at such a pace, hooves thundering on the rough ground.

Emilia took a deep breath and turned to face the rider, her hand clenched about the golden coin.

It was Luka.

On The Run

He was riding a black stallion, wet sides heaving, nostrils flaring red.

"On my trail. . ." he panted, leaping down and staggering as his legs gave way under him. "Baba! We have to get out of here."

"No use me trying to run," Maggie said. "I'm too old. I'll just slow you young things down. Here. I've packed you a bag with what food I had. There's not much. Emilia, I've put my crystal ball in there, and my cards. If those constables found them, they'd burn me for a witch. You must not let the soldiers find them else they'll burn you too."

Emilia nodded, gulping back tears. She knew how dangerous such things were. To the Rom, her grandmother was a *shuvani* – someone who knew how to cure and how to curse, how to mix poisons and potions, how to cast love spells and how to protect from evil spirits. Her role was more important and mysterious than that of a *drabardi*, though a *shuvani* could often see into the future too. A *shuvani* was the guardian of the secret ways of the Rom, the only woman permitted into the councils of the men. Yet the *gorgios* would think Maggie a witch, and thus a servant of the Devil. They would not care for her age or her wisdom, but burn her alive at the stake.

"Here, take my earrings. They may come in useful; they're gold." Maggie hurriedly unhooked the large hoops from her ears and pressed them into Emilia's hand. Emilia had never seen her grandmother without her earrings. She looked different without them, older and more vulnerable. Emilia gulped back tears and shoved the earrings deep into her pocket, as Luka danced about in impatience, urging her to hurry.

"Now go! Both of you. Get out of here before those constables arrive!"

Emilia embraced her grandmother fiercely. "Please, Baba, won't you. . ."

"Nay, nay, I'm too old now. I'll go and rest my weary bones in that gaol of theirs, and look after my family till you can come and get us out."

"But how? How am I meant to get you out?"

"You'll think of something, my darling girl, I know that."

Emilia could hear the sound of horses approaching. Maggie gave her a hard push, and so she bent and picked up the bag and slung it over her shoulder, then clambered up on to Alida's back, her legs trembling.

"Here, take this demon horse," Luka said, and thrust the reins into her hand. "I'll get Sweetheart."

Emilia hung on to the reins with all her strength as the stallion fought and danced, knowing they had to get him away from the campsite if Maggie was not to be charged with horse-stealing on top of everything else. The stallion was far too strong for her, however, and she could not make him budge a step. She took a few deep breaths, trying to calm herself, knowing her distress and fear were infecting the beast. She could never charm him into following her like a lamb while her breath came in short, sharp bursts and her sweat stank of her terror.

Luka came running back, Sweetheart ambling along beside him, pleased to be taken for a walk. Alida, of course, was used to the huge old bear, but the stallion went mad with terror. He reared, trumpeting, dragging Emilia off Alida's back and on to the ground, breathless, her arms almost jerked out of their sockets as she fought to hold on to the reins. The stallion reared over her, and she rolled away from his pounding hooves, the reins torn from her grasp. The stallion took off at top speed, the reins flapping wildly about his head.

"Well, he'll be in the next county before he stops," Luka said. "Shame, though. He was a good horse. I'll have to walk on my own two legs now."

"I didn't mean to let him go!" Emilia hurried after Luka as he ran towards the trees. "You couldn't have held him either!" She whistled to Rollo, who loped after them.

"Nay, he was devilishly strong," Luka admitted, holding up a branch for her and Alida. "It was all I could do to ride him here. He almost had me off a dozen times. That pastor must be stronger than he looks."

"He was the pastor's horse? You stole the pastor's own horse?"

"Aye, of course I did. If I hadn't, I'd be back in that filthy cell. Come on, let's get going."

Hidden in the shelter of the trees, Emilia cast a miserable glance back at the half-circle of caravans. The constables had arrived at the campsite and were shouting at Maggie, scattering clothes and cooking utensils everywhere.

Coldham had his pistol drawn and was watching closely as the constables tipped out baskets of clothes and opened chests and boxes. When the constables found nothing, he pressed his lips together and looked very angry.

Maggie sat on her caravan step, her lips clamped on the stem of her pipe, her arms folded over her chest. A constable stood over her, yelling at her, but she did not reply, her eyes hidden under her heavy lids. Coldham stepped forward and struck Maggie hard across the face. Her head snapped around, but she did not speak or respond in any way, and so he slapped her again.

Emilia took a deep, shuddering breath, fists clenched in futile rage, then turned and broke into a stumbling run, following Luka as he scrambled down the rough hillside, ducking and weaving from one blackberry bush to another, and leaping over the rocks and bracken, Sweetheart lumbering after him. Alida trotted behind, her ears pricked forward, and Rollo raced on ahead. Zizi was back on Luka's shoulder, her paw on his ear.

"South, we need to go south," Luka panted. "Jacob said to go and find Felipe Hearne and beg him for his help. He'll be horse-racing on the Downs, he said, at Epsom."

"Aye, Baba said the same," Emilia said. She put up her hand and grasped the gold coin hanging from the chain about her left wrist. It was warm to the touch.

The crown is for light and luck and magic. . .

"Are they following us?" she asked, turning to look back up the hill.

"Not yet," Luka said. "Come on, let's keep moving."

Emilia vaulted on to Alida's back, and held down her hand for Luka. In an instant he was up behind her, and Alida was cantering along smoothly. Grumbling and moaning, Sweetheart followed. She was not used to running.

There was a shout from behind them. Emilia glanced over her shoulder. Silhouetted on the hill behind them was Coldham, pointing and waving to the constables to follow him. She urged Alida on faster.

Even under their double weight, Alida soon left their pursuers behind. Both Emilia and Luka were very thin and light, and only thirteen years old, while the men were all heavy and beefy. However, the ground was too rough to canter for long. Emilia did not want Alida to break a leg. As soon as they were once again within the shelter of the trees, she slipped down to the ground. While Luka concealed Sweetheart behind a great gorse bush, Emilia rode Alida through a damp, marshy patch of ground where her hoof prints would leave a deep indentation. She then made the mare step daintily backwards, putting her hooves back in the same spot so that it looked as if she had gone on to drier ground. Walking backwards was a simple enough trick. What was difficult was making sure the mare did not make new prints, or blur the outlines of the existing ones.

Then Emilia concealed Alida behind the gorse bush, and swung herself up into the trees just as Coldham led the constables into the wood at a gallop.

They slowed their pace once within the trees, and Coldham leant from his saddle to stare at the ground. He saw Alida's trail, and spurred his horse on, followed close behind by his men. In a few minutes they were out of sight, but the two children dared not move or breathe until they were sure their ruse had not been discovered.

Exultant, they dropped down out of the trees and hurried back the way they had come, going around the bottom of the hill and crossing the highway once they were sure the road was clear. Together they cleared the stile, Alida hopping over it as nimbly as Rollo, and then disappeared once more into the woods, heading due south.

They reached the bottom of the valley, looking back over their shoulders so often Emilia began to get an ache in her neck. A broad stream wound its way through the glen. Sweetheart's eyes brightened, and she strained against her chain, eager to reach the water. Luka and Emilia stopped and drank deeply, and let Sweetheart splash about in the shallows as they discussed what they should do next. Emilia was all for staying in the wild, while Luka thought they should find the road so they could make quicker progress. He was tired of being scratched to pieces.

They scrounged in the bag and found some apples, which they shared with the animals, and then to their delight Sweetheart caught some fish. The first few she tossed straight into her mouth, but Luka was able to wrest the fourth one from her, and killed it with a stone. They would normally have lit a fire then and there, and enjoyed the fish roasted on the coals, but they dared not attract any attention to themselves. Luka wrapped the fish in leaves and stowed it in their pack, even though Emilia screwed up her nose at the thought of the fishy smell.

They waded downstream as far as they were able, glad of the opportunity to leave no tracks. The rocky floor of the stream was treacherous, though, so after a while they clambered out and went on, their feet numb with cold. Emilia walked behind, doing her best to conceal the deep tracks left by Sweetheart's heavy paws in the mud by the stream. Even the most inexperienced tracker could not mistake a bear print.

Both Emilia and Luka were growing tired, and the ground was steep and rough. Alida was having great difficulty scrambling up some of the big, mossy rocks, and Sweetheart dragged on her chain and moaned unceasingly.

"Can't we stop?" Emilia panted. "My legs are aching."

"We'll stop when we reach the top. We might be able to see something from there."

"Are you sure we're going the right way?"

"Nay, I'm not sure," Luka snapped. "You were the one who said we should cut across country. If we'd gone back to the road like I said, we would know where we were."

Emilia opened her mouth to snipe back, and then shut it again, too weary and sick at heart even to argue with Luka. They came up out of the cool woods into warm sunshine again.

It was late afternoon, and the heath was busy with the murmuring of bees, and the distinctive chirp of the male yellowhammer. "Little bit of bread and no cheese," he sang, and Luka said rather sourly, "I'd be happy with just the little bit of bread."

"We should save the food for later," Emilia said. "If we're hungry now, think how much hungrier we'll be at dinner time."

"At least this pack would be lighter. It's heavy as anything now."

So they shared a little of the bread and cheese Maggie had packed for them, lying on their stomachs in the long grass, Rollo panting beside them. Alida cropped the grass, and Sweetheart rolled, turning her hairy belly to the fading sun. Zizi went scampering off to explore. She was not tired, having been carried most of the way.

From the top of the hill they had a broad view. Below them lay the thick forest, and then the countryside falling away in green, rolling hills and valleys, under heavy clouds building up in the north. It all looked very peaceful. It was hard to believe that the horror and violence of the morning had really happened.

"Look! Look there!" Luka pointed.

Emilia looked and saw the sun glinting off the bridles of three horses, riding slowly along the far hillside. It was hard to see the men, for they were dressed in buff coats and leather breeches, but the flash of the sun on Coldham's steel gauntlet gave them away.

Emilia wondered anxiously if the sun was catching on Sweetheart's chain, or if her skirt was vivid as a flag amidst the dull colours of the heath. She wished she had had time to change into her everyday skirt, the same dull brown as the earth. *It would be easier to hide if it was raining*, she thought. On such a bright, clear, sunny afternoon, it must be easy for the men to track them. She rubbed the old coin, wishing for some luck.

"They're not far behind," Luka said, scowling to hide his fear. "We'd better keep moving."

Staying low, they crept over the rise of the hill and were able to judge where they were by the landmarks rising out of the broad valley to the south. Villages were scattered here and there, and they could see the tall towers of Nonsuch Palace rising from its vast green parkland to the south. Epsom was only a mile or two past Nonsuch. If they kept on walking, they could reach it in less than two hours.

"Come on," Luka said, hefting the pack on to his shoulder and clicking his fingers to call Zizi down from the tree. "Let's try and make the woods before those hellhounds pick up our trail."

Summer Storm

Emilia and Luka stood staring at the road which ran through flat fields and meadows. It was a broad road, lined by low walls of stone. There was nothing to hide a boy, a girl, a horse, a dog, a monkey and a huge brown bear from sight. They could see a man working in one of the fields, and a woman out in the garden of her cottage, gathering herbs. As soon as Emilia and Luka stepped out from the shelter of the trees, they would be seen.

A long, low grumble of thunder. A gust of air lifted Emilia's tangled curls and cooled the back of her neck. She glanced behind her.

Thick grey clouds were pouring over the top of the hill. She had never seen clouds move so fast. Within moments they were spreading halfway across the sky. The woman in the garden looked up, her apron flapping in the breeze, then went inside, calling to her children.

The man shouldered his tools and hurried home, having no desire to be caught in the storm.

"It's raining." Wonderingly Emilia put out her hand to catch the first big, fat drops.

"Aye. That blew up fast. Just what we need, to be slogging along in the rain."

"They won't be able to see us, though," Emilia said. "If it rains hard enough."

There was a crack of lightning, then the heavens opened and the rain came bucketing down. In moments they were drenched to the skin. They could see nothing but the crooked wall before them and a brief stretch of road, turning rapidly to mud.

"I suppose that's true," Luka said, his face brightening. "Come on, then. Let's hurry, before the rain blows over. Those soft constables will probably hide under a tree until it's gone. We could really get away."

Emilia laughed, and lifted her face to the streaming sky, sticking out her tongue so she could taste the rain. Her heart was suddenly lighter than it had been since her family had been captured. She glanced at Luka, and he grinned too. They were Rom and didn't care a snap of their fingers for a summer storm. Laughing, they ran out into the road and danced. Sweetheart rose up on her hind paws and danced too, though Zizi huddled under Luka's collar. She didn't like the rain at all.

"Come on!" Luka said. "Let's run!"

For five or ten minutes they ran, laughing and splashing each other by jumping with all their force into the puddles.

Soon they were muddy and bedraggled, and drenched to the skin. Then they began to get cold and hungry and tired. The rain was not so much fun after that. Sweetheart lumbered behind, her wet fur hanging in her eyes. Every now and again she lifted her snout and uttered one of her heartfelt moans, perfectly expressing the children's feelings. They too would have liked to stretch out by a fire with a bowl of hot soup and a foaming mug of weak ale. But they had no soup, and no ale, and no fire, and nowhere safe to stop.

"Maybe we could stop and rest at the Cock Inn in Sutton," Luka said.

"I have money," Emilia said, touching her purse, which hung down inside her skirt.

"Clever girl! Let's do that, then. I can't walk any further."

The idea of stopping for a drink and a bite to eat gave them fresh energy. They could see the village of Sutton clearly now. It lay just ahead, a scatter of houses about the green. It was dusk and smoke was rising from the inn, smelling of home.

A tall hedge rose up on one side, cutting out the light. They passed a set of iron gates, closed shut with a rusty chain that led on to a drive lined with rhododendrons that had grown so tall they gave the impression of a dark tunnel curving away. Above the hedge they could see the roof and chimneys of an old manor house, overgrown with ivy.

Wheels rattled behind them. Luka and Emilia looked

back in dread. A large black carriage drawn by four horses was just cresting the hill.

"Here! Quick!" Luka pushed his way into the hedge, dragging on Sweetheart's chain to make her follow. The bear widened the gap enough for Emilia to lead Alida through, Rollo at their heels. The branches sprang back to hide them, and two children crouched in the gloom under the dripping trees, hardly daring to breathe.

The carriage drew up, the horses whinnying and stamping, restless at the faint scent of bear lingering in the laneway.

"What is it? Why have we stopped?"

Luka and Emilia shrank back at the sound of the pastor's voice.

"I thought I saw something, sir," the coachman said. "Something moving in the shadows under the hedge like it was trying to hide. You told me to keep a good lookout, sir; I thought you might like me to get down and have a look."

"Very well, but be quick; I am on God's business and He shall not suffer to be kept waiting," the pastor said, leaning out of the window. It sounded as though he was looming right over them. Luka had his hand on Sweetheart's muzzle to keep her quiet, and she stood obediently still, looking puzzled.

They heard the coachman jump down to the ground. "Easy, boys, easy," he said to the horses. "Settle down. They're right spooked, sir. Something's got them twitchy."

His boots crunched on the dirt of the road as he walked along the hedgerow, sweeping through the wet branches with his whip. They heard him rattle the gates, and prowl about a bit more, and then he came back.

"Gates locked up tight, sir. No sign of anyone about."

"Nay, of course not. No one's lived here since Henry Tudor cut off Sir Nicholas's head. It's been empty for years."

"Maybe that why the horses are so twitchety. Ghosts about."

"Nonsense," the pastor said coldly. "Drive on! Stop at the inn ahead and see if anyone has seen any sign of those two gypsy children. They should be easy enough to remember, with their menagerie of wild beasts. A dog, a horse, a bear and a monkey, for pity's sake!"

The coachman climbed back up on to his box and snapped out his whip. The horses took off at once, anxious to be away from the strange predatory smell drifting from the undergrowth. On the other side of the hedge, Sweetheart yawned and scratched her ear, and nudged Luka's leg with her nose as if asking him for her ale.

"Lucky we didn't go to the inn," Emilia said.

Luka looked rather pale. "Aye!"

"I'm so tired, I don't want to walk any more."

"Me neither."

They lay on the wet ground with the black leaves dripping water all over them, their legs aching, their stomachs hollow.

"I can't believe they're still looking for us. Why does that mean old Fish-Face hate us so much? Why is he hunting us down?"

"Maybe it's because I made him sit down in some cow muck," Emilia said. "Or maybe he just hates the Rom. He looks the sort of man who hates just about everyone."

"How could anyone hate Mimi?" Luka bit his lip.

"Or Noah?"

Sweetheart moaned and put her paw over her eyes.

Emilia and Luka laughed ruefully, then heaved a big sigh and sat up. It was almost dark, and all they could hear was the drip, drip, drip of the rain through the trees.

"We're still miles away from Epsom."

"Let's go and have a look at this house, then," Luka said. "Maybe there's somewhere we can doss down for a while. It'll be good to cook our fish. I'm starving!"

"Me too," Emilia said miserably.

"Well, come on, then."

Emilia hung back. "But what if there's ghosts?"

"It was Sweetheart the horses were jibbing at, not ghosts," Luka scoffed.

"Aye, but. . ."

"Come on. It's almost dark. We won't be able to see a thing if we don't go now."

"Oh, very well." Emilia got up, shaking all the leaves and twigs off her wet skirts, which were now so muddy they were almost as brown as her everyday skirt. They pushed their way through the undergrowth and out on to the lawn in front of the house. It had stopped raining, and an eerie light hung over the silent house and garden as the setting sun shone out from under the clouds. Everything was very quiet.

Alida dropped her head and began tearing at the long grass. Sweetheart lay down on the flagstones with a sigh and rested her head on her paws. She did not understand where her master was, or why no one had set up camp and given her any supper. It was all very tiring and bewildering.

With Zizi scampering ahead of them, Emilia and Luka walked round the house, looking up at the shrouded windows and occasionally trying the handles of any door they passed. All was locked, though, and they had no desire to smash a window unless they had to. At the back of the house they saw a door standing ajar, and went into a musty-smelling scullery with a pump, where they were able to quench their thirst.

Baba had hung a small lantern on the side of their pack, and Luka managed to light this and set it on the sill. In doing so, he knocked over an old saucer, which fell to the ground and broke. Amongst the shards of china was a key. They glanced at each other in excitement. The key was stiff and rusty, but Luka managed to turn it in the lock. The door creaked open.

Keeping the lantern shuttered, the two children tiptoed into the house. The kitchen was dark and cavernous, with pots and pans and ladles still hanging over the long table, and dried bunches of herbs spun all round with cobwebs. More cobwebs hung from the ceiling, furred with dust, and they saw spiders scuttling away from their light. Luka shuddered. He hated spiders.

Beyond the kitchen was a corridor leading to the front hall, where portraits of long-dead people hung on the walls. It made Emilia shiver, seeing those eyes staring down at her from the walls. She pressed close to Luka, who was pretending to be brave and striding out nonchalantly.

Zizi jumped down from Luka's shoulder and scampered about, leaving little monkey tracks in the thick dust on the floor. Glancing back, Emilia saw the trail of their footprints behind them. Uneasily, she scuffled her bare foot back and forth, wiping her last few steps out, then lifted the sole of her foot. It was grey.

Zizi pushed open a door and scampered inside and the two children followed her, Luka casting his lantern from side to side so they could see. The ray of light fell upon a huge pale shape floating in the gloom. Emilia screamed. Luka fell back a step, and they pressed together, shivering, too frightened to move. Zizi leapt on top of the dreadful white lump and gibbered in terror as it suddenly slithered away under her paws. Immediately she bounded to the safety of Luka's shoulder.

"Look, it's just a couch, covered in some kind of cloth."

Emilia pressed her hand to her heart. "I thought it was a ghost for sure."

"Me too." Luka moved around the room, pulling more dustsheets off the furniture. Clouds of dust rose into the air, making Emilia cough and Zizi sneeze.

"Stop it!" Emilia cried. "I can't breathe."

"I just wanted to see what was underneath," Luka said. "Look, they're not too dusty under those sheets. We could sit on them."

He had uncovered several tall wooden chairs with hard backs, and a long bench made of oak by the fire. With a tired sigh, Emilia sat down, pulling her legs up under her damp, muddy skirts and wrapping the material about her icy feet. Luka cried out with joy as he found some firewood in a chest against one wall. He quickly kindled a fire in the hearth.

"I'll go and see if I can find a pan or something to cook the fish in, and then I'll bring Alida and Sweetheart in," he said. "Will you be all right here?"

Emilia nodded, even though she would have much preferred not to be left alone. She was too tired to move, though, and the warmth of the dancing flames was comforting. She rested her head on her arm, and wondered how Beatrice and Noah were. Tears rose in her eyes and she sniffed them back, determined not to cry any more.

Alone and half-asleep in the fire-lit, cavernous darkness, Emilia thought she saw people in old-fashioned garments laughing and talking, drinking wine from gem-studded goblets and eating from little trays carried about by servants in livery. She sat up, unable to breathe for terror, and rubbed her eyes, which were stinging from the smoke. The dream – if that was what it was – dissolved. She found herself with only the shadows of flames for company.

The door creaked open. Emilia sat up, stiff with fear. It was only Zizi scampering in, proudly carrying a ladle. After her came Luka, carrying a saucepan, while behind ambled Sweetheart and Alida, both damp and ruffled.

"I don't like this house," Emilia said.

"No. At least we're not sleeping in the ditch, though. It's pouring with rain. Sweetheart was not at all happy about getting wet."

Emilia looked at the bear and the horse, standing in the middle of the grand drawing-room with all its tapestries and carved furniture, and suddenly grinned. They looked as out-of-place as she felt. Luka grinned too. "Imagine the look on the squire's face if we'd brought a horse and a bear into his drawing-room? He'd pop a vein!"

"Not to mention a monkey!"

Sweetheart lay down before the fire with a sigh. Steam began to rise up from her coat. Emilia screwed up her nose and moved away. Wet bear was not a pleasant smell.

Luka cleared a spot for Alida to stand, and rubbed her down while Emilia put the water and potatoes on to boil. Luka had already scaled and gutted the fish, and cut it into chunks, for which Emilia was extremely grateful. She hated gutting fish.

She told Luka about her dream while she tossed the chunks of fish into the water. "I wonder who lived here, and where they've gone."

"I'm just grateful for it," said Luka pragmatically. "We'd have been in trouble if someone still lived here."

"Aye, I suppose so." Emilia stirred the stew. She was feeling very tired and melancholy. It seemed to her this house was full of the ghosts of sad people; that indeed, the world was haunted by sorrow.

Yesterday the world had seemed a safe and sunny place, where people were in general kind and fair, and tales of cruelty and injustice and war were just that – tales told about the fire to send a shiver down the spine, but then forgotten. Now, though, her family was facing death. She and Luka were alone. The world was suddenly vast and frightening.

Luka saw her face and took the ladle from her. "Here, I'll do that. You take off all your wet clothes and spread them out by the fire. We may as well get warm and dry. By then the stew will be ready and we can think what to do next."

"Baba said to find our kin and ask them for their help," Emilia said, unbuttoning her skirt. "She said if we joined all the charms together. . ."

"It would do what?" Luka asked.

"It would help us to better times." As she stepped out of her skirt and spread it to dry on the back of one of the chairs, she told Luka all that Baba had told her, and saw him frown. Luka was a practical boy, and did not have much faith in magic and miracles. Oddly, by trying to convince him – and failing – Emilia argued herself into a more positive frame of mind, finding her own faith renewed.

"Well, one thing at a time," Luka said at last. "We'll eat and sleep, and then in the morning we'll head to the Downs and look for the Hearnes. You can ask them for their charm if you think it'll help us. *I* plan to ask them to help us break everyone out."

"Break them out of prison!" Emilia cried. "But . . . how?"

"I don't know how," Luka said. "We'll have to think of a plan. I saw where the guard kept his keys. Maybe I can steal them."

"But surely they'll just chase after us and catch us again," Emilia said. "And what about our caravans and horses, how are we to get them out?"

Luka grimaced. "I can't think of everything all at once," he said. "But with a little bit of luck, we'll be able to save them, I'm sure of it."

A little bit of luck. . .

Emilia touched the old coin. "Aye, for sure."

The Royal Forest

Nonsuch Park, Surrey, England
13 August 1658

Emilia woke and looked about her. At first she did not know where she was. Then her eyes identified the black hump of the sleeping bear silhouetted against the glowing coals. Memory rushed back upon her. She pressed her hands against her chest, overwhelmed by dread and sadness. She wondered how Beatrice felt, waking in prison. She wondered if Noah was very afraid.

It was not yet dawn. She could not hear any birds, and the shuttered window was not leaking any light. She leant over and laid her hand on Luka.

Luka was awake at once. "What is it?"

"Time to go," Emilia said.

"It's morning?"

"Almost. But it'd be better if we tried to get through Sutton before everyone's about. We don't want anyone to see us and report us to that Fish-Face."

"Aye. All right." Luka stretched and yawned. "Ouch, I'm stiff! Is there anything left to eat in the bag? I'm starving!"

"A heel of bread and some old cheese is all."

Luka sighed. "Chuck them to me, I'll toast them on the fire. I wish we had some ale. I'm so thirsty."

"Me too. I feel really grimy too. I'd love a wash. I wish there was a stream so I could have a bath."

The Rom had very strict laws about where they washed – it must always be in running water, and always in a different spot to where clothes were washed, or animals watered, or water drawn for drinking and cooking.

"Maybe Sweetheart will catch us some more fish if we find a stream," Emilia said. "Really, she's a very useful bear."

"If a little hard to hide," Luka retorted. "Here, have some bread and cheese. Watch out, it's hot!"

Emilia blew on it and gingerly nibbled at its edge. The melted cheese burnt her mouth, but she was so hungry she did not care. She gave some to Rollo, who swallowed it whole, then begged for more. Sweetheart moaned, and Luka gave her some of his, which was gone in seconds. "We need to get some more food. The animals are hungry."

"Maybe I'll catch us a rabbit in the forest," Emilia said.

They had packed up last night before going to sleep, so that all they had to do was put on their outer clothes and pick up the bag. It clanked as Luka swung it on to

70

his shoulder. He had tied the pan and the lantern to the outside so there was room to fit his violin inside.

They went through the silent, echoing house, Alida's hooves clip-clopping loudly on the flagstones, and locked the kitchen door behind them, hiding the key on the scullery sill again. The sky was turning grey to the east, but they still needed their lantern to see their way through the gardens. The rain had blown over, but all was dank and wet, and Emilia's feet were soon freezing again. They squeezed out through the gap in the hedge, clambered on to Alida's back, and went on down the road.

All was quiet in the village of Sutton. The Cock Inn was dark and shuttered, with only one lantern hanging above the door. As they went by, they looked up and down the crossroads, but there was no sign of any black coach drawn by four black horses, or of any vehicle at all. Sighing in relief, they rode on.

A mile or so past Sutton, forest closed in around the road. The children were glad of this, for the sun was almost up and smoke was beginning to wisp up from the cottages in the fields. Along the eastern side of the road ran a high wall of red Tudor brick. Beyond the wall could be seen a few treetops and then, in the distance, the grand towers of Nonsuch Palace. When they came to a massive pair of iron gates, Luka and Emilia looked through in interest.

They saw a vast stretch of velvet green lawns, all silvered with dew, and intricate formal gardens of clipped hedges and trees cut in fantastic shapes. Beyond was an ornate building with tall octagonal towers topped with minarets and flying with flags. Every inch of stonework was heavily carved and fretted.

"Can't be a friend of Old Ironsides' living there, then," Luka said. "The Puritans don't believe in pleasure gardens. Only gardens grown in sober toil and godly labour." He put his hands together and turned his eyes up to heaven.

"I'd like to explore in there," Emilia said. "It's really pretty."

"Come on, no time for dabbling in the dew," Luka said.

Reluctantly Emilia turned Alida's head away.

Suddenly there was a clamour of barking. Emilia almost jumped out of her skin. Rollo barked back loudly. She kicked Alida into a canter, whistling to Rollo. Looking back, Emilia saw a man in a long coat with seven dogs on leashes, all straining to be free, hurrying down the drive towards them.

"Did he see us?" Luka panted, yanking on Sweetheart's chain. The lantern and the pan clanked together loudly, and Emilia winced.

"I don't know," she hissed, "but he's heard us for sure now."

"Get off the road, head into the forest," Luka said. "Maybe we'll lose them there."

They heard the sound of the gate being unlocked and swung open, and the excited baying of dogs on a scent. A horn rang out.

In and out of the trees they weaved, Sweetheart running behind them, Luka keeping a tight grip on her chain. Rollo ran ahead, nose to the ground. Still the dogs bayed behind them. Emilia glanced back. She could see them running full-pelt. A man was running with them, shouting and urging them on. They heard his horn again.

"Why's he chasing us? We did no harm. We were only looking."

Emilia bent low over Alida's neck and tried to think. Her mare could not gallop for ever, and the hounds were swift. She could perhaps have charmed them into friendship, if she had the time, and a bit of meat about her, but her hands were empty, and the scent of the bear was sending the dogs wild.

"Alida, I'm sorry, darling," she whispered, bending to pat her mare's damp neck. "Just a little bit more. . ."

Alida galloped on.

The path petered out in a thick tangle of blackberry brambles. The dogs cornered them a few seconds later, baying in triumph. Ferociously Rollo fought back, as Alida reared, trying to keep the hounds away with her hooves. Sweetheart roared. She rose up on her hind paws and swept one dog aside with her massive claws. Yelping, it tumbled head over heels. Another two dogs attacked. One went for her snout, the other for her flank. Sweetheart roared again, in pain and confusion, and fought back.

Luka, clinging desperately to Emilia's waist as the

mare spun and reared, drew the knife from his pack and tried to stab the dog leaping up at them. For a moment all was confusion and noise.

Then the huntsman arrived, breathing heavily, his leathers splashed with mud. He lifted his horn to his lips and gave a mighty blast, then, when his dogs would not come to heel, laid about him with his whip. The hounds slunk back, tails between their legs, growling still. The huntsman put away his horn and took out a pistol.

"The tinker brats," he said, observing Luka and Emilia with great satisfaction. "Pastor Spurgeon will be so pleased. When he told me to look out for you, I was not expecting to have you the very next morn."

Rollo crouched, licking his leg. Alida trembled with fear, her ears laid back, her eyes showing a rim of white. Zizi had her face covered with her paws. Behind the huntsman, the dogs growled and slunk about, showing their teeth.

Sweetheart stood up on her hind legs and lifted her snout high, moaning in distress and bewilderment.

"Can you control that bear, or will I shoot it now?" the huntsman said.

Luka gritted his teeth together, and tugged gently on Sweetheart's chain. She put her paws up to clasp her sore nose. "Come on, Sweetheart." Luka tugged on the chain again. She sighed and got down on all fours, ambling closer to him with an air of long suffering.

"Quite a clown," the huntsman said. "I'm guessing

she's not used to being baited by dogs. She's lucky she didn't kill any of them, for then I would have shot her, chain or not. Now, do not even think of trying to escape me. I'll simply set the dogs to hunt you down again, and have a fine morning's sport for my trouble. And do not let that bear get out of hand, else I'll shoot her down and that loathsome little monkey too. I suggest you ride back quietly, like good little children, and then no one will get hurt. Understand me?"

"Yes, sir," Luka said sullenly.

"Very good. Come along, then."

Nonsuch Palace was a truly magnificent building. A broad terrace ran its length, lined with great balls and heraldic beasts of white stone. Beyond stretched the grounds, with a formal knot garden bounded by hedges, leading on to lawns and groves of flowing shrubs. Swans floated on the lake.

Emilia and Luka were so dispirited they hardly noticed.

"King Harry knocked down a whole village to build this place," the huntsman said. "The church and all the houses. My grandfather was a little boy then. He and his family had to move to Ewell."

Luka and Emilia did not reply.

"See the decorations. King Harry had them built when his son was born."

Emilia stared. She had never seen anything so ornate. The panels seemed to depict a king about his various duties: sitting in judgement, touching the sick, feasting, hunting and fighting.

"Good Queen Bess loved this place," the huntsman went on. "That was when my father was head hunter here. She died here, you know."

It was clear from the huntsman's voice that he loved the palace and grounds. Emilia found her voice.

"Who . . . who lives here now?"

"Colonel Pride." His voice was carefully neutral. "Must've heard of him. Pride's Purge? It's famous."

Emilia had heard of it vaguely, but she was not much interested in politics and tended to slip away and play whenever the adults began arguing over the campfire. Luka considered himself almost a man now, though, and that meant taking part in, or at least listening to, adult conversation. His eyes widened in surprise.

"You don't mean . . . not the man who arrested all the Royalists in Parliament, so they could not stop the king's head being chopped off?"

"The very same," the huntsman said. "Colonel Pride was well rewarded for his purge, indeed he was. Living in the finest palace in the land, hunting and drinking and feasting like royalty himself."

For a moment they thought he would say more, but then the great door to the palace was flung open, and the huntsman bowed low, doffing his hat.

A grossly large man stood in the doorway, the buttons of his coat straining over his belly, a huge, stained napkin tucked under his chin. He held a pheasant leg in one hand and his mouth shone with grease. Behind him stood Coldham, looking very dour.

"Are these the gypsy brats?" the colonel boomed. "Good work, Jenkyns, good work! Bring 'em in, bring 'em in. Spurgeon's eager to see them."

"What of the animals?"

"Lord, man, I don't know. Shoot 'em or lock 'em in the stables, do you think I care? It's the brats Spurgeon's interested in, Lord knows why. Filthy little beasts."

Luka and Emilia were very frightened by this and clung to their animal friends, Emilia with one hand on Alida and one hand on Rollo, Luka cuddling his little monkey up under his neck, his free hand on Sweetheart's snout.

The huntsman said, "Give them to me. I'll put them in the stable for now."

Emilia and Luka shook their heads emphatically. Jenkyns sighed and cocked his pistol. "Else I could just shoot them, whatever you prefer."

"Please don't hurt them. Please," Emilia said, and the huntsman grunted and took Alida's reins in his free hand. After a moment Luka passed him Sweetheart's chain. "She's very hungry," he said.

"You expect me to feed your pet bear?" Jenkyns asked in exasperation. Then he rolled his eyes and said, "What does she eat?"

"Anything, really."

"She likes a nice drop of ale," Emilia said, her voice quavering despite herself.

"Don't we all," the huntsman said. "Give me the monkey, then. I suppose you want me to feed her too?"

"Not Zizi, please," Luka said. "She's never apart from me; she'll be frightened. Please."

The huntsman sighed and hefted his pistol. "Your choice."

Zizi suddenly leapt off Luka's shoulder and on to the huntsman's, dragging his hat down over his eyes. She bounded away at top speed, clambering up the sculptured frieze along the wall. Emilia could not help laughing as Zizi perched on the stone crown of the king at his feast. The huntsman lifted his gun and aimed, but Luka clung desperately to his arm. The pistol went off, shattering a stone urn planted with flowers. Startled by the noise, Zizi made a flying leap up to the top of the wall, then disappeared through an open window and into the palace.

"Nincompoop!" the colonel roared. "Now I've got a nasty flea-ridden monkey running amok in my house! You should have shot it!"

"Sorry, sir." Jenkyns gave Luka an evil look. "I did try."

"I thought you were meant to be a crack shot! A crack shot, I say! Can't even hit a monkey in broad daylight. Nincompoop!"

"Don't blame your hunter; it wasn't his fault. Blame those rotten little ragamuffins!" Coldham said in his harsh, grating voice.

"What will my housekeeper say, I ask you? A monkey

in my house! Fleas! Dirt! Breaking things! Should've shot it is what I say." The colonel turned and stumped back into the palace, consoling himself with another huge bite of his pheasant's leg.

The huntsman turned and led the dog, the horse and the bear away. The children were left with Coldham. He dropped his hands on their shoulders. They were unbearably hard and heavy. Squirming a little, trying to hide their anxiety, the children were pushed up the steps and taken into a vast hall, magnificently decorated and hung with shields and banners. Through one chamber after another they were pushed, each more lavishly decorated than the one before, till they ended up in a room dominated by a table groaning with all sorts of food. Emilia and Luka saw a platter of pheasants, a gleaming pink ham, a dish of eggs swimming in butter, smoked herrings and a steaming plate of roast beef, all flanked by jugs of foaming ale. Their mouths watered and their stomachs grumbled. They were so transfixed they barely noticed the pastor sitting at the table, a virtually empty plate before him, his fingers drumming impatiently.

"Here you go, Spurgeon, the gypsy brats you wanted. Nothing if not quick off the mark, hey?" The colonel grunted with laughter, his triple chins wobbling, then dropped into his chair. "But you're not eating, man. Eat up, eat up!"

The pastor ignored him. "Indeed, your hunter has done his work well," he said in a low, cold voice. "Better

79

than my man, who let these squalid little gypsies slip his net."

"I beg pardon, sir," Coldham said gruffly. "It won't happen again."

"Indeed it won't, because you shall take these spawn of Satan back to Kingston-upon-Thames this very day, and you will have them up before the magistrates by the end of the month, and you will see them hang."

The colonel looked up, startled. "Hang? You mean to hang 'em, my dear fellow? Not to say they aren't nasty little pests, but a little young, don't you think?"

"Never too young to stamp out the Devil," the pastor said.

The colonel had stopped chewing. His mouth hung open, showing a lump of grey, half-chewed pheasant meat. Then he shrugged and went back to eating. "Whatever you say, dear fellow," he mumbled. "I cannot think you do our cause any good, though, to hang such a pair of grubby brats. What is their crime? You know the Lord Protector abhors a judge too quick to hang."

The pastor was quiet for a moment, frowning and looking very displeased. "Coldham," he snapped. "Go through their bag. Let us see with our own eyes what Devil's wares they carry."

Luka clutched the bag closer. Both he and Emilia remembered, too late, what Maggie had said about her crystal ball and fortune-telling cards. They should have thrown the bag away during the chase through the forest. Coldham wrested the bag from them and upended it on the table. He found the crystal ball and tarot cards at once. He held them up for the pastor to see, almost smiling.

"Aha, behold the malignancy of their sin," the pastor cried, that strange burning light in his eyes again. "Indeed, they are about the work of the Devil. See there his prayer books, painted with all sorts of foul and loathsome idols; and their scrying ball, for contacting and communicating with his evil spirits. Did I not tell you? And what is the penalty for those wicked and devilish arts called witchcraft? Death! Only then can we stamp out the Devil in them!"

"So help me God," Coldham said piously.

Luka glanced at him in dislike. He found the pastor terrifying, but also strangely fascinating. But Coldham was just plain old mean.

The colonel shrugged and returned to his meal, piling his plate high with beef and eggs and fried potatoes.

The pastor looked displeased to have his oratory ignored in favour of roast beef. "Remember, Colonel," he said in a menacing voice, "that you must keep from temptation. Lay siege to your sins and starve them out, by keeping away the food and fuel which is their maintenance and life."

"Well said, well said," the colonel replied, cramming a huge forkful into his mouth. "Come, my dear fellow, you must be hungry after all that high talk. Sit down, man, and eat, before you waste away to a shadow. A shadow, I say!"

"I thank you, I have had enough," the pastor replied coldly. "Colonel, we still have business to discuss. When you have finished your meal, perhaps you could find some time to spare me? I am a busy man."

"Aye, indeed, indeed," the colonel said through a mouthful of beef. "In due time, of course, my dear fellow, in due time."

"Coldham, I'll need my horses set to, and my carriage prepared. Make sure all is ready for me within the half-hour. In the meantime, get these children out of here. We do not want to spoil Colonel Pride's appetite."

The Wheel Of Fortune

Coldham began to drag the children away, but the colonel saw the longing glance they cast at the food and raised a pudgy hand, saying wheezily, "Hold your horses, man, no need to lock 'em up just yet. Scrawny a pair of brats as I've ever laid eyes on. Hungry?"

"Aye, sir," Luka said, and Emilia nodded emphatically.

"May as well fill your bellies, then, plenty of food, hey? Plenty of food here." He wheezed with laughter again. "Pull up a pew, brats. What's your poison?"

"It all looks good, sir." Luka was so hungry he felt quite ill, and did not hesitate in grabbing whatever was closest and cramming it into his mouth. Emilia did the same. Any moment now the pastor could come back and order them thrown into a dungeon with nothing but dry bread and maggotty gruel to eat.

Today we feast, Emilia thought. *Tomorrow we'll starve. . .*

"So food's good, hey? Hey?" The colonel seemed torn between disgust and amusement.

They nodded but did not pause to reply.

"Aye, my cook is the best in three counties," the colonel said, folding his hands across his belly. He cast a look of dislike at Coldham and said, "Hadn't you best be about your master's business, man? Pastor Spurgeon strikes me as one who doesn't like to be kept waiting. What? Oh, no need to worry about the tinker brats. There's plenty of men here to keep them in hand." He waved at his footmen, standing stolidly against the wall in their grand livery. "I'll have them brought out to you when they've had a bite to eat."

"Yes, sir," Coldham said unwillingly, and went out of the room.

The colonel at once sat up and leant forward. "So, a fortune-teller, hey?" He waved his pudgy hand at the crystal ball. "Not good enough a fortune-teller to predict your own misfortunes, hey? Hey?"

Emilia was stung to the quick. "We have not had time to be stopping and laying out the cards, or looking in the ball," she said. "We've been on the run, chased by that horrible man, since yesterday morning! And all because he saw my sister singing in the marketplace."

The colonel looked solemn. "Oh, well, singing, you know. And fiddling too, he told me. Devil's work."

Emilia reached out her trembling hands and took hold of the crystal ball, warming it between her palms. It was her grandmother's, and she was glad she had not smashed it, even if it did mean Pastor Spurgeon had cause to condemn them.

"Well, well, fortune's a funny thing, ain't it?" the colonel said. "I mean, who could have guessed that me, a mere brewer's apprentice, would end up here, in Queen Bess's own palace, with an army of servants to pick up after me, and as much roast beef as I like? If a fortune-teller had told me that as a boy, I would have laughed in her face, aye, I would. Laughed fit to burst myself, I would. Yet here I am, jolly as you please. . ."

Emilia had been staring down into the crystal ball as he spoke. She felt strangely light-headed. It was as though the cloudy white ball had grown until it filled all her world, while the room shrank away and became misty. She felt her mouth open and heard words come out, but even though it was her voice that spoke, she did not know where the words came from.

"Yet those that rise can fall, and the wheel of fortune raise up those who were ground into dust. So know that you are bound to the wheel of fortune too, and it shall see you die before the year is out, and in time they shall order your rotting body to be dug up and hung on the gallows at Tyburn, and you shall suffer a second death, a traitor's death, for the deeds you have done, and it is as a traitor and a killer of kings that you shall be remembered, when nothing of this palace remains but stones and weeds. . ."

As Emilia spoke, she raised her eyes from the crystal ball and fixed them on the colonel's face, and she saw it turn purple. He half-rose from his chair, gasping and clutching at his collar, his eyes bulging. Then he fell, crashing to the floor. His footmen all scrambled to his side, loosening his collar, dashing water in his face and endeavouring to lift up his massive weight.

Luka grabbed the bag, swept all their belongings back into it, along with all the ham and roast pheasant and smoked herrings that he could reach; then he grasped Emilia's arm and dragged her to her feet.

"Not bad," he said. "Risky, but it seems to have worked. Come on! Let's get out of here."

He swung open one of the windows and pushed Emilia out of it, holding on to her wrists and lowering her down to the lawn below. She went without a word, her gaze still fixed on the gasping, purple face of the colonel. She felt utterly bewildered, as if she had been woken in the middle of a dream. Then Luka landed lightly beside her and began to run, dragging her along with him.

"Old Pride-Before-A-Fall had an absolute apoplexy," he chuckled. "Did you see his face? I wonder you dared, spouting such stuff at him, Emilia. Come on! Where do you reckon the stables are?"

Behind them, a footman was leaning out of the window and shouting, shaking a fist at them, but no one attempted to climb out after them, possibly because their trousers were so tight.

"They'll be after us," Luka said. "Let's look smartly! I wonder where Zizi is?" He lifted two fingers to his mouth, and gave a high, shrill whistle. A few minutes later he whistled again.

They came to the corner of the building and looked around it carefully. Before them lay the stable wing, where Coldham was busy giving orders to the grooms harnessing the four black horses to the pastor's black coach. Beyond was an orchard where Sweetheart dozed in the sun, occasionally twitching an ear at the flies.

All was peaceful and quiet. News of the children's escape had yet to reach the stables.

"Do you reckon you can sneak into the stables and get Alida out?" Luka said. "Rollo will be in there too. I'll get Sweetheart, no one's minding her."

"But what will we do then?" Emilia asked. "We still have to get out of the grounds."

Luka was only half-listening, staring back at the palace. His eyes lit up as he saw Zizi come scampering down one of the towers, using the carved stonework like a ladder. She had evidently heard his whistle.

"Darling girl!" Luka cried, and she leapt into his arms and cuddled her tiny arms about his neck. "Where have you been?" he scolded. "I was that worried."

She chittered back at him, as if giving him a full explanation, and he listened gravely and then said, "Oh well, no harm done. I hope you made a right fine mess, monkey girl."

Emilia rolled her eyes at this touching reunion.

"Come on, Zizi-girl, let's go and get Sweetheart," Luka said to the monkey.

"But what then?" Emilia asked again. "How will we get out of here?"

Luka considered. "Do you think you could steal that coach?"

"Steal the pastor's own coach?" Emilia cried, then clapped her hand over her mouth to stifle her giggles. "Sure, and why not?"

"The trick will be getting out the gates, but hopefully, if we gallop fast enough, they'll open them for us before they see it's not the pastor."

"With a bit of luck, we'll get through," Emilia said, rubbing the golden coin at her wrist.

"Right, let's do it," Luka said.

Together they sneaked quietly round to the back of the stables; then Emilia tiptoed inside while Luka ran and got Sweetheart, Zizi clinging to his shoulder. It was dark and quiet inside the vast stables, with horses resting inside their stalls. All the grooms were out in the courtyard, talking with Coldham. The four horses were all in their harness, and the coachman was at the leader's head, holding his bridle as he waited for the pastor to appear.

Alida was inside a stall, looking over the gate expectantly, her ears pricked forward. Rollo lay in the straw beside her, licking his wounds. At the sound of Emilia's footsteps, he got up, wagging his tail.

Emilia quietly opened the gate to the stall, propping it open with a brick. "Stay," she whispered to the two animals, holding up one finger imperiously. "Stay till I whistle."

Rollo's tail sank, but he sat down obediently, his brown eyes fixed on her face. Alida pawed the ground, shook her mane and hurrumphed.

Emilia ran quietly down the stables and crept round to the side of the coach, pressed between it and the wall. The coachman would have seen her if he had turned his head, but no one was looking back at the stables. Nimbly she clambered up on to the roof of the coach, then lay there, waiting for the right moment.

She did not lie there very long. A footman came running out of the palace and excitedly told them about the colonel's fit and the gypsy children's escape. Everyone crowded around him, demanding more details. As the footman told his story with great vigour, Emilia lowered herself into the driver's seat and took the driver's whip out of its stand.

With a great *crack!* she brought the whip down about the horses' ears. They reared and whinnied, and took off, knocking over the coachman and scattering the grooms and other servants. At a great pace the coach-horses galloped off down the drive, and Emilia whistled loudly. At once Alida came cantering out of the stables and raced after them, her white tail flying. Rollo bounded along beside her, barking with joy.

The drive led past the orchard. At its furthermost point, Emilia – who was well-used to driving her grandmother's caravan but was finding the four horses infinitely more challenging – managed to bring them to a snorting, prancing halt. Immediately Luka came running out from behind a tree with Sweetheart lumbering along behind him. The horses went mad, but Emilia managed to hold them long enough for the bear to clamber up into the coach, Luka pushing her ample behind in through the narrow door. Then he swung himself up too, Zizi on his shoulder. Emilia gave the horses their heads.

At the sound of the galloping hooves, the gatekeeper came running out and opened the gates wide. Then he bowed and doffed his hat. It was not until he had straightened up that he realized that the coach was being driven by a tangle-haired gypsy girl with a grubby face and a very bedraggled pink skirt. By that time it was too late. The coach was veering out of the gates and on to the road, and rattling away at high speed, the mare cantering along behind it.

It was not long before they heard hooves drumming along behind them.

Luka, hanging out of the coach window, saw Coldham racing along the road behind them, bent low over the outstretched neck of a big bay.

"Criminy, does he never give up?" Luka cried, and shouted to Emilia to whip up the horses.

Emilia cracked her whip, thinking fast. They could not outrun Coldham, not dragging a heavy coach behind them. They would have to trick him. She drew a deep breath, and turned left at the next crossroads, taking the road away from the Downs. As soon as the road fell down into a dip behind some trees, she drew the horses up and let Luka, Zizi and Sweetheart out to hide in the nearby woods. The horses, spooked by the overpowering smell of bear, needed little encouragement to break into a headlong gallop again. She whistled to Alida, who followed swiftly behind.

She tied the horses' reins to the coach-rail, then stood up on the driver's seat, arms spread. She whistled to Alida, who galloped close alongside. Emilia took a deep breath, then leapt across to Alida's back. The coach rattled on, drawn by four galloping horses. Emilia jumped her mare over the hedge into the field beyond. In an instant Emilia was off Alida's back and urging the mare to her knees, ducking down behind the hedge.

Soon they heard the thunder of galloping hooves. They crouched lower. Then Coldham raced past, pursuing the bolting coach. As soon as he had disappeared over another hill, Emilia was back on Alida's back and going as quietly as possible back to the crossroads, where Luka and Zizi and Sweetheart were waiting.

"Did he fall for it?" Luka whispered.

"I hope so," Emilia whispered back.

"With a bit of luck they'll gallop halfway across the country, and that Cold-Pig will have no idea where we got off," Luka said, grinning.

"We've been mighty lucky escaping him so far." Emilia gave a superstitious shudder, thinking what strange turns their fortunes had taken these past few days.

"Luckier than we deserve," Luka said, cuddling Zizi close.

"It's been too lucky to be just luck," Emilia argued. "It's magic!"

"Magic!" Luka snorted. "You and your magic! No, it's luck, pure and simple. All we need do now is lie low a few hours and then go find the Hearnes' camp."

. . .*and the charm of the silver horse*, Emilia thought.

PART TWO

The Silver Horse

Gypsy Gold

As dusk fell over the high, rolling downs, Luka and Emilia crept out of a stand of trees and jumped over a ditch full of thistles on to a potholed road. Sweetheart lumbered at their heels, and Zizi clung to Luka's shoulder as usual.

"Come on, the coast's clear at last," Luka whispered.

"I'm dying of thirst," Emilia groaned, coaxing her mare to jump the ditch. "And so is Rollo. Look how far his tongue's hanging out. Couldn't we have found somewhere to hide that had a stream or a spring or something?"

"Rollo's tongue is always hanging out," Luka said. "Don't worry, we'll get a drink as soon as we find those Hearnes."

The two children had spent the afternoon hiding in the copse of trees. To the west lay the town of Epsom. To the north ran the road to London. Many carts and carriages had rattled one way or another all afternoon. There was a well beyond the town, the children knew, that was said to have miraculous healing properties.

On the far side of the road rose the great Downs. All afternoon Emilia had lain on her stomach, her chin propped in her hands, staring at them. They rolled up into the sky like the humped shape of a giant sleeping under a green counterpane. The shadow of clouds drifted over them and, as the sun had begun to set, they had slowly turned a strange, eerie purple. Now they were black against the translucent sky, and looked very lonely and mysterious.

Emilia had found it very difficult to lie still when her every instinct was to hurry on and find help for her family. She had nothing to do all day but worry about the terrifying visions she had seen in her grandmother's crystal ball at Nonsuch Palace, and Colonel Pride's dreadful fit. Luka thought she had been very clever, pronouncing her prophecy so that they could escape. What Luka did not realize was that, although it was Emilia's mouth that had spoken the words, it was not Emilia's brain that had framed them. It had been like someone else had spoken through her. This had never happened to Emilia before. She did not understand it. It gave her a nasty feeling, like she was nothing but a glove puppet, with some stranger's hand making her bow and twirl and speak. She wondered if this was how Maggie felt when she prophesized the future. If so, Emilia never wanted to do it again. She was glad to get moving again, and leave the memory of the prophecy behind her.

The children went slowly along the road, their eyes fixed on the ground, searching for a patrin that might tell them which way the Hearne family had travelled. After a while, Luka gave a joyful exclamation. There, near a bridle path up to the Downs, was a loose circle of leaves arranged around a red rock, with an arrow formed of sticks pointing away from the road. The leaves were held down with little twigs.

To anyone else, the muddle of leaves and sticks would have looked like something blown together by the wind, but to the two gypsy children, it was a patrin, a signpost. The Hearne family had gone this way.

The gypsies often left such secret messages behind for their kith and kin, to signal a new direction, to warn of danger, or to pass on news of a friendly farmhouse where a hungry gypsy family might be able to barter for a bit of food.

"There's no cover," Luka said anxiously. "Let's just hope no one comes riding by."

They left the road and followed the bridle path, which soon began to climb steeply. Luka saw some deep ruts left by caravan wheels in the grassy verge and pointed them out to Emilia, who nodded eagerly. It was scary being out in the dark by themselves. Both were eager to huddle by a fire and tell someone their troubles.

The two children paused on the top of the Downs, the wind blowing back their hair. It felt like they were on the top of the world. The sun had almost set, marking the horizon with carmine and gold, but all else was just shadowy dips and undulations, with the sharp spires of the churches and the tall poplar trees stabbing up into the darkening sky. Then Emilia turned to look back the way they had come, and gasped aloud, for there to the north was a false sunrise, a distant glare of orange light.

"That must be London," Luka said beside her.

Emilia was amazed. She could not begin to imagine how many candles and lanterns must be burning, to make such a glow in the sky. "I've always wanted to see London!"

"Well, now you have. Come on, I smell wood-smoke!"

Before long they saw the warm glow of a fire some way ahead of them, illuminating the dark, square shapes of caravans. Luka and Emilia stumbled forward, the animals close on their heels. Dogs began to bark, and Rollo answered furiously.

A lantern was held high. "Who's there?" a man's voice called.

Luka cleared his throat. "It's Luka Finch!" he cried. "Jacob Finch's son. And Emilia, my cousin."

The Hearne family all exclaimed in surprise. "What are you doing here?" cried Felipe, the Big Man of the tribe. "Is there trouble?"

"Aye," Luka said. "Big trouble."

"Have you been followed?" Felipe asked sharply.

"We hope not," Luka answered. "There's a thief-taker on our heels, but we think we lost him."

"You better have," said Cosmo, Felipe's younger brother, a thin man with a face like a ferret.

"Is Beatrice with you?" Sebastien demanded. About sixteen years old, he was long and lean and wiry, and wore a new coat and a gold hoop in his ear.

"She's in gaol!" Emilia's voice wobbled.

There was an exclamation of horror and surprise. "Come to the fire and tell us what's happened," said Janka, a wrinkled old woman who wore gold clanking at her wrists and in her ears. Emilia looked for any sign of the silver horse charm, but it was too dark. It did not seem the right time to ask for the charm, so she sat down shyly, holding her hands out to the fire.

"Look, Mam, they've brought the bear!" a little boy cried.

"Will it play football with us?" another demanded.

"Not tonight, darling boy. Hush now," his mother said, rocking him on her lap.

"Look, there's the monkey too!" sniggered Nadine, a bony girl who had unfortunately inherited her father Cosmo's face. "It's a travelling zoo!"

"Nice horse." Cosmo ran an expert eye over Alida. Even muddy and exhausted, the mare's beautiful lines were obvious. Felipe whistled in admiration, and stepped forward to run his hand down the mare's curving neck, and lift her lip to examine her teeth.

The Hearnes were well-known horse-traders and,

since it was not unknown for a fine horse to disappear when they had been nearby, Emilia drew Alida a little closer to her. Felipe took no notice, lifting her hoof and then expertly counting her ribs. When he saw that Alida had only seventeen ribs, one less than most horses, he glanced at his brother Cosmo meaningfully.

"So, an Arab," Felipe said. "Out of Maja, is she?"

Emilia opened her eyes wide in surprise. Maja had been her mother's horse, and was indeed Alida's dam. Emilia's mother had died five years earlier, from the smallpox. She had given Maja to Emilia to care for, but Maja had been confiscated by Roundheads three years ago, when Alida was little more than a foal. They might have taken the filly too, but Emilia had hidden Alida in her own bunk, under a blanket. It had been like losing her mother all over again, having Maja wrested away from her, and Emilia had been inconsolable for days afterwards. Sometimes it seemed Alida was all she had left of her mother.

"How did you know about Maja?" Emilia demanded, keeping a tight grip on Alida's halter.

Felipe grinned, showing a mouthful of crooked teeth. "Your mother, Elka, was my cousin. I grew up with her. Maja was her dowry when she married your father. She was a fine mare, descended from the great mare Baz, or so my dado said."

Emilia knew the story, of course. Baz was a horse out of mythology, said to have been captured and tamed by the great-great-grandson of Noah. She was the root-stock

100

of all the horses bred by the Bedouins of Arabia, famous for their fleetness, grace and beauty. Emilia had always liked knowing her Alida was bred from such magical stock.

"Look at her dished face," Cosmo said. "Pure Arab, by the look of her. Who was her sire?"

"A stallion owned by our local squire, Sir Hugh Whitehorse. His ancestor rode to the Crusades and brought back some mares and a stallion, all greys. That's where they get their name from, they say. They're famous for their horses."

"So how did ye get a foal out of the squire's stallion?" Nadine demanded. "You must have snuck your mare in late at night." She sniggered.

"Enough, Nadine," Felipe said sharply.

She pouted and flicked back her hair, leaning to whisper something into Sebastien's ear. He frowned and shook his head, moving away from her.

"The Whitehorse family has been good to us," Emilia said defiantly to Felipe.

Felipe made an expansive gesture. "I've heard your dado speak of this family," he said to Luka. "You are lucky to have found safe haven in these troublesome times."

Luka nodded and made an affirmative noise through a mouthful of stew. It was very good. Someone brought them ale, and they drank thirstily. Sweetheart sat up expectantly, and Emilia passed her the cup. The big bear drank it down to the dregs, burped noisily, and then wiped her paw across her snout and held out the cup, begging for more. That made everyone laugh, and some of the awkwardness eased.

Sebastien leant forward, looking anxious. "So what happened? Is Beatrice all right?"

"We went to Kingston Fair, to earn us some gold," Luka said.

"Not singing and dancing?" Felipe said in dismay. "It's a nest of Puritans there now. Best for our kind to stay away."

"You were the ones who told us about the fair," Luka said angrily.

"I never told you any such thing," he said, frowning.

"She did!" Luka said, pointing at Nadine. Everyone looked at her.

She tossed back her hair. "I never thought you'd go to the fair! I thought everyone knew it was a Roundhead town. I guess you've been holed up in the Great North Wood too long." There was a faint shade of contempt in her voice that made Luka flush.

"We'd have warned you if we'd thought you'd go to the fair." Felipe sounded troubled. "But your dado said you'd be heading back Norwood way."

"We changed our minds," Luka said shortly. He was the one who had suggested visiting the fair and he could not help feeling it was all his fault.

"What are the charges?" Cosmo said. When Luka told him, he shook his head and looked away.

"Well, there's nothing we can do, then," Felipe said.

"They'll never pardon a gypsy involved in a constable's death."

Emilia looked wildly at Luka, then back to Felipe. "Please, you've got to help us!"

"I don't see how," Felipe replied, looking apologetic. "I'm sorry, weans. They'll hang for sure."

"Gypsy gold does not glitter," Emilia's grandmother always said. "It gleams in the sun and neighs in the dark."

Lying in the cocoon of her blanket, watching the firelight make strange patterns on the canvas flung over a stick above her head, Emilia remembered these words and felt her despair deepen. The Hearne family was as rich as any gypsy family could be. They had a whole string of horses quite as fine as Alida. Yet they planned to do nothing to help Emilia's family. Nothing!

They had soothed her with soft words and promised to think on the problem overnight, but Emilia could tell by their eyes that they didn't want to stir up trouble for themselves. Felipe, smiling, had asked Luka to play his fiddle for them, which he had done gladly, filling the night with his music, wild and fierce and heartrendingly sad all at once. None of the Hearne family could play like Luka, and they demanded song after song until at last he laid down his fiddle, trembling with weariness.

The Hearnes had given her a blanket and said she could share a tent with some of the other girls. Sweetheart had drunk a bucket of ale and was now snoring by the fire, while Rollo was curled up in the crook of Emilia's knees, his nose on his paws. She did not know where Luka was. He had gone off with Sebastien, and Emilia could only hope he was doing his best to persuade Beatrice's betrothed to break her out of prison. Somehow.

Now the older gypsies were sitting round the fire, smoking their pipes and telling tales, as was their custom. Emilia should have been feeling warm and comfortable and safe, but she felt as desolate and lonesome as she had ever felt. Not wanting anyone to see, she shut her eyes and pretended to sleep.

"Have you heard," Cosmo said, "The Tale of the Wild Hunt?"

"Not for a while," Felipe replied. Janka gave a little cackle, and sucked noisily on her pipe.

"It's on a night like this, when the wind tears across the sky, and howls through the valley, that you might see the Wild Hunt. It is led by Herne the Hunter, and is well-known in these parts. Why, Good King Harry is said to have seen him many times, racing through the Forests of Windsor."

Someone laughed and made a wry comment about the trustworthiness of King Henry the Eighth. Cosmo paid him no heed, but went on, lowering his voice in such a way that Emilia could not help feeling a little thrill.

"Herne the Hunter is dressed all in deer skins, with a helmet on his head made from a stag's skull. A large horned owl flies before him, and a band of wood-demons rides behind him. Their horses are all coal-black, with fiery red eyes, and smoke gushes from their nostrils as they race through the forest, faster than the wind, a pack of hellhounds at their heels. It is said that the sight of the Wild Hunt means death."

"Or at least death to one of your wives," someone called. "How many times did you say Good King Harry saw the hunt?"

Janka chortled. Cosmo gave a grimace, saying sourly, "I just hope you don't see old Herne riding out one wild night. Then you won't be so bold." He tapped out his pipe and leant forward, saying in a meaningful voice, "And if any of you weans wonder why it is our name is so like that of Herne the Hunter, well, think on this. Who else do you know that rides on horses faster than the wind?"

There was a little sigh from the children, who rolled over in their blankets and went off to sleep, imagining themselves galloping over the woods on night-black horses with fiery eyes and breath that gushed like steam. One by one, the grown-ups muttered goodnight and crawled into their tents or climbed up their steps into the caravans. Only a few sat hunched by the fire, smoking their pipes in silence.

"So are the weans asleep?" Felipe said, after a long while.

"Think so," Janka said, and she got to her feet and came over to the tent where Emilia lay quietly, the other young girls sleeping about her. Janka lifted up the edge of the canvas sheet. Rollo stirred, and growled softly in his throat. "Sssh, sssh, all's well." Rollo put his head down again. "Snug as a bug," the old woman said to the men by the fire.

"So, Felipe, what are we to do?" Cosmo said. "The whole Finch family, locked up in gaol!"

"It's bad," Felipe said. "And us connected to them through the betrothal! It could not have come at a worse time. Janka, what do you think? Is there anything we can do to help them?"

"What can we do?" Janka gingerly lowered herself back to the ground. "We don't have the kind of money it would take to get all of them out of prison, and if we did, the Finch family certainly couldn't be paying it back; they haven't two pennies to scratch together."

"I'll wager that's why they took the risk of going into town in the first place," Cosmo said. "To raise the dowry."

"It's a shame, but we're best keeping our noses out of it," Janka said.

"But, Janka, they're our kin. That girl Emilia is the daughter of my cousin, and Beatrice and the blind boy too," Felipe said.

"Show me a gypsy who's not kin somewhere under the skin," Cosmo said sourly. "Are we to risk our necks for every Rom in the land? We'd be dead long ago. No, keep ourselves to ourselves, I say."

"A betrothal is as binding as blood," Felipe said. "That

girl, Beatrice, she is like my daughter now. Would you be leaving Nadine to rot in gaol?"

"Of course not," Cosmo said angrily, "but Nadine's not in gaol, thank the stars. If you're worried about the betrothal, hitch Sebastien to the skinny little sister, and then at least you'd get the horse. She's a beauty, isn't she?"

"Indeed, she is," Felipe said in a soft, caressing voice.

Emilia knew it was Alida, her dapple-grey mare, who brought that tone into the men's voices.

"We could do with a new brood-mare," Cosmo said. "The blasted Roundheads keep taking all our best horses, and half the time they don't come through with the money they promised. Which is why we'd better win tomorrow, Felipe!"

"Don't worry, we'll win," Felipe said. "Russet is the best filly in the whole county; no one can outrun her."

"I bet that grey filly has a motion on her like that," Cosmo said.

"I wonder if the little girl has any idea what she's worth?" Felipe said.

"Probably not." A younger woman's voice spoke for the first time. "But I can tell you one thing, you men. That little girl loves her horse, and at the moment it's the only thing she's got left to love. So don't you go trying any of your tricks on her, do you hear?"

"Julisa, you wrong us, truly you do!" Cosmo's voice was mocking. "We're merely admiring the horse from afar."

"Make sure it stays from afar," Julisa said.

"Now, now, Julisa," Felipe said. "The last thing we want is the attention of the constables. It's a big race tomorrow, there's gold riding on it, and we could get a good price for the mare if we win."

"Horse-racing and gambling, no wonder you don't want any constables nosing around." Julisa's voice dripped with scorn.

"That's right. *We* don't want to end up in gaol."

"Felipe, please, can't you cancel the race? It's too dangerous!"

"I can't, Julisa," Felipe said shortly. "The bets are all laid, and if I back out, I'll be forfeit. I can't afford to call the race off. We'll set lookouts all round, and make sure we have warning of any constables approaching."

Julisa expelled her breath in exasperation. "There's no talking to you men; you always do just what you want, and damn the consequences." Her skirt swished on the grass as she walked to her caravan and climbed inside, shutting the door with a snap.

"I'm off to my bed too." Janka groaned as she struggled to her feet. "There's a damp mist rising, and it makes my poor old bones ache."

Felipe stood too, knocking out his pipe on the log. "We should all sleep. It'll be a hard race tomorrow, and dirty too, with all the rain we've had."

"Not just because of the rain," Cosmo said. "We need to win that race, Felipe."

"Aye, I know."

"Bad luck to have those brats land on our step just now," Cosmo said. "Best send them on their way first thing in the morning."

"How can we? They're only weans."

"They're thirteen, not three," Cosmo said. "Don't be soft, Felipe. They must have other kin they can go to. Send them on their way, and concentrate on winning us that race!"

Felipe grunted in reply, and shut his caravan door. As Cosmo made his own way to bed, Emilia drew her knees to her chest and sobbed quietly into her arms.

Three Chains

Emilia was woken by the sound of Rollo growling softly. How long had she been asleep? It felt as though it was only a moment.

Her eyes were swollen and gritty from crying, but she climbed out from under the canvas. Mist floated along the ground, in pale ghostly wisps that swirled about the caravans. Then a hand reached down out of the darkness for her.

Emilia stifled a scream.

"Ssssh," Sebastien said. "It's only me."

He looked round as a few people shifted in their sleep, and waited until all was quiet again before turning back to Emilia. "What's wrong?" she whispered.

"Luka and I saw the man that's chasing you down in the town," Sebastien said. "It'll only be a matter of time before he finds his way up here. I've got a place where you can hide out until he's gone."

"All right." Emilia pulled her bag towards her. The frying pan tied to it clanked, and Sebastien shushed her again. "Sorry," she hissed, and followed Sebastien as he tiptoed through the campsite. A great shape loomed at her out of the mist, and she caught a whiff of the familiar scent of damp bear. "Sweetheart?" she whispered.

"Sweetheart was easy enough to find; she was sleeping so close to the coals of the fire I thought she'd singe her fur," Sebastien whispered. "But I couldn't find your mare; she seems to have wandered off. Did you tie her up?"

For answer, Emilia pursed up her lips and whistled softly. At once her mare came trotting out of the darkness, ears pricked, tail raised high like a white silken banner.

"She comes when you whistle?" Sebastien was impressed.

"I raised her from a foal. She's better trained than most dogs!"

"Aren't you worried about her being stolen? She's a fine mare."

"I've put a charm on her to keep her from straying, and another to keep her from being stolen." Emilia looked over at Sebastien, who was walking beside her along the top of the downs, Sweetheart ambling behind. "Do you not do that?"

Sebastien shrugged. "My dado's not really one for charms. How does it work, this spell?"

Emilia could not tell from his voice if he really wanted to know or if he was just humouring her, like Luka always did. But she answered him seriously, saying in a hushed voice, "You must cut a lock of your own hair and plait it into the horse's mane, underneath, where it cannot be seen. And you say, 'Stay thou, stay here, thou art mine! Three chains I have, to bind thee to me; one is the wind, one is the sun, one is the earth beneath thy hooves. Where I goest, so must thee; where I stayest, so stayest thee.'"

Emilia took a deep breath. "Then you gather up a little earth from under the hoof of its left foreleg, and take some hairs from its mane and tail, and three drops of its blood, and you sew them into a little bag with some grass, or straw, and bury them somewhere deep, where it will not be dug up by a dog or a badger. As you bury the bag, you say, 'A straw, a hair! May you never be hungry. May he who steals you die, like the hair and the straw, may he go into the ground, never to come out. Earth, these things I give to you, may this horse be strong and fleet and tireless, and forever mine.'"

"And you did all this? You buried this charm and spoke this spell?"

"Aye."

"You think that's why she never strays?"

"And because she knows who feeds her," Emilia said practically.

They walked on in silence for a while, Sebastien's eyes on the path, which floated before them in the darkness like a pale, undulating ribbon. To the south the Downs fell away very steeply, and it was dangerous to wander them at night, when the ground could suddenly dissolve into emptiness.

All was quiet. Even their footsteps were silent, muffled by the mist that flowed up around their waists like water. Emilia shivered. Everything was strange and dreamlike, the fog stroking her cheek with pale, clammy fingers, the wind keening softly in her ear, the Downs rolling away, empty and unchanging. She thought she heard someone following them and snapped her head around, but could see nothing but drifting mist.

"Where are we going?" she whispered, as much to hear a human voice as to satisfy her curiosity.

"I know one of the stable lads at one of the big houses down near the town," Sebastien answered. "Luka and I went down to the inn in Epsom, to let everyone know about the race tomorrow, and this lad, Dicky, told me a fellow had been asking after some gypsy weans with a dancing bear and a monkey. It has to be you two! So I hid Luka in the stables, with Dicky to watch out, and came to get you. The stables there are enormous; they'll be big enough for all of you, even Sweetheart."

The path forked, one leading straight on into the darkness, the other tumbling and falling down the steep slope, towards the lights in the valley below. Sebastien turned to follow the path down the hill, tugging on the bear's chain so that she followed him. Stumbling in her weariness and fear, Emilia followed. Again she thought she heard a footstep behind her, but could see nothing but darkness. She shivered and walked faster.

After about ten minutes, a tall iron fence rose up before them. Emilia gazed through the railings at a long, low house with tall chimneys and rows of windows, some of which still showed a light, even though it was well past midnight. Idly Emilia imagined what it must be like to live in such a house. She wondered what people did with so many rooms. Tom Whitehouse had once told her that his father's manor had one room for eating breakfast, another room for afternoon tea, one for dinner when it was just the family eating, and yet another dining room for when they had guests. There was a banqueting hall to eat their dessert in, and a room for the men to smoke their cigars in, and yet another room to arrange flowers in. Emilia had not known whether to believe him or not. It seemed an awful lot of work, having to walk from one room to another every time you decided to do something different.

They came to a small gate set in a high wall. Sebastien rapped on it gently with his knuckles, and almost immediately it swung open. A boy in the leather gaiters and rough coat of a stable hand stood on the other side. He put his finger to his lips and jerked his head for them to come in. Alida's hooves clopped on the cobblestones, much to the stable boy's alarm. He hurried them across the yard, and in through a big door, split horizontally across the middle. Inside, it was black as pitch.

"Sebastien?" came Luka's voice. "Is that you? Have you got Emilia?"

"Luka!" Emilia cried in relief.

"Ssssh!" said the stable boy.

There was a scrabbling noise, a scrape, scrape, scrape, and then the flare and hiss as the flint struck sparks from the steel. Luka bent over his tinderbox, blowing on the glowing red flame, then hastily lit a taper and held it to a candle, which flickered alight. He blew out the taper and stowed it away carefully in its box with his tinder and flint.

"You owe me big time," Dicky the stable hand said to Sebastien. "If we're caught. . ."

"We won't be caught," Sebastien assured him. "It won't be for long. Besides, the whole house will be up on the Downs today, watching the big race, you know that."

"Your horse had better win," the boy said bad-temperedly. "I've put my whole month's wages on her."

"She will," Sebastien said with the same easy confidence. "Dicky, this is Luka, and this is Emilia. I'm betrothed to her sister, which sort of makes her kin."

"My daya was your dado's cousin, and your baba was my baba's cousin, which definitely makes us kin," Emilia said. She was still upset and angry that the Hearne family had done so little to help them.

"Right," Sebastien said. "I knew it was something like that."

Dicky nodded his head at them and muttered a greeting under his breath. He looked at them with intense interest, his eyes wide as he took in the sleepy-eyed bear, yawning behind one massive paw, the big shaggy dog, and the monkey peeping out of Luka's shirt.

"Thanks for hiding us," Luka said.

"It's fine," Dicky said. "You'll need to lie low, though. Old Matthew, the head groom, will have my hide if he finds you here." The children nodded. "There's plenty of straw to sleep on and I dug out some old blankets. They're a bit smelly, but I guess you won't mind that."

Emilia opened her mouth to protest, but Luka gave her a warning glance and she closed it again. Dicky had some reason for his comment, rude as it was. After all, they were both very grubby after two days on the run, and the combined smell of bear, horse, dog and monkey was already rather overpowering in the small stable.

Dicky had pumped them a bucket of water and put out a battered tin cup, not too dirty, and some bread and cold mutton for them.

"Blow the candle out when we've gone," he said. "Old Matthew will come looking if he sees candlelight, and besides, it's dangerous with so much straw about."

Emilia and Luka nodded.

Sebastien yawned, and then covered his mouth hastily with his hand. "I'd better get going," he said. "I've got to climb back up the Downs again and it's really late. Try and get some sleep, and I'll come and get you when the coast is clear."

"All right. Thanks a lot," Emilia and Luka said, and he grinned and gave them a friendly wave before going out.

"Don't forget about the candle," Dicky said as he followed, pulling the door shut behind him.

Emilia and Luka looked at each other.

"Cold-Pig was in the village?" Emilia asked.

Luka nodded. "Asking after us. He's hot on our trail."

"They won't tell him where we are, will they?"

"I hope not. I think we should get going, though. As soon as it's light enough to see, we'll sneak out of here and get on the road. We'll head to the New Forest, we've kin there."

"We can't," Emilia said.

"Why not?"

"The charm of the silver horse," she said. "That old woman, Sebastien's grandmother – she's got it. I didn't have a chance to ask her for it."

Luka made an impatient movement. "It's just an old charm, Emilia," he said. "It's not going to help us get our family out of gaol. Only people can do that. And the Hearne family made it quite clear that they're not going to help us."

"We can't go without the silver horse charm," Emilia said. "Baba said. . ."

"But we don't have time to be hanging around and hoping they'll give us their charm," Luka said impatiently. "We only have till the end of the month to get our family out of gaol. That's when they go up before the magistrates."

Emilia's chest tightened so much that she could not speak.

Luka saw her face, and said roughly, "It's all right. We're going to get them out. I've got a plan of sorts already. You snuggle down now, and try and get some sleep. We've a long way to go tomorrow."

Emilia could not look at him. It seemed a gulf had opened up between them. Maggie had told her she must find the lost charms. Emilia trusted her grandmother with all of her heart, and in her absence, put that trust into her words. She could not ride on and just leave the charm of the silver horse behind her. Yet the prospect did not seem to bother Luka at all.

Emilia huddled her shawl about her and lay down in the straw. Rollo lay down in the crook of her knees, sighing heavily. Luka spread one of the blankets over her, and said, "Don't you worry, Milly."

She did not reply.

Horse-Trading

Epsom Downs, Surrey, England
14 August 1658

Slowly the darkness changed to day. Emilia had not slept again. All night she had lain awake, worrying about her family, trying to think of some way of saving them from the gallows, and brooding over the crystal ball. She badly wanted to look into its cloudy depths again, and see what was happening to Baba and Beatrice and Noah, but she did not dare.

Rollo lifted his head and growled. The door opened and Emilia sat up, stomach lurching. Luka woke with a jerk and was on his feet in a moment, his knife in his hand.

There was just enough light for them to see Sebastien. Luka groaned in relief and dropped his knife. "I thought you were the constables! You gave me such a fright."

Sebastien did not smile. "You need to come back to the camp."

"Why? What's wrong?" Even as Luka spoke, he was gathering up their belongings.

"That man that's after you, he showed up at the camp this morning with the local garrison," Sebastien said. "He wanted to know where you were, and when we said we didn't know, the soldiers requisitioned our horses."

"No!" Emilia was shocked. "All those beautiful horses?"

"Aye. Every one. And not a penny did they pay."

"I'm so sorry," Luka said. Zizi cuddled her thin arms about his neck, crooning softly, and Luka put up his hand and stroked her fur.

Sebastien looked grim. "My dado wants to see you right away."

"But why? He's not turning us in to the constables, is he?" Emilia cried.

"He wouldn't do that."

"Not even to get his horses back?" Luka demanded.

Sebastien did not answer. He looked troubled.

"We're not going," Luka said. "Even if your dado doesn't intend to turn us in, that Coldham fellow is probably hanging around waiting for you to lead him straight to us. Come on, Emilia, let's get out of here!" He swung the bag on to his shoulder and turned to face Sebastien. "I'm sorry," he said. "But we can't take the risk. If we get locked up too, there's no way we can help our family."

"Forget the constables!" Sebastien cried. "He wants your horse for the race today."

"He wants Alida? But why?"

"She looks fast," Sebastien said.

"She is fast," Emilia boasted. "No other horse can catch her!"

"Good," Sebastien said. "Because if we don't have a horse to race today, there's going to be trouble."

"I'm sorry for that." Luka picked up Sweetheart's chain. "But it's too much of a risk."

"No. Wait." Emilia turned to Sebastien. "Will your dado promise to help us if I bring him Alida? And will your grandmother give me her charm of the silver horse?"

"Forget the charm, Milly," Luka said.

Emilia shook her head. "No. Baba told me to get it. I'll go, and I'll race Alida for them, and win them their bets, and then I'll come away with you. You stay here with Zizi and Sweetheart and Rollo. Without them, I'm just another gypsy girl. Cold-Pig won't know who I am. Even better! I'll wear Sebastien's clothes and look like a boy."

"And what am I supposed to wear?" Sebastien cried indignantly.

"Nothing," Emilia said. "You'll stay here with Luka. You're a hostage, in case I don't come back."

"And what are you going to do then, kill me?" Sebastien said sarcastically.

"If your dado turns Emilia over to a thief-taker who wants to hang her, then I'll see you into the hands of the constables too," Luka said, his voice hard. "We'll see how your dado feels about having one of *his* kin facing the gallows!"

Sebastien looked taken aback, then angry, but he

began to strip off his clothes, wrapping one of the blankets around him against the chill. Ordering the boys to turn their backs, Emilia then dressed quickly in his breeches and shirt and jacket, all of them much too big for her, then twisted her hair up into a rough knot that she jammed under his cap. She could not help feeling rather odd and vulnerable without her skirts. She gritted her jaw together, though, and pretended not to care.

Luka said, his voice uneven, "Be careful, Emilia. Any sign of trouble, just get out of there, all right?"

"All right," she said. "See you later."

Outside, the fog still hung low over the buildings. Emilia looked about her cautiously, then, when she was sure no one was watching, turned Alida's head towards the Downs. The fog was so thick they could not go any faster than a walk, for the road was rough with stones and potholes. Emilia had plenty of time to grow sick with trepidation.

She reached the steep path up to the Downs, and Emilia slipped off Alida's back and led her. The chalk path was slippery with dew. Everything was still and quiet. No birds called, no dogs barked. The mist pressed close about them.

Then, unexpectedly, Emilia stepped out of the mist, and found herself on a broad spine of green land which rose before her out of a vast sea of cloud. The sky above was clear and blue, the mist below was white, and where it rose in soft, billowing peaks, it cast shadows of an intense and vivid blue. As far as Emilia could see, this landscape of clouds stretched, building palaces and temples in the sky, all gilded with the rising sun.

Emilia stood and stared, awed and humbled, her eyes unexpectedly hot with tears. Then Alida nudged her with her nose, and gave a soft enquiring whinny. Emilia vaulted back on to the mare's back and kicked her into a canter, so that together they flew along the narrow isthmus of land as lightly and fluidly as if the mare had wings, and this ethereal construction of air and water was their natural element.

All too soon they crested one of the rolling undulations of the hill and saw below them the rough circle of caravans about the ashes of the fire. As Alida galloped down the hill towards them, her pale mane and tail flying, her ears pricked forward, Felipe lifted his face from his hands, then stood up and took a few eager steps forward.

Emilia brought her mare to her usual abrupt halt, Alida tossing her head and prancing as if aware of all the eyes upon her. Emilia looked at Felipe.

"I am very sorry about your horses," she said. "May they pay for their shame."

Felipe nodded. His eyes were on the mare.

"Sebastien has said that you want my Alida, to run in the race for you," Emilia said. "You are my kin, and you are in trouble. I would be happy to do what I could to help you, except that we came to you in the time of our great trouble, and you turned your faces from us."

Felipe frowned and looked away. Cosmo chewed on

the end of his pipe, his hands in his belt, his eyes measuring the distance between him and Emilia. She had stopped Alida well away, however. She could wheel her mare about and escape before anyone could come within reaching distance of her.

"It is dangerous for me to be here. That thief-taker and his soldiers could be hiding under the cover of the mist. I could have slipped away and gone, and you would have had no chance of winning this race of yours. But I have come with Alida, despite the danger, because you are my kin, and because I wish to make a bargain with you."

Felipe's eyebrows shot up. He and Cosmo exchanged glances, and a smile creased Cosmo's pockmarked skin. Emilia knew what they were thinking. They were horse-traders, used to making canny deals, and she was nothing but a little girl. All around the campfire there was a sigh as everyone relaxed and smiled.

"First, before I run this race of yours, I want the little silver charm that your mother, Janka, wears," Emilia said, trying to sound brave.

There was a murmur of surprise. Janka put her hand up to her neck and closed it about something that hung there. Felipe raised his brow. "It's ours, it belongs to our family, it's our luck."

"Yet your luck has gone," Emilia answered. "And with it, your horses."

"Do you think the little charm will make your horse run faster?" Felipe asked. From the tone of his voice,

Emilia could tell that he was like Luka, and set more store by his own wits and strength than any power a small silver trinket could have.

She turned her eyes to Janka. "Ever since the chain of charms was broken, the gypsies have suffered hard times, you know that."

"You want to keep my charm?" Janka sounded furious. "Not just wear it for the race?"

"At least until my family is free," she said pleadingly, and wished she could control her voice better. One must never show weakness when bargaining, she knew.

"Absolutely not." Janka folded her arms.

"Then I'll be on my way," Emilia said, and wheeled her horse about.

"Wait, wait!" Felipe cried. He turned to his mother. "It's only a little thing, you have much better jewels. Give it to the wean, if she wants it so bad."

"It's the charm of this family!" Janka cried. "Given to me by your dado."

"We are all kin," Emilia said. "Our caravan is our family, and the world is our caravan."

The old woman scowled and held on tight to her charm, but Felipe went to her and spoke softly in her ear. She shook her head obstinately, and he whispered some more. After a little while, she shrugged and said something crossly. He answered soothingly. Emilia's spirits lifted as she saw Janka shrug once more and reluctantly pull something over her head and give it to her son. Felipe turned to Emilia and held it out on his hand.

"So?" he said. "You want the charm?"

Emilia shook her head. "It's not so simple," she said. "I also want your promise to help us free my family from Kingston Gaol."

Felipe's hand closed over the charm. "What sort of help?"

Her brain racing, Emilia said, "We must get them out before the magistrates sit at the beginning of next month. Before then, we will be asking for help from the rest of our kin. We'll ask them – and you – to come and meet us at Kingston by the last day of the month, and we will tell you then what we need you to do."

Felipe and Cosmo glared at her, and then put their heads together, muttering furiously. Emilia waited, so tense that Alida fidgeted and danced, curving her neck. She could always sense what Emilia was feeling.

Cosmo turned back to her. His face was hard and cold. "Who are you to try and bargain with us? You are nothing but a worthless girl. Your family is imprisoned, you have no money, you wear borrowed clothes. How dare you try and tell us what to do?"

"Fine," Emilia said, and spurred Alida away.

Alida, as always, moved as smoothly and lightly as the wind through a meadow of grass. Emilia was surprised. Her heart was so heavy, she felt sure it should have weighed her mare down.

"Wait!" Felipe called again.

Emilia drew Alida to a halt at the very crest of the hill.

"The day is running away," she said coldly. "You are wasting my time. If you want me to stay and run this race for you, I need to know. Otherwise, I'm for the road."

Cosmo laughed. "Girls don't race. If your mare is to run today, I'll be on her back."

Emilia shook her head. "She's my mare."

Cosmo leant in towards Felipe and whispered. After a long moment, Felipe nodded his head. "Here's a bargain for you, little girl," Cosmo said mockingly. "You take my mother's charm, and you race for us today. If you win, you get to keep the charm as long as you need it, and we swear to help you if we can."

Emilia's heart leapt with joy.

"But you must leave us with some kind of surety. That seems only fair. So if you win for us today, you have our precious family charm and our promise of help, but we get to keep the mare. Agreed?"

Emilia could only stare at him, aghast.

The Silver Horse

The silver horse was no larger than the first knuckle of Emilia's smallest finger. With all four hooves lifted in a gallop, its tail was lifted high like a banner, and its mane flew in the wind. It was warm from lying against the old gypsy woman's skin.

Emilia cradled it in the palm of her hand. Then, her fingers trembling, she hooked the charm on to the golden chain she wore about her wrist, next to the ancient coin her grandmother had given her.

"An Arab mare in return for an old piece of junk," Felipe said to his brother in an undertone. "It doesn't seem fair."

Cosmo rubbed his hands together. "As long as both parties come out of an agreement happy, that's all that matters."

But Emilia was not happy. She felt as if her heart was breaking. She had helped Alida struggle out of her mother's womb, she had helped her stumble to her feet and find her way to her mother's side, and she had fed the filly her first handful of grain. Girl and horse had never been separated since. Both were orphans, their mothers cruelly stolen away from them. Emilia had thought she would rather die than give her mare away.

Yet if she did not give Alida up, she would have no chance of freeing her family. Emilia believed in the story of the five lost charms with all her heart. Felipe Hearne may think the little silver charm a piece of worthless junk, but Emilia knew that its worth was incalculable, mysterious and unexplainable as this was. To have refused the bargain would have been to have lost all chance of adding the silver horse to her chain of charms, and to Emilia, this would have been like condemning her family to death.

"Now, my wean, it's time to get ready for the race." Felipe's voice was surprisingly kind.

"It's ridiculous to let her ride the mare," Cosmo said. "She's nothing but a child; what does she know about horse-racing? It's our mare now; tell her that I'll be the one riding her."

"No," Emilia said angrily. "You want to win, you have to let me ride. She's used to me. No one else has ever ridden her." Tears spilled down her face, and she wiped them away.

"She'll have to get used to me eventually," Cosmo said. "If she's as good as you say, we'll be running her whenever we can, to try and earn back some of the gold we've lost today, thanks to you."

"It wasn't my fault," Emilia protested. "Did I take your horses away?"

"You led that Coldham man to us," Cosmo said implacably. "If it wasn't for you, he'd never have bothered us."

Emilia took a ragged breath, but Felipe dropped his hand on her shoulder. "Come, child, no need for tears. You'll upset your mare, and we want her happy and eager for the race. It's a shame you've already galloped her this morning; we don't want her to be tired. I'll get her some of my special oats and molasses, and you have a bowl of hot soup and a sup of ale. Nothing heavier, we don't want you weighed down. Cosmo, leave the child be. You've no time to be schooling the mare today anyway, and you'll have plenty of time to get used to her once Emilia's gone."

"All right, then," Cosmo said ungratefully, "but I'd better be giving her some coaching. We don't want her thrown at the first corner."

"Alida wouldn't throw me," Emilia cried. "I haven't had a toss since I was a little girl!"

"What, last week?" Cosmo said.

She glared at him, fists clenched.

Felipe laughed. "Come now, Cosmo, stop teasing her. Emilia, I know you think no one could ride Alida as well as you, but Cosmo's right. It's a tough course. Let him lead you round it slowly, and tell you what he knows."

Reluctantly Emilia agreed.

The sun had burnt off most of the mist, so that the Downs were bathed in warm sunshine. Here the slope was not so steep, falling down in a broad sweep towards the valley. Cosmo led Alida around the course, which was shaped like a skewed horseshoe, and was one mile and four furlongs long.

"You must lift your weight off the horse's back," Cosmo told her. "Stand up in your stirrups and lean right forward over her shoulders, so she can run freely. The further forward you lean, the easier it will be for her. How is your balance?"

For answer, Emilia lifted her feet and set them upon Alida's narrow back, then stood up, balancing easily as the mare walked forward. Then she bent and laid her hands on the mare's shoulders and did a handstand, her feet pointing straight into the air. Alida, used to Emilia's tricks, did not even twitch an ear.

Cosmo snorted. "The idea is to be as streamlined as possible, to offer no resistance to the wind," he said. "You won't win this race standing on your head."

"You must admit my balance is good, though," Emilia replied sweetly.

"I hope it's good enough," he answered sourly.

Emilia did a neat somersault, her feet landing where her hands had been, and sat down again.

"Now, she'll be full of oats, so watch her at the beginning, don't let her dance or fight the bit too much." Cosmo said. "Hold her steady, and get her off fast – then you won't be eating the other riders' dirt."

Emilia nodded her understanding.

"Remember, horses have two blind spots," Cosmo said, "directly before them and directly behind them. She'll be wanting to look behind her, to see who's on her tail, but you mustn't let her. Keep her head steady, and let her know you're doing the looking for her."

Emilia nodded, although she was not at all sure how she was to do this.

After the crest of the hill, the track curved down to the left, falling steeply at one point and dropping into a muddy patch. Cosmo showed her where the ground was firmest, and warned her that many horses slipped and fell here.

"That won't matter to me," Emilia said. "They'll all be behind me."

To her surprise, that made Cosmo grin and give Alida a friendly slap on the rump. Past the mud, the path swept down and around, falling another fifty feet, before straightening out for a stretch, and then rising gently to the finish line.

"Sit down hard here. Drive her home." Emilia nodded. "I just hope you know your horse as well as you say you do," Cosmo continued, as they turned back towards the gypsy encampment. "You've never raced before; you don't know the stresses it places on you and the horse. Did you know a horse can lose up to twenty-five pounds during a race like this?"

Emilia did not know. It seemed an awful lot. She patted Alida's neck apprehensively, and the mare twitched an ear towards her.

"Alida will tire easily on this course," Cosmo went on. "These hills are tough on any horse, and she's still only a filly. You're going to have to judge how much strength she has left in her, and how blown the other horses are, and if they have any heart left in them. You're going to have to know, instinctively, the right moment to spur her on for that final desperate effort, and yet not ruin her by whipping her on too hard."

Emilia's heart sunk down to the pit of her stomach.

"Can you do all that?" Cosmo demanded, turning his pockmarked face up to hers, his eyes squinting against the sun.

"I don't know. I hope so," Emilia said. She was beginning to wish she had just ridden on with Luka, and not made this Devil's bargain with Sebastien's uncle.

He shrugged. "So do we all."

They arrived back into the gypsy encampment, which was a hive of activity. The sight of so many *gorgios* made Emilia feel very apprehensive. She was never very comfortable around those who were not her kind, and the last time she had been surrounded by a crowd of *gorgios,* her whole family had been thrown in gaol. Alida sensed the tension in her hands and body, and shied sideways. Cosmo soothed her, and looked up at Emilia consideringly.

"You all right?"

"Aye," Emilia lied, and wiped her palms on her breeches.

Cosmo lifted her down. "At least you're a light little

133

thing," he said, as he put her down on the ground. "I just wish I knew you were strong enough."

"I'm very strong," Emilia assured him.

"Aye, for your age, perhaps, but you'll be riding against grown men. You must watch out for them. They'll be as desperate to win this race as we are. Not just gold but reputations ride on a race like this. Do you understand?"

Emilia nodded.

Cosmo gave her a little push. "Go and eat, rest up a bit. I'll look after the mare."

Emilia was feeling so keyed-up and nervous she could not rest.

She put down her bowl after only a few mouthfuls and followed the other gypsies as they went over to the racetrack, getting ready for the races. They set up makeshift stalls to sell their produce, which mainly consisted of cures for various horse ailments, or home-woven baskets and chair bottoms.

Already many people had turned up, milling about in their excitement and placing bets with each other. Many were local farmers, but to Emilia's surprise there were a great many gentlemen in the crowd too. Some were there with their horses, and stood around giving last-minute instructions to their jockeys, who were generally thin, young stable hands in livery. None of them were as thin and young as Emilia.

The other gentlemen huddled in a group, talking in undertones. They wore their hair in the long curls of the Cavalier, and had large buckles on their shoes and feathers in their hats. They looked about themselves constantly, as if fearing eavesdroppers.

One in particular caught Emilia's eye. A tall, blue-eyed man with broad shoulders, he was dressed in a green velvet coat that had definitely seen better days. His tall boots were worn too, but carefully blackened and polished, and the lace at his wrists, though darned, was very clean. Although he was no longer young, he moved with the upright briskness of a soldier. It was not his military manner that caught Emilia's attention, however, nor his shabby dress, but the contrast between his very black hair and his fair brows and lashes. Emilia had never seen anyone with such black hair who did not have eyebrows to match. It intrigued her.

A servant brought a tray of wine and fine crystal glasses and poured it out for the little group, bowing with great deference to the man in green and passing him his glass first. They all raised their glasses in a silent toast, looking south towards the far-distant sea, then drank deeply, some obviously in the grip of strong emotion.

Fascinated by their behaviour, Emilia stepped closer, wondering suddenly if they were Royalists plotting the return of the king. It occurred to her that a horse-race would be the perfect cover for such a meeting. One of the problems that Royalists had in furthering their plans was that any large gathering of people was banned. The mail was all opened and searched, and even letters written in code were not safe, as Cromwell had expert code-crackers amongst his staff. So it was very difficult to organize meetings where sympathizers could be introduced, and plans made for action. A horse-race was the perfect excuse, since people of all kinds came together and mingled and talked, and notes could be passed from hand to hand as easily as money. A sharp watch was kept out for the constabulary, and even if the race-track was raided, the penalty was usually no more than a fine and a reprimand, while the punishment for treason against the Parliament was death by hanging, drawing and quartering.

Emilia had disliked the Roundheads ever since her father had been killed by them during the war, and she had a natural distaste for the puritanical views of those who ruled the country, as they contradicted everything Emilia thought most good and beautiful about life. So she came closer and closer to the Cavaliers, hoping to catch a word or two.

Suddenly her eyes widened in surprise. Tom Whitehorse was there at the black-haired lord's elbow, bowing deferentially.

"Master Whitehorse!" Emilia cried. "What are you doing here?"

His head snapped round, fear and horror on his face. He did not recognize her in her boy's clothes. "Who wants me?" he demanded.

"It's me. Emilia. Don't you recognize me?"

"Emilia!" He was incredulous. He cast a quick apologetic glance at the black-haired lord, seized Emilia's arm and steered her roughly away. "What on earth are *you* doing here?"

"I'm racing."

"You can't race; you're a girl."

"Not today," she said coolly, indicating her breeches with a wave of her hand.

He looked scandalized. "Surely you're jesting."

"No. I'm entirely serious. If I were you, I'd be putting money on me and Alida, because we're going to win this race."

He put up his eyebrows. "I'm not here to gamble," he said.

"No? Then why are you here?"

He flushed and bit his lip. "Visiting friends," he said shortly.

"That man in the velvet coat? But he's old enough to be your father. Surely he's no friend of yours?"

"Friend of my father." Tom's flush deepened. Emilia opened her mouth to ask more questions, and he said quickly, "He too is visiting in the area. We are staying at the . . . at one of the big houses around here. I'm . . . ah . . . I'm staying only a few days. Lord Berkeley, my host, is . . ." he fumbled for words, and came up, rather lamely, with ". . . ummm . . . interested in horses."

Tom waved his hand towards an elderly man in an ornate mulberry coat, leaning lightly on an ebony stick with a silver knob as he talked earnestly to the black-haired lord. Neither was paying any attention to the horses.

"Surely he's not racing himself!" Emilia said.

"Of course not. His groom will be riding the horse."

"Of course," Emilia said mockingly. "How could I be so stupid? Gentlemen do not ride their own horses."

Tom stared at her, in half a mind to be affronted, then suddenly grinned. "Not in a race they want to win, anyway," he admitted.

Emilia was relieved to see him smile. She had not been able to understand why he was so fidgety and uncomfortable with her, when they had known each other for years.

"I'd better go," she said. "My race starts soon. Wish me luck!"

"All right, good luck!" he said.

She waved her hand at him and went back to find Felipe and Cosmo. When she turned round a few moments later, Tom was gone.

Devil's Bargain

"Where have you been!" Cosmo cried. "The race is about to begin. Come, quickly! I've got your mare bridled and saddled and raring to go! I've given her a good slug of my special brew, and there's no holding her now."

"Why, what's in it?" Emilia demanded.

"A bit of this, a bit of that. Come on! Here are some spurs for you, and I'm lending you my own lucky whip. I've won more races than I can tell you with that whip."

"I'm not wearing those!" Emilia cried, recoiling at the sight of the cruel-looking spurs. "I've never needed them before!"

Cosmo was angry and told her curtly to do as she was told, but Emilia was adamant. She had never used such instruments of control on Alida before, and she would not start now.

In the end Felipe just shrugged. "No time for this. Put her up!"

Cosmo scowled and threw Emilia up into the saddle. She took a moment to familiarize herself with the stirrups, which felt quite odd after a lifetime of riding bareback.

"They give you much more control," Cosmo told her. "Remember what I told you! Use them!"

Emilia's mouth went dry and her mind completely blank. She could not remember a thing Cosmo had said. Sensing her panic, Alida reared. A few of the other riders looked across and grinned. Emilia felt a hot flush burn up her cheeks. She brought Alida down sharply and took the reins into her left hand, so that she could rub the lucky charms at her wrist.

First she touched the coin, the golden crown. *The crown is for light and luck and magic. It's why they call me the Queen of the Gypsies*, Maggie had said.

Then Emilia touched the little silver horse, galloping through air.

The charm of the running horse . . . it is silver, the moon metal, and has the power to charm all the beasts of field and forest, the charm to wheedle that you have, my darling girl.

Tears stung her eyes at the remembrance of her grandmother's words.

"Are you ready?" Cosmo demanded.

"Yes," she cried.

Felipe undid his red kerchief and held it high. There was a roar from the crowd. Alida shied at the sound, but

Emilia forced her to the starting line, keeping her knees hard against the mare's side. The boys around her were tense and focused, leaning low over their mounts' necks. The horses trembled with eagerness, throwing their heads up and down, snorting through their flared nostrils.

Emilia dropped one hand to stroke Alida's satiny neck. "Run like the wind, my darling girl," she whispered.

The flag dropped. The horses took off. Emilia found herself jostled on all sides. Whips cracked in her ears. Someone elbowed her sharply in the side. She cried out and flinched. Alida's stride faltered, and the big bay to her right drew ahead. Gritting her teeth, Emilia leant forward, urging Alida on. As the mare's stride lengthened, she remembered what Cosmo had said, and stood up in her stirrups, lifting her weight clear of the saddle, leaning so far forward that she threatened to bang her chin on Alida's neck, which plunged up and down below her. Most of the horses fell behind. She felt Alida twitch the reins as the mare strove to turn her head, but Emilia held her firm. Ahead of them, the bay mare sent great clods of earth flying back, hitting Emilia in the face and showering her with mud. Emilia fixed her gaze on the track beyond the mare, and drove Alida forward.

"Fly like the wind, my darling," she murmured. "Fast as the hot desert wind."

Alida responded to her voice, her hooves seeming to barely touch the ground as she surged ahead, her nose at the bay mare's tail, then at its heaving withers, then racing past its rigidly held head. As Emilia galloped past, she felt the sudden sting of a whip across her face from the rider beside her. She gasped aloud but did not falter, only lifted herself higher in the saddle so that Alida could begin the hard, heart-breaking gallop up the steep rise of the track.

Alida's breath gasped in her throat. Her nostrils flared red as she struggled to suck in air. Emilia felt her hooves sinking into the soggy ground. "Come, my darling, my beauty," she whispered. "Fly for me."

She could hear hooves thundering up behind her, could feel the earth shake. "Please, darling girl, please. . ."

Blood was running down her face, and the salt of her sweat stung in the whip-cut. Alida was faltering. Above them was the green curve of the hilltop and the blue arc of the sky. Emilia imagined them taking flight into the sky, spreading wings of golden and silver light, and launching off the top of the hill. "Come on, darling, come on. . ."

Alida leapt forward, touched the hill's crest lightly with one hoof, and then surged on down the broad sweep of the track. Emilia risked a quick glance back. Two horses, the big bay mare and another fleet-footed chestnut, both bearing down at her at incredible speed. Their riders were wielding their whips cruelly. Emilia just had time to see the blood that ran down the bay mare's sides before she had to look forward again, sensing a change in Alida's stride.

Ahead of them was the bend, and the muddy stream. Emilia shifted her weight forward, bent to one side as they took the curve, then lifted herself high over the mare's neck as Alida soared over the ditch, landing nimbly on the far side and accelerating as the track once again began to climb. She heard the thud of hooves behind her, then a heavy thump and the dreadful sound of a horse screaming. The bay horse had taken the corner too fast, and had slipped in the mud and fallen.

The chestnut mare came past at a canter, took the ditch at the far side, and broke once more into a gallop. The groom riding her drove his spurs into her side, and she leapt forward, foam flying from her grimacing mouth.

Emilia fixed her eyes upon the finishing line, where Felipe stood with his red kerchief held high, flapping in the wind. "Now, Alida!" she whispered. "Run like you've never run before."

The mare was exhausted. Her hooves rose and fell more and more slowly; her breath wheezed in her chest. Behind them came the relentless rhythm of the other mare's hooves, slowly but inexorably gaining on them. Emilia was flecked with flying foam as the chestnut galloped up on her inside.

Emilia took a deep breath and wished desperately for the help of the lucky charms. "Please, Alida," she whispered. "Fly for me!"

Alida made one last great effort. Her muscles bunched beneath her mud-spattered skin; the rhythm of her hooves quickened. For a moment dapple-grey and chestnut were poised, neck to neck, and then Alida stretched out and raced through the finish-line, a scant hand-span ahead of the chestnut.

The crowd went wild, throwing up their hats and waving their kerchiefs. Emilia drew Alida up and slipped off her back, her trembling legs barely managing to hold her up. She pressed her face against Alida's shivering skin and let the tears well up. Everything was a roar. Dimly she heard Felipe crowing with triumph and calling out, "Pay up, my fine gentlemen! What a race! And against such odds! Who would have thought that little grey mare had it in her? Pay up, my dear fellows."

Cosmo slipped his hand under Emilia's elbow. "Steady, lass," he whispered in her ear. "Swoon on me now, and we may have your secret discovered. Here, have a sip of this."

"What is it?" she whispered.

"My special brew," he answered, then, when she turned her face away, said with a laugh, "I'm joking! It's just peach brandy."

She drank, and felt a sudden shock of warmth and giddiness. She found she could stand again and turn to receive the excited congratulations of all those mobbing around her. Her hand was shaken so vigorously, she feared it might fall off, and Alida was petted and praised extravagantly. One man offered Felipe a bag of gold coins for her there and then.

Suddenly, she heard a high, shrill whistle. At once

144

Cosmo turned and threw her up into the saddle. "Get out of here, Emilia," he said. "Take Alida, and get to wherever it is that you and your cousin have been hiding. Tell Sebastien we'll meet him on the road, all right?"

Emilia nodded, too scared to speak.

"Make sure he brings that mare with him," Cosmo warned. "Else I'll curse you myself."

"The Rom don't curse the Rom," Emilia managed to say.

"They do when they steal other people's horses. That mare is mine now, lassie."

"Only until I give you back the silver charm," Emilia protested, and then saw by his face that he did not expect her to live long enough to return the charm.

Cries of alarm rang out from the crowd. Emilia looked back to see a company of Roundhead soldiers, the sun glinting on their helmets and pikes. Emilia's pulse jolted. At their head was Coldham!

He raised his face, scanning the crowd, and then saw her. For an instant, their eyes met. Then he raised his arm and bellowed a command. Emilia had already dug her heels into Alida's side, and the mare broke into a heavy-footed trot.

Coldham seized the reins of a horse that had been about to run a race. It was fresh and full of vim. As he swung his heavy bulk into the saddle, cursing to find his stirrups much too short, the horse reared and sidestepped, almost toppling the thief-taker from the saddle.

Toss him off! Emilia pleaded silently, touching a finger to the charm of the silver horse.

To Emilia's intense pleasure, the horse bucked wildly. Coldham was thrown to the ground. Emilia grinned and kicked Alida forward, urging her away from the racetrack as Coldham, cursing, endeavoured to mount the horse again. When Emilia next glanced back, he was up in the saddle again, with two grooms holding the horse steady while he adjusted his stirrups.

The Downs were bare and empty and wind-scoured, falling away steeply on either side. There was not a tree or a rock for miles. If Emilia was to hide, she had to get down into the valley. But Coldham would catch up with her long before she reached the downhill path. There was only one way out: straight down the steep drop to her right.

Alida put one hoof forward, then stepped back again. Emilia patted her neck. "I know, I know. But you can do it, I know you can!"

Alida reared, shaking her head. Emilia glanced over her shoulder desperately. Coldham and his men were galloping towards her, and she could see his mouth stretched wide in a grin of triumph.

Pure Magic

"Come on, Alida! Down!" Emilia cried.

Alida bunched her muscles and leapt over the edge.

They slipped and slithered, rocks rattling around them. Emilia leant back, one hand on the reins, the other held aloft to help keep her balance. The mare's hooves skidded on the wet chalk. She spun and lost her footing and slid some way on her side. Emilia clung to the saddle, afraid they would both end up at the bottom of the cliff, broken into pieces. But Alida recovered her footing, bounding first one way, then another, across deep crevices in the hillside. Nimbly she leapt towards the valley floor and landed safely, cantering away into the woods.

Emilia glanced back. At the top of the Downs stood Coldham on his stiff-legged horse. No matter how hard Coldham whipped the horse, and dug in his spurs till the blood ran red, the horse would not budge. Emilia laughed, and waved her cap joyfully as she disappeared into the trees.

She knew she had not gained much time. It would not be long before they found another way down, and then they would be searching for her. Emilia slipped off Alida's back, and together they hurried through the forest.

Emilia had travelled to the manor house in darkness and mist, and while half-asleep, and she had no clear idea of where to go. But she had been raised to absorb directions and distances, and to note key landmarks, almost unconsciously, as no gypsy ever liked to be lost. Even as she forced her way through the trees, she was remembering their journey and calculating which way to go.

They did not make very good time. Emilia's breath came in great, ragged gasps, and her legs trembled. She did not think she had ever been so worn out. Alida walked slowly, her head hanging, her hide matted with mud and sweat. When she could, Emilia broke into a run, but it was not long before she needed to slow again, pressing one hand to the stitch in her side.

At last she reached the road, and recognized the high iron railings on the far side. Emilia hurried along the side lane to the gate where they had been admitted the night before. It was locked.

For a moment Emilia was overwhelmed with panic. She just wanted to be back safe with Luka. She clasped her hand around her charm bracelet, drawing strength from its familiar warmth and weight, stood up on Alida's back and clambered on top of the wall.

The stable-yard was quiet. Emilia slipped down the other side and ran across the yard to the stable. The door stood ajar. Gently Emilia pushed it open and stepped inside.

No one was there.

Emilia stood frozen, looking about her in shock. Her heart beat so fast, it hurt. Where could they be?

In the shaft of sunlight slanting in through the door, motes of dust floated peacefully. Straw was piled up in one corner, and Emilia experimentally nudged it with her foot, uncovering what was unmistakably a pile of bear droppings. The sight of it relieved Emilia, since it showed her that Sweetheart had at least been here, and Emilia had not somehow gone to the wrong place. She kicked the straw back and looked around for some clue as to where Luka may have gone. Behind the door, she found two straw stalks laid one over the other in the shape of a cross. She was examining them thoughtfully when she heard the sound of marching boots and angry voices.

Emilia looked about rapidly. There was nowhere to hide except under the straw, and Emilia had no desire to crouch in a pile of bear manure. She glanced up and saw a thick crossbeam running the length of the stable. It was high off the floor, but Emilia was able to climb up the back of the door, using the studs as footrests, then reach out and grab a giant hook which hung from the beam and quickly climb up it. She lay down on the crossbeam just as the door below her swung open, and Coldham stepped inside.

The hook was still swaying slightly, and he absent-mindedly reached up and stopped it with his hand so it would not knock his head. Then he stood, looking around him.

"As you can see, there is no one here," an aristocratic voice said. "These stables have not been used in months." Stepping in to the stable behind Coldham was Lord Berkeley, the man in the coat of mulberry velvet that Emilia had last seen up at the racehorse. He was accompanied by a wizened old man in rough wool and leather, who Emilia thought might be the head groom, Matthew.

Coldham ignored them, staring around the stable with narrowed eyes. Emilia clutched the crossbeam with her damp palms and prayed no one would look up. A troupe of soldiers marched in and began to thrust their pikes through the straw and look inside the barrels.

"I would like to know, sir, who has laid such a charge against me?" the lord said coldly. "It is completely baseless, and is, indeed, slanderous. I shall be speaking to my lawyers."

"Our sources of information are always reliable," Coldham said in his harsh, unpleasant voice. "We know the dirty gyps have been here. We just want to know where they are now. You'd better tell us what we want to know, else it'll go the worse for you."

"My dear man, if I had any idea where these gypsies of yours were, I would tell you so, naturally. *I* have no desire to have my silver stolen. I have little enough left as it is, thanks to your damn Royalist tax. I can assure you I know nothing about any gypsies, apart from the horse-traders up on the Downs. I know you are already acquainted with *them*."

"We know you've been hiding the Marquis of Ormonde here," Coldham said menacingly.

"I'm afraid I'm not acquainted with a gentleman of that name. I do have guests staying with me, of course. Young Thomas Whitehorse is the son of an old friend. He is very interested in horses too, which is why we went up to see what new stock the horse-traders had for sale. If we had had any idea that an illegal horse-race was being run, we would not, of course, ventured anywhere near. But how could we have known?"

Emilia listened intently. Luka had told her that Coldham was hunting for a marquis that had been sent over to England by the young king-in-exile, to make contact with the Royalists and plot for a way to return the king to his throne. Emilia had seen Lord Berkeley and Tom Whitehorse in the company of a man who looked like he had dyed his hair. Was it possible the man with the very black hair was indeed the Marquis of Ormonde, the king's spy? Was Tom mixed up with some plot to overthrow the Lord Protector? Emilia could hardly believe it. She and Luka were always laughing at Tom for being so obedient and well-behaved!

"We'll find the marquis, that you can be sure of," Coldham said. "Even if I have to rip your house apart brick by brick, Lord Berkeley."

"Well, you certainly won't find any marquis here, nor any gypsy children," Lord Berkeley said. "I hope you intend to pay for any damage you do? For I'll be writing a very strongly worded letter to the Lord Protector, I promise you. I've paid my fines and been pardoned, and you have no right to persecute me because of some mad notion you've got about a few gypsy children."

"Those gypsies sneak around all over the country," Coldham said. "Who better to carry secret messages, or even hide a hunted man?"

Lord Berkeley shrugged. "Perhaps you are right, man. What do I know of tramps and thieves? They may hide an army of spies for all I care. I do not see what that has to do with me. If I saw a gypsy on my land, I'd get out my gun and hunt them off again."

Coldham scowled. "But I was told they were hiding here!"

"I'd find better informants." Lord Berkeley sounded bored.

Coldham looked around the stable one more time, then stamped out, calling to his men to search the house. The soldiers hurried after him.

There was a long moment of silence. Lord Berkeley said to the old man in leather gaiters, in a much-altered voice, "It is no longer safe for the marquis to be here, Matthew. We must get him away. As soon as those bloody blue-noses are gone, will you have my coach brought round? There's a safe house in Salisbury I know of."

"Aye, My Lord," Matthew said. "You can count on me, My Lord."

"I know, old friend," Lord Berkeley said. His thin, blue-veined hands gripped the silver knob of his walking stick tightly. "That it should come to this!" he burst out. "The Marquis of Ormonde, forced to travel in disguise like a common criminal, hounded by the likes of that dreadful man, Coldham! What has the world come to?"

"Hush, My Lord," Matthew said. "Don't be getting yourself into a state. All will be well. We will get the marquis away safely, don't you fear."

"At least he can go back to the king, and tell him there are still men loyal and true in England, ready to rise up and die for him!" Lord Berkeley's voice quavered with emotion. He began to tap his way out of the stable, but on an afterthought turned back and said, "What of these gypsy children Coldham was after? They've not been here, have they?"

Matthew frowned. "I cannot tell you, My Lord. I have not seen them. But something in this stable stinks to high heaven, and it's not good, clean horse manure, that I know."

"I see," Lord Berkeley said. "So they may well have been here after all?"

Matthew nodded. "Though they're gone now, thank the Lord!"

"What luck!" Lord Berkeley exclaimed. "Imagine if that Coldham fellow had found them here!"

His words faded away as the two men went out to the empty yard. Dizzy with relief, Emilia dropped her head down on to her hands. It seemed Luka and Sebastien had had a lucky escape indeed. She wondered how they had got away, in broad daylight, when Sebastien was wearing nothing but a blanket, and they had with them a dog, a monkey and a bear. That was not luck. That was pure magic!

Following the Patrin

When all was quiet, Emilia slipped back across the stable-yard, climbed back over the wall and found Alida waiting patiently on the other side. She stroked the mare's soft nose and led her swiftly away. She did not want to ride along the roads, in case Coldham had more soldiers out hunting for them. Instead, she made her way cross-country, keeping to hedgerows and copses of trees.

Slowly the light faded. Emilia set her sights on the one constant landmark in the valley – the narrow spire of the church – and slowly crept towards it, Alida plodding along behind her.

The graveyard was lined with ancient yew trees, bent and crooked. The gravestones were covered in grass and weeds, and Emilia could see many of the church's windows were empty of glass.

Inside the church, all was cold and dark and dank. Long pews stretched from side to side, thick with dust and cobwebs, and there was a dead bird lying amidst a litter of old leaves on the altar. Statues with shattered faces held broken arms to the shadows. Alida's hooves on the paving was the only sound. Emilia began to think she had misunderstood the patrin Luka had left for her.

Then she heard a soft gibbering sound. Zizi dropped to her shoulder from the shadowy heights. Emilia cuddled her close in delighted relief. "Luka?"

"We're here, Milly." Her cousin called softly from behind the altar. She led Alida up the steps, and found Luka and Sebastien lying on some pews, hidden from sight. Sweetheart lay beside them, her muzzle on her paws, looking sleepy and content.

Luka leapt up at once to embrace and question her, but Sebastien lay motionless, stretched out on his stomach. He rolled one agonized eye her way.

"What's wrong? Is he wounded?" Emilia asked in sharp concern.

Luka grinned. "He was stung by some bees."

"Bees? But . . . how?"

"Sweetheart raided the beehives."

Emilia tried to bite back her grin. "Oh, no! I'm so sorry, Sebastien." She bent over him, saying consolingly, "Do you want me to have a look?"

"No, thank you," he cried, huddling the blanket closer.

"He was stung in rather a tender spot," Luka said. "That's why he's lying down on his stomach."

Emilia could not help laughing.

"Ha ha, very funny," Sebastien said.

Emilia sniffed the air. "You stink," she said to the boys. "Even worse than usual!"

"We hid in the rubbish-cart," Luka explained. "Dicky saw Cold-Pig heading our way, and rode hard to warn us in time. He helped us escape. It was a close call!"

"Me too!" Emilia said. "Cold-Pig almost had me a couple of times."

"Thank heavens you're all right," Luka said. "I thought you were nabbed for sure."

"*I* thought *you'd* been nabbed. I'm so glad to have found you." Emilia gave her cousin's arm a little pat. It had been a horrible feeling, finding the stable empty and Luka gone.

"So what happened?" Sebastien demanded.

"Alida won the race and your dado pocketed heaps of gold but then Cold-Pig turned up with soldiers. I thought I'd shaken him off, but he turned up at the stable right on my heels. Someone must've told him where we were."

"Tom Whitehorse!" Luka exclaimed angrily.

"Tom? But . . . how could he have known where you were?" Emilia asked, startled.

"He was at the inn last night when Coldham turned up. He must've followed me and Sebastien when we went to the stable."

"But why would he. . ." Emilia suddenly remembered how Tom had disappeared from the racecourse, and how Coldham and the soldiers had appeared soon after.

She told Luka this, but went on passionately, "Tom wouldn't have told Cold-Pig, Luka! He's caught up in some Royalist plot. There was some lord there in disguise. I think he's the Marquis of Ormonde. Remember you were telling me about him? How all of Cromwell's men were hunting him, but he kept slipping through their fingers? Well, I think Tom's helping to hide him."

"How do you know he was in disguise?" Sebastien asked.

"His hair was all black, but his eyebrows were still fair," Emilia said. "You know how careful you have to be, when you dye a horse's coat, to make sure its whiskers are dyed too, else you'll have a bay horse with white whiskers?"

Sebastien grinned and shrugged, not wanting to admit he knew anything about dyeing the coats of stolen horses.

"Anyway, I thought I heard someone following *me* and Sebastien from the camp," Emilia said. "When he brought me down to meet you."

"No one from my family would've told the constables," Sebastien said angrily. "Why would they? They took our horses away, remember?"

"I heard someone following us," Emilia insisted. "I bet it was Nadine! She's jealous of anyone you spend time with. Maybe she told Coldham where we were this afternoon, to get him off your family's backs. That was how he knew just where to come!"

Sebastien frowned. "She wouldn't . . . would she?

Maybe if he threatened to arrest everyone . . . but no! I bet it's that stuck-up *gorgio* friend of yours . . . he was probably trying to get Coldham off *his* back."

"Well, we'll probably never know, cause we're out of here tonight. We've got to go and find *someone* who's willing to help us." Luka's voice was sharp with sarcasm.

"The Hearnes have promised to help," Emilia said. "They said they'd come and meet us in Kingston by the end of the month. And Felipe gave me the silver horse charm. See?" She lifted her wrist to show him the bracelet, even though it was now too dark to see anything.

"He said that? My dado said that?" Sebastien asked incredulously.

"I had to give them Alida," Emilia said in a muffled voice. "Not for ever. Just until I give them back their charm."

"You gave them Alida?" Luka spoke very gently. He knew what the mare meant to Emilia.

His understanding undid her. Too choked with tears to speak, Emilia could only nod her head. She felt his hand groping for hers in the darkness, and let him take it and give it a little squeeze.

"But what use is the mare? We can't get any foals from her in only a few weeks."

"They'll race her," Emilia said, sniffing and wiping her eyes on her sleeve. "No doubt they'll run the poor darling to death. They made a fortune on her today. Your dado was very pleased."

"I bet he was," Sebastien said. "He may be able to bribe the soldiers to give us back some of our horses. Or he'll go and buy some more. There's the big horse fair coming up in Horsmonden in September."

"He said he'd meet me in Kingston by the end of the month. Though I don't know where. We didn't have time to set up a meeting place. Where would be a good place?"

"Richmond Park is near Kingston," Sebastien said. "We often camp out there, especially now there aren't any royal huntsmen to drive us out. The closest place would be Gallows Pond, which is near the Kingston Gate. I guess you won't have any trouble remembering that name!"

"No." Emilia gave a little shiver. "All right. Gallows Pond it is, near Kingston Gate, on the last day of the month."

"Well, then, I guess I'll be seeing you then," Sebastien said.

"Wait!" Luka cried. "Just one thing. The Wood family, from the New Forest. Know what happened to them?"

"No. Sorry," Sebastien answered. "Haven't heard of them in years. One got hanged, I think, for fortune-telling in Salisbury. I do remember that."

"What about the Smiths?" Luka asked.

"Oh, they're at Horsmonden, at the cannon foundry there. We see them every year when we go to the horse fair. Why? You going to go find them?"

Luka nodded. "I'm sure they'll be able to help us. We'll go to the New Forest first, though; it's closer."

"Well, good luck." Sebastien took Alida's bridle, preparing to lead her away. It was now so dark they could barely see the white blur of each other's faces. Emilia was glad, for she was perilously close to tears. Alida baulked and would not go, dragging against Sebastien's hand and turning her head to look for Emilia.

"She won't come," Sebastien said. "Emilia! Your spell. The one you put on Alida. You've got to take it off. I don't want to end up in the cold earth like your spell-bag."

Emilia said, very roughly, "Can't take off the spell, for Alida's still mine. I'm lending her to you, that's all. But I'll cut out the charm hung in her mane, so she'll go with you, at least. Make me some light."

Luka scrabbled in his pocket until he found his tinder and flint, and lit the small lantern they carried hung to the strap of their bag. Yellow light flared up. Emilia scrubbed at her eyes, furious to be so revealed, then took out her knife. Very carefully she ran her fingers through the mare's silvery mane and found the little plait of entwined white and black hair, hidden beneath. Gulping back tears, she carefully cut it and stowed it away in her pocket, then stroked Alida's soft nose.

"Goodbye, darling girl," she said. "It's not for long. Don't let them run you to death."

"We'll take care of her," Sebastien said. "Don't you worry. Horses are our business, remember."

161

Emilia nodded. "Tell your dado and your uncle if they try and cheat me, I'll curse them to the very ends of the earth," she said, unsmiling.

"I will," Sebastien said, just as solemnly.

She gave Alida one more pat, and then stood back, unable to help the tears that ran down her face.

"Hey, Sebastien," Luka called out. "Remember you promised to take Sweetheart for me?"

Sebastien looked dismayed.

"Thanks so much," Luka said. "We'll get along much faster without her. I'll get her from you when we see you at Gallows Pond."

Reluctantly, Sebastien took Sweetheart's chain into his other hand, and then slowly led the horse and the bear out into the night.

Luka turned to grin at Emilia. "That'll make sure he comes to meet us as promised," he said cheerfully. She nodded. "You all right?" he said. She shrugged. "Come on, then," he said. "It's just you, me and Zizi now, on our way to the New Forest."

"And Rollo," she said. The big dog wagged his tail, sending up a cloud of dust.

"And Rollo," Luka agreed. "Let's hope he catches us a rabbit, because I'm starving!"

"Yesterday we feasted, today we starved. . ." Emilia said.

"Tomorrow we'll feast again," Luka said, giving the old proverb its usual buoyant ending.

"Let's hope so." Emilia felt in the darkness for the

little silver horse that hung from her wrist, galloping endlessly upon the air. It had cost her greatly, winning this charm. She could not help wondering what sort of price she would have to pay for the charm of the sprig of rue, the bitter herb of grace.

PART THREE

The Herb of Grace

The Angel Inn

Guildford, Surrey, England
17 August 1658

"It'll cost a fortune to catch the stagecoach!" Luka said, holding his coat shut so no one would see Zizi buttoned up inside. "It goes against the grain, having to *pay* to travel the roads."

"I have the money from the fair still," Emilia said. "And we don't have much time. We could be in Southampton by tonight!"

The two children were standing outside an inn with an angel painted on its sign. Being the largest inn in Guildford, the stagecoach to Southampton stopped there overnight on its way down from London.

Emilia could not help feeling apprehensive being in such a big town, but it had been three days since they had escaped Coldham and they had been careful not to draw any attention to themselves as they made their way across the country. The previous night they had stayed at a ramshackle manor house owned by an impoverished

Puritan widow, who had given the children clean clothes and some food in return for their help around the farm. Emilia was now wearing a plain grey dress, with her black hair braided back neatly and hidden by a white cap. Even Luka looked quite respectable, with his hair combed and a plain brown coat worn over a pair of woollen breeches. Only the fiddle in his hand and his nut-brown skin gave him away.

In the inn's bustling courtyard, the coachman was overseeing the disposal of the luggage on the roof of the coach. He was a big, beefy man with a red face and a heavy cape, and he was complaining loudly about the noise he had had to endure overnight.

Emilia hung back against the wall, Rollo sitting at her feet, as Luka went to enquire about the time of departure from the grooms. They were busy and impatient, but one shouted over his shoulder that the coach to Southampton would be leaving soon, and they could purchase a ticket from the public bar. Luka pushed open the swing door and went inside to the dark, smoky, crowded taproom. There was a roar of conversation.

"Tell us, is it true Old Ironsides fears he's been poisoned?" one man demanded.

"The Lord Protector has been threatened with many assassination plots this past year," a wizened old man in a lawyer's gown said. "It is not surprising that he fears this latest bout of illness may have an unnatural source, particularly given its proximity to the death of his beloved daughter."

"If you ask me, it's all a set-up," the other man retorted. "They just want us to fear for Old Ironsides' life, so we'll keep on paying taxes for his soldiers."

"I assure you the threat is very real," the lawyer said stiffly. "I have had reports of a Royalist plot being uncovered this very week. One of Charles Stuart's right-hand men has been travelling incognito about the country, trying to raise another rebellion. We are lucky the plot was unmasked in time!"

"I've heard that the King of Scots has his army drawn up at the waterside in France, ready to be shipped for England," the innkeeper said, drawing another mug of ale.

"Rubbish!" another said, with a grin and a wink. "That young gentleman is too busy dancing and flirting at the French court to worry about us. I've heard he has a bevy of mistresses, each one more beautiful than the last."

Luka squeezed through to the bar and asked for two tickets to Southampton. He was very glad to get back outside, because Zizi was wriggling about like an eel, trying to get out of his coat. He went to stand with Emilia, watching as passengers came out of the inn, sleepy and bleary eyed.

"Better take Rollo for a bit of a walk," Emilia said. "Once we get on that coach we won't be getting off for a while, and we don't want him whizzing all over our feet."

"Good idea." Luka whistled to Rollo and took him round the back. While Rollo cocked his leg against a post, Luka let Zizi out of his coat for a scamper around.

She did not want to be shut up again, and refused to come when he called. It took him a while to catch her and button her up in his coat again. With his fiddle banging on his back, Luka raced towards the coach and cannoned into the wizened old lawyer, who was just coming out of the inn door.

"Oops, sorry!" Luka cried.

The lawyer frowned and drew his black gown closer about him. Suddenly his expression sharpened. Looking down, Luka realized Zizi's bright, dark eyes were peering over the top buttons of his coat.

Hastily Luka clutched his coat lapels together, muttered, "Excuse me," and went hurrying back to join Emilia. He glanced back over his shoulder and saw the lawyer grab one of the inn's messenger boys and press a coin into his hand. Feeling uneasy, Luka joined Emilia at the steps up into the coach.

"Where have you been?" she hissed.

"I couldn't catch Zizi," he muttered back.

"Better keep her hidden," she said. He grunted, not wanting to tell her someone had already seen the little monkey.

"Let's get on before they see Rollo," Emilia said. They clambered on board, Rollo scrambling up after them, much to the dismay of the other passengers.

"Coachman! They've brought a big smelly dog on board," a fat woman said, shrinking away from Rollo, who panted amiably and scratched his ear.

"He's not smelly," Luka said indignantly.

"Still, no dogs allowed," the coachman said. "Get him off."

"Oh, please," Emilia said. "He's all we've got left in the world. Our parents have died, and we're being sent to stay with some grumpy old godfather we've never even met. We've had Rollo ever since he was a puppy; we can't leave him behind. What would become of him? He'd starve. Please, please, don't make us leave him behind." Tears began to roll down her face.

The fat woman clasped her hands together. "Oh, you poor little mites."

The coachman hesitated. Emilia nudged Luka with her very sharp elbow. "Could we offer you some coppers?" he said at once. "For the cost of sweeping out the coach once we've gone."

"Thank you, that's very kind," the coachman said, his big fist closing over the coins Luka offered him. "Now let's get rolling, we're already late!"

As the coach moved slowly out of the stable-yard, Luka heaved a sigh of relief and relaxed back against the cushions.

Then a thin, dry voice cried, "Wait! Wait! I have a ticket for that coach."

The door was yanked open and the lawyer climbed in, his withered face all red and hot, his gown rumpled. Luka could only stare at him in dismay.

"So?" the lawyer said, looking intently at Luka and Emilia as the coach clattered over the cobblestones. "Heading for Southampton?"

Luka nodded, for there was no point lying when they were all on the Southampton coach together.

"Two small children, travelling all on their own?"

"Aye," Luka said, though he very much disliked being described as "small".

"We're not on our own," Emilia broke in, smiling. "We have Rollo."

"Not to mention the creature you're carrying inside your coat," the lawyer said drily, nodding at the small bulge that was Zizi.

Emilia's smile faded. She glanced at Luka, who said stolidly, "That's right."

The fat woman gave a little scream. "What? What are you carrying?"

"Another pet," Luka said. "A dear little thing."

"It's not a mouse, is it?" the woman said fearfully. "Or a . . . a rat?"

"No," Luka said, "she's not a rat."

"Is it a cat?" the woman asked, leaning forward and peering with interest at the bulge. Luka just smiled and said, "No need to worry, she's fast asleep," and after a moment the woman lost interest and began checking through her basket.

The lawyer, however, did not lose interest. "What are your parents thinking, allowing you to travel on your own?"

"Their parents are dead, poor mites." The fat woman looked up from her basket. "They're off to stay with their godfather."

172

"Indeed?"

Luka made an affirmative noise in his throat and looked out of the window, hoping that would discourage any more questions. The coach was moving slowly up the road, pushing its way through a muddle of other vehicles.

"That's a very large dog you have there," the lawyer said.

"Aye, Rollo is big," Emilia said politely.

"I've never seen a dog quite like it before," the lawyer said. "What breed is it?"

"I don't know," Emilia said. "He's just a mongrel, I guess."

"So when did your parents die?" the lawyer asked.

Emilia turned back to him, looking woebegone. "Last week," she said.

"Oh, poor mites," the fat lady said.

"Both together, at the same time?" The lawyer sounded sceptical.

"Aye," Luka said. As the lawyer raised grey, bushy eyebrow, he added hastily, "Plague," just as Emilia said, "Smallpox."

They cast quick, anguished glances at each other.

"So which was it, plague or smallpox?" the lawyer demanded.

Emilia gave a little sob and shrugged, and Luka said, in a tone of deep unhappiness, "Plague, pox, what does it matter? They're dead."

"They . . . they had spots," Emilia volunteered, scrubbing her eyes hard with her kerchief so that they looked suitably red.

"And a cough," Luka said.

"A fever," Emilia said, frowning a little at him.

"So now we're orphans," Luka said sadly.

The fat woman shook her head. "Oh, what an unhappy story. Such terrible times we live in. I do hope your godfather will be kind to you."

"I'm sure he will," Emilia said in a very small voice, making it quite clear that she did not expect so. The fat woman was so affected she rummaged through her basket and gave the children some toffee, which had the happy effect of making it impossible to answer any more questions.

The day rumbled past.

Emilia was feeling very jolted and bruised, and was glad to be allowed out of the coach in Alton while the horses were changed. The coachman disappeared into the inn to consume some more beer and some lunch, but the children wanted to get away from the other passengers, and so they quickly climbed the hill, searching for a cool, green spot where they could eat some of their supplies and let Zizi out for a play. The little monkey had woken as the coach had jerked to a stop, and she was doing her best to wriggle from inside Luka's coat.

"Don't be too long, dears," called the fat woman, who was called Mistress Hudson. "The coach will only stop for half an hour or so."

They waved at her and hurried away, not liking the

way Mr Pettigrew, the lawyer, was staring after them. As soon as they were out of sight, Luka let Zizi out of his coat and she leapt about like a mad thing, gibbering loudly. She swung through the trees overhanging the lane, leapt down on to Luka's shoulder and pinched his ear sharply, then dropped down on to Rollo's back, riding him like a pony. Rollo twitched his ear back, but otherwise tolerated her.

"I don't like the way that scrawny old man keeps asking questions," Emilia said. "Do you think he knows about us?"

"I'm afraid he might. He saw Zizi at the inn, and I'm pretty sure he sent someone a message about it. I hope it's not to that Cold-Pig!"

"But how could he know about us?"

Luka shrugged. "How does Cromwell find out about all these plots to restore the king? There are spies everywhere. They must have some kind of message network. If Fish-Face worked for the government – I mean, as more than just a pastor . . . I mean, I remember he said something about how he had been sent to Kingston to stamp out rebels. . ."

"We're not rebels!"

"We're not God-fearing Puritans either," Luka said drily. "And you know Baba could be burnt as a witch for looking in her crystal ball or laying out the cards. We're Rom, and we have our own way of doing things, but these pastors . . . they cannot abide anyone not thinking or believing the same way as them."

They reached the end of the laneway and spied an old white church with a square tower topped with a tall spire, surrounded by grass and flowers. The churchyard was quiet and empty, so they went in through the lychgate and sat under one of the trees, spreading out Luka's coat so they did not have to sit on the damp ground. It was very peaceful, with only the hum of bees and the warbling of birds to disturb the quiet.

"So you think Pastor Spurgeon has written news of us to all his cronies all over the country?" Emilia sawed at their loaf of bread with their very blunt knife.

Luka nodded, his mouth full of hard-boiled egg. "I think he's angry we got away."

"But why? Why is he so angry?"

"I don't know. Maybe he hates us because we're gypsies. Some people do, you know."

"Maybe he thinks we're caught up with this Royalist spy," Emilia said. "I mean, Cold-Pig saw us talking to Tom Whitehorse in Kingston, and Tom's up to his eyebrows in some kind of plot. And Coldham said something about gypsies being able to carry secret messages around, and maybe even hide a hunted man. I know it seems ridiculous, but maybe Coldham thinks we'll lead him to this marquis. . ."

"We're in big trouble, then," Luka said. "If Coldham thinks we're mixed up in some plot to restore the king, no wonder he keeps on chasing after us. . ."

The two children stared at each other in consternation. "What should we do?" Emilia whispered.

"Get away. Surely we're small fry compared to the king's best friend? We'll lose ourselves in the country, and let Cold-Pig get back on the marquis' trail. . ."

Rollo rose to his feet, growling, his hackles rising. Luka whipped around and saw Mr Pettigrew peering at them over the church wall.

"Hello!" The lawyer stretched his thin, wrinkled cheeks into a smile that looked very unnatural. "Having a picnic, are we?"

The children nodded.

"I . . . I've come to look at the church. It's very old, you know. Eleventh century. There was a famous battle here, you know, during the war. You're meant to be able to see the bullet holes in the wall." Mr Pettigrew spoke quickly, smiling all the while, and Emilia wondered if he was trying to justify his presence there so that they would not suspect him of following them. If so, he failed miserably.

"So where's your monkey?"

Luka was taken by surprise. Involuntarily he glanced up into the tree, where Zizi was perched, enjoying an apple.

"Unusual pet," the lawyer said.

"Not really. Lots of people have monkeys. The old queen had one called Pug, which is a pretty stupid name, I think."

"The widow of the tyrant also had a dwarf that was only two feet high. She collected strange creatures. But it is certainly a peculiar animal for a young boy to own."

177

"Zizi is not peculiar," Luka flashed. "She's a sweetheart. Don't you dare call her peculiar."

Emilia gave a little cough and nudged Luka with her foot. She knew he was capable of saying almost anything if he lost his temper, and she did not want to antagonize this lawyer if she could help it.

Zizi, knowing she was being talked about, threw her apple core at the lawyer and knocked his hat off. Angrily he snatched the hat up and jammed it back on his head, staring at them with narrow eyes. Zizi gibbered, jumping up and down. Luka held up his hand to her. At once she swung down to his shoulder, holding his ear with one paw.

"Not at all the sort of pet a normal young boy would have," the lawyer said in a cold, hard voice. "A queen with a taste for follies, perhaps. A sailor back from foreign parts. Or maybe a *gypsy* boy."

Luka's cheeks flushed hotly. He jumped to his feet. "I think I'd like a look at those bullet holes. Where did you say they were?"

The lawyer looked taken aback, but he walked with them into the church, giving them a dry lecture on the civil war. Luka nodded and smiled, doing his best to look like a well-brought-up child. As they passed through the big arched door, Luka gave Emilia a meaningful glance and mimed turning a key in a lock. She grinned and slipped away. Luckily the keys were kept in the locks, and she was able to quietly lock the back and side doors while Luka pretended to be interested in the spray of bullet holes in the wall.

"So how many men were killed here?" he asked the lawyer.

"I'll just go out and keep an eye on Rollo, else he'll start howling," Emilia called. "Don't be long."

She went out of the front door and stood quietly, waiting. A moment later, Luka came hurtling out the door, Zizi clinging her thin arms about his neck. Emilia slammed the big door shut and locked it.

As they ran, laughing, out of the churchyard, they heard a faint pounding and yelling behind them. "That should hold him a while," Luka said in satisfaction. "Come on, else we'll miss the coach!"

Stand and Deliver!

It was very late when the stagecoach at last rattled into Southampton. Luka woke and yawned, stretching out his arms, then roused Emilia. Quietly they slipped into the dark street, the bag slung over Luka's shoulder and Zizi snuggled up inside his coat. A cold breeze was blowing dead leaves and rubbish along the gutter. Luka looked up at the night sky, for his sense of direction had been disoriented by the day spent in the swaying, rumbling coach.

Rollo growled deep in his throat. Walking towards them were two dark-clad men. Luka stepped further back into the shadows, one hand on Rollo's neck. He expected the men would pass them by, but they approached grimly.

"Go on your way, sirs! We have nothing worth robbing, and if you try, I'll set my dog on you."

"If you do, I'll shoot him," a familiar voice said gruffly.

Luka's blood turned to ice. Coldham!

He turned and bolted, Emilia running beside him. Every step, he expected to hear the bang of a pistol, but Coldham evidently did not want to fire in the middle of the high street. Instead, he heard the thud of running boots. Luka put on speed, but it was no use. He was seized roughly. Rollo sprang to his rescue, but was knocked down with a heavy cudgel. The big dog fell with a whimper, then lay still.

"Rollo!" Emilia screamed. "Rollo!"

A hand was put over her mouth, and she was dragged towards a large black coach drawn up in the shadows. Though both Luka and Emilia fought with all their strength, they were tossed through the coach door.

Coldham climbed in after them, slamming the door behind him and throwing himself down on the seat opposite as the horses were whipped into motion. The only light came from a lantern hanging by the driver's seat. It swayed back and forth over the interior of the coach, so that Coldham's face sank in and out of darkness. It was a face that had haunted their dreams the past few nights: heavy, black-jowled, with mean slits of eyes and a flattened nose. One hand rested on the pistol he wore thrust through his belt.

"Rollo!" Emilia panted. "You've killed Rollo."

Coldham grunted. "Let's hope so."

"Why? Why?"

"Savage brute. Bit me once. Won't do so again."

"How could you?" Emilia sobbed.

"Easily," Coldham said, sounding amused. "Do it again in an instant."

Emilia wiped her nose on her sleeve and slowly groped for the chain that hung about her wrist. Her fingers found the familiar shape of the misshapen coin, and closed upon it. *Please . . . please. . .*

"Where are you taking us?" Luka could barely manage to frame the words.

"Back to gaol."

"Why? Why chase us all over the country?"

Coldham cleared his throat and spat. "Got my reputation to think of. Can't have a couple of grubby gypsy brats show me up. No one would hire me again."

"But we're just weans. We haven't done anything wrong."

He snorted. "Gypsy brats like you? Taught to steal before you can walk."

"That's not true," Emilia cried.

He snorted with laughter. "I'm not a fool, girl. I know what you've been up to. Where's the marquis?"

"We don't know any marquis!"

"Likely story. Better tell me what you know."

"I don't know anything!"

"Bad choice, girlie. Well, we'll see what you choose to tell the Lord Protector's spymaster. My advice is, squeal like a pig. It's not pretty what they do to people who don't tell them what they want to know."

Emilia shrank back against the hard cushion. Luka gripped her hand reassuringly. They could only stare at the dark hulk of a man brooding in the far corner. As the coach rattled on through the darkness, he kept on talking at them, describing some of the things he had seen done in the Tower of London's torture chambers to men who defied the Lord Protector. All courage and strength and hope drained out of the two children.

There was a loud bang, right outside the window, and a bright flash.

The horses reared and plunged, the coach swerved and skidded to a halt, and a loud and cheerful voice cried, "Stand and deliver!"

At once Coldham slid off his seat and crouched by the door, his hand going to his pistol. There was a commotion outside, horses neighing, men shouting, and the door was wrenched open. As Coldham lunged forward, his pistol ready, Luka leapt up and landed a heartfelt kick in the thief-taker's posterior. Coldham fell sprawling out of the coach. His pistol discharged harmlessly into the dirt, much to the startled relief of the highwayman.

"Oddsblood!" he cried.

"Please!" Luka cried. "Help us! We've been kidnapped. . ."

"He's a bad, bad man," Emilia said. "Please help us."

Coldham groaned and tried to get up, but the highwayman gave him a hard crack over the head with his cudgel. He lay still.

"Is he dead?" Emilia whispered.

"Lord, no. I'm no murderer." The highwayman raised

the lantern high so its light illuminated Emilia and Luka. "Heavens above, it's a couple of children. I thought you sounded young. Now what bramble have I landed myself in? I heard there was a government agent travelling this road, and thought to have a little fun, and maybe some gain as well, but the kidnapping of children? That's serious stuff."

"He *is* a government agent," Luka cried.

"He grabbed us. . ."

"He wants to throw us in gaol."

"He killed our dog," Emilia said.

The highwayman was frowning. "He does sound most unpleasant. Now what am I meant to do with you? Two brats don't fit into my plans at all! I suppose you had best come back with me. Just give me a moment to see what goodies this dear sweet-natured man has for me."

The children nodded and sat down together on the stony bank by the side of the road. The highwayman riffled through Coldham's pockets and pulled out a bunch of keys and a heavy bag of coins. He pocketed the bag of coins, then went to toss the keys down by Coldham's unconscious body.

Luka cried, "No! Please. Wait."

The highwayman paused in surprise as Luka hurriedly found a candle. He pressed the candle against the lantern until the wax was warm, then carefully took an impression of each of the keys.

The highwayman busied himself tying up the two men and dumping them in the coach. He shone the lantern into every corner, then expertly opened up some kind of secret drawer under one of the seats, extracting a folder of papers. He made a noise of intense satisfaction in his throat, thrust his finds into his saddlebags, then hid the coach behind a large bush, and unhitched the coach-horses.

"Should get a pretty penny for this lot," he said to Emilia. "I know a fellow in Salisbury who will paint them up and sell them for me, none the wiser."

She nodded her head. "It's a shame they're black. Much easier to disguise a grey."

He raised an eyebrow. "What's a pretty young lass like you doing knowing such things?"

Emilia flushed. "Oh, I'm guessing."

"Good guess."

She smiled and dropped her eyes.

"A boy who knows how to take an imprint for a key to be copied, and a girl who knows how to disguise a stolen horse. What kind of company have I fallen into?"

"I could say the same," Emilia retorted, and he laughed.

"Can you ride?" he asked. "Because I'd like to get away from here fairly quickly."

She gave him a scornful glance and vaulted up on to the back of one of the coach-horses.

"I guess that means *yes*," the highwayman said.

Luka carefully tucked Coldham's keys back into his pocket, making sure there was no wax left on them to make the thief-taker suspect they had been copied. He then joined Emilia and the highwayman with a smile of pure joy on his face.

"I have a feeling these could be very useful," he said to Emilia. "We'll ask the Smiths to make us copies."

"You think they're the keys to the gaol?" she whispered sceptically. "But would Cold-Pig have them?"

"Maybe, maybe not," Luka said. "Only one way to find out." He winked at her. "Besides, even if they're the keys to his dear old father's cottage, they still may come in useful. I like to be prepared."

"After all, they could be the keys to his coin-laden strongbox," Emilia replied, grinning.

"Exactly." Luka deftly leapt on to the back of one of the other horses, his monkey's tail whipping round his neck as she fought to stay on his shoulder.

"Let's go!" The highwayman gave a wild cry, whipping up his horse. At once the bay was off, the two other coach-horses racing along behind him.

Thrilled to be free, Emilia and Luka followed at breakneck speed, huge clods of mud spraying up from the hooves of their horses, the darkness hurtling past them.

Close on an hour later, the highwayman led them to a rough camp in a small hollow on the moors. A tent was slung over a rope tied between two bushes, and there was a dead fire in a circle of stones.

"Home sweet home," he said, dismounting gracefully. He unsaddled and hobbled his mount, then laid a fire. Emilia and Luka were so tired, it was all they could do to dismount. They slithered down and unbuckled the bridles with fingers that did not seem to want to work properly. At last they all sat around the fire, grateful for its warmth.

By the light of the fire they saw the highwayman was young, long-limbed and lean, and dressed like a gentleman in a velvet coat. His face was pale-skinned and bony, with hollows in the cheeks above a neatly trimmed beard.

He swept off his hat and bowed low. "Lord Harry Morrow, at your service."

"If you're a lord, why are you working the bridle lay?" Luka demanded.

"I prefer to call myself a knight of the road," Lord Harry responded.

"Whatever you want to call it, it's not what you expect a lord to be doing," Luka said.

"What else am I meant to do?" the highwayman replied bitterly. "My estate has been stolen, my house burnt to the ground, my family are all dead. . ." He sighed. "Tell me what you were doing in the coach of a government agent?"

"It's a long story," Luka said.

The gentleman leant back against his saddle. "I'm in no rush."

So Luka and Emilia told him a short version of their tale. As Lord Harry listened, he smoked his pipe in silence, his brows drawn close together.

"So you say this Coldham man has been chasing you across the countryside? It seems a most unlikely tale."

"But it's all true!" Luka exclaimed hotly.

"I don't necessarily disbelieve you, lad. I did, after all, find you in his coach. I'm just wondering if there's not more to this than meets the eye. If my information is correct, he's a government agent whose job it is to hunt down Catholics and Royalists."

The children nodded.

Lord Harry regarded them through heavy-lidded eyes. "Tell me, are you for the king or for Parliament?"

Luka was too tired and dispirited to be tactful. "I'm for myself, My Lord," he said bluntly. "We gypsies say, 'Bury me standing, for I've been on my knees all my life.' Well, it's true. We were branded and whipped and hanged when a king sat on the throne, and there's no difference now a Lord Protector sits there instead, as far as I can see."

Lord Harry frowned and examined his shabby boot.

"Well, me, I'm for the king," Emilia said. "The Roundheads killed my dado and took our horses and left us with nothing. I was only a baby when the old king had his head cut off, so I don't remember what life was like back then, but I know things could hardly be worse than they are now. Maybe if the new king came back, he would have learnt some kind of lesson and rule better than his father did."

"And maybe he'd be worse," Luka pointed out.

"Oh, no, he's a great man! I fought with him and a braver prince never lived! We had to beg him to flee when it was clear the day was lost. He would've fought to the death, but we knew our only hope was to keep him alive." Lord Harry sighed and looked into the flames. "It was a miracle he got away. Indeed, it is a sign of God's favour that he was preserved." He lifted his cup to the stars, then drank deeply.

"The Puritans say it's a sign of God's favour that Parliament won the day," Luka said.

Lord Harry glanced at him and, unexpectedly, laughed. "Indeed, I guess we all believe it is by God's providence that we are delivered, when in truth it is probably nothing more than blind luck."

Emilia caressed the gold coin at her wrist and said in rather a shaky voice, "It was more than luck that saw you save us tonight. If it was not for you, we'd be on our way to the gallows."

"Luck or providence, who knows?" Lord Harry bent and patted his saddlebags, where he had thrust the papers he had taken from Coldham's coach. "Either way, I got what I was after, as well as some nice swag. I'll be off to Gypsy Joe's in the morning to sell those nags, and. . ."

"Gypsy Joe?" Both children sat up.

"Aye, do you know him? The innkeeper of The Herb of Grace in Salisbury?"

The children looked at each other, torn between hope and disbelief. The name of the inn was definitely a good sign. But what would a Rom be doing running an inn in Salisbury?

"We think he may be the man we are looking for,"

Luka said carefully. "He's a relative of ours. But we thought he lived in the New Forest."

"All the gypsies were cleared out of the New Forest. Cromwell's cutting down all the trees to build new ships for his navy."

"What happened to them all?" Luka said.

Lord Harry glanced at him, then said gently, "I heard most of them were transported to Jamaica, to work on the sugar plantations."

Luka drew in a sharp breath. "But . . . that's slavery!"

Lord Harry looked away, his face grim. Zizi looked up at Luka's face, then patted his arm.

"Why don't you come with me to the Herb of Grace?" Lord Harry said, after a long moment. "Then you can see if Gypsy Joe is the man you seek. We'd need to leave bright and early, though, as I have no desire to ride into Salisbury in broad daylight with four horses that belong to one of Cromwell's spies!"

"All right," Luka said.

Emilia yawned, and rested her head on her hand.

"Get some sleep in the meantime," the highwayman suggested kindly. "It's very late."

Emilia lay down, pulling her shawl about her, but Luka felt in the dark for his violin, which lay in its case next to his knee. "Would it be safe for me to play my fiddle?" he asked. "Just for a little while. We've been running and hiding for so long, it's been ages since I've played, and she should be played every day. It's bad for her to lie quiet."

"We're miles from anywhere here," the highwayman said. "Play away."

Luka took out his violin and fitted it to his chin. He tuned the strings carefully, then began to play, glad to fill his ears with music. The lack of it had been a hollow ache inside him all these days.

His fingers found their way into a lament. Luka shut his eyes, and the music soared out into the starlit darkness, wild and plaintive. When Luka laid down his fiddle and opened his eyes, he felt much calmer and happier.

"I haven't heard a fiddle in a very long time," the highwayman said, clearing his throat. "I'd forgotten how beautiful its music can be."

Luka smiled and stroked Zizi's fur. The little monkey was sitting bolt upright, her black-button eyes fixed on his face, her head cocked a little to one side. She knew when Luka played music to dance and tumble to, and when he wanted her to sit and listen.

"I want my mother back," Emilia suddenly sobbed. "I want her back and alive, and Beatrice and Noah out of gaol, and Baba . . . I want. . ." Her voice failed. "I want to go galloping on Alida . . . and I want Rollo! Oh, Rollo!"

She buried her face in her hands, her whole body shaking.

Luka patted her arm awkwardly. "Never mind, Milly. We'll get them out of gaol, don't you worry. Haven't we got this far already? Try and get some sleep, and we'll go find that rue charm tomorrow, and see what Gypsy Joe can do to help us. All right?"

Emilia did not uncover her face, but she nodded her head, cradling her charm bracelet in her hand.

Emilia woke with a jerk, her breath harsh in her chest.

She had been trapped in a dream, a terrible dream, where she had been running through endless stone corridors and cells, looking for her family. She had called and called their names, but her voice was strangled. She had not been able to find them.

Something had woken her. Lying still, every muscle rigid, Emilia listened. The sound came again, and Emilia threw aside her shawl and scrambled to her feet, straining her eyes to peer through the darkness. The only light came from the fire, where the log had collapsed into smouldering coals. The sky above glowed faintly, filled with stars.

She heard it again, a faint whine, and stumbled towards it. Her shins bumped into something soft and hairy. She flung herself to her knees, throwing her arms about the neck of the big dog. "Rollo, Rollo," she cried. "You're alive! You found us! Good dog, good dog!"

He gave a faint whuff and licked her face, then laid his head on her knee. Emilia stroked the dog's rough fur, and found a wet sticky patch between his ears. Although she at once flinched away, Rollo whined again.

"Did you smell where we had gone? Did you follow the coach? Oh, what a clever dog." Rollo licked her fingers. "Come on, boy, I'll get you some water. You must be so thirsty. Come lie here, near the fire, and I'll wash that cut, and get you a drink. Good boy!"

As Emilia stirred the fire up again and added some wood so she could see, Rollo lay down and put his aching head on his paws. Emilia brought him a pan of water to drink, then lay down beside him, stroking his ears.

"I'm so glad you're here," she whispered to the exhausted dog. "I'm so glad you found us, Rollo!"

She thought to herself, *Everything's going to be all right. Already the magic of the charms are helping us, protecting us. Tomorrow, maybe, we'll find the rue charm. . .*

The Herb of Grace

Salisbury, Wiltshire, England
18 August 1658

It was a mad ride through the darkness before dawn. Lord Harry crouched low over the saddle, never losing his balance as his bay swerved and leapt over the worst of the ruts. The only sound was the heavy hooves hitting the road, the jingle of the harness and the blowing of the horses' breaths.

"Aren't you afraid you'll take a tumble and break your neck?" Luka demanded when at last the highwayman slowed down. Emilia looked back anxiously at Rollo, who was toiling along behind them, his tongue hanging out. She wished Lord Harry would remember Rollo's sore head.

Lord Harry laughed. "Better to die in the saddle than at the end of the hangman's noose."

"But why become a highwayman?" Luka asked. "You could have turned yourself in, and taken your pardon, and paid the fine for the return for your land."

"With what?" Lord Harry replied. "We were utterly ruined by the war. Besides, to beg pardon would have meant betraying everything we fought the war for. This way I am still fighting for my king, in the best way I can, and raising money to restore my lands once he is back on his throne where he belongs."

"How is holding up coaches helping to restore the king?"

"I only rob Roundheads," Lord Harry replied shortly.

"But how do you know?"

Lord Harry glanced at him in exasperation. "I get information, from innkeepers and stagecoach drivers and anyone else willing to pass on news for a few coins."

"But what do you do if you pull up the wrong coach?" Emilia asked.

"I ask them to drink a toast with me to the king," Lord Harry replied. "If they refuse, I rob them and reprimand them and let them go on their way, but if they agree, we share a nice drop of brandy and we part friends and comrades."

Luka laughed out loud.

"I don't just rob coaches," Lord Harry went on. "I work for the Royalists too. I carry messages, and information about troop movements, and help guide the king's agents about the country. Quite a few of us knights of the road do that, for we can move about freely while many who support the king cannot. You know it is against the law for a known Royalist to move more than five miles from home? That makes it very difficult to plan an uprising, particularly since Cromwell's spymaster reads all the mail."

"So are you planning an uprising now?" Emilia asked in high excitement.

"That would be telling," he smiled, and spurred his horse on.

It was not long before Lord Harry rose in his stirrups and pointed. "Look! There lies Salisbury."

They saw a small grey town set within medieval walls. A cathedral spire soared upwards, so fragile it seemed impossible it would not snap. It was like a sword point held to the heart of the brightening sky, sharp and infinitely dangerous. It was the highest church spire in all England, Lord Harry told them. Luka wondered that the Roundheads had not torn it down.

"Let's get a move along," Lord Harry said, tapping his heels to his bay gelding's side. "I'd like to be within the walls before the city begins to wake up."

The town rose on its hill on the other side of the River Avon, roofs and towers rising from behind the thick walls. A stone bridge crossed the river, and they clattered across to the barred gate, which was manned by two guards with pikes. A wink, a quick flash of gold, and the gates were hauled open and the five horses and three riders were allowed through, Rollo panting at their heels. As they rode down the narrow street within, the buildings leaning over them and almost obscuring the sky, the gate swung shut behind them. Emilia gave a little shiver.

"Isn't it a bit of a risk, letting the guards see us all like that?" she whispered.

"No way into Salisbury except through the gates," Lord Harry said cheerfully. "They're good fellows, though, those two, and goldmines of information. They won't give me away."

"Are you sure?" Emilia asked.

He shrugged. "Let's say I hope so."

The town was a maze of narrow streets and narrower houses, but Lord Harry showed no hesitation as he led the way, the horses' hooves clip-clopping on the stones. Emilia kept glancing behind to make sure no one was following them, and to keep an eye on Rollo, who was plodding along slowly, his head hanging.

People were beginning to stir. Maids were flinging open windows and shaking out rugs, or scrubbing the front doorstep on their hands and knees. A water cart clattered down one street, and people came out with jugs and stood chatting as they waited for their turn to fill them up. A young woman went from door to door selling eggs from a basket, and someone else led a cow around, calling loudly, "Milk-o! Milk-o!"

By the time they reached the Herb of Grace, the sun was up, gilding the river so it hurt to look at it. The inn was long and low and white, cross-hatched with heavy oak beams, with tall chimneys sprouting from the thatched roof. Hanging above the front door was a large, vividly painted sign depicting a yellow flower growing from a bunch of grey, three-lobed leaves. Already coaches were preparing to leave, with luggage piled high on their roofs, and coachmen in their heavy coats perched on the driving seats, shouting and swearing as they tried to squeeze past each other.

Lord Harry took them down an alley into the stable-yard behind the inn. Here all was quiet and peaceful. Horses stood in dim stalls, heads in nosebags, their tails whisking at the flies. A groom was mucking out one of the stalls. He nodded his head at Lord Harry and said, "You're late. I'll get Joe."

A few minutes later he returned with a short, broad, swarthy-skinned man with a soft belly that hung over his belt and thick, brown hands. He ignored the highwayman and the two children, casting his eyes over the four black coach-horses with a critical eye, then running his hands down their legs to check their feet and lifting their lips to look at their big yellow teeth. He grunted and stepped back, wiping his hands down his apron.

"You're late," he said to Lord Harry. "This is my busiest time. Too many people around to see you and wonder about you."

"We came as fast as we could," Lord Harry said, cheerful as ever. "I had two gypsy brats to slow me down. Kin of yours, they say."

Gypsy Joe flicked them a quick glance but said nothing. He jerked his head at the groom and together they led Coldham's four black coach-horses into a large barn at the back of the stables. Working quickly, they unharnessed the horses, rubbed them down well and fed them, while the children found Rollo some water.

Joe jerked his head at the groom and said, "Go make sure the kitchen's not on fire, would you, Bob?"

He then took out a pot of white paint, and delicately began to alter the appearance of Coldham's coach-horses. He gave one a white sock and a blaze; another four white socks and a white stripe; the third he gave a half-pastern of white on the forelegs and a star; and the fourth received a tiny splodge of white on its nose, a marking called a snip, then a crown of white on each of its four hooves. Lord Harry had obviously seen this done before, for after he had attended to his own horse, he went whistling into the inn, calling for ale and bacon and eggs. Luka and Emilia sat on upturned barrels, though, staring in fascination. Evidently Joe did not mind them watching, for after a while he said quietly, "So, who do you know?"

Luka gave Joe his parents' names and his grandparents' names, and it was soon established that Joe's aunt had married Luka's mother's cousin, some time back, and that his father was a second cousin to Emilia's father. All the Rom were linked together in an invisible cobweb of kin.

"So why are you here in Salisbury?" Joe asked.

Luka took a deep breath. "They've arrested our family in Kingston-upon-Thames, and say they are all to hang. Only Emilia and I managed to get away. Baba told us to seek out our kin and ask them for help."

"And what kind of help are you seeking?"

"Any kind," Luka said rather hopelessly. "The gaol is in the centre of town, near the church. I thought maybe we could storm the gaol, if we could get enough men . . . break them out by force."

"The Sealed Knot did that here in Salisbury a few years back," Joe said, concentrating on the white he was painting about one of the horse's fetlocks.

"They did? Here?" Emilia was enthralled. She loved tales about the Sealed Knot, which was one of the secret organizations that worked to restore the throne to the king.

"Aye. The plan was for men to rise all over England, but the spymaster's spies did their job too well. Cromwell had troops brought in all over the country, and most of the rebels' hearts failed them."

Luka and Emilia settled down for the story.

"Only here in Salisbury did the uprising go ahead, and that was because of a brave and foolhardy man called Penruddock. He and his men entered Salisbury late one night, and stormed the gaol and begged the help of the prisoners. They arrested the sheriff and took him hostage, still dressed in his nightgown, and then they marched out, only to be met by Cromwell's army. Penruddock and all his men had their heads cut off, and that is what would happen to you if you tried to do the same."

"But we don't want to start a rebellion; we just want to save our families."

"Tell that to the Lord Protector. He thinks there are spies and assassins under every bed these days."

"There must be something we can do," Luka said. "If I can get copies made of the gaol's keys. . ."

Joe added a few delicate strokes of white, saying nothing.

"You have to help us!" Emilia burst out. "My brother is only nine . . . and he's blind! And my sister . . . my grandmother. . ."

"My little sister is only nine too," Luka said. "Please!"

"They probably won't hang the weans." Joe carefully hid the pot of white paint. "Put them into the workhouse, probably."

"But my daya, my dado, my baba," Luka cried, at the same time as Emilia said passionately, "I don't want them to go to the workhouse, I want for things to be the way they were before."

Joe looked at her pityingly. "Is there anyone who does not at some point wish that? The past is the past, and nothing can change that."

"But you can change your future," Emilia exclaimed. "If anyone must know about the possibility of becoming something new, you must!"

He regarded her for a long time out of eyes so dark it was impossible to read them. Then he said, very quietly, "Aye, I do, I suppose. Which is why I am a gypsy no longer, but an innkeeper. So I'm afraid you must go elsewhere for help. I have my hands full at present."

"With what? Serving ale?" Luka said in bitter contempt.

Joe's mouth quirked up. "Actually I have a house full of Royalist rebels, a stable full of stolen horses, and a spy for Cromwell who will no doubt be arriving on my doorstep any minute. I'm guessing he won't be in a happy mood."

Into The Oven

A bell hung over the stable door clanged loudly.

"Quick, run!" Gypsy Joe cried. "That's the sign that soldiers are on the doorstep. We've got to get you hidden. Here, hide your dog in here!"

He pushed his hand against the back wall. Unexpectedly a wooden panel sprang open, revealing a small, dark cavity inside. Hurriedly Luka and Emilia pushed Rollo inside. He looked up at them, whining, his tail between his legs.

"Stay, Rollo, stay," Emilia said, patting his rough head. Joe shut the secret panel, then they ran across the stable-yard, hearts pounding with fear.

The kitchen was full of people peeling potatoes, stirring pots on the stove and turning a big lump of meat on a spit over a roaring fire. The heat hit Emilia in the face as soon as she stepped inside.

"Troupe of Roundheads," said Bob, the boy they had

seen in the stable. "Headed by a big mean-looking fellow with a steel gauntlet."

"Coldham!" the two children cried.

Joe narrowed his eyes. "I'd like to know how he knew to come straight here. There's a spy in our ranks, for sure."

"The guards on the gate saw us," Luka said. "Could they have told him?"

"For enough money, they'd sell their mother," Joe said. "They'll live to regret it if they have, though. Quick, you two, into the oven."

"What?"

"Into the oven. Don't worry, we make our bread in the evenings; the oven will be quite cool now."

The children glanced nervously at the oven, which was an iron tunnel set into the wall at about hip height, above an open fireplace. The grate was swept clean, they could see, but the idea of being locked inside was daunting.

"Don't worry, I'm not going to cook you," Joe said. "Quickly! I can hear their boots on the stairs!"

So could Luka and Emilia. They let Joe lift them up so they could slide into the oven, feet first. There was just enough room for them to lie side by side, though they were very squashed. It was terrifying. Zizi whimpered, and Luka cuddled her close, whispering, "Sssh, sweetie, sssh."

Emilia could hear very little through the heavy iron door. She strained her ears. "But I'm just a simple innkeeper," Joe was protesting. "I know nothing about highwaymen or Royalists."

There was an answering rumble which made the children catch their breath as they instantly recognized Coldham's harsh voice.

"Oh, of course," Joe said. "Your men are welcome to search the house from attic to cellar if you wish. You will not mind if we keep on about our work, will you? For we're very busy at this time of the day, as the coaches come and go. Which reminds me! Bob, the London coach needs a change of horses, quickly! Give them Star, Blaze, Stripe and Snip, would you? They're fresh."

Luka and Emilia stifled giggles as they realized that Gypsy Joe was talking about Coldham's own coach-horses. What a clever way to get them out of the stables before the soldiers discovered them.

There was another low rumble, then Joe said, "Certainly, sir, of course. At once! I'll get the girls to bring it to you in your bedchamber."

The children lay in the stifling darkness for a long time before the door was at last heaved open and they were able to crawl out. They had no chance to say even a word. People hurriedly tied long aprons on them and thrust large laundry baskets into their arms, piled high with sheets and blankets. One woman hurriedly seized Emilia's long mane of wild black hair and twisted it up under a big white cap, pinning it on ruthlessly.

"Hide your monkey well," Joe said tersely.

Luka nodded and coaxed Zizi into the basket, hiding her under some sheets. She tried to lift the sheet and peep out, her eyes wide and anxious, but he pressed her down firmly, tucking her tail out of sight.

"Go with Daisy and Rosie," Joe instructed, jerking his head at two plump, dark-eyed girls who stood nearby, baskets on their hips. They looked so much like Joe they had to be his daughters. "Just nod and smile if anyone talks to you."

Luka and Emilia nodded.

"I'll keep your dog safe, don't you worry. You'll have to lie low all day. I'll get you out under cover of darkness. Just keep that monkey quiet!"

Emilia would have liked to ask him about his family's lucky charm, but Joe strode away before she had a chance. She gazed after him unhappily, then heaved up a basket and followed the two girls upstairs. Soldiers marched along the corridors, roughly searching every room. They took no notice of the children.

"Right," Daisy said, as soon as they reached a big bedchamber at the top of the house. "You, strip the bed, and if anyone comes in, cough, all right? Rosie, take the empty basket back down to the kitchen and bring something else back, so they see you coming and going."

The other girl nodded and went out and Emilia began to strip the bed as she had been commanded. Daisy took

Luka to the fireplace and showed him how to creep inside and stand upright. Emilia watched in amazement as he suddenly disappeared from sight, only his feet dangling down from the chimney.

At that very moment she heard the door open. Coldham came in, accompanied by two soldiers. Panic seized her by the throat. She coughed violently into her hand, then bent and seized a sheet and shook it out so it hid her from view.

"I'm sorry, sir, we're not quite ready for you," Daisy said respectfully, standing in front of the fireplace, dustpan and brush in hand.

Coldham grunted and went out again but left the door standing open. Emilia could hear him barking orders at the soldiers. Daisy beckoned urgently. Emilia threw the sheet down and hurried across to the fireplace. She crawled inside and found within a much larger space than she had expected. Shallow grooves in the wall led up the chimney like a ladder. Emilia climbed up nimbly, and heard Daisy hurriedly begin to lay a fire below her.

Emilia hauled herself into a narrow alcove. Below her, Daisy turned and said, "Almost finished, sir. I'll just light the fire for you."

"Where's the other girl that was here?" Coldham asked. Emilia's pulse jumped, and she pressed back into the alcove. The wall behind her gave way under her weight, and Emilia bit back a gasp of surprise.

"She just went to get some other sheets, sir, didn't you

notice her?" Daisy spoke above a great clatter of fire irons, and Emilia realized she was trying to cover up any sound.

Coldham grunted in response, and Emilia heard the scraping of a chair being pulled out. She pushed back with her hands and felt the wall swing away noiselessly, revealing a greater cavity inside. Emilia stepped through and found herself in a long, narrow room crowded with people. Her eyes opened wide in surprise. Luka beckoned her inside and closed the door behind her.

Luka was crouched beside Lord Harry, Zizi on his lap, while a tall man with a mop of thick black hair and a shabby green velvet coat sat on the far side. Emilia recognized him at once. It was the Marquis of Ormonde. She could not believe she was so close to him they were bumping knees. No wonder Gypsy Joe had been so anxious to hide him. If he was discovered, the Marquis of Ormonde would have his head cut off – if he was lucky.

Beside the marquis sat his servant, a burly man dressed in neat brown wool with a red scarf around his neck. Beside him sat Tom Whitehorse, glaring at her in angry suspicion.

The marquis frowned at her and lifted his finger to his lips. Emilia could hear the scratch of Coldham's quill on the paper, so she understood the need for silence. She nodded.

Somewhere, a dog howled. Luka and Emilia gazed at

each other in an agony of anxiety. They recognized Rollo's deep voice.

Coldham's quill stopped scratching over the paper. Then the howling stopped and Coldham's writing resumed. Emilia bit the soft mound of flesh at the base of her thumb, feeling quite sick with fear. She barely dared to breathe.

After a while, Coldham got up and went out of the room, a packet of letters in his hand. At once Tom turned to the Marquis of Ormonde. "My Lord, I know these two! They're gypsies! They work on my father's farm sometimes."

"Are they friend or foe?" the marquis asked swiftly, in a low voice.

"My Lord, I do not know, but everywhere I've been these past few days, they've turned up, with that man Coldham on their heels. I think they're spies!"

"We're not spies!" Luka cried indignantly. "Coldham's been chasing us all over the country!"

"Coldham chasing you?" Tom sneered. "What would he want with two grubby gypsy brats? It's my lord he wants!"

"He's been on our trail for days," Luka said. "He wants to drag us back to gaol."

"He's been chasing *us* for days," Tom responded hotly.

"Sssh, lads," Lord Harry hissed. "Do you want the whole inn to hear you?"

The two boys fell silent, though they glared at each other angrily. On Luka's shoulder Zizi jumped up and down, gibbering, and baring her teeth at Tom.

"Keep the monkey quiet," the marquis said.

Luka dug around in his bag and pulled out a prune, which Zizi at once snatched in delight and began to nibble. Lord Harry put his eye to a peep-hole, then made a gesture to show the coast was clear.

The marquis looked back at Tom. "These two are friends of Lord Harry, and some kind of kin to Gypsy Joe," he said softly. "I do not think Joe would have hidden them in here with us if he was not certain of their loyalty. Do you indeed suspect them of being spies?"

Luka made a quick movement but the marquis held up one hand, and he subsided.

Tom, when he spoke, was much more subdued. "I do not know, My Lord. But I saw them in Kingston, when I was there to see the Leveller, Gerard Winstanley, and beg him to join our cause. The next thing I know, Winstanley is thrown in gaol, and constables are everywhere in the town, and the thief-taker Coldham directing them. I barely managed to escape!"

He took a deep breath, and cast an angry glance at Luka. "Then we manage to get you away to Epsom, and again I see these two, and again the thief-taker turns up with soldiers and we barely manage to get you safely away. Then here we are in Salisbury, and lo and behold! Here are Luka and Emilia again, with Coldham on their heels!"

"They are young to be spies," the marquis said.

Tom flushed. "Luka is only a year younger than me," he said. "You said it was because of my youth that I was likely to be useful!"

"True," the marquis said, smiling. He rubbed his bristly chin. "So what is your explanation, my boy?"

Luka glanced at Emilia, who stared at him intently, willing him to think before he spoke. He must have heard her silent pleas, because he replied quietly and steadily. "We know nothing of you, My Lord. We were in Kingston to try and raise some money for Emilia's sister's dowry. But the pastor saw Beatrice singing and had us all arrested. Coldham was there, he chased after us when we escaped, and he's been chasing us ever since. He nabbed us in Southampton and if Lord Harry hadn't held up the coach. . ."

"They said they'd been kidnapped and begged me to rescue them."

"But you don't know whether their story was true?" the marquis asked.

Lord Harry shrugged. "Nay, My Lord."

Just then they heard the bedchamber door scrape open, and the rap of boots on wood. Everyone fell quiet.

"What do you mean, you can find no trace of them?" Coldham said irritably. "I tell you, the guards on the gate said this inn was where that highwayman always brings his stolen nags to sell! We know he's a Royalist spy, we know he took those gypsy brats from me, and we know the Marquis of Ormonde was heading for a safe

211

house in Salisbury! So if we find that highwayman, we'll find those gypsies, and more importantly, we'll find the marquis."

"But, sir, we've looked everywhere!"

"Start ripping out the panelling," Coldham said. "They're here somewhere."

Fish Berries

All day Emilia heard the thump, thud, thwack of soldiers breaking down walls and ripping up floorboards. Sometimes the sound was so close she felt sure they were about to be discovered. She could do nothing but sit, gnawing her fingernails, hardly daring to breathe.

It was even more difficult for Luka, who was always as restless as a hen on a hot griddle. It was torture for him to be cooped up in that narrow space, unable to even hum or drum his fingers.

Occasionally Coldham went out to shout at the soldiers, or to send a letter somewhere, and then the hiders were able to move their cramped limbs, and cough and clear their throats, and even whisper to one another. Luka told Tom and the marquis how they were trying to come up with a plan to break their family out of gaol, and Tom told them of some of his adventures this past week trying to keep the marquis from being discovered. The respite never lasted long, though, and as soon as Coldham returned, the unnatural immobility was forced upon them again.

Eventually Luka stretched out on the floor, with his coat pillowed under his head, and went to sleep, Zizi curled against his shoulder. Emilia lay down beside him, and they slept all afternoon, the men's legs stretched over them. Both felt much better as a result. The marquis' servant also fell asleep at one point, but he snored so loudly that Lord Harry had to clamp his hand over his mouth and wake him up.

At last the inn grew quiet, and they heard Coldham make ready for bed. The hours snailed past. Emilia dozed again, and was woken with a painful stab of terror at the sound of furtive fumbling at the secret door.

Gypsy Joe was looking through the secret door, beckoning them urgently, a candle in his other hand. All the men stirred and stretched, pale and dishevelled.

One by one they clambered down the chimney. Emilia clung close to Luka as they crept through the dark bedroom. There was a snoring lump in the bed that must be Coldham, and every creak and sigh made Emilia hold her breath in case he should wake.

"They've torn my inn apart, but they still didn't find you." Joe grinned. "How do you feel? Are you all right?"

"I'm damn thirsty," Lord Harry said. "You could have locked us up with a keg of ale."

"I'll make sure one is kept there always from now on. Come on! Let's get you all away from here."

A guard was lying slumped in a chair on the landing, fast asleep, snoring loudly, and another slept at the bottom of the stairs, a tankard rolled from his hand.

"What did you do, Joe, drug them?" the Marquis of Ormonde asked, his blue eyes dancing with merriment in his unshaven face. Emilia was amused to see how fair the stubble on his chin was compared to his black hair.

"Let me guess, Joe. Fish berries?" Lord Harry asked.

Joe grinned and nodded.

"It's a berry from the New World. The Indians used to throw it into rivers to stun fish," Lord Harry explained. "Wily innkeepers like our Joe here use it to lace their ale, so no one realizes how much they've watered it down. Add enough of it to the ale, and everyone gets very merry and then passes out cold. It's a jolly useful little berry."

Luka grabbed Joe's sleeve. "Can I have some? Please?"

Joe looked down at him. "You thinking of using it to drug the prison guards?"

"Maybe."

"All right, then," Joe said.

Luka and Emilia exchanged exultant looks.

"I'll go and get you some. Harry, you take everyone out to the jetty, will you? Keep it quiet, just in case."

Lord Harry nodded and everyone followed him through the dark, silent inn, which was in a dreadful mess. Everyone looked at each other and grimaced.

"You know, I thought Gypsy Joe was either a fool or a villain for giving the thief-taker the very room in which we were hidden, but now I see how clever he was," the marquis said. "It was the only room not torn apart."

"Poor Joe," Lord Harry said. "His inn is a mess."

"I wish I could leave him some money as compensation, but I have none to leave," the marquis said with a wry twist of his lips. He fingered the ring he wore on his index finger. "I would leave him my signet ring, which is all I have left of any value, but it has my coat of arms on it and would be most dangerous for him to be caught with."

"He knew the risk of sheltering you," Lord Harry said. "At least he and his family are still alive."

"There is something in that." The marquis sighed, and let Lord Harry lead him through the stable-yard and out to the riverbank. A boat bobbed up and down on the dark rushing water, moored to an iron ring in the wall by a long rope. Lord Harry hauled it in, and helped hold it steady while the Marquis of Ormonde clambered in, huddling his cloak about him.

Emilia hung back, looking for Gypsy Joe and wondering where Rollo was. The very next moment the big dog came bounding through the door, his tail wagging joyfully. He jumped up to lick Emilia's face, whining loudly in his throat, his whole body wriggling frantically. "Good boy." Emilia wiped her face dry. "How's your poor sore head? All better?"

"A roast mutton bone kept him quiet and happy most of the morning," Joe said, coming up behind them, "and then he slept all afternoon, perfectly content. I think he'll be fine now, though it was a nasty cut. Can't say I like a man who would hit a dog so hard. A cat, now, that would be a different story."

Luka grinned.

Joe passed him a small brown bottle. "Keep that safe now," the innkeeper advised. "Don't mistake it for salt and eat it on your eggs."

"We won't," Luka promised, taking it gratefully and tucking it away in his bag. "Thanks so much."

"There's food here too," Joe said. "No roast mutton, your dog ate all that, but some cold chicken and bread and hard-boiled eggs."

They thanked him and shoved it all into the bag, glad to feel it heavy again.

"What's the plan now, Joe?" the marquis called from the boat. "I cannot say I feel easy in my mind about this Coldham fellow. His sources are too good. I have no desire to be hanged, drawn and quartered!"

"If you're lucky, you'll be able to get all the way to Bournemouth by way of the river," Joe said. "Search for a ship there back to France. You must move swiftly, though, and be careful of the bridges; they are all rather low."

"All right," the marquis said. "Thanks for your help, Joe. You'll be remembered when His Highness returns!"

Joe gave a wry smile. "That's something to look forward to." He turned to Luka and Emilia. "What about you two?" he asked. "What will you do?"

"We'll go and find the Smith family and see if they can help us," Luka said. "We know they're in the Weald near Horsmonden, wherever that is."

"I know where it is," Joe said. "Head east along the South Downs till you reach the coast, then turn and head straight north. It's just past Tunbridge Wells."

"Thanks!"

"I'm sorry I could not help more," Joe said.

"You have helped," Luka said earnestly.

"Please," Emilia said. "The rue charm of the Wood family. Do you have it?"

He looked troubled. "No," he answered. "I have not seen it for years."

Emilia sighed in disappointment.

"My daya used to wear it, but she's dead now. But my sister may have it."

"Where can we find her?" Emilia spoke with great intensity, clutching her hands together.

"Beaulieu, maybe," Joe said. "That is where I last saw her. I must warn you, though. . ."

"What?"

"She's a witch," Joe said. "And quite, quite mad."

Down The River

The New Forest, Hampshire
19 August 1658

"Does he mean it, do you think?" Luka asked.

They were all sitting huddled in the boat, being poled slowly and steadily downstream by the marquis' servant, Nat. Salisbury slipped past, a huddle of black buildings silhouetted against the starry sky.

"If she lived in the New Forest, she would have seen some terrible things," Lord Harry said. "Cromwell's soldiers are not known for their mercy."

"They sold my kin into slavery," Luka said. "Sent them to the New World against their will."

"These are dreadful times," the marquis said soberly.

"One madman makes many madmen, and many madmen make madness," Emilia whispered.

Luka knew she was repeating an old gypsy saying, yet Lord Harry was much struck and repeated it softly to himself several times.

Salisbury fell behind them, and they went on down

the river in the darkness, the men taking it in turns to pole the barge along. The river was treacherous with weeds and sandbars, and several times they passed under bridges, many of them so low the boat barely fitted underneath.

Some hours before dawn, they drew close to the sea. The air had a salt tang to it, and the low hills had given way to flat stretches of marsh rustling with rushes. Emilia was very tired. She laid her head on her arms and gazed at the rippling black water. The moon hung in a tangle of dark branches, and in the water, another moon drowned.

"Not far now," Lord Harry whispered. "We'll get as close as we can to the sea, then abandon the boat. My Lord, we should have no trouble finding you a ship here. Ships are in and out all the time, the soldiers cannot search them all, and I have many friends in the harbour."

"Thank you," the marquis said. "I must admit I'll be glad to be safely away."

"Please, My Lord, I beseech you," Tom said. "I cannot bear to just go home and twiddle my thumbs again, after the excitement of this past week. May I not come with you? I would so love to meet the king!"

"Hopefully, if all goes well, Tom, you will see him soon enough," the marquis replied gently.

Emilia saw, in the dazzle of moonlight on the water, a tall, dark man with heavy curls, most gorgeously dressed, riding on a fine horse, while all around him a vast crowd cheered and shouted and flung their hats in the air. She shook her head in wonder and disbelief. "He will win back his throne, and the people of London will sing and dance and throw flowers, and all without a single drop of blood being spilt."

"By the Grace of God, let it be so," the marquis said indulgently.

Emilia could tell he did not believe her. "I see true," she whispered. Nobody heard her. She gazed again into the water, but the vision was gone. It left her feeling shivery-cold and weepy with weariness. Emilia shut her eyes and rested her face against her hands.

Soon a great stone bridge loomed over them, spanning the river, which had grown broad and fast. The River Avon was streaked with red, reflecting the light of flaming torches along the bridge's length. Emilia could see the dark, hunched shapes of the men in the boat, and the ripples from their passage rocked the red reflections, causing them to shake like candle flames in a breeze. The suck of the pole in and out of the water seemed very loud. Emilia crouched lower in the bottom of the boat, her arms about Rollo's neck.

Nat sighed and arched his back, then gave a great jaw-cracking yawn.

"Sssh!" Lord Harry hissed.

Nat poled onwards. On the bridge, soldiers were patrolling. Emilia could see the glint of the torches on their pikes. Then the pole slipped from Nat's hand. The crack of wood against wood, and the following splash, seemed very loud.

"Ahoy! Who goes there?" A voice shouted.

Everyone in the boat lay still, hearts pounding painfully. A soldier leant over the bridge, torch in hand, but the boat had drifted under the shadow of the bridge.

"Probably just a fish," a distant voice said. The wavering reflection of the torches retreated.

Nat suddenly sneezed, very loudly. He would have sneezed again, but Lord Harry ruthlessly muffled his face in his red scarf. Nat fought him off. "Leave off!" he muttered angrily. "You're suffocating me."

"Sssh, you fool," Harry hissed back.

Everyone glanced anxiously back at the bridge, but no one seemed to have heard. Emilia allowed her breath to whoosh out.

Then Nat threw down the pole and leapt to his feet. "Ahoy! Ahoy! Down here! Traitors and spies! Down here!"

"Nat! What are you doing?" the marquis demanded sharply.

Nat called out again and waved both his arms. Tom threw himself on top of him and brought him crashing down to the bottom of the boat, but it was too late; the damage was done.

A soldier on the bridge shouted. "Beware! Invaders! Call the alarm!"

The shore was alive with the sound of shouting and running feet and the sudden kindling of lanterns. A bell tolled. The red fire of torches illuminated the little boat and its cowering cargo of horrified passengers.

Shots rang out. Water sprayed up where the bullets hit the river's surface. Emilia gasped and crouched lower. Rollo whimpered.

"Get us away," the marquis commanded. There was no sign in his voice of the terror or desperation he must have felt. As light from the shore flickered over his face, Luka saw that the marquis' eyes were bright with determination, his shoulders square. Luka felt a reluctant admiration for him. He was a brave man, there was no doubt of that.

Lord Harry seized the pole and sent the boat skidding along the water. Nat heaved Tom off his back and pulled out a pistol, turning it on the marquis. "Here! Traitors aboard! You must stop them!"

Tom scrambled up and launched himself at Nat, who turned and casually fired point-blank.

"Nat! No!"

But even as the marquis shouted in horror, Tom cried out and fell backwards, hitting the water with a great splash.

"Tom!" Luka cried and dived overboard. Shrieking with terror, Zizi clung to the bulwark with her tiny paws, looking for her master.

Emilia searched the fast-moving black water with desperate eyes. "Luka? Tom?"

Zizi leapt into her arms, and Emilia cradled her close, sick with fear. There was no sign of the boys.

Nat levelled his pistol at the marquis. "Hands up, My Lord."

"But, Nat. . ." The marquis was so shocked that

realization came slowly. "It was you! You're the one who's betrayed me at every turn! In London . . . do you know how many men died because of you? And then again at Whitehorse Manor . . . in Epsom . . . in Salisbury. . . Nat, surely it cannot be true!"

"That's enough talk," Nat said stolidly. He turned and cast an anxious glance back at the bridge, where soldiers were piling into boats and rowing swiftly towards them. Emilia took her chance. She leant back on the side of the boat and swung her legs up, hitting Nat hard in the chest with both bare feet. He was not expecting it, and he cried out, staggering back. The pistol flew up into the air, and Emilia tried desperately to catch it. But it flew past her hand and splashed into the dark water.

The next instant there was a flash of orange and another loud report. Nat screamed in agony. He fell back into the river. Lord Harry shoved his pistol back in his belt and seized the pole, sending the boat skimming away into darkness. Bullets sprayed up water on either side and splintered the boat as the soldiers fired after them.

"Luka! Tom!" Emilia cried in despair.

"The tide will have carried them this way," the marquis whispered. "Now hush! We must not be caught!"

Emilia cast one last desperate glance at the black water, then bowed her head over the charm bracelet, frantically rubbing the golden coin between her fingers. Rain had come once before to hide them. Was it too much to expect such luck again? She looked up at the star-scattered sky, the heavy orb of the moon, and felt the darkness of despair fall down upon her spirit. Then Emilia remembered how desperate she had been in the coach with Coldham, and how Lord Harry had come and held up the coach and rescued them. She pressed her braceleted wrist against her chest and searched for the spark of life inside her, what Maggie called the *mi del zee*, which meant the heart of God. *Let me find the boys, let us get away safely*, she said silently. *Help me. . .*

Emilia opened her eyes. Mist began to snake up from the river. Soft and white, it wreathed about the dark trees and billowed across the water, drawing a net across the moon and the stars. Soon she could see little but its muffling whiteness. She bent her head and anxiously scanned the dark rushing water for any sign of the boys. Suddenly she saw two heads bobbing together some distance down the river. Jubilantly she turned her face towards Lord Harry, pointing. He nodded and sent the boat racing that way. Within seconds they were drawing up beside the two boys. Luka was dog-paddling furiously, Tom lying unconscious in his arms. He looked up at them and opened his mouth to speak, but the marquis silenced him with a gesture. Hurriedly he dragged the two boys on board, as Lord Harry again began to pole with deep, powerful strokes that sent the boat racing across the water. Mist curled up around its prow.

She knelt beside her cousin and clasped his arm with

both hands, trying to show him without words how very glad she was to see him. Zizi leapt to Luka's shoulder and petted him all over his face with her tiny paws. He gathered her close.

Emilia turned to Tom, lying in the bottom of the boat. His eyes were shut. There was blood on his shirt. She caught her breath in dismay. Lord Harry silently passed her his hipflask. She dribbled a little brandy between Tom's pale lips and he swallowed and coughed. She sighed in relief as his eyelids fluttered open. He saw her face and smiled weakly. As he tried to speak, Emilia shook her head and laid her finger on his lips. He nodded his understanding. Indeed, the sound of the boats in pursuit came clearly across the water.

Emilia carefully eased open Tom's shirt. The material was stuck to the wound, but she was able to moisten it with some water and lift it clear. Emilia had never seen a gunshot wound before. It looked very ugly. She bit her lip and quickly tore her bedraggled petticoat into strips, making a soft pad to press against the wound. Tom looked sick and exhausted, and she gave him more brandy, then passed the flask back to Lord Harry. With a grim smile, he gulped a mouthful and passed it to the marquis. He drank as deeply, then insisted on Luka drinking a mouthful, for he was shivering violently, the wind blowing against his wet clothes.

Tom bit back a groan. "Not far now," Lord Harry whispered. "Let us just get away from the soldiers, and then all will be well."

Once they were round the curve of the river, Lord Harry sent the little boat shooting under the cover of some willow-trees trailing their long fronds in the water. "Let's dump the boat here."

Emilia nodded and clambered out, Rollo leaping after her. Together Lord Harry and Luka helped Tom out. His face was white and shining with sweat.

"Thanks for diving in after me," he whispered to Luka. "I'd be a goner otherwise!"

"Not a problem," Luka whispered back.

Together they all lay on the riverbank and watched the ghostly flotilla of soldiers sail on down the river and disappear into the fog.

Lord Harry expelled his breath in a long sigh. "That was close! I wouldn't be surprised if you find my hair and beard bleached all white in the morning light."

"I cannot believe Nat would betray us like that. He volunteered for this job! I guess he was a spy all along. No wonder I kept falling out of the frying pan and into the fire. He must've been betraying me every step of the way." The marquis' voice had grown so choked he could barely speak. He took a moment to compose himself, then said roughly, "Tom, I have one more task for you, if you're up for it."

"Of course I am, My Lord!" Tom struggled up, pressing one hand to his wound.

The marquis drew his signet ring from his finger. It was a dark red stone, carved with a shield, and set in gold. "Will you pawn this ring for me and give the money to Joe, to help him repair his inn? I would hate him to lose everything because of me. And give some money to those friends who sheltered me in London too, to thank them for their help."

"I will, My Lord."

The marquis looked down at the ring a moment later, then shrugged and gave it into Tom's hand.

"Maybe you can buy it back again when the king returns," Emilia said.

"Maybe." The marquis spoke heavily.

"My Lord, before you seek to find a ship, you should blacken your eyebrows and eyelashes," Emilia said earnestly. "They are too fair for such a black head."

He laughed out loud. "Believe me, I'm lucky I have a hair left on my head at all! I near burnt it all off in my first attempt to dye it. I do not want to lose my brows and lashes too."

"You do not need to dye it. Just use some charcoal from the fire. And shave well. Your stubble is blond too. A man with a black head like yours would have a blue chin by noon."

"Thank you, my dear," the marquis said, and gave her a low bow. He then cast Tom a mischievous glance. "And you thought her a spy! She's given me the best advice of all of you."

Tom looked crestfallen. The Marquis of Ormonde saw it, and bowed towards him as well. "Indeed, I could not have managed without you these past days, Tom."

"I just wanted to help," he whispered passionately.

"You have! I will tell the king," the marquis said. "I will tell him all that you have done, all of you. I thank you from the bottom of my heart. I just hope one day you will receive the reward you deserve."

"So what will you two do now?" Lord Harry asked. "I need to get Tom to a safe house and get that shoulder looked at, and find a ship for the marquis. Will you travel with us?"

Emilia and Luka exchanged a quick glance. Then Luka said, "We can't, I'm afraid. We have to go on to Beaulieu."

"We have to find the rest of our kin," Emilia said. "There must be someone who can help us break our family out of gaol!"

"How can Gypsy Joe's mad sister possibly help you?" Tom asked.

"She has a lucky charm," Emilia said hesitantly. "Once there were five of them, hanging on this chain, see?" She showed him the bracelet about her wrist. "But when the chain was broken, bad luck came to the Rom. We're trying to find the five families and see if they will give us back the charms. . ."

". . .and help us rescue our families," Luka broke in.

"The charms . . . they help us and protect us. They have magic."

Luka rolled his eyes, but Tom nodded, his pale face serious. "Well, I hope you find all the charms, and some way to save your family."

"Thanks," she whispered.

"Maybe I could help somehow? Would you like me to come to meet you in Kingston too?"

Emilia nodded eagerly, and Tom smiled. With his fair curls all tousled, and his coat torn and filthy, he looked a far different boy to the young lord she had known.

The Witch

By dusk, Luka and Emilia finally reached Beaulieu.

It was a small village, overshadowed by great trees. Across the river, glowing warm and red in the rays of the setting sun, were the ruins of an ancient abbey. High walls set with gothic arches soared above the trees, but most of the walls were broken, and Emilia could see a sweeping staircase of stone steps that climbed into nothing more substantial than air.

"How do we find Joe's sister?" Luka wondered.

"Ask for her?" Emilia suggested. "It's only a small village. They'll know her. We'll wait here, in the cover of the trees."

While Luka went quietly into the village, Zizi tucked up in his coat, Emilia lay on the grass and stared at the ruins of the abbey. As the sun slipped down behind the trees, the stones lost all colour and became ghostly grey. She thought she heard, faintly, a bell, and then rising high into the air, the soft, eerie, heartbreakingly beautiful sound of chanting. All the hairs rose on Emilia's arms, and she started to her feet. Rollo growled, his hackles rising.

The singing lasted only a moment, like a fragment of sound blown by a change in the wind, but it was enough to unnerve Emilia. She paced to and fro, rubbing her arms, wishing for Luka to come back, wishing for the calm wisdom of her grandmother. Emilia missed her baba dreadfully. She did not know how to manage these strange omens and premonitions. They were coming more and more often, leaving her feeling worn out, as if she had been ill.

Emilia wondered if it was the two charms hanging on her bracelet that had so sharpened her inner eye, or if it was just that she was getting older. She was at the age, her grandmother had told, that most *drabardi* discover their skills. Emilia would very much have liked the comfort of telling her grandmother all that she had seen. Maggie had the eye herself, and knew how frightening it could be to see what others could not. But Maggie was locked away in a cell, facing the gallows. Emilia might never see her again.

The evening was still. There was no sign of Luka. Emilia sat down and let Rollo flop beside her, his head on her knee. She drew the pack towards her and took out her grandmother's crystal ball. It was cold and heavy in her hands. Its clouded surface reflected the fading light. Emilia took a deep breath. Another. Another.

She bent her gaze and looked into the ball.

"Baba. . ." she whispered.

She saw a crossing of dark lines. Bars, not twigs or branches. She saw her grandmother hunched against a stone wall. Maggie looked up with an effort. *Emilia. . .*

"Baba!" Emilia cried.

Beware . . . black. . . Her grandmother's voice faded away. Instead Emilia saw an inky-black pond seething with sinuous dark forms. As they writhed and rolled, she saw the flash of a narrow eye and a mouth full of needle-sharp teeth. She barely had time to recoil before the vision changed. She saw a hare being chased by a fox, and seized and dragged down. She saw a white hind pierced with arrows, leaping and failing and falling. She heard a peacock scream, and an owl hoot. Last of all, Emilia saw a dead man, wrapped in a green shroud, and hanging from a gallows before a jeering crowd. She saw the corpse cut down, and his head hacked from his body and stuck on a spike. She clearly saw his face, wizened and discoloured, still with warts upon chin and brow, and eyebrows bent over hollow eyes.

A sort of swooning came over her. The crystal ball fell from Emilia's hands into the grass and rolled away. She bent her face into her hands, dazed and dizzy. Even as the visions dissolved, Emilia tried to seize them again and make sense of them. Eels. A hare. A hind. Peacock and owl. A corpse dancing upon air. A rope knotted.

It was almost night. Emilia was very frightened. She hugged Rollo close to her, and he licked her face and put his paw on her knee. Emilia rolled the crystal ball up in her grandmother's shawl, knotting it three times, and thrust it deep into the pack. *Never again*, she swore.

At last Luka came back through the trees, looking very gloomy.

"What's wrong? Can't you find her?"

"Oh, yes. Everyone here knows Marguerita the Mad. She lives in the ruins of the abbey and poaches rabbits as bold as you please. No one dares try and stop her, not even the foresters, in case she curses them. They are all terrified of her. Her mother was hanged for a witch five years ago, in Salisbury, they told me."

"Her mother?" Emilia whispered. "So that'd be Joe's mother too?"

Luka nodded grimly.

They stood for a while, wishing it was bright morning-time, wishing they were not alone. But eventually, without a word to each other, they turned towards the abbey. With Rollo trotting at their heels and Zizi riding on Luka's shoulder, the two children slowly crossed the bridge in the fast-gathering twilight and made their way into the vast maze of broken-down stone.

Everything was eerily quiet. No birds sang, and the wind was silent amongst the stones. They smelt wood smoke, and followed their noses. They came to a long arcade, with delicate fluted columns forming narrow archways on one side.

A great arched doorway led into darkness. Above the

curve of the door were the smashed remains of a stone cherub's face. A woman stood in the doorway, watching for them. She was much younger than Emilia had expected. Her hair was wild and black and matted with knots. She was dressed in brown rags that showed the flesh of her arms and legs through the holes. Her feet were dark with dirt, and her nails were black half-moons. Amidst the wild profusion of her hair, her face seemed very thin and bony. Her nose crooked out of it like the prow of a boat. Her mouth was marred with sores.

"You come for what is mine," Marguerita said.

"Aye," Emilia replied. "I'm sorry."

"At least you speak true. Come in . . . if you can bear the smell."

The children hesitated.

"I'm not going to eat you," she said. She sounded so like her brother Joe that the children relaxed and went inside, Rollo slinking at their heels, his tail between his legs.

It did stink inside, though mainly of bitter smoke. It was a long hallway made of grey stone, with a flagstone floor and a high arched ceiling held up with great buttressed beams. A fire glowed in a massive great hearth, large enough to roast an ox. Around the hearth was set up a small camp, with beds made of dried bracken with furs thrown over the top, and a rough table and stools made from old logs and wooden boxes. On either side the hallway stretched, dark and cold and empty, but the camp itself was cosy and warm, with a bunch of wildflowers in a broken urn, and a pot bubbling over the flames.

Wooden stakes had been hammered into the cracks between the stones of the wall, and from these rough pegs hung bunches of plants and the uncured skins of animals. Emilia saw rabbit, and fox, and badger, and deer, and wondered that this wild gypsy woman had not been hanged for poaching long ago.

As they came in, a little boy scuttled sideways and hid in a pile of old furs. He stared at them fearfully through a tangle of black curls.

"It's all right," Marguerita crooned. "Don't be afraid. You can come out. They're only children."

But the little boy would not come out, shrinking down further into the bed.

"He does not like strangers," Marguerita said.

Emilia squatted down by the bed and held out her hand to the little boy, asking his name, but he only huddled deeper, turning his face away.

"His name is Abram," Marguerita said. "He does not talk. He has not said a word since he saw his father killed."

"How dreadful," Emilia said. "Poor little boy."

The witch stared at her. After a moment, Emilia dropped her gaze, feeling clumsy and afraid. There was a strange ferocity in the gypsy woman's gaze.

"You have a fiddle," she said to Luka. He nodded, clutching his violin a little closer.

"I have not heard a fiddle played since they took my family away. If I give you some of our supper, will you play for us?"

"All right," Luka said. Zizi clung tightly to his neck, not liking the smell and darkness of the cavernous hall. Rollo pressed close to Emilia's legs.

"We're hungry," Emilia said.

Marguerita snorted. "Weans your age are always hungry. You'll have to share a bowl; I haven't many." She bent and stirred the pot, then began to ladle it out into three battered tin bowls, one of which she pushed towards the shelter of the furs. A small, grimy hand sneaked out and caught it, drawing it under the fur.

"It smells good," Luka said, sniffing the air. "What's in it?"

Marguerita laughed. "What's not? There's chicken and pheasant and bacon and lamb and venison and hare and potatoes and carrots and beans and peas and corn and mushrooms and whatever else I've found in the woods. Nothing poisonous, though. I save my poisons for those I hate."

Rather gingerly, the children tasted the stew, but it was quite simply the most delicious meal they had ever eaten. They could not get the spoons from the bowl to their mouths fast enough. Marguerita laughed, and silently served them some more.

"Today we feast," Luka said with a grin at Emilia.

"Tomorrow we'll starve," she replied, with an exaggerated shrug.

". . .and the next day we'll feast again," Marguerita finished off the Romany proverb, and they smiled a small, complicit smile, the smile of people who knew they shared each other's language.

"So, play to us," Marguerita commanded when they had licked out their bowl. "My husband was a fiddler. He could play the birds down out of the trees, and the fish out of the streams."

"That's what they say about my dado," Emilia said.

"They'll say it about me too one day," Luka boasted, and lovingly took his violin out of his case, tuning it gently.

Emilia expected him to play a wild lament, like he had played for the highwayman, but instead he played a tender lullaby, so sweet and loving it drew tears to Emilia's eyes. The witch stared at him and did not seem to even breathe. Very slowly the furs slid back and the little boy crept out, his eyes fixed on Luka's face. He came closer and closer, until he was crouched right at Luka's elbow, and when at last Luka laid down his bow, he put out one hand and touched the fiddle reverently. "More?" he whispered.

So Luka played more. The little boy pressed his hands together, his eyes shining, and his mother, the witch, wept silently, her whole body shaking.

At last Luka wearied of playing. It was dark and the wind was rising, and he could no longer hear his own music. He laid down the bow and let the little boy touch it. Abram was as gentle as if the violin were a living thing, running his hands over its curving sides and caressing its silky wood before, tentatively, plucking at one of the strings. At the shimmer of sound, he raised his transfigured face, and then he bent over the violin again, experimenting with the sounds.

"So, tell me, who do you know, and what do you want with me?" the witch demanded, turning away so they could not see her face.

They told her, and Marguerita listened quietly.

"Do you have the charm?" Emilia asked when they had finished.

The witch nodded.

"Can I have it? Please?"

Marguerita crossed her arms over her chest. Her hair was so thick and frizzy it rose out around her body like a thunder-racked cloud. "Why not? What good has it ever done us? What luck have we had? It's worthless, useless, a funny old trinket my baba used to wear."

She got up and rummaged in a chest by the wall while her son plucked the violin's strings, totally absorbed. The smell and the darkness seemed to grow thicker, and the sound of the wind in the ruins, stronger. She turned from the chest with something in her hand.

"See? It is a sprig of rue, wrought in silver. It is very, very old. I do not wear it. It's meant to guard against black magic."

"What do you mean?" she asked, even as she half-snatched the charm from Marguerita's hand. It felt very light and flimsy.

The witch laughed. It was a high, shrill, scary sound. "I would not want it to stop me."

Abram stopped strumming the violin strings. The only sounds were the rush of the wind and the low crackle of the fire.

"Stop you from doing what?" Luka asked.

"I shall have my revenge," the witch answered. "Oh, yes. He shall suffer the agonies of grief, like I have, and then he too will die."

"Who?" Emilia whispered.

Marguerita stared at her without seeing her. "Cromwell," she answered, as if it was obvious. She lifted down a box and took out what looked like two small rag dolls. They smelt bad, like rotting nettles. Emilia shrank away. One was a limp little doll in the shape of a man, dressed in a scrap of dark material crudely cut to look like a jacket and breeches. It had a tuft of gingery hair sewn to its head, and features roughly drawn with charcoal. The other wore a grey dress and carried a baby in its arms. Two long hatpins protruded from their breasts.

"The daughter and her little baby gone already," Marguerita said softly, "and soon you too, Oliver Cromwell." She took another pin from the box and jabbed it cruelly into the rag-doll, again and again. "Shall you die tonight, Cromwell? Or shall I make you suffer a little longer?"

"What are those?" Luka asked roughly. Emilia wondered if he too felt the thick, dark odour of hatred and menace that writhed out of the rag-dolls like smoke.

Marguerita smiled. "Poppets," she answered. "After they killed my husband and took away my boys, selling them like cattle, I walked all the way to Fernhurst, where I had heard the Lord Protector was staying. It took me days, with Abram on my back. My feet were so sore and swollen I could barely take another step, but I went up to the house, and I went into his bedroom, and I took the hair out of his brush, and I cut some material out of his suit, the bit that would rest just over his heart, and then I went into his daughter's room, and I took her hair too, and I cut up her dress, and then I walked all the way home again. No one saw me, no one stopped me, for I'd changed into the shape of a black hare."

She laughed wildly. "And then I made my little poppets, and I stuffed them with nightshade, and I sewed them with up with black thread, and chanted every curse and evil spell I knew over them, all in the dark of the moon, and every day I take them out and I jab him and stab him and jiggle and wriggle the pin, and laugh as I think of him shrieking and falling about in agony. And then I take the pin out, and let him rest awhile. For I want it to be slow. I want him to feel every bit as much pain and grief that I have felt since they hanged my daya for telling true what she saw, and murdered my husband, and stole my sons away."

Emilia and Luka were horrified. They backed away from her. Emilia had the charm clutched in her hand.

The witch stared at her. "You can have it," she said. "What good has it done us? I'll make my own magic, a stronger, blacker magic! But I must have something in return."

"What?" Emilia spoke through stiff lips.

"We have nothing to give," Luka replied unhappily, though Emilia saw how he clutched his little monkey closer.

"But you do," Marguerita said.

"What? We have nothing."

She pointed at Luka's violin, which Abram held pressed to his chest, staring at them wide-eyed and frightened. "He spoke for the first time since his father died," she said. "One word! Only one word, but it is the gladdest word I've ever heard. Give him your fiddle."

"No!" Luka cried.

"Give it to him, else I'll curse you with all the power at my command. You came here wanting my rue sprig. Well, now you have it, so go. Go!"

Luka cast one last look at his beloved violin, then he seized Emilia's hand and they ran, Rollo bounding after them.

If ghosts pursued them through the moonlit ruin, they were not benevolent. As she ran, Emilia clutched tightly in her hand the sprig of rue, the bitter herb of repentance, and trusted in it with all her heart to guard them against such black magic.

Thorns and Tangles

All night Emilia and Luka stumbled through the thorns and tangles of the forest, the twigs and briars weaving themselves into nets that caught at their feet as if the trees themselves were alive and hungry. Sometimes roots writhed up out of the ground to trip their feet and send them sprawling. Other times they found themselves trapped in a thicket of brambles, sharp as teeth and claws. Each time Emilia's fingers found their way to the rue charm that she had hung from the chain at her wrist. In the darkness, she could not make sense of its shape. It was smooth and complex, a writhing tangle of metal tendrils. Yet as her fingers traced the sinuous knot of metal, they would suddenly burst free of the thicket and find a moonlit path winding through the black murmuring shadows.

By the time they reached the shore, the darkness was fading. Delicate colour bloomed in the eastern sky.

Fishing-boats were already out on the River Solent and smoke was rising from the chimney of every cottage. They dared go no further. Huddled together under some bushes by the shore, the children tried to get some rest. Luka lay curled with his back towards Emilia, his arm flung over his eyes, his mouth twisted in misery.

Emilia lay quietly, examining the charm they had won from the witch of the New Forest. Her grandmother had told her it was very old and very powerful. Emilia certainly found it mysterious. Forged from silver, and no larger than the circle she could make with her first finger and thumb, it was formed by slender coiling tendrils, tarnished and black. Entwined within the rue leaves were a flower, a dagger, a rooster, and a crescent moon twined about with a snake. Tracing their shape with her finger, Emilia wondered what they meant. They gave her an odd, shivery sensation, as if she crouched outside a forbidden door, sensing danger.

Baba had told her the charm of the Wood tribe was imbued with the power of all growing things, which all the Rom knew had a potent magic of their own. All her life Emilia had been taught to look out for certain leaves and flowers and roots and berries, some to boil up with water to make gypsy tea, some to throw into the pot with meat to make stew, some to tuck inside their clothes-box to keep their linen sweet-smelling, some to use as remedies for all sorts of illnesses. All the Rom were taught the lore of the hedgerow – it was their larder and their apothecary.

Yet sometimes the most gorgeous flower was the most dangerous. Foxglove was grown in many a garden for its tall spires of bright, drooping bells, yet make gypsy tea from its leaves and your heart would beat so fast it felt as if it would burst from your chest, until eventually it failed to beat at all. Black hellebore was called the Christmas rose for its delicate winter beauty, yet its roots, powdered, could kill a man. Deadly nightshade was also called belladonna, for it was a beautiful plant with bell-shaped purple flowers and round black berries. Many a small child had died from popping a few of those juicy-looking berries into their mouth, and every part of the plant was poisonous.

Yet all these plants, if used wisely, could heal too. Baba made a potion from foxglove leaves that could restore a stilled heart to life, and she added just one of the toxic berries of bittersweet to the tea she drank for her rheumatism. Even deadly nightshade could be used in a poultice to ease the inflammation of a wound.

Life, death. Healing, hurting. Growing, dying.

Emilia traced the delicate silver tendrils of the rue charm with her finger, round and round, thinking and wondering. She and Luka had travelled so far already, the two of them, and yet their journey was only half over. Three charms hung on her chain, and another two were yet to be found. Emilia could not help being afraid of what lay ahead. They had paid so dearly for what they had won that her spirit quailed within her. Yet. . .

Rue for pity's sake, Baba had said.

Emilia smiled a little wryly. Certainly she and Luka had seen cruelty and malice, but they seen courage and kindness too, and found friends in unexpected places. They had the beginnings of a plan, at least, and promises of help.

She gave the sprig of rue one last thoughtful rub, then got to her feet. Through the sunlit groves she wandered, picking handfuls of leaves from various plants that grew wild in the forest – creeping thyme, meadowsweet, lemon balm, and then, with a glad leap of her heart, a bunch of dried angelica flowers. Tea made with angelica comforted the heart, blood and spirits, her grandmother had told her, and indeed Emilia thought they could both do with some comfort now.

She lit a fire, boiled up some water, then tossed the herbs into the pot. When the water had turned a rich, fragrant brown, she carefully scooped out the leaves and twigs and flung them away. They had no mugs, so she deftly made cups from bark that she cut from the tree.

With a cup in both hands, Emilia went and sat down next to Luka, who glanced at her moodily, then, seeing the steaming tea, rolled over and sat up. He wiped his nose on his sleeve and gave his face a surreptitious scrub, then took the cup and drank. Emilia drank too, pushing her cold feet into Rollo's thick fur to warm them. The big dog thumped his tail in response, but did not open his eyes.

"Better?" Emilia asked after a while.

Luka nodded and shrugged, draining the cup to its dregs, then tossing it into the undergrowth. Bark cups did not last very long.

Emilia reached to pick a leaf out of his hair. He looked as grubby and disreputable as ever after a night slogging through the forest.

"We'll go on east, shall we, looking for the Smith family?" she said.

"Aye. They could be really useful! They'd know all about locks and keys, wouldn't they? And they could make copies of Coldham's keys for us." Luka's eyes lit up with new enthusiasm.

Emilia gave a quick smile of relief. She had not liked seeing her cousin so quiet and miserable. "Maybe they'll have the next charm too."

"Aye. What was it again?"

"A lightning bolt," Emilia answered. "Forged from the heart of a falling star."

Luka grunted in response, rummaging in the bag for some food to share with Zizi and Rollo.

Emilia clasped her cup close to her. What powers would such a charm hold? Something fierce and dark and hard, she thought. Something cruel.

She shivered in sudden fear.

PART FOUR

The Lightning Bolt

The Knight of Swords

Horsmonden, Kent, England
25 August 1658

Emilia woke in the hush before dawn. Luka was still sleeping, and Rollo opened one eye, thumped his tail, then shut his eye again. Emilia huddled her skirts about her cold feet and looked about her.

Fields stretched away on either side of the road. The farmer had recently ploughed, so the furrows lay across the dark earth like puckered seams. A hare sat up in the verge to stare at her. Although Emilia was hungry, she did not call to it, to see if it would come leaping into her arms. They had no cook-pot, and anyway, Emilia liked to see it running wild over the bare earth.

For six days, Emilia and Luka had trudged down narrow tracks, through sunken lanes, up steep bridle-paths and along lonely by-ways, making their slow way towards Horsmonden. Only their innate sense of the compass kept them from wandering in circles, for they had not dared to stop and ask directions or beg for food.

They ate berries from brambles, foraged for mushrooms and fungi from the forest floor, and gathered nuts and acorns and the tender tips of nettles. Once Rollo caught a rabbit and they managed to wrest away its hind legs to roast over a fire. Another evening Luka caught a fish with his bare hands, while twice Emilia found hedgehogs, which they rolled in clay and baked in the coals of their fire.

It had not been nearly enough.

Emilia had never much noticed the passing of time before. Now she was acutely conscious of every minute, every hour. Each evening, as the sun set in bloody streaks in the west, it reminded her cruelly that her family was one day closer to their trial, one day closer to being condemned to death. *Hurry, hurry, hurry*, her heart told her, and her tired body tried its best to obey.

At least they had left Coldham far behind them, and Luka was hopeful that the thief-taker would have given up the chase altogether. Emilia was not so sure. She wished she had her grandmother's skills. She could have searched for Coldham in her crystal ball, and read her tarot cards for clues of his intentions.

Yet Emilia was too afraid. She had been haunted for days by the visions she had seen in her grandmother's crystal ball at Beaulieu. The image of the hare and the hind hunted to death; the apparition of the hanging corpse, rope knotted about his throat; the scream of the peacock, bird with one hundred eyes; and the warning hoot of a night-hunting owl: these omens had disturbed her dreams these last five days, and returned to her in moments of reverie, always with that chill, as if winter had breathed down her neck.

The image of the hanging man wrapped in a green shroud had odd echoes with one of her grandmother's tarot cards, though Emilia could not quite remember which one. So, in this moment of quiet between night and day, Emilia dug through the satchel until she came to her grandmother's things, wrapped up in a gaudy scarf that smelt, faintly, of her baba. Emilia laid the crystal ball aside on the grass, not daring to even glance at the prism of light reflected from its smooth surface, and slowly looked through the shabby old tarot cards.

Emilia had grown up with these cards. It had been a rare day when her grandmother had not laid them out, either for herself or someone else. Emilia had always watched as Maggie read their mysteries, utterly fascinated by what she saw. The cards seemed to tell fantastical stories, of love and war and fate and disaster. Laying them out about her, fingering their bright, strange pictures, of stars and roses, flaming comets and winged lions, bodies pierced with swords, laughing devils, weeping queens and dancing fools, Emilia had to wipe her eyes with the back of her hand.

She found the card she half-remembered. It showed a man hanging from a gallows from a rope bound about one foot. He was dressed like a fool, in red, green and white, and a pool of water had gathered on the ground below him. Emilia stared at it for a long time. The

Hanged Man was a card, she remembered, that often showed when someone was suspended between choices, unable to see which way to go. Maggie always said it was a card that urged submission to one's fate. Only by surrendering to the inevitable, Maggie said, could you take the first steps towards truly understanding your destiny.

The echoes between card and vision rang now with the heavy toll of truth. Emilia knew that she too hung between choices.

Maggie said she had known Emilia had the eye from the moment she was born. Her mother had laboured all night, out in the open as all the Rom did, during a wild lighting-racked storm. Emilia had been born at dawn, in a burst of sunshine and bird-song, with both her eyes wide open. Maggie said she had never seen a babe with such wide-awake eyes. "She will be a *drabardi*," Maggie had said right away, "and maybe even a *shuvani*."

Maggie had begun training Emilia as soon as she began to talk. Emilia had loved knowing she had something that made her special. Beatrice was the pretty one, while Noah – God bless the poor boy! – was blind, and like Luka, had his fiddle. All Emilia had was the eye. She liked feeling she knew things no one else did, and that she was trusted with the deeper mysteries of the Rom.

Emilia had never doubted she was destined to be a *drabardi*. Then the visions had begun. So often, it seemed, they foretold death. Maggie said she would grow used to it, but Emilia did not want to grow used to seeing death. It chilled her to the very marrow of her bones. For the first time in her life, she was not at all sure she wanted to follow her destiny and become a *drabardi*. In the thirteen days since her family had been thrown in gaol, Emilia had felt layer after layer being peeled away, leaving her raw and vulnerable. So Emilia had hidden away her grandmother's crystal ball. She had tried to pretend the dreams and omens and strange certainties that came upon her were just moods, passing like the shadows of clouds.

Surrender to one's fate, the card of the Hanged Man told her. Accept that the gift of the *drabardi's* true-seeing eye was both a curse and a blessing, and learn to use it.

Emilia nodded to herself ruefully. It was no use flinching away from the visions, or longing that Maggie was there to tell her what to do. She had to grapple with her gift and try to force it to her will. She had to find some way to use it to help save her family.

She shuffled the cards slowly and rhythmically, then laid three out on the grass. *What is to become of us all?* she asked silently, feeling a quickening of spirit within her, as if a part of her that had been restrained was now, at last, being unbound. *What lies ahead?*

Emilia turned over the cards, one by one, and saw:

A tower struck by lightning. That meant calamity, a reversal of fortunes, a stroke of fate.

Seven swords crossed. A trial that can only be overcome by inner strength and courage.

The Knight of Swords. A treacherous man.

Emilia stared down at the three cards, then, as Luka stirred and sighed, swept them up and wrapped them quickly in the bright scrap of scarf, tucking them and her grandmother's crystal ball back in the satchel. These were the tools of the *drabardi*, and as such were women's mysteries, not meant for the eyes of thirteen-year-old boys who thought they knew everything.

"I'm starving." Luka scratched his dark mop of hair. "Any more food?"

Emilia shook her head.

Luka sighed. "Do you think the Smiths will feed us?"

"Probably cold pottage and beans."

"What I'd really like is some roast rabbit and potatoes hot from the coals." Luka tucked his cold hands into his armpits. Rollo barked eagerly, his tail wagging.

"Rollo does too," Emilia said with a giggle.

"My darling monkey girl wants some plums." Luka swung Zizi on to his shoulder. She pushed his cap so she could seize hold of his ear and croon something into it in her own liquid monkey language. Luka listened solemnly, then said, "And some fresh figs."

"I can just imagine the Smiths having fresh figs. She may as well ask for a satin cushion and a new velvet dress at the same time."

"Nothing but the best for my little monkey girl. And she does need a new dress."

"So do I!" Emilia's grey dress was very grubby after she had spent a week sleeping in ditches and haystacks.

"Well, the sooner we find the Smiths, the sooner we can be begging them for some food. Come on!" Luka set off down the path that ran through the copse.

"And the lightning charm," Emilia murmured as she followed behind, her shawl wrapped tight about her shoulders.

The path led them down through the woods, all tangled with sloe berries and crimson rosehips and the fluffy grey seeds of clematis. The leaves of the beech trees above them were bright as new coins against the pale blue sky. Ivy smothered the ground, its invisible flowers sending a faint wild fragrance into the chilly air. Emilia's feet did a little dance as she went down the path, the bracken brushing against her skirt. Luka began to whistle. She knew how much he had missed his music since he had given away his violin. It made her heart lift to hear him whistling as gaily as any blackbird.

They came out of the woods, and stopped.

Aghast.

A ruin of a landscape lay before them. There were no trees, no hedges of blackthorn, elder or wild rose, no late drifts of wild parsley, no birds singing or rabbits bounding about. The ground was pitted and poisoned, littered with dead trees and piles of ugly slag and raw gaping holes from which sounded the dull ring of metal on stone. Smoke from the smouldering fires of charcoal-burners hung over the scene. Shallow pools of poisoned water were edged with nasty red slime like the inflammation of a wound.

The only living things to be seen were grey-faced men in filthy smocks, working away with axe or pick or hammer. At the far end of the valley, a huge building loomed over a huddle of low houses, its chimneys belching smoke, its windows flaring red.

"What . . . what is this place?" Emilia stammered.

"I guess . . . I guess it's the gun foundry."

"It's awful."

"We won't have to stay long," Luka promised. "Let's just find the Smiths; then we'll go."

They came at last to Horsmonden, a small village of red-brick houses built around a large green. The inn had a picture of a gun hanging above the door, but, much to Emilia's surprise, there was no church. She had never before seen a village that did not have a church.

In the middle of the green was a makeshift pen built of sharpened sticks. Impaled upon one stick was a large crudely drawn poster showing a snarling bear beset by a pack of rabid dogs. The children frowned at the sight of it.

"Don't they know that bear-baiting's against the law now?" Emilia said angrily. "It's the only good thing the Puritans have done, banning such cruel sports!"

Luka put up one eyebrow. "What makes you think the Puritans banned bear-baiting because it's cruel to the bear?" he asked mockingly. "They only banned it because the audience enjoys it!"

"Well, no one should enjoy it, it's horrible." Emilia would have liked to have torn the poster down, but she did not want to draw attention to themselves. Already two women gossiping over a front fence had turned to stare at them in open curiosity. A big burly man with a shock of black hair and a huge beard was smoking a pipe on a bench outside the inn, a mug of ale in his hand. One of his eyes was miscast, so it was hard to tell if he was staring at them or at some point behind their shoulders.

"Let's go ask those women there if they know where we can find the Smiths." Emilia led the way across the road, Rollo at her heels.

The women looked her over assessingly. "Gypsies, are you?" one said. "Come for the horse fair too? You're all early this year."

"No, we're here to see the Smiths."

"Which one?" the other woman said. "There's seven of them – eight if you count the girl!"

"The Big Man," Luka said.

The women exchanged glances. "That'd be Stevo now, I suppose," one said hesitantly. "But his brother Dax is just here, you could ask him. . ." She turned and glanced at the inn, but the man with the beard was gone. She shrugged and turned back to the children. "They're all up at the foundry. You shouldn't go there. It's not the place for children. Wait until tonight when they knock off work. They'll all be here at the Gun, wetting their dry throats."

"We'll be all right," Luka said cheerfully. "Thanks for your help."

The women stared after them all the way up the street.

*

The foundry was an immense dark hulk of a building, spewing forth smoke and great bursts of fire as if a dragon was imprisoned inside, fighting to escape a massive iron collar and chain. The air was so acrid that Emilia and Luka's eyes stung, and the ground beneath their feet shook.

A banging and a clanging assaulted their ears, like the sound of a thousand giant iron hammers pounding on a thousand giant anvils. Then came a great roar, and fire glared from the window slits. Rollo whined and pressed against Emilia's leg. Inside Luka's coat, Zizi whimpered.

Bang, clang, clash, rattle, boom boom boom!

"I don't like it." Emilia pressed her hands over her ears.

"You stay here. Here, take Zizi! Don't let her escape. I won't be long." Luka went on alone, staring up at the foundry in fascination. He had never seen anything like it.

Inside, all was darkness and smoke and fire. Men with soot-black bodies were silhouetted against a waterfall of liquid flame that poured ceaselessly down from above. Massive hammers pounded away, making Luka's teeth shudder in his skull. He could feel the vibrations jolting up through his bare feet, all the way to the delicate bones behind his ears. There was a long hiss, like a giant serpent, and he jumped violently and spun. Behind him a pair of enormous bellows worked, more than twice as long as Luka himself.

Sparks flew wide, like burning bees.

"More charcoal!" a stentorian voice roared. "Tell the men, more charcoal!"

Luka peered towards the voice. Then a great black shape loomed up over him, a huge, hairy hand seized him by the scruff of the neck and he was lifted and heaved away from the falling river of fiery gold, away from the *clang* and *bang* and *boom*, out into the smoke-hazed sunshine.

"Idiot boy!" the voice roared in his ear. "A blast furnace is no place for weans! Do you want to be cooked like pork crackling?"

Luka wriggled free. "I'm looking for Stevo Smith."

A giant of a man glared down at him. He had fierce black eyes, a thick mane of curling black hair and a bushy beard that jutted out over his massive chest. His arms were near as thick as Luka's waist, and bulged with muscles. He wore nothing over his breeches but a leather jerkin pitted with scorch marks.

"I'm Stevo Smith. What do you want with me, boy?"

Luka stumbled through his story. The fierce scowl deepened. "I cannot help you. I have my work to do here. We cannot leave the blast furnace once it's fired up. I'm sorry." Stevo Smith spoke with no hint of apology in his voice, but as a way of terminating the discussion.

"But you are our kin! If we cannot call on our family in time of need, who can we call on?"

Stevo shrugged and walked back inside the foundry.

Anger roared up Luka's body. He ran back inside the black, stinking belly of the foundry and seized Stevo by his arm. "You can't just walk away like that! You're a Rom too. The Rom need to help each other, for no one else is going to!"

Stevo glared down at him. "We're not Rom any more. We've given up the roads."

"Once a Rom, always a Rom," Luka said.

Stevo jerked his arm free. "What do you think I can do to help you? All I'll do is get myself and my family into trouble. I tell you, we've given up the roads, we've got work here, our noses are clean. You're bad news, you are. I've no desire to get myself tangled up with one of Ironsides' thief-takers!"

Luka swallowed. "How do you know about the thief-taker?"

"Word's gone out, little man. He's looking for you. A boy, a girl, a dog and a monkey. He knew you'd come here asking for help. So you see, I'm not such a hard man as you think. I could send word to him, and claim that reward for myself. But I won't. I'll warn you instead. You'd better get out of here fast, for that thief-taker doesn't like to be crossed, and by all accounts, you've been crossing him at every turn."

Even though it was stifling hot in the foundry, Luka felt chilled through. "Coldham's here? Here in Horsmonden?"

"He is indeed," Stevo said. "Better get moving, little man."

"What about the lightning bolt charm? Do you have it?"

He snorted. "You'd have to ask my father about that. Now, go on, get out of here."

"Your father? Where is he?"

"They live up the far end of the valley, near the church." He made a broad gesture to the south. "As far away from the foundry as they can get!"

Luka pushed out past Stevo Smith, then broke into a run. He did not stop running until he had found Emilia.

Rose Honey

It was impossible not to imagine the thief-taker lurking behind every slagheap. Luka and Emilia did their best to keep out of sight as they hurried south, but it was impossible. The whole valley was bare as a licked bowl.

After about half an hour, they came again to fields and felt their steps slow in some kind of relief. Ahead was the church, its square tower rising high above the towering poles of hops. A little further round the curve of the hill was an oast house next to an apple orchard, with three tall conical towers, each topped by an angular white wind-funnel that swung round every time the wind moved. The house was surrounded by a colourful profusion of flowers – foxgloves and lavender and roses and columbines, with a thick wood behind.

A girl stood in the middle of the garden, her hands full of roses. Her apron and cap were snowy-white, and her shoes were as black and shiny as her hair. She smiled when she saw Luka and Emilia trudging wearily up the path, Rollo at their heels. "Good morning! Have you come to buy some honey?"

"We're not here for honey," Luka said. "We're looking for a man called Smith. Father to Stevo Smith."

"Well, you're at the right place. My name's Fairnette Smith, and Stevo is my brother. What do you want with my father?"

"We need his help."

She frowned. "My father's help? I'm not sure. . . You had better come in, I think, and tell me what it is you want."

This kitchen was the neatest room Emilia had ever seen. The furniture gleamed, smelling of beeswax, and the big iron stove and oven had recently been blackened. Lined up along the mantelpiece was a row of pewter plates, as precise as soldiers on parade. On the top shelf of the dresser were jars of honey, arranged in order of colour from the darkest to the lightest.

A young boy was slumped over the table, a plate full of cake crumbs before him. He had a round, plump face and a round, plump body. Kicking moodily at the table leg with one sturdy boot, he crammed a very large piece of cake into his mouth.

"Van! You didn't eat my cake, did you? That was for morning tea!"

"Well, you shouldn't leave it out if you don't want me to eat it." Van spoke sulkily through his mouthful.

Fairnette sighed, and turned to Emilia and Luka with a little helpless shrug. "I'm sorry. Are you hungry? There's no cake left . . . but I can cut you some bread and honey."

"Thanks, that'd be great. We're starving!"

Fairnette took a loaf of bread out of a tin and neatly cut off a few slices. "What kind of honey would you like?"

"Criminy, I don't know. There's a difference?" Luka asked.

"The rose honey is very rich and strengthening, and heartens you when you are weary. That would be best; you both look worn out." She got down the darkest jar from the shelf. It was the colour of toffee. She spread it on the bread and gave them each a slice, then poured them a mug of cold, frothy milk.

Luka sat down gratefully and unbuttoned his coat to let Zizi out. Fairnette and Van exclaimed in surprise.

"You got a monkey! I wish I had a monkey!" the boy said enviously. He bounced to his feet, reaching out as if to grab Zizi. The little monkey shrank back, baring her teeth.

"She doesn't like strangers," Luka said. "I wouldn't grab at her like that, she'll bite you."

"I want to hold the monkey! Let me have a hold!"

"Don't frighten her," Fairnette said. "Oh, isn't she a funny little thing?"

Luka cradled her protectively in one arm as he ravenously ate his bread and honey. He tore off a small piece for Zizi and she ate it daintily, licking the honey off her fingers.

"So what are you doing here? You look like you've travelled many miles," Fairnette asked, putting down a bowl of water for Rollo, who drank thirstily.

"We have!" Emilia crammed the last of the bread into her mouth. "You see, we're kin of yours . . . and our grandmother sent us to find you and beg you for your help."

"To beg *me*?" Fairnette sounded startled.

"All of your family," Emilia said impatiently. She and Luka quickly told the other two children some of their adventures, and showed them the wax imprints of Coldham's keys.

"I can make keys for you," Van cried. "Father's no use any more, but I can do it!"

"You know you can't," Fairnette said. "You're not big enough yet, Van."

"Everyone always says that," Van replied sulkily. "It's so unfair." He thrust his hands into his pockets, rattling his fingers through what he carried there.

"You're only seven, Van. Plenty of time for learning to use the forge."

"Except who's going to teach me?" he blazed up. "You? Father? He can't even remember how to do up his own buttons!"

"Don't say that, Van, it's not fair. Father has good days sometimes." She looked apologetically at Luka and Emilia. "Father's old now, you see, and wandering in his wits a little."

"A little!" Van snorted.

"We also wanted to ask you about your family's lucky charm," Emilia asked. "Do you know where it is? Does your father have it?"

"The lightning bolt charm?" Fairnette looked puzzled. "Stevo's got it."

"I asked Stevo and he said your father had it," Luka said angrily.

"It went missing," Fairnette said. "Father said Stevo stole it. . . He wanted it, you know, when he took over the running of the foundry, but Father wouldn't give it to him. They fought over it. Stevo knocked Father over and snatched the charm away. That's what happened, isn't it, Van?"

Van shrugged, and looked away. "I guess so."

"Stevo says he didn't take the charm, but Father says he's lying and he should give it back. They haven't spoken since," Fairnette said. "Father was angry that Stevo took over the foundry. . ."

"It was dangerous," Van said. "Father kept forgetting how much charcoal he'd put in, and stuff like that. He could've blown the whole place up."

"We moved out here, where we can't see the foundry or smell it," Fairnette explained. "It's best, really."

"For you and Father, maybe, but not for me," Van burst out. "Why should I be stuck all the way out here just because Father keeps blowing his top? I wanted to stay at the foundry."

"It's too dangerous for weans." Fairnette spoke wearily, as if she had said it many times before. "You know that. You can go and work as an apprentice when you're twelve. . ."

"That's five years away!"

Fairnette turned back to Emilia and Luka. "I'm sorry. I guess Stevo didn't want to admit he'd taken the charm from Father. It's forged from the iron of a meteor, did you know? It's our family's most precious thing. The Big Man always wears it. It means . . . I guess it means strength."

"But we need it. Without it we'll never be able to save our family!"

"But why? I don't understand."

"The charms are the luck of the Rom." Emilia showed them the three charms she wore at her wrist. "They bring good luck, and help guard and protect us. It's a kind of magic."

Luka was frowning. She knew he did not have the same faith in the charms that she did. So far, he had humoured her insistence that they search for all of the charms because he had wanted to get more practical help, like the sleeping drug Joe Wood had given them. She put her hand up to finger the charms, rubbing them one after the other. "It's hard to explain. Things have happened just when we've needed them to. Rain coming when we needed it, and Alida winning that race."

"Luck, pure and simple," Luka said.

"It's too uncanny to be just luck," Emilia argued. "And it's happened too often. On the river, when those soldiers were after us, I begged the charms to help us get away safely and next thing I knew, that mist rose up and hid us from their sight."

"That's just coincidence," Luka said.

"Well, what about Lord Harry? You can't say it's just a coincidence that he was there, lying in wait for Cold-Pig's coach, just when we needed him most? And that he knew Gypsy Joe, and where the inn was, and everything?"

"Of course it was a coincidence. He's a highwayman that likes to hold up Roundheads. He would've held up that coach whether we were in it or not."

"It's the magic of the charms," Emilia insisted. She did not like talking about the charms in this way; it made her faith in the charm bracelet seem foolish. She cast about for another way to convince Luka and the others of what she felt instinctively to be true. "It's not just that they're good luck. They give me . . . some kind of power too. The longer I wear them, the more clearly I seem to see things. It's like. . ." She struggled for words. "It's like on a really bright, frosty morning, when you can see for miles, and everything is so sharp against the sky, and you can *smell* things, like you were a fox, and hear them too. Everything seems so much clearer. That's what it's like, wearing the charms. And each time I add a new one, the powers of the ones I already have get stronger. I can't explain how. I just feel it."

"What kind of powers?" Fairnette was fascinated and afraid.

"Making things happen," Emilia said after a moment. "Changing things."

"Well, I wish you could turn rocks into gold, and then we could buy our family free," Luka mocked. She sent him a hurt and furious look. He raised his eyebrows and shrugged.

"Without them we would not have come so far," she insisted.

Van stared at her, his hands thrust in his pocket, his eyes troubled.

"Well, let's go and see how Father is faring today. Maybe he'll be up to making the keys for you. That'd be something, at least." As she spoke, Fairnette rose to her feet. The other two rose too, Luka swinging Zizi up on to his shoulder. Van stayed where he was, scowling at the table, his fist thrust in his pocket.

Outside, the sun had gone behind a great bank of grey clouds. Fairnette led them through the kitchen garden, towards a long, low stable at the end of the yard.

"That's my father's forge. He works in there sometimes, on his good days. Not so often any more."

An old man sat on a bench in front of the forge, staring down at his hands. They were huge and hard and calloused, and lay idle on his lap. A pipe smouldered from the corner of his mouth.

"Father?" Fairnette said hesitantly.

He looked up, taking the pipe out of his mouth. He was huge, the biggest man Emilia had ever seen. His beard was vast, streaked with grey, as if he had wiped his ashy fingers through it.

"Father, it's me, Fairnette. Your daughter."

He stared at her without recognition, then moved his vacant gaze to Luka's face. "Do I know you?"

"No," Luka said, "though we're kin, way back."

"I think you may know their grandmother, Maggie Finch," Fairnette said.

"Maggie? But she's only a young thing, with black hair hanging down her back. They say she's got the eye."

"Her hair's grey now." Luka thought of his grandmother, bent and crippled with rheumatism.

"Can't be the same Maggie. Why, I saw Maggie just last month, dancing at the horse fair. They married her off to that boy with a bear, I can't remember his name."

Neither Luka nor Emilia wanted to say that Sylvio and his bear were both long dead. They looked to Fairnette pleadingly. She said gently, "Maggie Finch is in gaol now, Father. Emilia and Luka want to get her out. Can you help?"

"I've got wax imprints of some keys." Luka rummaged in their bag until he found them. "Could you make copies for us?"

The old man looked at them suspiciously. "Why? Who are you? I don't do things like that any more! Why, I'm the master smith at the foundry. I'm no gypsy-boy, to make keys and lock picks for thieves."

"Lock pick?" Luka asked eagerly. "What's that?"

"You trying to trick me? What are you, some kind of spy? Get out of here, I say!"

"Father, no, Luka's our kin, he's no spy or a thief. He

just wants our help." Fairnette held out both hands imploringly.

"Who are you? I don't know you. What do you want? Coming round, trying to trick me and steal from me. I won't allow it!" He surged to his feet and at once all three children scrambled back a few steps, frightened. He shook a huge fist at them. "Get out of here, I say!"

Sugarplums

"Come on. There's no point talking to him when he's like this. We'll come back later. He'll have forgotten all about it, and we can ask him again." Fairnette's voice was stiff and unhappy.

"Does he not remember you? His own daughter?" Emilia felt this would be worse than not having a father at all.

"Sometimes he remembers. Sometimes he thinks I should still be only a baby, and does not believe I'm me. Other times he does not remember he has a daughter at all."

"That's terrible," Emilia said. "What about your mother. Where's she?"

"She's dead. She died when I was eight."

"My mother's dead too," Emilia said. They looked at each other sadly. There was no way to explain the dark absence in their lives to anyone who had not lost their mother too. Only those who had suffered the same sorrow could understand.

"Come back to the house. I have a lot to do, I'm afraid. I need to bring in the washing, it looks like it might rain, and soon I'll need to start cooking dinner. You will stay for dinner, won't you? Father may feel better after a little sleep."

"That'd be lovely, thank you," Emilia said gratefully. "If you have enough."

When they came back into the kitchen, Van had his head bent over something in his hand. He scowled at the sight of them and shoved his hand back in his pocket. "I'm hungry. When's dinner?"

"I just need to get the washing on first, Van, else it won't dry," Fairnette replied, sounding harassed. "I'll start making some soup in just a minute."

"But I'm hungry now."

"I could cut you some more bread. . ."

"I don't want bread! Can't I have some sugarplums?"

"But, Van, you've already had that whole honey cake. . ."

"But I'm hungry!"

"All right, Van, but just a few." Fairnette got down a jar of sugarplums from a high shelf in the pantry, then put a pot of water on to boil.

Luka and Emilia offered to peel the potatoes and chop the vegetables for Fairnette while she hung out the washing. They worked together steadily, watching Van as he rattled his fingers in his pocket, kicked the table legs, and ate sugared plums out of the jar till his face was red, shiny and sticky. He managed to coax Zizi to go to him by offering her plum after plum, and was delighted when she leapt up to his shoulder so she could reach the jar more easily.

"Zizi, stop it! You'll make yourself sick!" Luka did not at all like to see his monkey perched on another boy's shoulder.

"She's all right," Van said. "She's better than all right! Where did you get her?"

"I got her when she was just a baby," Luka said shortly. "My father saw her in a basket at one of the markets, all sick and covered in sores. He bought her for me. I've had her ever since." He held out his hand and gave a little chirrup, and at once Zizi leapt over to his shoulder.

Emilia had been watching Van curiously. She did not like the way he ordered his sister around, and did nothing to help her in the running of the house and garden. Something about him bothered her. It was not just that he was greedy and cocksure, for she had met small boys like that before. It was more than that, an aura of brawn and sinew that did not fit comfortably with such a small, plump, smug little boy.

"You've got the lightning bolt charm," she said suddenly, acting on a hunch.

Van almost choked on his sugarplum. "I do not," he answered feebly, when he got his voice back. Luka looked from one to the other, his hands stilling in their task.

"You do. I can feel it."

"Nay, I don't. Stevo's got it."

"You must've picked it up that day your father and brother had the fight. Where did you put it? In your pocket?" Emilia had noticed the way he kept fingering something in his pocket, and when she saw him jump and snatch his hand away, she was sure she was right. "Will you not let us borrow it? Our family faces the magistrates in less than a week. Your lucky charm, it has power, you know it does."

"Don't know what you're talking about."

Emilia said gently, "I have the eye, you know, Van." He shot a scared look at her, and her suspicion hardened into conviction. "Please, Van. I'm begging you. We need your help. It need only be for a little while. . ."

"My guess is Van is too scared to admit he's got the charm," Luka goaded. Van glared at him, but the look of obstinacy did not leave his face.

Emilia tried a different approach. "Isn't there something we can do to convince you, Van? There must be something you'd like. . ."

Van's eyes flicked towards Zizi, combing Luka's hair lovingly with her tiny paws. Luka went white. "No! Not Zizi!"

Van crossed his arms over his chest. "I've always wanted a monkey," he said, as if musing aloud.

"You can't ask it of him!" Emilia's voice shook. "It's not fair. He's already given up so much. He gave away his violin. . ." But even as she spoke, she was thinking of her own mare, Alida, whom she had loved at least as much as Luka loved Zizi.

Fairnette came in from the garden, a basket of washing on her hip. "I'll just get the soup on, it won't take long."

Van got up and went towards the back door. "Let me know if you change your mind," he said to Luka, who clutched his monkey close.

Emilia and Luka sat in silence as Fairnette, noticing nothing, chattered away making the soup. Emilia did not know what to say. She knew how Luka loved his monkey. She knew he also loved his family. It was a cruel choice.

In a way it had been easier for her. A horse was a simpler creature than a monkey. Emilia had known Alida was unlikely to pine away to death once she had given her away. Zizi, though, was a monkey who had never known another monkey. Luka was her mother and father, the Big Man of her monkey tribe. She would simply not understand.

Luka suddenly stood up. Looking up at him, Emilia could not guess his intention. She got to her feet too, holding out one hand to him.

Just then, Rollo lifted his head from his paws and growled, deep in his throat. Luka and Emilia looked at each other in sudden alarm. Rollo rose to his feet, the hair on his neck standing up. He was staring at the door.

"Fairnette," Luka said in a low, urgent voice. "It could

be Coldham, that thief-taker we told you about! Someone must've told him we were headed here. We have to hide."

"Quick, hide in the old oast house," Fairnette said.

"Is there any way out of there?" Luka asked.

"There's a door where they used to load the bags of hops on to the cart, but it's bolted on the outside," Fairnette said.

Luka grimaced. "What about through that white thing at the top?"

"You mean through the cowl?" Fairnette asked doubtfully. "But how would you get up there? And the hole is very small. Zizi could get out, I guess. It's really a chimney, you know, that cowl, and it's just as narrow as a chimney."

"I can climb a chimney," Luka said.

"He can climb anything," Emilia added loyally. "He's a monkey boy."

"And Milly's a monkey girl." Luka gave her a wan grin, sharing a very old joke.

"Hopefully you won't need to try," Fairnette said, opening a door in the side of the kitchen. "It's an awfully long way down to the ground!"

The door led into a round, dark, cavernous room. Along one wall was a huge fireplace, cold and bare of anything but cobwebs. The floor was covered in brown leaves and petals that crunched underfoot and sent up an odd smell in dizzying waves. Everywhere were barrels and sacks and peculiar equipment covered in dust.

A ladder led up to the next floor. Luka and Emilia

scrambled up it, Zizi leading the way. Rollo put his paws up the ladder and whined, but it was too steep for him to follow.

Above was a vast, empty space. The floor was wooden, and scattered with dried hop cones. The roof narrowed to a point far above their heads, and there was the white post of the wind vane, letting in a thin beam of light and a faint draught to move the dried hops so they murmured about the children's feet.

Luka stared up at it, wondering. "Could we, if we had to?" he whispered.

Emilia frowned. "It's very narrow."

"We're only skinny."

"Aye, but skinny enough?"

"Lucky we didn't eat much breakfast," Luka grinned.

"What would we do about Rollo?"

Luka did not answer, only pressed his lips together.

They crept back down the ladder and put their ear to the door.

"Open up, else I'll knock the door down!" a rough and all-too-familiar voice was roaring. Coldham!

They heard Fairnette open the door, and then her voice, sounding scared, "What is it? Who are you?"

"We're looking for a couple of gypsy brats," Coldham snarled. "They had a dog with them, a savage, hairy brute, and a horrible flea-bitten monkey. They were last seen coming this way."

"No, I'm sorry, I haven't seen anyone," Fairnette said.

"Things will go badly for you if you're lying!"

"No, I'm not lying!" Fairnette's voice shook. "Please, I haven't seen anyone. . ."

"Is there a reward?" Van's voice suddenly piped up, shrill with excitement. Emilia and Luka looked at each other in horror.

"Why? Have you seen them? Have they been here?"

"What's it worth to you?" Van said. Next moment there was the sound of a sharp slap, and then sobbing.

"That's the reward for cheekiness in my part of the world," Coldham said. "Right, men! Rip this place to pieces. If those gypsy brats are hiding here, I want them found."

They heard a great clatter of boots, a cry of dismay from Fairnette, and then the crash of furniture being overturned, plates falling, pewter jugs clanging, glass smashing, iron clanking, fists hammering, and doors banging.

Emilia exchanged an agonized look with Luka. "We'll climb out the cowl," he decided.

"But . . . Rollo!"

Luka seized the dog by his thick rug and dragged him over to a pile of sacks by the big double doors that led out to the courtyard. "Down, boy, down. Stay!"

Obediently Rollo lay down on the sacks, and Luka draped more sacks over him. "We'll get out the cowl and then open the doors and let him out. Come on!"

Emilia and Luka quickly climbed to the next floor, and looked up at the tiny crack of light so far above them. "No help for it," Luka said, and grabbed the end of the dangling rope that was used to pull the wind-vane round to catch the breeze. Emilia climbed quickly up the rope. The hole was not much bigger than Emilia's head, and outside the mossy red tiles of the roof fell away steeply. Emilia breathed out till her lungs were flat and empty, then squirmed through the vent, clinging to the wind-vane. Then she slithered down towards the edge of the roof, hoping the noise the soldiers made would conceal the clatter of the tiles. The roof was so steep she slid at great speed, and only just managed to grasp the gutter and swing her body round. Her feet found a thick branch of ivy. Panting, she clung to the side of the tower, and rested her hot face against her scratched and filthy arm.

Zizi and Luka followed swiftly. They could hear Coldham shouting. Hurriedly they clambered down to the ground, and dragged back the bolts to open the door to the oast house. Rollo leapt up, barking with joy, and they shushed him, dragged him out, bolted the door again, then ran into the woods, Rollo bounding at their heels.

"Did they see us?" Emilia panted.

Luka shook his head. "They must've heard Rollo, though. You're a bad, noisy dog! We told you to be quiet."

Rollo wagged his tail happily.

"It could be any old dog," Emilia said. "They've got no way of knowing it was Rollo barking."

"Coldham will know," Luka said grimly.

A Hungry Beast

Emilia hid under a thick bush with Rollo, while Luka climbed up a tall tree from which he could keep a good lookout. After about twenty tense, uncomfortable minutes, he slithered down and came to haul Emilia out.

"They've marched off down the road, back towards Horsmonden," he said. "They must've given up looking for us."

"I can't believe Coldham found us again!" Emilia crawled out from under the bush and dusted herself off.

"We told the Hearnes we were coming to find the Smiths," Luka said angrily. "Remember? They must've told Cold-Pig! That's how he knew to come here to Horsmonden."

"But they're Rom. The Rom don't talk to thief-takers."

"Do you really think they would risk getting on the

wrong side of the law for our sake? What if Cold-Pig threatened to throw them in gaol too?"

"They could've said they didn't know anything," Emilia said. "They didn't have to put Cold-Pig back on our trail. I bet it was that Nadine girl! I'm sure she was the one who told him that we were hiding out in those stables."

Luka nodded and shrugged at the same time. "Maybe." He stood still, biting his lip, stroking Zizi gently. Emilia looked at him questioningly. "Do you think its safe to go back?" he burst out. "I mean, will Cold-Pig be watching the house?"

"You want to go back?" Emilia felt both joy and horror. She knew going back meant Luka must give Van his darling monkey-girl.

"I don't *want* to," Luka said fiercely. "But we have to, don't we? I mean, we've come all this way. We can't just give up. That lock pick sounded like it could be just what we need! And if that rotten little kid really does have the Smith's lucky charm. . ."

"You'd give up Zizi so I can have the lightning bolt charm?" Emilia flung her arms about his neck and hugged him hard, then bent her head and pressed her face against Zizi's soft fur. There was a big lump in her throat. Zizi seized hold of her curls and tugged them sharply, then, as Emilia sprang away, shrieked with laughter.

Luka nodded, looking as miserable as Emilia had ever seen him. "But I'll sure as hell make him get us those keys and that lock pick too!"

Emilia nodded. "I'm so sorry," she said hesitantly.

Luka walked away from her. "He'd better not feed her too many of those sugarplums."

The two children went slowly back towards the oast-house. Emilia wrapped her shawl about her shoulders, for the day had grown gloomy and cold, as if the weather felt the same heavy misery as she and Luka. Emilia could not imagine Luka without his monkey perched on his shoulder. It seemed so unfair.

The blustery wind changed, and blew with it the smell of burning. Emilia looked up. Above the trees billowed a thick column of black smoke.

"Luka!" she shrieked. "Come on! We've got to run. Fairnette's house is on fire."

"What?"

"I'm telling you, their house is on fire!" She seized Luka's hand and broke into a run.

"But what can we do?" Luka panted.

"Must do something," Emilia panted back.

The smell of burning grew. They saw the red glare of fire as they burst out of the wood into the garden, and heard the hungry roar of flames.

One of the roundels was up in flames. Old Man Smith was drawing water from the well and passing it to Fairnette, who ran to throw it on to the blaze. Van was standing helplessly nearby.

Luka and Emilia ran to help, but it was of little use. With only one bucket, they could not move the water fast enough. The fire leapt and gibbered at the gaping windows, and tore great chunks out of the pointed roof.

"Van!" Luka shouted. "Find us another bucket!"

"I can't! I'm scared!"

"Get it, Van!" Fairnette shouted. "This is your fault! If you hadn't told that horrible man . . . if you had not been so . . . so greedy . . . and faithless. . ." Her voice failed, and she dashed one angry hand across her eyes. "How could you! Luka and Emilia are our cousins. They came to us for help. How could you betray them like that?"

"But . . . I. . ." Van stammered.

"I'm ashamed of you. Our caravan is our family, and the world is our caravan. Don't you know that?"

Van's shoulders were hunched, his hands shoved in his pocket. He looked angry and sulky.

"If you don't help, the whole place will burn to the ground," Luka shouted. "Come on, Van! Run."

Van ran to the forge. He staggered out with the smithy's big quench-bucket and flung it to Luka, then went back for another. Soon there was a desperate chain of buckets passing back and forth between the well to the fire.

With a roar, the roof collapsed and fell in. Charred and blackened timbers fell on the roof of the cottage, smouldering coals raining everywhere.

"The whole place will go up in flames now!" Luka cried. "We need more water."

Van thrust one hand into his pocket. Emilia knew he was rubbing the lightning bolt charm for courage, as she touched the charms at her wrist. When he saw Emilia watching him, he turned scarlet.

Emilia grasped him by the arm. "Give me your charm! Please, Van. I need it."

He stared at her, eyes wide, and instinctively shook his head.

"Please! If I had it, I think I could save your house. Nothing but a downpour will put this fire out. But I'm not strong enough without the lightning bolt charm."

Van hesitated, then withdrew his hand from his pocket. In his palm was a small piece of iron, forged into the jagged shape of a lightning bolt. He rubbed his thumb over it, then held it out to Emilia. "Here you are," he said. "I'm sorry I didn't give it to you before. I . . . I wanted it to be all mine. It's got power, you know."

"I know," Emilia said. She hung the jagged iron charm on her bracelet. It swung to and fro, black as night, hard as hate, hot to the touch. At once she felt the surge of power around the chain, like a lick of blue lightning. A little shiver ran over her, half dread, half excitement.

Emilia shut her eyes and ran her fingers swiftly over her charms, every atom of her body begging for rain to come and help kill this dreadful hungry beast of red flaming eyes and red devouring mouths. Rain had come before when she needed it. She believed absolutely that it would come again.

And it did. A sudden rain-burst that drenched them

all to the skin. They stood in the grey downpour, jumping up and down and cheering. Emilia felt so weak with relief that she fell to her knees in the mud. Slowly the fire sizzled and went out.

"I can't believe it," Old Man Smith said. "That rain . . . it came at just the right moment."

"Magic," Emilia said confidently.

"Luck," Luka said, not quite so confidently.

"A miracle," Fairnette said.

Emilia smiled and hugged her.

"So who are our saviours?" the old man said. "Friends indeed in our time of need!"

Fairnette flashed a quick look at Emilia and Luka. "Father! Let me introduce you. This is Luka and Emilia Finch. They're the grandchildren of Maggie Finch, who I think you know. . ."

"Of course, I remember Maggie. She married Sylvio Finch, who had a dancing bear. I wonder what happened to that bear?"

"We have one of his cubs, though of course it's not a cub any more," Luka said. "We call her Sweetheart. She loves to dance too, and play football. . ."

The old man laughed uproariously. "Sylvio's bear liked to play football too. I'll never forget it!"

Luka and Emilia exchanged a glance of wry amusement.

"So what brings you here to Horsmonden? It's too early for the horse fair, isn't it?"

So, once again, they told him their story. He nodded

when they mentioned the Graylings tribe and said, "Aye, that's right, they went to London, hoping to make their fortune there. Last I heard old Mala's daughter had married a *gorgio*, some lawyer fellow."

Luka was very interested to hear this and pressed the old man for details, but if he had ever known any more, he did not remember it. So Luka hurried on to his next urgent need, and this time, when he mentioned the wax imprints, the old man nodded his head jovially. "Sure, that's easy enough. I could do that in my sleep." He chuckled. "It's been a while since I've been asked to copy keys. In the bad old days, that's all we Smiths ever did, half the time."

Luka leant forward, intent. "You said something before about a tool? For picking locks?"

"Aye. Simple enough to make, if you know what you are doing."

"Do you think you could make me one of those tools too?" Luka asked.

"Me? I can make anything," the old man boasted.

"It's true, he can. Father, could you make one for Luka? Please?"

"Sure I could. Give me five minutes, and I'll whip one up for you."

Luka and Emilia's eyes met in pure joy.

Old Man Smith went striding out to get the fire in the forge going, and the children began to help Fairnette tidy up. Van stood watching for a moment, then silently got a broom and began to help.

"I didn't mean for our house to get burnt," he said after a while. "Or for you to be caught. I just wanted. . ." His voice trailed away.

"Water washes away everything but shame," Emilia answered quietly, pausing in her scrubbing. It was a favourite saying of her grandmother's, but she thought she was only just beginning to understand it.

Van nodded. "I'm sorry."

Luka said unhappily, "I guess you want Zizi now."

Van shook his head. "No. I mean, I do, of course I do, but I couldn't take her away from you. Not after you helped us and everything."

Luka grinned in relief and cuddled Zizi close.

"Oh, Emilia, I almost forgot," Fairnette said. "Before that awful man set the house on fire, he gave me this." She passed Emilia a crumpled piece of paper. It was a copy of the poster advertising the bear-baiting. "He said that if I saw you again, I should be sure to tell you that he was looking forward to watching your bear being ripped apart tonight."

A feeling of cold horror stole over Emilia. She stared down at the picture of the great bear, surrounded by a pack of snarling dogs, then passed it with a shaking hand to Luka. "Coldham's got Sweetheart! She's to be baited by dogs tonight."

"But . . . how? He must've got her from the Hearnes! But why?"

"It's a trap," Emilia said. "He knows we'd never let Sweetheart be attacked by dogs."

"But how are we meant to stop them, Milly? There'll be soldiers there. How can we possibly fight them?"

Emilia narrowed her eyes in thought. "You know what Baba always says? 'Surrounded by *gorgios*, the Rom's tongue is his only defence.'"

"Aye, so?"

"Well, so tonight I'll use my tongue as a weapon."

Fire and Smoke

Night had fallen and all was dark, but torches planted all around the village square cast a flickering red light over the crowd gathered together in the street before the Gun Inn.

An improvised bear pit had been built with rough stakes in the centre of the green. Sweetheart sat in the middle, chained by the leg. She looked very sulky. She did not like the noise of the crowd, shouting and jeering as they drank beer and laid their bets. She did not like the smell of the half-starved dogs snapping and snarling nearby. She was covered with cuts and bruises where she had been beaten with a stick, and her nose was very sore. Sweetheart just wanted to go home.

No one paid much attention to a couple of boys loitering near the dog-cart. The owner of the fighting dogs was busy taking bets, and so he did not notice when the boys surreptitiously threw the dogs half a dozen lumps of meat before creeping away. Soon the snarling died away as the dogs settled down to devour the meat. It did not take long for the powdered fish berries to take effect. One by one the dogs lay down and put their heads on their paws, yawning and sighing. Some began to snore.

It was more difficult to reach Sweetheart. Luka had to clamber over the fence, first folding his coat over the sharp points of the stakes. Luckily a thick mist had begun to drift in over the town – Emilia would have called it magic – and so no one saw him. He crept right up to Sweetheart, talking softly to her as he wrestled with the lock that chained her leg to the stake. He had practised all afternoon with the lock pick Fairnette's father had made for him, but it was much more difficult to pick a lock in the dark and the mist, with a disgruntled six-hundred-pound bear growling at the other end of the chain, than it was in the light of the day.

He gave the slender little hook another wriggle and suddenly the padlock clicked open. Luka was able to hastily unfasten it from the chain and quickly creep away.

Shouting and jostling, the audience began to call for some action. The dog-man drank down his beer and swaggered across to the cart. When he found his dogs sleeping, he cursed and began to lay about him with his whip. The dogs yelped and staggered to their feet, and he dragged them from the cart towards the bear-pit.

Sweetheart growled. The dog-man clambered over the fence, seized the chain that hung from the ring in Sweetheart's nose and gave it a vicious yank. She reared on to her hind paws and bellowed her displeasure. At once everyone cheered, and Sweetheart snarled and struck out with her paw. The dog-man drove the half-drugged dogs into the bear-pit. With tails slunk between their legs, they staggered around, whining. One even lay down and went back to sleep.

"Poor show!" one man shouted. "What's wrong with your dogs?"

"What kind of bear-baiting is this?"

"Tie some fireworks to their tails, that'll get them jumping!"

Suddenly there was a loud *bang* and *whoosh*. Purplish smoke billowed up from the grass, and sparks sprayed everywhere. Everyone glanced around, startled.

Emilia stepped out of the smoke. She was dressed in her vivid gypsy skirt, with a gaudy scarf tied over her head and big golden hoops in her ears. Her black curls hung down her back. She held her grandmother's crystal ball in one hand. With the other she pointed three fingers at the startled crowd.

"Curse the voices that cry for blood!" Emilia called. "Curse this town, which lives by fire and iron and death! May your foundry crumble to dust and ashes."

The crowd stood still, shocked and afraid.

Emilia turned her pointing fingers towards the dog-man. "Curse the hand that strikes a poor dumb beast!

May you feel the sting of the whip, the bite of the chain."

He stumbled backwards, terrified. At once Sweetheart lunged forward, lashing out with her sharp claws. Shrieking, the dog-man stumbled back and fell over one of his huge, pug-faced mastiffs. The dog snapped at him. The dog-man screamed, wrenched his leg away and ran, limping, the dogs snarling and leaping at his heels. The crowd shrank away.

Emilia was as shocked as anyone. She had not expected her curse to work quite so quickly. Her hand sought the comfort of the charms hanging from her bracelet. Golden crown, silver horse, the sprig of rue. . .

"Seize her!" Coldham strode out of the crowd, flanked by burly soldiers. "We have the little witch now!"

Emilia's fingers touched the last of her charms, the unfamiliar serrated shape of the lightning bolt charm. Her hand flashed up again. She pointed her three stiff fingers directly at the thief-taker and cried, at the top of her voice, "And I curse you, Coldham. With fire you fought, and so with fire you shall be struck down!"

Luka, hidden in the crowd, at once threw more handfuls of saltpetre into the flickering flames of the torches, while Van ignited another smoke bomb. Again there was a loud *whoosh*. Sparks flew high, and acrid smoke billowed out, obscuring Emilia from sight. She ran forward and seized Sweetheart's chain, drawing her away.

People were screaming and running in all directions.

Coldham stood, pale-faced and sweating, struck dumb with terror.

Emilia wrapped her black shawl about her waist, trying to hide the rose-pink and crimson of her multi-layered skirt, and dragged her grandmother's gilt-threaded scarf away from her hair, shoving it into her pocket too.

Those smoke bombs Van made for us really worked! Emilia thought exultantly. *Now all we have to do is get away from here.*

Emilia ran as fast as she could into the darkness and the mist. Sweetheart ran beside her, glad to get away from the smell of smoke and dogs. Behind her she heard shouts and the thud of running feet. Emilia recognized Coldham's voice and ran faster. Then her foot fell into a pothole, and she stumbled and fell to her knees. A big hand seized her elbow.

"If it's not our little *gule romni*," a familiar voice murmured in her ear.

Emilia swung round in fury. "You sold us out!" she hissed. "How could you?"

Felipe made a deprecating sound. "Don't take it so hard, my wean. With one behind you cannot sit on two horses, you know that. I did what I could to save my family."

"What about mine?" Emilia was trying hard to hold back her tears, but her voice quivered so much, she knew Felipe heard them.

"I'm sorry about your family, little one, but what could I do? Coldham is a bad man to cross."

"May he burn in hell!"

"Is that another curse? I swear you made my blood run cold with those curses of yours, my little *shuvani*. Will it come true, what you said to him?"

"I don't know," Emilia said. "Words have power. Maybe."

"Well, I just hope you don't ever curse me, Emilia Finch."

"May you pay for your shame!" Emilia flashed.

There was a brief silence, then Felipe let go of her elbow. "Who am I to stop a Rom from running where she wills? Go, little one. I'll try to throw them off the scent."

Emilia did not hesitate. With a little jerk to the chain, she was off and running again, Sweetheart bounding beside her.

"No little girl here!" Felipe called loudly. "I think they've slipped your net again, Coldham!"

"I'll see that girl hang," Coldham replied nastily. "And you too, you dirty gyp, if you don't find her!"

"I swear, she must've slipped through a crack in the ground and gone down to find her master," Felipe said, in mock-piousness. "For she's not to be found anywhere!"

"Kindle some fire!" Coldham shouted. "Let us have some light here!"

"Are you sure that's wise, Coldham?" Felipe said, very coolly. "Given her curse and all?"

There was a long moment of silence. Emilia quirked

her mouth up in a rueful smile. She could not help liking Felipe.

Fairnette was waiting for her with a pony and cart on the road out of Horsmonden. She held the pony steady while Emilia coaxed Sweetheart up into the cart, covering her with straw. Moments later, Luka and Van slipped out of the mist, flushed and excited.

"I can't believe you got the bear away," Van said. "I never thought your plan would work, Emilia!"

"I had my doubts as well," she said drily. "We could never have done it without your smoke bombs."

"They're so easy to make! It's just sugar and saltpetre which I scraped off the floor of our henhouse," Van said exuberantly.

"They did the job beautifully," Luka said. "And how about those flames! Zizi was terrified." He patted the bulge in his coat, where the little monkey cowered.

"Thank you so much for helping us," Emilia said.

"Thank *you*!" Fairnette hugged her goodbye, and then the two Smith children ran back into the darkness. Luka clicked his tongue and slapped the reins on the pony's rump, and the old mare ambled down the road.

"Criminy, but I can see that lock pick coming in useful!"

"And we've got four of the charms now."

"And maybe we can find that lawyer fellow the Graylings girl married," Luka said. "A lawyer could be just what we need!"

Emilia thought of the last of the charms, the butterfly

in amber. It meant change and transformation, Maggie had said. It made her heart leap with hope.

The cart crested a high hill and came to a crossroads. There was a way-stone, with a big letter carved so deep into it they could see it even in the dark, and an arrow pointing to the north. Emilia had never learnt to read but she had seen this letter on way-stones before. It looked like a man sitting down, at ease, his legs stretched out before him. It stood for London, she knew, where everyone was so rich they rode about in carriages, instead of on their own two feet.

She smiled.

PART FIVE

The Butterfly in Amber

Falling Down London Bridge

London, England
29 August 1658

"There's London Bridge!" Luka cried. "We're almost there, at last!"

A great stone edifice loomed over them. Shops lined the street, each with houses piled on top, higgledy-piggledy, with gables and windows and chimneys that filled the air with a brown haze of smoke. People were walking home from the evening service, dressed in their best Sunday black. The men all wore tall, stiff hats that mimicked the shape of church steeples, while the women hid their hair under flat white caps.

Stern glances were cast at Emilia and Luka, for travelling was not permitted on the Sabbath. Puritans were not permitted to cook or clean or wash their dishes, or cut wood, or even make their beds. Once upon a time everyone had been allowed to relax and enjoy their one day of rest in the week, as long as they attended church services first, but now any kind of activity at all was forbidden on the Sabbath. You could not even shave your chin, or clip your toenails.

The children exchanged quick glances and slid down from the cart, not wanting to draw any attention to themselves. Sweetheart stirred and sat up, straw falling away from her bulk. "Sssh, Sweetheart, down, Sweetheart," Emilia murmured. Grumpily the old bear lay down again.

"Stupid old bear," Luka said. "I wish we didn't have to drag her about with us everywhere."

Emilia bit back a sharp retort, reminding herself that both she and Luka were exhausted from eighteen days of constant running and hiding, and weighed down with worry over their families. It was harder for Luka, though. She had all her faith invested in the magic of the chain of charms, but Luka had no such comfort. He thought the fate of his family rested solely in his hands and, if he could not come up with some way to rescue them, they would all die.

We'll find the butterfly in amber, don't you worry, Emilia promised her family silently. *Somehow. . .*

The cart passed under the heavy portcullis. Screeching birds wheeled overhead. Emilia looked up, only to recoil in horror.

Impaled on long sticks on top of the gate were a number of grotesque human heads, some no more than bone and gaping cavities, others still covered with rotting flesh, their long thin hair blowing in the breeze.

The smell was foul. Emilia gagged and pressed her hand over her mouth.

"Come to London-Town for work, have we, sweetie?" an impudent young man shouted. "I hear the Keeper of the Heads needs a hand. I could recommend you?"

One of his friends howled with laughter. "Bad choice of words! The Keeper of the Heads has too many hands up there already, and legs and feet too. Watch out one doesn't fall on you!"

Emilia shuddered, and the young men laughed again. Luka urged the pony on, and Emilia gasped, "What did they mean? Hands are up there too, and feet?"

"Traitors are cut into four, and a limb placed on every gate into the city," Luka said flatly. "Didn't you know?"

Emilia shook her head.

"That's what would have happened to our friend the marquis if they'd caught him," Luka said. "Hanged, drawn and quartered."

"Aye, I'd heard that, but I didn't realize. . . They'd have cut him in four?"

"Eventually," Luka said drily. He would have said more, but one look at Emilia's face stopped him. "Don't you worry, all our friends got away safely."

"Cromwell's head will be stuck up like that one day," Emilia said. "They'll dig him up and cut off his head and stick it on a stake."

"How can you say such things?" he hissed. "Do you want to be taken for a witch? Hush your mouth."

Emilia shut her mouth and did not speak again. *Luka*

is right, she thought. She must learn not to blurt out the things she mysteriously knew to be true. She must learn when it was wise to speak, and when it was wiser to hold her tongue.

The cart moved out into sunshine, crossing a wooden drawbridge that rattled under the hooves of their pony. With nothing but flimsy wooden railings on either side of them, Emilia was able to have her first view of London. She gasped. It spread as far as the eye could see on the opposite bank of the river, narrow hovels of timber and straw leaning up against great churches and mansions of stone, which in turn jostled against warehouses and wharves with tall peaked roofs. The water of the Thames rushed through the arches of the bridge, a long way down.

Then the view of the city was cut off as the cart moved into a narrow, dark tunnel, the buildings on either side leaning together and arm-wrestling for space. The hair on Emilia's neck prickled. "I don't like it. Can't we go back?"

Luka glanced back. Marching quickly behind them was a company of soldiers. He bit his lip and seized their pack, clicking his tongue to Zizi and grabbing Sweetheart's chain.

"What are we going to do?" Emilia slithered to the ground, Rollo leaping down behind her.

"I don't know. Hide? If we get into one of those shops, maybe. . ."

People had begun to exclaim at the sight of the huge

old bear clambering reluctantly down from the cart. Luka and Emilia glanced around for somewhere to hide, but it was too late. The soldiers had seen them.

"There they are!" one shouted. "Seize them!"

Clinging to Sweetheart's chain, Luka dodged and weaved through the crowd, Emilia at his heels. Hands seized Luka's coat and almost dragged him off his feet. Zizi leapt out, clawing and biting. The soldier yelped and let go, and Luka ran on.

"Stop or I'll shoot!" a soldier cried.

Everyone shrank back against the walls or threw themselves down. There was nothing between Luka and the tense black mouth of the pistol but a span of air.

Luka somersaulted over the nearest shop counter. He landed with a thump and was on his feet in an instant. Sweetheart clambered after him, sending vials and bottles of precious spices crashing to the floor. A man in a white turban wrung his hands and wailed. Luka had no time to listen.

A pistol shot rang out. Time seemed to slow. Then Luka was knocked flying by a big, hairy shape. Rollo! An instant later Emilia was diving across the counter, smashing all the bottles Luka had somehow managed to miss.

"Hurt?"

"Nay!"

"Let's get out of here!"

"How?"

Luka glanced around wildly. He saw a long, dark,

narrow room, the floor covered in smithereens of glass, dried leaves, flowers, bark, dust. The furious face of a dark-skinned merchant. Beyond, a small window out to the river, a trapdoor in the rush-strewn floor, and a ladder to the rooms above. Luka seized the handle of the trapdoor and hauled it up. Below, far below, torrents of water raged through the narrow archway.

He had time only to glance back and see soldiers framed in the dark wood of the shop-front, pistols raised. Luka gulped and looked at Emilia. She shrugged, then dived through the trapdoor, down, down, down towards the river. Luka heaved Rollo after her, and the big dog went tumbling down, howling in dismay. Luka crossed his arm protectively over Zizi, then jumped, his other arm dragging at Sweetheart's chain. Sweetheart leapt too, a huge black shadow crashing down upon him.

Luka could do nothing but fall.

He smashed into the water, and was driven deep under the wild white rapids. All the breath burst out of his lungs. Sweetheart hurtled after him, blotting out all the light and air. Luka saw her go past him in a burst of bubbles. He swam for the surface, feeling the remorseless drag of the tide on his body. His legs weighed like lead. His head burst free of the water, and was sucked down again immediately. Luka fought his way up again, and managed a quick gulp of air.

Zizi scrambled up his body and perched on his head. Her weight, slight as it was, pushed him down under the water. Then Sweetheart burst out beside him, swimming strongly. Luka hauled on her chain and managed to grab her collar. Sweetheart dragged him clear of the stone arches, water gushing all about. Desperately he looked for Emilia.

At first Luka saw nothing. Then he saw Rollo's wet, sleek head held high. Beside him was Emilia, struggling to keep her head above water, her hand on the dog's neck. Sweetheart swam back towards Emilia, who grabbed weakly at the thick collar. The bear turned and swam for the far shore, the two children towed along behind. Rollo dog-paddled behind.

Gasping, shivering, water gushing from their clothes, the two children crawled out of the river, still clinging to the collar of the huge old bear.

"Sweetheart," Luka said hoarsely, coughing up river water. "I will never call you stupid again!"

Boatmen on the river lifted their oars and waved, laughing, while workmen on the busy wharves leant down and shouted at them in high good humour. Emilia and Luka ignored them, too busy trying not to cut their feet on the barnacles that encrusted the rocks.

"What a good bear you are," Emilia said, letting Sweetheart haul her up the steep steps. "You saved us, you good girl."

Luka patted her muzzle. "Just as soon as I can, I'll get you a whole bucket of ale!"

Sweetheart's eyes brightened at the word. She surged up on to the wharf, looking around for the promised treat.

"I'll have to get us some money first. We're broke!" They did their best to wring the water out of their clothes and hair. "Criminy, but I'm cold! We'd better try and find some shelter, Milly. Night's coming on."

Emilia suddenly remembered her charm bracelet. Checking quickly, she was greatly relieved to find it was still safe upon her wrist. "Imagine if it'd fallen off into the river!"

"Lucky! Zizi darling, I know you're cold. We'll try and find a fire somewhere where we can get warm and dry again."

They hurried along the wharf, damp and shivering. Everyone they passed turned to stare. Someone barged past Emilia, knocking her arm, and disappeared into the crowd. Emilia groped at her wrist in sudden suspicion.

The charm bracelet was gone.

Emilia gasped. Frantically she dragged back her sleeve and shook her arm. Her wrist was bare.

Her chest so tight she could not breathe, Emilia spun on her heel, searching the cobblestones behind her, looking all around her in case it had simply slipped off to the ground. There was no sign of it.

"Luka!" she cried. "My charm bracelet! It's gone!"

"What? But you just had it. . ."

"That boy who bumped me. . ." Emilia was finding it hard to breathe. She started forward a few steps, her eyes searching the gloom, but there were people hurrying everywhere, all of them looking the same with their pinched faces and dark coats. Emilia's knees would not hold her. She sat down on the cobblestones and bent her face into her hands. Luka put a clumsy hand on her shoulder.

"I told you to be careful!" he scolded. "You should've hidden it away. These pick-pockets can take a ring off your finger without you even noticing, I told you that."

Emilia could not speak. The shock was too overwhelming. Her brain could not begin to grapple with the consequences. *Baba had trusted . . . all their kin had trusted . . . the charms were irreplaceable . . . how could they rescue their family now?*

"Nothing we can do about it," Luka said. "It's gone now. No point blubbering about it. Come on, Milly, get up."

Emilia only shook her head.

"Come on, Milly, there's nothing we can do." Luka tried to speak gently, but he was tired and damp and cold, and so his voice was sharper than he meant.

Drying her eyes on her sleeve, Emilia got to her feet and trailed disconsolately after him. She still could not believe her charm bracelet had been stolen. It had been so quick, so deft. Every few steps she put her hand up to check, just in case the charm bracelet had miraculously returned. But her wrist remained bare.

Luka asked a few people if they knew where they could find some gypsy folk, but everyone shook their heads and hurried away. Miserably, Emilia thought it was no wonder. She and Luka were bruised and filthy and barefoot, and their animals looked thin and unhappy.

In the countryside, they would have knocked on a cottage door and offered to cut firewood, or tell a fortune, or fix a fence in return for food. There was no wood to cut in the city, no fences to fix, no kind farmer's wife willing to exchange a cup of tea for some harmless gossip and a bright view of the future.

Luka and Emilia began to beg for help.

People pushed past them impatiently, muttering, "No, sorry." A beggar in a tattered Roundhead uniform yelled and shook his walking stick at them. "Get out of here, this is my corner," he shouted. "Go beg somewhere else."

A few streets later, they passed an inn. The smell of hot food wafted out the window, where a woman was stirring a big pot on the fire. The smell made their stomachs growl.

"Do you think they'd give us some food if Sweetheart danced for them?" Luka said.

"It's worth asking," Emilia said hopefully.

Suddenly they were soaked with a deluge of filthy, stinking water. They gasped and cried out, then looked up. A red-faced chambermaid in a frilly white cap was shaking a chamber-pot at them from the window of the upper storey. "Get out of here, you dirty thieving gypsies!" she cried. "We don't want your kind round here."

"We weren't doing any harm!" Luka yelled back. "What did you do that for?"

"Get out of here," she bellowed back. "Go on!

Luka glowered at her, holding his arms out stiffly so the muck could drip down on to the cobblestones. The chambermaid snorted with laughter and banged the casement shut. Luka looked around. Emilia knew he was looking for a rock to throw at the window. His eyes fell on the shelf just inside the kitchen window. There lay a tray of loaves cooling, and a small row of bottles. She waited for him to snatch something and run, feeling a weight of sadness like a stone in her chest. Her Uncle Jacob had always said, "You can't walk straight when the road is bent," but it seemed to her that the road of the Rom was always being twisted awry under their feet.

Luka heaved a deep sigh and turned away, scraping away the worst of the muck and throwing it on the ground. "Come on," he said. Quietly she followed him.

Silently they plodded on down the street, Zizi a shivering ball of wet fur on Luka's shoulder, Sweetheart lumbering behind. Luka generally never walked in a straight and steady line. He always had to find the most dangerous and difficult route anywhere – over stiles and along walls, up a tree and down a vine, on the narrow edge of a gutter, or along a ridgepole. If he had to walk on flat ground, he would skip and run, turn cartwheels or walk on his hands. At the very least, he would put on a funny walk, pretending to sway his hips like his mother, Silvia, or jump up and down and gibber like Zizi. He was always in motion, always laughing and talking and whistling and singing at the top of his voice. Not tonight.

Tonight he dragged his feet along like a donkey going round and round in a treadmill. Emilia followed, so worn out and weary she could have wept. Even Rollo slunk along, his tail between his legs and his ears drooping.

It grew darker. The streets began to empty. The wind nipped at their ankles and insinuated a cold finger down their necks. Something rustled behind them, and they edged closer together. Emilia kept her hand on Rollo's back, her fingers deep in his fur, occasionally sniffing and wiping her eyes with her sleeve.

Then she saw fire shadows leaping against a towering stone wall at the very top of a steep alley. She caught Luka's arm and jerked her head towards it.

"What is it?" she whispered. "It looks like a campfire."

They stood, hesitating, staring at the orange reflections.

"Only one way to find out," Luka said at last, starting forward. "At least we might be able to get warm and dry!"

The Cradle and The Coffin

The campfires were built in the grounds of a great ruin of a cathedral, surrounded by booths and barrows and makeshift huts where, during the day, people sold beer and books and baskets of bread, and brown eggs and muddy potatoes, and green bunches of watercress, and broken tiles, and many other things beside.

Looming high above the seething, fire-lit crowd was the broken hulk of the cathedral, like a massive toppled giant, arms spread wide, its chest weighed down with a ramshackle tower, cross-hatched with tatters of wooden scaffolding. The roof had fallen in at many places, and all the windows were smashed.

Luka and Emilia sidled near the closest fire, tended by a woman as thin as a stick, in a long dress with a hem all bedraggled with mud, and a big grey apron that had a wooden spoon sticking out of its pocket. She was chopping up onions on the top of a wooden barrel.

"We're really cold." Emilia hugged her arms about her. "Can we just warm ourselves by your fire?"

"Guess so," the woman said. "Don't think you can go pinching anything off me. Got nothing to pinch."

"We wouldn't steal anything! We've just been robbed ourselves. It's a really mean thing to do to someone."

"Robbed, were you? Not surprising, couple of country bumpkins like you."

Emilia sat down wearily and stretched her hands to the blaze. Her legs ached.

"How come the church is all wrecked?" Luka asked, swinging Zizi down from his shoulder.

"It was hit with lightning, you know, years ago, but the king was going to pay for it to be fixed out of his own pocket. Then the war came, and the Roundheads nicked the funds and chopped up all the pews for firewood. They even baptized a foal in the font! A thousand years the cathedral's been here, and now look at it!" She flung the chopped vegetables into the pot and swung it over the fire. "It's a crying shame, I say."

Emilia let the woman's voice wash over her. Although she was so tired her bones seemed to ache inside her skin, needle-sharp anxiety twisted inside her. *I've lost the chain of charms.* Tears stung her eyes, and she blotted them away with her sleeve.

Luka gazed longingly at the pot, which was beginning to smell, if not exactly appetizing, at least a little like food. The thin woman scowled and hunched her shoulder. "Warm enough yet?"

"We need to earn some money," Luka said. "Do you think the people round here would pay us if our bear danced for them?"

The woman looked them over. "Maybe."

"She's very funny," Emilia said. "Especially when she dances with the monkey."

"We could all do with something to laugh about," the thin woman said. "Heavens knows life has given us enough to weep over."

Luka looked about, making sure there were no soldiers about. He knew the risk they ran performing in public again, but they had spent all their money on the stage-coach to Southampton, and it had been many hours since they last ate. He had to make some money somehow.

"I wish I had my fiddle," he said unhappily. His eyes fell on the barrel that the woman had been cutting onions on. He rapped it with his knuckles. It boomed in a deeply satisfying way. "Can I borrow your barrel? And some wooden spoons?"

She frowned. "What's in it for me?"

"The pleasure of knowing you're helping two poor little orphans," Emilia said.

The woman guffawed with laughter.

"I'll give you some of whatever we earn," Luka said. "But only if you give us some soup first; we're starving."

"And what if all you get is stones and curses?" she demanded.

"Then you'll get a fair cut of those," he answered at once, and she laughed again.

317

"Fair enough, I suppose." The woman, whose name was Annie, gave them each a bowlful of the thin, tasteless stew. They ate ravenously, then put the half-empty bowls down for the animals to share. It was not nearly enough, but it was better than nothing, and at least it was hot.

Then Luka dragged out a few of the barrels into the light, and sat, experimenting with Annie's wooden spoons, enjoying making music again, no matter how primitive. Annie sat and listened, nodding her head and tapping her toe. A few people nearby stopped and listened too.

Sweetheart's eyes brightened. She knew that music meant dancing, and dancing meant praise and plenty of ale. She rose ponderously on to her hind legs and began to sway to the music. Then Zizi swung down and scampered over to meet her, holding up one tiny paw. Sweetheart bent down and took it, and the bear and the monkey danced clumsily together. Round and round they went, one so great and heavy, the other so little and light. Zizi spun and pirouetted and turned deft cartwheels, and Sweetheart tried her best to copy her. The watchers roared with laughter and applauded vigorously. Soon a large crowd had gathered, and coins were clinking into Luka's hat.

Emilia stared into the fire, hearing the drumming as if from a great distance. She felt very light, almost as if she was not her own self, but merely the thin, crooked shadow she cast on the ground. Flames roared in her ears, filled her eyes.

She saw the cathedral burning, flames as tall as the sky, devouring the stones as if they were dry leaves. She saw the whole city burning, churches and palaces and shops and the narrow, huddled hovels of the poor, all consumed in a great conflagration that destroyed everything in its path. The stench of ash and brimstone was in her nostrils; she heard the sharp crackle and snap of the flames, and the shrill cries and screams of the dying.

Emilia shut her eyes. The *boom-boom-boom* of the drums filled her ears. She wanted to wrench her mind away from this dreadful vision of disaster, she wanted to bury her head in her arms, and thrust her fingers in her ears.

Instead she thought of her family. *Show me. . .* she begged.

She saw Beatrice, weeping. She saw her grandmother hunched over, the whites of her eyes quivering in the slit of her half-shut eyelids. She saw Noah coughing, coughing, coughing, a bloody rag held to his lips. She saw her uncle, holding him up so he could breathe. She saw her aunt, wan and filthy, trying to drive off a pack of rats. Then she saw the door of the cell open, and the shadow of the pastor fall upon the floor, like an accusing finger. Emilia heard a dull clang, as if of a funeral bell. . .

"Wake up, Milly!" Luka cried. "Look, we got quite a few coins, and I've bought us some bread and cheese, and a bottle of elderflower wine. You know how Baba loves that. Annie says we can doss down here for the night, and maybe earn more in the morning. . ."

Emilia blinked and looked about her. The crowd had drifted away, and Sweetheart had her muzzle thrust in a large jug of ale, slurping it down with pleasure. Zizi was perched on Luka's shoulder, cracking a nut with her sharp teeth, and Rollo was asleep at her feet. The only light came from the fire, which had fallen into coals.

"What's wrong?" Luka asked.

"We've got to go on. We haven't got time to be sleeping. We've got to find Mala Graylings."

"But it's late. It's black as the Devil's waistcoat out there."

"I'm just afraid that if we stop and sleep, we'll lose our chance," Emilia said. "We really only have tomorrow to find her, else we'll never get back to Kingston in time."

"But I'm so tired," Luka said, sitting back on his heels. "And we can make money here. . ."

"We need to get out of the city," Emilia said. "Coldham will be on our trail."

"But the city's so huge, how could he find us?" Luka said, even though he knew as well as Emilia did that their menagerie made them conspicuous, and Coldham seemed to have friends – or at least fellow-spies – all over the country.

"I just know we need to get moving," Emilia said.

Luka sighed and put his hat back on his head. He swung Zizi up to his shoulder. "Safer that way, anyway," he said.

"You heading off again?" Annie said in surprise, looking up from the coins she was counting in her hand.

"You know us gypsies, we can never rest," Emilia said, attempting to smile.

"Have you seen any gypsies roundabouts?" Luka asked, settling the pack on his shoulder.

"Heard there's a mortal lot of gypsies out at St Giles," Annie answered.

"Could you show us where that is?" Emilia begged, and Annie drew them a rough map in the mud. She backed away when Emilia and Luka bent down close to see, wrinkling her nose.

"You'll have to run if you want to get out the city gates tonight," she said.

"Thank you for letting us sit by your fire," Emilia said in a small, forlorn voice, and helped Luka haul Sweetheart to her feet. The bear had been quite comfortable by the fire, and did not want to leave. They had to tug hard on her nose-ring before at last she lumbered after them, complaining every step of the way.

The streets were dark and quiet and scary. Emilia was glad of Sweetheart's bulk, and Rollo's swift strength. A fog was rolling in from the river, smelling of frog-slime and fish-eggs. It bandaged their eyes and gagged their mouths. Walking through it was like a game of blind man's bluff. Only the clatter of Rollo's claws on the cobblestones stopped them from bumping into walls.

"I see a lantern ahead," Luka said, peering through the mist. "It's hung high. Do you think it's the city gate?"

"Could be," Emilia said. "Come on."

They hurried forward, holding hands. Church bells began to toll the curfew. Luka and Emilia broke into a run. The glow of the lantern was blurred by the fog, but by its indistinct light they could see a large gate being dragged shut by the hunched shapes of two men.

"Wait!" Luka hollered. With Sweetheart lumbering along behind, and Rollo bounding ahead, they ran full-pelt down the hill, Zizi clutching on to Luka's flying hair with both paws. The watchmen paused and stood aside, letting them run through before closing the gate behind them. They heard the bolts being slammed home.

"We're safe now," Luka said.

"With any luck," Emilia answered. Without thinking, she put her hand up to touch her charm bracelet, only to feel her wrist bare and bony. She let her hand fall, and trudged after Luka, her heart aching.

St-Giles-in-the-Fields had grown up around a leper hospital, Annie had told them, which had been built out in the marshes to keep the lepers away from the city. But St Giles was the patron saint of beggars and cripples as well as lepers, and so the church had a reputation for charity towards those who were stoned out of town elsewhere.

So of course gypsies ended up here as well, Emilia thought bitterly.

The village was a dark maze of alleys and laneways, courtyards and cobbled squares. Emilia was so tired it seemed as if she wandered in a nightmare. The air smelt of cinders and cesspits. Slimy things squelched under her bare feet. In the thin ray of light from the lantern, she saw the damp, crooked walls of ramshackle houses, a rat dragging a dismembered hen, a runnel of green slime, piles of old gnawed bones and filthy rags, and scuttling cockroaches.

"This is a fool's errand," Luka muttered. "We could've been sleeping by the fire, getting back our strength. What are we doing wandering round this hell-hole at midnight?"

"Sweetheart will keep us safe." Emilia's voice shook, and she took a deep shuddering breath. She felt small and vulnerable. Her left wrist was too light and bare, the absence of her charm bracelet weighing her down as the chain had never done. Footsore, heart-sore and unutterably weary, Emilia trudged on.

The only light came from lanterns hung outside the doors of the inns, illuminating the shabby signs that hung above the step. The inns all seemed to be called something black, like the Black Jack or the Black Lamb.

An old man was hunched over a fire, toasting what looked like a rat.

"Seen any gypsies?" Luka called.

"Try the Cradle and the Coffin," he called back, and jerked his thumb down a side-street.

"I hope that's the name of an inn," Luka muttered, and

they went nervously down the alley into a dark square where the rickety wooden buildings all leant upon each other's shoulders like melancholy drunks.

"There's an inn," Emilia whispered. By the light at the front door, she saw the inn sign hanging above it. It was roughly painted with a picture of a cradle and a coffin. Lying in the doorway was a bundle of noisome rags. Then the pile of rags stirred, and mumbled.

The children inched closer, their breath tight in their chests.

It was an old woman. She looked about two hundred. Her skin was scrunched and spotted like old parchment, and two massive, hairy moles sprouted from her chin. She half-woke as the light shone in her face, and cracked open an eye like a toad's, dark and protuberant between brown, leathery lids. She winced away and muttered something, showing rotten, diseased gums where only a few broken teeth remained. She wore three vivid skirts of different colours, and so Luka and Emilia knew at once she was a Romni.

"Sar'sharn, Baba?" Luka whispered the traditional Romany greeting.

At once the old woman cracked open her eyes. "Si'n Rom?"

"Aye, we're Rom. We're looking for one of our kin. Baba Mala Graylings."

She stared at them suspiciously. "What do you want me for?"

Emilia squatted down on the cobblestones. "Greetings

to you, Baba Mala," she said softly. "We're your kin, the grand-weans of Maggie Finch."

"So?" The old woman hunched down again.

Luka had an idea. "Look, Baba Mala, I have a present for you." He found the bottle of elderflower wine, yanked free the cork and offered it to the old woman. Her face lit up; she seized the bottle and gulped down a few mouthfuls. She wiped her mouth with satisfaction, and said, rather indistinctly because of her lack of teeth, "What you want?"

"We want to ask you about your amber charm, the one with the butterfly in it." Although Emilia's charm bracelet was gone, she could not help hoping it would somehow, magically, be restored to her. Besides, she reasoned, even if it was gone for ever, surely she should not give up looking for the last charm. One lucky charm was better than none.

The old woman spat. "Fancy took it."

"Fancy? Your daughter?"

"Little snake."

"Your daughter took your charm?" Emilia asked. "Where is she now?"

The old woman glanced at her sideways, then had another swig from the bottle. "Fancy gone."

"Where has Fancy gone?"

The old woman rocked back and forth, muttering. Her grey hair hung in rats' tails, so thin they could see the bluish colour of the skin beneath. She held the flask to her lips and drank down the last of the liquid, shaking it to try and get the last drops.

"We heard she'd married a lawyer. Is that true?"

"Fancy thinks she's too good for her poor old ma. Stole my charm and my crystal ball, and ran off to marry a *gorgio*. Haven't seen her in years."

"Do you know the name of the *gorgio*?" Luka asked.

"What you want her for?" the old woman said. "She's no good, I've told you that."

"We need the charm," Emilia said, at exactly the same moment that Luka said, "We need a lawyer."

They made a face at each other, then Luka went on, "I don't want to spend the rest of our lives afraid of being caught and dragged back to gaol. It'd be better if we could find some way to get them out legally – or at least, with the appearance of being legal. . ."

"If you would tell us about your daughter?" Emilia begged. "Did she really steal your charm? Why? What did she do with it? And did she really marry a lawyer?"

Mala snorted. "Much good it did her. As much good as it'll do you. He's as blue-nosed as they come."

"What was his name?" Luka asked desperately.

"Pure something or other. Henry Purefoyle. Pure by name and pure by reputation, I've heard," Mala said. "Not that I've ever met him. Too good for the likes of me."

"But she took the charm from you, the butterfly in amber? You're sure?" Emilia asked.

Mala nodded. "Aye, she took it, when she was not much older than you. I hope it brought her luck, is all I can say. I certainly haven't had any since it was gone."

Emilia sighed and looked at Luka questioningly.

"I guess we need to try and find her, if we can," he said. "We have only one day left before we need to head back to Kingston. It's worth a try, I guess."

"I know where Henry Purefoyle lives," Mala said unexpectedly. "He lives near Gray's Inn, not so very far from here. All the lawyers live round there, near the Inns of Court. You could be there in less than half an hour, if you walked swiftly."

"I'm so tired I don't think I can walk another step," Emilia said.

"It's either walk out of this place, or spend the night sleeping on these disgusting stones," Luka said, getting up with fresh energy. "I say we get out of here and make camp in a field somewhere. Then we can go and find this Henry Purefoyle in the morning. What do you say?"

Emilia's words were swallowed by an enormous yawn. When it was finally over, she said, "Sounds good! As long as we find a field soon. All I want to do is sleep."

"And sleep and sleep and sleep," Luka said. "But not here! In a field somewhere, under the stars. One with a stream so we can scrub away all this filth." He looked back at Mala, rolled once more in her stinking blanket. "I just can't understand it," he said in a low voice.

"She's forgotten her roads," Emilia answered sombrely.

Obedience

Gray's Inn, London, England
30 August 1658

Luka and Emilia lay under a weeping elm tree in a small square fenced with wrought-iron and abutted on all four sides by a road lined with large, gracious houses that all looked exactly the same.

It was a fresh, clear morning with the promise of heat to come. Luka felt much better after a good night's sleep in a haystack, a wash in a stream, and some bread and cheese. Emilia, however, was still drooping with misery over the loss of her charm bracelet.

"At least we've found the lawyer's place," Luka said. "Maybe he'd come and talk to the judges for us, and then we won't need any good luck."

"It's not just that. Baba trusted me! And the others too. How can I tell them I lost their lucky charms?"

"Well, it can't be helped," Luka said impatiently. "Stop sniffling and help me think what to do next. Should we just go up and knock on the door?"

Emilia looked across at the house doubtfully. "It's very grand."

"Look, the door's opening!" Luka flattened himself in the grass.

Out came an elderly woman, sharp and upright as a fence post. Her dress and hood and folded hands were black, and under her stiff white face spread a stiff white collar. Her sharp blue eyes were set so close together, she had to peer down her long, bony nose to see her way. She walked as if her shoes hurt her.

Behind her, in descending size, came three girls, all dressed identically in severe black gowns with white collars and black hoods. The four of them turned one by one to the right and promenaded around the outskirts of the square, in single file, each one exactly three paces behind the other. Their skirts rustled, and their boots made little tapping noises on the pavement.

Luka and Emilia stared.

Then the middle girl trod on the hem of her dress and grimaced as it tore. She gathered up the trailing hem in her hand, revealing tight black button-up boots and black stockings with holes in them. Suddenly, as if feeling their gaze on her, she glanced at the tree. Her eyes widened in astonishment. Sweetheart was peering through the canopy of leaves. Although Luka jerked on the bear's chain so she lay down again, grumbling, the girl continued to stare the whole time the four of them walked round the park and back to their front door.

"It is not so hot today, Aunt Grace," she said, in a

329

clear, refined voice. "May we promenade about the park?"

"Very well, Obedience, but only for a few minutes. You girls are sallow enough as it is; I do not wish for you to get sunburned."

Luka and Emilia glanced at each other, stifling giggles. What had she called the girl? Surely her name could not be Obedience?

Aunt Grace unlatched the gate and settled herself on the bench. The three girls walked demurely about the perimeter of the garden until they were out of sight, behind the weeping tree. Then Obedience seized both of her sisters by the arm and dragged them forward. Three sets of dark brown eyes peered through the leaves at Luka and Emilia, Zizi, Rollo and Sweetheart.

"Gypsy children!" Obedience whispered. "Look! With a bear and a monkey! And what a lovely big dog!"

Rollo beat his tail on the ground, and she bent to pat his head. "I wish we had a dog," she said enviously. "And imagine having a pet monkey!"

"I do not think gypsies are permitted in the park," the elder one said. "We must inform Aunt Grace at once."

The third girl said nothing, just stared, her thumb in her mouth.

"Don't be such a spoilsport, Humility! When are we ever going to get a chance to see a monkey again?"

"I could see a monkey any day of the week, if I wished to go to St Bartholemew's Fair and hobnob with riff-raff," Humility said. "But I have no desire to do any such thing, and neither should you, Obedience."

"We're not riff-raff," Luka said indignantly. "We're your cousins."

"Cousins? How dare you?" Humility said. "We do not have any cousins, and if we did, they would not be grubby little guttersnipes!"

"Who do you think we are?" Obedience asked in lively curiosity.

"The children of the lawyer Henry Purefoyle and the gypsy Fancy Graylings," Emilia replied promptly.

The girls looked puzzled. "Henry Purefoyle is our father. . ." Obedience began.

"But you should call him *Mister* Purefoyle," Humility struck in.

"But we've never heard of a gypsy called Fancy," Obedience finished. "Our mother is named Faith."

"What peculiar names you all have," Luka said. "Are you really called Obedience?"

"They are not peculiar names; they are excellent, god-fearing Puritan names," Humility said, her nose in the air.

"They could have been worse," Obedience said. "We have friends called Meek, and Lamentation, and one called Tribulation." She giggled. "Imagine being called Tribulation!"

"You are a tribulation," her elder sister said sternly.

Obedience laughed again. "What are your names?"

"Emilia and Luka," they answered.

"How heathenish," Humility said condescendingly. "Far more peculiar than ours."

Luka scowled. He liked their names. At least they were not completely inappropriate. As far as he could see, Humility was not at all humble, Obedience was not at all obedient, and Aunt Grace was far from graceful.

"What's the little one called?" Emilia said, smiling at the thumb-sucker.

Obedience grinned. "Justice."

Poor little thing, Emilia thought. But she smiled and said, "I have a brother just your size called Noah. And Luka has a little sister called Mimi. Are you called Justice? Or do they have a love-name for you?"

Justice did not reply, just sucked her thumb harder.

"We call her Cherub," Obedience said. "And I'm usually called Beedee. We don't shorten Humility's name, though; she doesn't like it."

"Humility! Obedience! Justice!" Their aunt's voice rang through the square. "What are you doing?"

"Coming, Aunt Grace," Obedience sang. As her sisters hurried away, she bent and hissed at them. "Come to the back gate in half an hour and I'll let you in. I want to hear more about this so-called kinship of ours. I always *knew* there was a mystery about my mother!"

Half an hour later, Luka and Emilia waited nervously outside the back gate. Obedience let them in with her finger at her lips. Like her sisters, she was a plain child, skinny and sallow, but her eyes were sparkling with such mischief Luka and Emilia felt a stir of kindred spirit.

"I thought you could hide the bear in the shed," she whispered. "Will she make a fuss?"

"Got any honey?" Luka whispered back.

Obedience made a face and shook her head.

"Anything sweet? Fruit cake?"

"Not allowed anything sweet. Devil's food."

"So I'm guessing no ale?"

Obedience snorted. "Of course not. We drink asses' milk, or water."

"Even your father?" Emilia was amazed.

"Especially my father."

"Got any food at all? Fish?"

"I'll see what I can find. Wait here." Obedience pushed them inside a small, dark shed that smelt unpleasantly of the compost heap outside. She was back some time later with a string of fish, their scales gleaming softly in the dimness.

"What's it like having a pet bear?" Obedience asked, as they settled Sweetheart down on some sacks, attaching her chain to a hook on the wall.

"Lovely," Emilia said.

Luka said gravely, "She saved our lives yesterday. If it wasn't for Sweetheart, we would have drowned."

"Really?" Obedience was fascinated. "And you have a monkey too. Isn't she sweet? She looks just like a little baby. . ."

"Only much hairier," Emilia said.

333

Obedience giggled. "What fun," she said. "Will she stay out here too, with the bear?"

"No, she'd shriek till I came back," Luka said. "She always stays with me."

Obedience looked dubious. "She won't get into any mischief, will she? I mean, not that I mind, it'd be great fun to see her. It's just that I'd be whipped if it's discovered I've brought a monkey into the house. Though, mind you, I'll be whipped if they discover you too."

Luka assured Obedience that Zizi would stay close to him. "She does everything I tell her to," he boasted, which made Emilia roll her eyes.

The lawyer's house was tall, dark and narrow, and smelt of soap. Obedience did not need to lay her finger on her lips to keep them quiet. Luka and Emilia were quite overawed by the heavy silence of the house. They tiptoed down the hall, Rollo's claws clicking so loudly on the wooden floorboards that Obedience turned an agonized face towards them. She eased open a door and they ducked into a large, book-lined room dominated by a huge desk covered in neat piles of paper. Framed documents were hung all over the walls, and there was a large glass case hanging near the fire in which dead butterflies of all colours and sizes were pinned. Another glass case held rocks and bits of dead wood, all neatly arranged and labelled.

A small fire flickered on the hearth. It brought warmth and comfort to the room, and at once Luka went to stand in front of it. Rollo flopped down at his feet, sighing in contentment.

"Father's library," Obedience said in a low voice. "They'll never look for me here, because they'd never believe I'd dare to come in. Father's library is strictly out-of-bounds."

"So do you come in here often?" Luka said with a grin.

Obedience grinned back. "All the time. I like to read Father's books, and look at his maps. He's hardly ever here; he's always at Gray's Inn, or at the palace."

"At the palace? How come?"

"He's a lawyer, you know," Obedience said. "He was one of those that prosecuted the tyrant Charles Stuart. His Highness relies on him greatly."

"So he's one of Old Ironsides' . . . I mean, the Lord Protector's men?" Luka was filled with dismay. *There goes any chance of him helping us*, he thought.

"Indeed, one of his right-hand men," Obedience said proudly, noticing nothing. "But enough of my father. Tell me why you have conceived this strange notion that my mother is a gypsy? Indeed she is the most boring, godly woman you could ever imagine. She does nothing but sew and reads nothing but the Bible, and even then only at random to see what advice it gives her."

Emilia opened her eyes, sudden excitement giving her new energy. "That sounds like she foretells the future through the Bible. How?"

"It's not exactly foretelling, is it? I mean, all she does is let the Bible fall open and put her finger on a verse."

"Do you know much about your mother's childhood?" Emilia asked. Luka fidgeted, the loud ticking of the clock on the mantelpiece reminding him of time scurrying away.

Obedience shrugged. "Nothing. That's why I said she was a bit of a mystery. She never mentions her family, and neither does my father. I had always supposed she had a deadly dull, deadly respectable upbringing, just like ours, except that she never talks about it. Aunt Grace is always telling us about how good *she* was as a child."

"Do you know her maiden name?"

"Grey," Obedience said. "Her name was Faith Grey. Could it get any more tedious?"

Fancy Graylings. Faith Grey. There was just enough of an echo for Emilia's interest to quicken. "Have you ever seen her with a small yellow jewel, a piece of amber?"

"Jewellery? My mother? Of course not! She will not even have buttons on her clothes in case anyone thinks she's vain."

"It can't be her," Luka said. "Come on, Emilia, let's go. It's a wild goose chase. She isn't Fancy, she doesn't have the amber charm, and her husband isn't going to help a couple of grubby gypsy brats. He's more likely to turn us in. Let's get out of here while we still can."

"But can't I help?" Obedience said. "If it's legal advice you need, I know nearly as much as Father, really I do."

"We do need help. Our families are in gaol, and come Monday morning, are facing the court. We need to get them out!"

"Why are they in gaol?" Obedience asked. "What have they done?"

In fits and starts they told her, trying not to reveal too much about their adventures. Obedience was enthralled with their tale, however, and asked so many eager questions they ended up telling her nearly the whole story.

"There's lots of things a lawyer could do to try and reduce the sentence," Obedience told them, "but to get the whole family out of gaol, scot-free, and no record against them, that's impossible. It'd take a miracle."

Luka's shoulders sagged.

Emilia put her fingers up to her wrist and was reminded once again, sharply, of her missing charm bracelet. "You must be able to think of something," she said unhappily. "You're so clever, you know so much more than we do. Isn't there something we can do to help our families?"

"No, I'm sorry," Obedience said. "Unless. . ."

"Unless what?" Luka sat up eagerly.

"You could apply to the Lord Protector for a pardon," Obedience said. "He's been known to issue them. Why, my father drew up a whole swathe of pardons for His Highness only a couple of months ago. Look, there are copies here in his desk."

She rummaged through one of the drawers. "It was

after the beheading of Charles Stuart's old chaplain. He was arrested in June, you know, for sheltering the Marquis of Ormonde when he was here in London."

Luka and Emilia both jumped as if stung by a nettle, and exchanged a quick, horrified glance. Luckily Obedience did not notice, still looking through her father's desk. "He was a silly old fool, really, Doctor Hewett. He used to ask his parishioners to remember an 'absent friend' when he passed round the collection plate. Of course he was sending the money to the king! Anyway, he was arrested, along with about forty other Royalists, but Lord Cromwell ended up pardoning half of them. I think everyone in London was sick of watching people being hanged, drawn and quartered! Look, here they are!"

She came up flourishing a pile of thick parchment, affixed with large blobs of red wax in which they could see the imprint of a soldier on a horse.

"That's his signature! Look how shaky it's got. He used to have a bold hand, Father says."

Emilia and Luka looked at the parchment she held out with great interest. It was covered in close lines of ornate black script, like the tracks of a worm with a bellyache. Down the bottom, in a different, frailer hand, was a large sprawling signature with an *O* like a scandalized mouth.

"Well, I can't see Old Ironsides pardoning a whole bunch of gypsies, so I guess we just have to break them out of gaol," Luka said. "Maybe we can burn the whole stupid place down so that they think everyone's dead and won't come chasing after us."

Obedience did not know whether to be shocked or admiring of Luka's boldness. "I wish I could come with you," she said wistfully. "How I'd love an adventure!"

"You'll have adventures of your own, in time," Emilia said, then bit her lip, realizing she'd once again spoken of something she instinctively and mysteriously knew to be true.

But Obedience only sighed. "Most unlikely, I'm afraid."

"We really need to go," Luka said, bending to pick up his pack and swing it to his shoulder. "It's been a complete waste of time coming here."

"Are you sure you haven't seen a little amber stone?" Emilia asked anxiously. "It has a butterfly inside it."

Obedience shrugged. "It sounds like one of my father's fossils. Look, he has a whole table full of them." She waved one hand at the glass display table. "Why do you want it?"

Emilia rubbed her wrist unhappily. "It's the lucky charm of the Graylings family. We thought your mother had it. I've been collecting the charms, you see, hoping they'd . . . well, it makes no difference now, I suppose. My bracelet's gone." She tried to shrug as if she did not care, but it was impossible. "Someone took it."

"Oh, no, really? The pickpockets in London are dreadful, I know. Was it very valuable?"

"It was to me," Emilia said.

"You need to go along to a pawnshop," Obedience said. "The pickpocket would want to get rid of the loot as fast as he could."

"Where would we find this pawnshop?" Luka asked. Emilia was speechless, her spirits bounding with new hope.

Obedience made a face. "How on earth would I know? I daresay there are hundreds of pawnshops in London, if not thousands. I wouldn't know where to begin looking."

Emilia felt a telltale prickling in her eyes and leant over the glass display case, trying to hide her expression.

Displayed within were stones and shells, bones and fossils, each labelled neatly. Emilia's eye was caught by a smooth lump of clear yellow, like solidified honey. Her pulse leapt. About the size of a man's thumbnail, its lucidity was marred by something crooked and dark inside. Something with wings.

"I love that one," Obedience said, leaning over the display case beside her. "Father sometimes lets me take it out and hold it, though only so he can lecture me about the properties of amber. It's meant to be magic, you know. Once it was worth more than gold. Do you know the old story of how amber came to be?"

The children shook their heads, staring longingly at the small lump of stone.

"Phaeton was the son of Apollo the sun god. Every day he watched his father driving the sun-chariot across the sky, and he longed to drive it himself. One day he persuaded his sisters to help him steal his father's chariot, but of course the horses bolted. The sun-chariot came so close to the world that fires blazed up beneath it. It seemed the whole world would be destroyed, but Zeus, the king of the gods, struck Phaeton dead with a thunderbolt. Phaeton's body fell down beside a river, and his sisters were turned into poplars along the river bank. As they wept over the dead body of their brother, their tears fell into the river and became amber."

"That's sad," Emilia said after a moment.

"The Greek myths are always sad."

"Is it true?" Luka asked.

"True? Of course not. Though it illuminates the truth, like so many old stories do. For amber's made from the sap of long-ago trees, turned somehow to stone."

"How did the butterfly get inside it?" Luka asked.

Obedience gave a little shrug. "Father says that once, a very long time ago, the butterfly's feet got caught in the sticky sap. It struggled and struggled, but could not get free. Slowly the sap oozed down over it and trapped it, and then the sap slowly, over many more years, turned into amber. The butterfly is still inside it, trapped for ever."

The children were enchanted and repulsed at the same time.

"The Greeks called amber *elektron*," Obedience continued dreamily, "which means 'the sun'. Amber is always the colour of the sun, whether it is pale yellow like the dawn or orange-red like the sunset. And also

341

because when it is rubbed, it gives off sparks of light. I wish I could get it out to show you."

"Can't we get it out?" Emilia tried to open the lid of the display case, but it was securely locked.

"I don't know where Father keeps the key."

"We could smash the glass," Luka said.

Obedience looked shocked. "Oh, I couldn't do that! I'd get into so much trouble."

"Your father doesn't need to know it was you."

"You want to steal my father's amber!"

"It's not your father's," Emilia said. "It belongs to your grandmother, Mala Graylings."

"I didn't even know I had a grandmother." Obedience sounded dazed.

Just then, Rollo sat up and looked at the door, growling. Emilia looked round and saw the door handle turning. Luka swept up Zizi, Emilia grabbed Rollo by his ruff, and the three children scrambled behind the curtains, just in time.

Can These Bones Live?

Emilia put her eye to the crack where the curtains did not quite close. She just hoped no one could see her.

"I cannot understand it; His Highness seemed so much better on Thursday!" A tall man in a long, dark robe swept impatiently into the room. He had the same large, bony nose of Aunt Grace, with blue eyes under thick frowning brows.

Behind him came a woman in a severe black gown. Her hair was parted in the middle and smoothed back into a sleek coil. Its severity did nothing to detract from her exotic beauty. Everything about her was delicately formed, her skin was the colour of old ivory, and her hair and eyes as black as sable. Emilia had to bite back a gasp of surprise, for Mrs Purefoyle looked very much like her sister, Beatrice. She nudged Luka and he nodded, his face alive with sudden interest.

"I thought we must be over the worst!" Mr Purefoyle

walked with quick, impatient steps to the fire and stood before it, scowling at the hearth-rug. Emilia shrank down, her hand on Rollo's muzzle to keep him quiet.

"So His Highness has taken a turn for the worse?" Mrs Purefoyle shut the door quietly behind her and turned, her hands folded before her.

"Indeed, he is suffering exceedingly. None of us can understand it. This is not the way an ague normally progresses. He has had the usual run of fever and sweating, and should now be recovering. Instead, though, he is in terrible pain. We are all nonplussed."

Emilia gave a little shiver. She could not forget the witch Marguerita Wood, stabbing the little poppet of Cromwell with hatpins, and laughing as she thought of the agony she was causing him. She glanced at Luka, and saw by his face that he was remembering the poppet too. They grimaced at each other.

"Oh, sir, what shall become of us if the Lord Protector should die?"

"Are you so ill-named, my dear? Have faith. Our Lord God has not yet finished with the Lord Protector."

"But, sir, this illness of the Lord Protector's is unnatural. You have said so yourself. I fear. . ."

"You fear some secret assassin?" Mr Purefoyle laughed. "My dear, the Lord Protector wears armour even to bed!"

"Sir, I must tell you . . . I prayed for guidance, and then, when I opened the Bible and laid my finger on the page, it fell upon Ezekiel, chapter thirty-seven, verse three."

"Can these bones live?" her husband murmured, much struck.

"So you see why it is I fear that the Lord Protector may not survive this sickness of his. Sir, you are the master of this household and I know you have a care for us all. But I cannot help but think we must look to the future. I fear what will happen if the king comes back!"

"You may rest easy on that account, my dear," Mr Purefoyle said bitingly. "The king lost his head and his crown together, and the young gentleman, his son, has not the nerve or the money to start another war. I've heard he lives on charity, pawning his watch to pay for bread. How could he afford to raise an army? No need for fear on that account."

He took a turn about the carpet, his hands clasped behind his back. "I must admit I am troubled by what the Bible has told you," Mr Purefoyle said. "You know I scorn such superstitious nonsense, but the Lord moves in mysterious ways and perhaps you are the unworthy instrument of his will. The verse revealed to you is ominous indeed. I think perhaps you are right, my dear, and we must put our house in order."

"I have heard, sir, that there are fortunes to be made in the New World. . ."

"And leave all I have worked for here? I think not!"

"As you see fit, sir. I know you will do what is best for us all." Mrs Purefoyle's head was bent meekly, but Emilia saw how she clenched her hands behind her back.

Emilia had kept her hands clamped close around Rollo's muzzle all this time, trying to keep him quiet, but the conversation had gone on too long and Rollo was tired of it. He gave a small whine, and tried to shake his head free.

"What on earth was that!" Mr Purefoyle exclaimed.

The next instant the curtain twitched back, and the lawyer's hand fell upon Emilia. She and Rollo were dragged out into the centre of the room.

"What is this? A thief? A spy? Call the constables!"

Rollo barked furiously. He lunged at Mr Purefoyle, snarling. The lawyer seized a poker, whacking the big dog across the back. Rollo yelped, and Emilia clung to the lawyer's arm, shouting, "Stop it! Don't hurt him. We weren't doing any harm!"

Luka flung the curtain back and ran to her rescue. Zizi leapt at the lawyer's head, biting his ear savagely. He yelled and flung her away from him. Nimbly she landed on the back of the chair and sprang from there to the mantelpiece. Luka grabbed Emilia's hand and ran for the door, Rollo bounding behind them. Zizi swung from the chandelier to Luka's shoulder, sending hot wax spluttering everywhere.

Luka opened the door with a crash, but the next instant the lawyer's heavy hand fell on their shoulders, dragging them back into the room. He slammed the door shut again and stood against it, his face white with fury.

"Why, I've heard about you," he said. "How many ragamuffin children can be running around the country with a dog and a monkey? I never expected to see the criminals Pastor Spurgeon described in my very own study!"

Luka and Emilia stared at him unhappily.

"Faith, will you go and bring me back something to tie up these thieves? And be quick!"

"Please, we're not thieves!" Emilia spoke quickly. "We're just children. We don't mean any harm."

Mr Purefoyle snorted in disbelief.

"Father, please!" Obedience came out from behind the curtain, looking scared. "These are my friends."

Her father was flabbergasted. "Obedience! What are you doing here? How dare you!"

"I . . . I'm sorry. It was so cold. We wanted to sit by the fire."

"*You* brought them into my study? How dare you?"

"I . . . they're . . . they're sort of long-lost cousins. We needed somewhere quiet to talk."

"Obedience, go to your room. I will deal with you later."

"But, Father. . ."

"Do not argue with me or I'll give you the whipping of your life!"

Obedience did as she was told, casting an unhappy look at Luka and Emilia.

"Please, sir, it's true," Luka said.

"Shut your mouth, boy, else I'll take my belt to you too."

"It's true, really it is. Please, Fancy . . . Mrs Purefoyle!

We came looking for you. We're your kin, really we are. Maggie Finch is our grandmother."

Mrs Purefoyle had been standing immobile, her eyes lowered, her hands set flat against the wall. At Emilia's words they clenched. She gave no other sign of having heard.

"Faith, go and get some rope. Hurry! I think we have ourselves some clever spies here. Who can believe those Cavaliers would stoop so low, using children to sneak about and spy for them!"

In just a few moments, Mrs Purefoyle was back with some kitchen twine. "It was all I could find, sir," she said, bowing her head.

Mr Purefoyle took the twine and made a grimace of disgust at its thinness. In a moment, he had bound Luka and Emilia together, pulling the knots uncomfortably tight.

"I will go and get the constables, my dear," he said. "I may be a while; it is still early and I do not know where they might be. Call Grace to come and help you guard them. I do not trust them not to escape, for indeed they are slippery and sly. Gaining entrance to our house by pretending to be related to us! I am surprised by Obedience. I had not thought her such a fool."

"She is young, sir, and naïve. She has been much protected. What does she know about the trickery of this world?"

Mr Purefoyle sighed. "You are right, my dear. She is

only a child. One cannot expect the wit and wisdom of a man to be found in the empty head of a girl."

"No, sir," Mrs Purefoyle answered, as he went quickly out of the door.

Mrs Purefoyle stood silently, listening. They all heard the sound of his footsteps going down the hall, and the front door opening and shutting. Then there was a long moment of silence.

Mrs Purefoyle heaved a great sigh and picked up her husband's pipe from where it lay smouldering on the mantelpiece. She sat down in the wing-chair, stretched out her button-up boots, and puffed pleasurably at the pipe. Clouds of fragrant smoke rose up around her sleek, black head.

"So, you're Maggie Finch's grand-weans, are you? What in blazes are you doing here?"

They gaped at her in utter surprise.

"I thought you'd blown it when you blurted out that you were kin of mine!" She laughed and blew a smoke-ring. "Fortunately, poor dear Henry never listens to anyone. He's always so sure he knows what's best."

"So you *are* Fancy Graylings!" Luka cried.

"There's a name I haven't heard in a long while! Fancy! What a name to give a girl. I ditched that as soon as I could."

"What about your mother's tarot cards?" Emilia said coldly. "Did you ditch those as well?"

"I sold them just as soon as I could, and bought myself a Bible and a good black dress. You think I

349

couldn't see which way the wind was blowing?" Fancy got up and stood before the case of dead butterflies, puffing luxuriously on the pipe stuck in the corner of her mouth. "I gave Henry the charm. He likes such things." She put out one finger to touch the fragile wings of one of the butterflies. "It's got a butterfly in it, you know, a crushed-up little thing. That's how we got our name, you know. From the Grayling butterfly. The Grayling angles its wings when it is resting, so it leaves no shadow. It makes them very hard to catch."

Like you, Emilia thought. *How well you have camouflaged yourself amongst these Puritans.*

"But what do you care? Is that why you came to find me?" Fancy knocked the pipe out and put it back in its stand. "Criminy, but my heart was in my boots when I saw you lot. I just knew my wicked past had come back to bite me on the buttock!"

"Our family's been thrown in gaol," Luka said angrily. "We heard you had married a lawyer, and were hoping. . ."

She laughed. "You thought Henry would help you get them out? He's more likely to press the judge to a harsher sentence. Nay, no help for you here, weans."

Luka said fiercely, "Well, you'd better give us that amber charm and help us get away or we'll tell him everything. We'll make him believe us! And we'll tell him how you robbed your own mother and left her to starve on the streets. We can tell him where to find her so he can ask her herself!"

350

"What, the old hag's still alive?" Fancy's beautiful dark eyes narrowed in calculation. "Fine. I'll let you go, but I want your word of honour you'll never come back and bother us again."

"You have it! Unlike you, our word actually means something!"

"No need to get nasty." Fancy quickly untied their bonds, then went to the clock and extracted a key from underneath it. "These are dangerous times, especially for a young girl with no one but a half-crazy old crone to look after her. Do you blame me for wanting to be safe and comfortable? Henry's one of the most powerful men at court. You think I could ever have lived in a house like this if I had not married him?"

"Meanwhile, your poor mam is sleeping on the streets," Emilia said.

Fancy frowned. "Well, she wasn't sleeping on the streets when I left her. Daya made a good enough living telling fortunes." She unlocked the glass case and removed the small golden stone, cupping it in her hand.

"Until you stole her tarot cards."

"Think of it as my dowry. Though I must admit, I've been sorry ever since. I would do much to know what the future holds. Tea leaves in the bottom of my cup and reading the Bible just don't show me clearly enough." She looked down at the amber charm, and closed her fingers over it.

Emilia held out her hand. "You promised you'd give me the charm."

"Amber's worth a pretty penny," Fancy said. "And it's belonged to my family for generations."

"We don't have any money," Emilia said unhappily.

"Henry will notice it's gone. He'll know I gave it to you."

Emilia did not want to stand here, arguing with Fancy, when Mr Purefoyle would be back in any moment with the constables. She thought fast. "What if I gave you my grandmother's tarot cards? They're small and easily hidden. You could lay them out for yourself whenever you wanted."

Fancy's hand at once flashed out. "Deal!"

It cost Emilia a pang to dig out her grandmother's beautiful old cards. She hoped her baba would not mind. Fancy took them eagerly, dropping the amber into Emilia's palm without a second glance. She then locked the display case and hid the key again, saying, "With any luck, he won't even notice it's gone! For a while, anyway."

Emilia held the amber up to the candlelight. It glowed softly golden, the colour of afternoon sunshine. Emilia could see clearly the crooked shape of a trapped butterfly within, its wings bent. Emilia rubbed her thumb over it, her mouth curving. She had the butterfly in amber!

"Now, how will you manage to escape me? I know! I went out to fetch Grace, finding it all too frightening, and while I was gone you got loose and snuck out of the back door."

"Sounds possible." Luka tucked Zizi up in the crook of his arm.

"Very well, then. I'll go and distract Grace. You two get out of here fast. And don't think of going back on your word – if all goes according to plan, we'll be leaving here soon anyway. I've had enough of dreary old London! I think we should try our fortune in the New World."

"That would be wise," Emilia said deliberately. "I think you have some of your mother's second sight, Fancy. For you were right. Cromwell will die before the week is out, and then the king will return. He will hang Cromwell's dead body and stick his head on a stake before the palace gates, and he will seek a bloody revenge on all those that helped his father to the scaffold. I've seen it, and I know I speak true."

"Oh, that husband of mine is a fool!" Fancy whispered. She opened the door, laid her hand against her forehead, and ran out, calling in a fading voice, "Oh, Grace, I think I'm going to swoon! Those dreadful gypsy children. My heart's all a-flutter!"

Luka swung his pack on to his shoulder. "Right! Let's get out of here."

"I wish we could say goodbye to Beedee," Emilia said sadly. "She was nice."

"And clever," Luka said approvingly. He glanced about, ensuring they had left nothing behind, then, on an impulse, snatched up the thick sheaf of parchment Obedience had showed them and stuffed it into his pack too. Then they bolted out of the back door and across the small yard to fetch Sweetheart, who, bored by her long, lonely wait, had made a great mess. As they hurried out of the shed, Sweetheart for once pushing ahead of them in her eagerness to be gone, they glanced up at the house and saw, with a leap of their hearts, Obedience leaning out of one of the windows, waving madly. They grinned and waved back.

Rough Justice

The two children ran till they were out of breath.

"We should try and get on a boat to Kingston," Luka panted, pausing in the shade of a tall house to wipe his face with his kerchief. "We'll get along much faster that way. We're really running out of time now. They go up before the magistrates the day after tomorrow, and after then it'll be too late."

Emilia nodded, her face sombre. She knew that her family would all be hanged the same day as the magistrates passed sentence on them. The magistrates only came to town once a quarter, so that they heard each court case one after the other in quick succession. People were either fined or punished and then released, or were hanged there and then, so that the travelling magistrates could see justice done before they moved on to the next town and the next court. The faster they got through each court assize, the sooner the magistrates could get home. It was a rough sort of justice, and left little room for a change of heart.

"We need to get my bracelet back first," she said.

Luka looked troubled. "We can't, Milly. We just don't have the time. It's a long way to Kingston from here, even if we get a boat."

"We have to at least try," Emilia said. "Let's just ask if anyone knows where we can find one of these pawnshops. We may get lucky." She caressed the lump of amber in her pocket with desperate hope.

"Fair enough," Luka sighed. He knew how much the charm bracelet meant to Emilia.

But though the children trudged the back-alleys and laneways of London for hours, they had no luck. They were shown numerous gold necklaces, bracelets, lockets, rings, earrings and jewelled combs, but no one they asked had ever seen a dainty gold chain hung with four mismatching charms. At last Luka said gently, "I'm sorry, Milly. We can't wait any longer. If we want to catch a boat up the river, we need to go now, before the tide turns."

"But my bracelet . . . all the charms . . . we went through so much to find them! Was it all for nothing?" Her voice wobbled.

Luka gave her a quick, awkward hug. "None of it was for nothing. We've got powdered fish berries to drug the guards, and a lock pick to open the cell doors, and big strong men coming to help us. And don't forget those pardons I nicked! We'll have no trouble saving our families now. Maybe it was the luck of the charms that helped us get all those things, I don't know. We certainly do seem to have had providence on our side."

"Until now." Emilia wiped her eyes on her sleeve.

"At least we still have one of the charms," Luka said. "That's better than none. Come on, let's just get to Gallows Pond now, and start laying some plans."

"So you'll think the Hearnes'll be there to meet us?"

"Sure they will. Sebastien promised they'd come by the last day of the month, and that's tomorrow. They may even be there already."

"What about Tom? Do you think he'll come?"

"I doubt his father would let him. With his wound and all, I mean."

There was a long silence.

"I wish I had my charm bracelet. I don't want to face anyone and tell them their charm is gone."

"It was just bad luck," Luka said. "You aren't the first person in the world to be robbed."

Emilia nodded unhappily.

They found a boatman who was willing to take Maggie's gold earrings in return for some food and drink, and a berth on a boat heading west along the River Thames to Kingston. Both the children were hot and weary after their day trudging the hard cobblestones of London, and it was a relief to sit down and stretch out their dusty feet and lift their faces to the breeze.

Soon the sun set into clouds as high as castles, and an early dusk settled over the countryside. The water was purple-grey, and rocked under the prow of the boat, parting and falling away in two long white curves.

Sweetheart was hidden under a canvas awning, her snoring bulk curled around an empty barrel of ale. Zizi was tucked up inside Luka's coat again, fast asleep, while Rollo slept on Emilia's foot. Luka yawned so wide his jaw cracked. Emilia sighed and let herself rest her heavy head against her cousin's arm. In moments, they were both asleep.

She was shaken awake some hours later. The boat had reached Kingston-upon-Thames. The children were afraid that the wharf would be guarded, and so they had begged the boatman to come to shore some distance before the bridge. It was dark, and the moon was obscured by heavy clouds. It was hard for Emilia and Luka to be back in the town where their family had been imprisoned. Every shadow seemed to hide a soldier, every creak or rustle was Coldham waiting to pounce. Emilia kept a tight hold of the lump of amber in her pocket as they hurried round the outskirts of the sleeping town, heading along King's Road towards Richmond Park.

The gates stood open, and they tiptoed in fearfully, looking around them. The road ran before them, showing pale against the rolling meadows. Slowly, wearily, the two children followed it.

"Let's find somewhere to camp and go looking for Gallows Pond in the morning," Luka whispered. "There's no way we can find it tonight. It's black as the Devil's waistcoat!"

"I can smell smoke. Look! Is that a campfire?"

"It may not be the Hearnes," Luka said softly. "Let's keep quiet until we see who it is."

They crept through the trees, keeping Sweetheart on a tight chain. The wind was high, rustling the leaves above them and hiding any small noise they made. They came to a clearing beside a stretch of water. There were no caravans pulled up under the shelter of the trees, no bender tents made from canvas thrown over hazel saplings. Instead, there was just a slender figure bent over a small campfire, toasting bread on a stick. The warm light flickered over his face and played on his long blond ponytail.

"Tom!" Emilia came forward in a rush.

He jumped to his feet, grinning widely. "Milly! Luka! I'm so glad to see you. Gallows Pond is rather creepy at night all by yourself."

"No one else is here?"

"Not yet, but it's still only Monday. I'm sure they'll be here by morning."

"How's your arm?"

"Much better. A bit stiff and sore." Tom moved it experimentally.

"I never thought your father would let you come," Luka said, dropping his pack and bending to warm his hands at the fire.

"He probably wouldn't have . . . if I'd asked him." Tom laughed. "I haven't actually been home. I took a week or so for my arm to heal and then I went to London. The marquis had asked me to pawn his ring for him, remember? I decided the best place to do it would be in London. I didn't want anyone tracking it back to me. So I rode up to town yesterday and pawned the ring, and then came straight here. But that reminds me, Milly. I found something for you at the pawnshop." He drew out a small golden chain from his pocket and handed it to her.

Emilia stared at it, dumbfounded, then threw her arms about his neck and kissed him. "Tom! My charm bracelet! But how on earth did you find it!"

Tom rubbed his cheek, looking surprised but pleased. "A man brought it in to sell while I was there. I recognized it at once. I didn't think the marquis would mind if I used some of his loot to buy it back for you. What happened to it? Did you lose it?"

"It was stolen." Emilia was so happy she felt as if she could float up into the sky like the sparks from the fire. She carefully hung the butterfly in amber from one link, then fastened the chain about her wrist again. At once she felt a sizzle of excitement, as if golden fireworks were igniting in her blood. At the same time, all her senses sharpened, as if cotton wool had been unwound

360

from her head, allowing her to see and hear and smell and sense more clearly. "Oh, I can't believe I got it back again. I'm so happy!"

"Now, that's too strange a coincidence," Luka said. "The thief bringing it in to the very same pawnshop as Tom? I'm beginning to believe in your lucky charms, Milly!" Although he grinned as he spoke, there was not the usual mocking tone in his voice. She smiled at him.

Luka settled down against Sweetheart's bulk, his feet stretched to the fire, and rummaged through their bag for some food, telling Tom about their adventures at the gun foundry.

Emilia sat down too, but she found it hard to relax. Gallows Pond was an uncanny place. The trees crowded down close to the water, twigs rattling together in the wind. The darkness seemed to loom over their small fire. She found herself clasping the charm bracelet close for comfort.

"I think we should put the fire out," she whispered.

"Oh, but it's cold now!" Tom protested. "And awfully dark without the firelight."

"We saw your campfire miles away. I'm worried in case someone else sees it."

"There's no one for miles," Tom said.

"You're not worried about Cold-Pig, are you? He'll have given up weeks ago," Luke said.

"He'll want his revenge on us for showing him up as

a fool. And I bet you he won't get paid unless he nabs us."

"But he has no way of knowing where you are," Tom said.

"I bet you he's lurking around somewhere, just in case we come back to try and save our families. I would if I was him." Luka got up and began to kick dirt on to the fire. "Better safe than sorry. Let's find somewhere else to camp the night."

As the fire died, the night grew vaster and darker. The three children pressed close to Sweetheart, taking comfort from her vast furry bulk as they pushed their way through the bushes towards the road.

"Let's go back towards the gate. That way we can keep a lookout," Luka whispered.

They had just reached the edge of the wood when they saw, ahead of them, a troupe of soldiers marching along the road, carrying flaming torches. At once the children melted back into the shadows. Emilia hardly dared to breathe.

"Are you sure you saw a fire? There's no sign of it now." Coldham's familiar growl reached their ears, petrifying the children into stone.

"Aye, sir, I'm sure. It was in that copse of trees just over there. It was not so long ago, sir, no more than ten minutes."

"Very well, men. Spread out. Search the wood. Leave no stone unturned. If those gypsy brats are here, I want them found, else I'll have your guts for garters!"

The children crouched down as the flaming torches came closer and closer. There was nowhere to run. They could only hope to hide in the shadows.

"Sir! Sir!" a soldier shouted. "Look here! Surely that's a bear print, here in the dirt?"

Emilia sucked in a panting breath. She shook her charm bracelet free of her sleeve and groped for the charms in the darkness. One by one her fingers danced over the familiar shapes. *Help me*, she prayed. *Hide us, keep us safe. Help me save our families.*

The last charm her fingers found was the smooth lump of amber. She thought of the long-dead butterfly imprisoned in its heart, the butterfly that cast no shadow with its wings. She coiled her fingers about the amber charm, and wished with all her heart.

Torchlight probed through the leaves. Soldiers came running. Luka dragged Emilia to her knees just as the soldiers went charging past. They passed so close that the children were able to see each other's faces clearly in the light of their torches. It seemed impossible that the soldiers did not see them, but they ran on past and disappeared.

"Follow the bear prints," Coldham ordered. He was only a few feet away. "See, there's one, heading that way. Those gypsies can't be far away!"

They listened as his footsteps crunched on the dead leaves, closer and closer and closer, the red wavering light staining the leaves above them. Then Coldham was standing right on the other side of the bush. His boots were so close Emilia could have stretched out her neck and licked them. She ducked her head down, knowing that it was often the gleaming whites of the eyes that gave away those that hid. Her heart thumped so loud she thought he must be able to hear it. *Wind blow, clouds hide the moon*, she thought. *Rain come! Wind and rain come and hide us.*

Coldham stood silently, listening. But the cold wind was blustering now, rattling sticks together, ripping leaves from the branches to blow in tiny black whirlwinds along the ground. Seconds passed. Minutes.

Coldham grunted and walked on down the path. The torchlight faded away.

"Lucky he didn't look down," Luka whispered. "We were right at his feet. And how could he have missed Sweetheart? Even if he didn't see her eyes gleaming red, you'd think he would've been able to smell her. She stinks!"

Luka rose cautiously to his feet, his back hunched, and risked a look over the top of the bush. The soldiers' torches were gusting out into smoky red ribbons on the far side of the pond. Rain began to patter down. He nodded at Tom and Emilia, who rose stiffly to their feet. Emilia's knees hurt, and she bent and dusted off the little bits of rocks and twigs embedded in her skin.

"Let's try and get away," Luka whispered. "With any luck they'll be so busy searching the wood they won't see us going down the road."

Together the three children crept along the edge of the wood, looking nervously back over their shoulders every few steps. The only sound was of low rumbling thunder and the wind in the trees. Emilia saw the road only a few feet away, and some distance away, the gate out of the park.

She glanced at Tom and Luka. Luka nodded, anxious to be gone. Together they darted across the broad expanse of open ground, straight towards the gateway.

"There they are! Get them!" Coldham shouted. He had been standing concealed in the shadow of the trees, only a few paces away. They heard the unmistakable click of a pistol being cocked.

The children raced on, breath sobbing in their throats, but Sweetheart surged around, raking her great claws at Coldham.

"No!" Emilia screamed.

Coldham fired.

Sweetheart bellowed in pain. Coldham quickly reloaded. Luka tried to pull the bear away, but ignoring Luka's dragging arm, Sweetheart sprang forward, just as Coldham fired again. The bullet buried itself deep in the bear's breast. Sweetheart yelped. Another soldier fired, and then another. Bullets seemed to come from every direction, whining cruelly. Sweetheart roared, twisting about, looking for something to rent with her claws. Again Coldham fired, at point-blank range. Sweetheart cried aloud, and fell with a crash that sent up a cloud of dust.

Coldham cried out in triumph, then swiftly reloaded again. This time he pointed his pistol straight at Luka.

Luka dropped Sweetheart's chain and ran, yelling at Tom and Emilia to follow. He put up his hand and wiped his cheek. His fingers were wet and sticky. It was Sweetheart's blood, he realized, which had sprayed across his face. Tears stung his eyes. Never had he seen anything so dreadful, so final, as the great bulk of his father's beloved bear collapsing to the ground.

A dark tangle of twigs sprang at him. Luka ducked and twisted, running full-pelt through the wood, his arms up to protect his face. He heard heavy feet pounding along behind him, and harsh panting. Then a steel hand seized his collar and brought him down. Luka kicked out, rolled over, and was up once more and running. Again he was dragged down. Coldham held him down, a knee heavy in his back, his gauntlet hard and cold across Luka's mouth.

Zizi shrieked and leapt for Coldham, clawing and biting at his face. He swept her away as if she were no more than a fly. Emilia flew at him, trying to drag him away from Luka, but he seized her by the hair.

"Thought you'd made a fool of me, didn't you? I'll show you!"

He gave Emilia a blow across the ear. She cried out in pain, and at once Rollo gave a blood-curdling snarl and leapt for Coldham. The thief-taker had no time to reload, so shifted his grip on his pistol, using it like a club to beat the big dog around the head. Rollo did not

366

seem to notice, his teeth clenched in Coldham's boot. Coldham tried to kick him away, all the time shouting for reinforcements.

Panting, his mouth full of earth, Luka tried once again to twist free. He heard Zizi gibbering with rage from somewhere in the trees above him. Then the orange, flickering light of torches fell upon him. He could see each blade of grass outlined, like a mighty forest at sunset. Boots came running at him out of the darkness, too many pairs for him to ever fight. He lay still, closing his eyes, trying to gulp air past the boulder that had lodged in his throat.

"Well, you two led me a pretty chase, but I got you in the end," Coldham gloated. "The little lordling too! Pastor Spurgeon will be pleased. So will Cromwell's spymaster. He'll have some questions for you lot, I think."

"But we don't know anything," Tom said, his voice choked. He was holding his wounded shoulder with one hand.

Coldham snorted. "Likely story. Haven't you lot been gallivanting round with spies and traitors for the past two weeks? In it up to your necks, you are."

"We're just children," Emilia said. She was crouched nearby, her hand gripping Rollo's ruff, holding the growling dog back. Her black eyes stared defiantly at Coldham through a tangle of wild black curls.

"Old in sin," Coldham said, and jerked his head at the soldiers. They lifted Luka to his feet, and went to drag Tom and Emilia up as well. Rollo snarled and lunged for them. Coldham loaded his pistol.

"No, no, please don't shoot him too!" Emilia flung her arms about Rollo's neck. "He won't bite, I promise!"

"That's for sure," Coldham responded and cocked his pistol.

"Go! Go, Rollo!" Emilia cried and, grabbing a fallen oak-apple from the grass, she hurled it with all her strength into the darkness. Rollo bounded after it, his ears cocked. Emilia threw all the oak-apples and branches she could find, shouting, "Home, Rollo, go home!" Tears flowed down her face, and she wiped them away angrily. "There, he's gone," she wept. "He's gone. You can't kill him too. Oh, Sweetheart, darling Sweetheart! Why did you have to shoot her?"

Coldham huffed out his breath in exasperation.

"See if you can't find that dog and kill it," he said to two of the soldiers. "And there's a monkey round here somewhere too, I want it shot as well. You, go and get rid of that bear."

"What am I meant to do with it?" the soldier said blankly.

"I don't know, dump it, make a rug out of it, you think I care?"

Emilia pressed the back of her hand to her mouth.

"What do you want us to do with these three?" said the soldier who was holding Luka, shaking him roughly.

"I'll take them back to gaol," Coldham said. "Get me a horse, and some rope to tie up these brats. And hurry up! It's late, and I wouldn't mind getting some sleep tonight."

"May you pay for your shame!" Emilia flashed. "I hope you. . ."

"And gag them too, will you? I've had enough of that little witch's curses!"

PART SIX

The Gypsy Curse

By Fire Struck Down

Thunder grumbled. Leaves battered their faces. Luka, Tom and Emilia stumbled through the dark, a rope about their wrists biting cruelly into their skin. The other end of the rope was tethered to Coldham's stirrup. He rode ahead of them, a looming shadow amongst shadows.

The night was so black it felt as if they had been blindfolded as well as gagged. Not a star or a candlelit window could be seen anywhere; only the red glaring eye of the lantern hung from Coldham's saddle. Emilia felt more desperate and miserable than she had ever felt in her life.

All their hopes of rescuing their families had been turned to ash. She and Luka had travelled so far, and faced so many dangers, for nothing. Tomorrow they would all be dragged before the magistrates, and by the sounds of it, a quick hanging was the best she and Luka could hope for. Better to be hanged than sent to London to face Cromwell's spymaster, she thought. Emilia had heard all the stories about the spymaster John Thurloe, who was said to have a special room at the Tower of London where he interrogated people suspected of being spies and traitors. No one ever said exactly what he did there, but from the way people shuddered and winced, she guessed it must be something dreadful. And Emilia had seen the severed heads and decomposing limbs of such traitors displayed upon London Bridge. It was impossible not to feel cold with fear at the possibility of such a death.

She grieved too for their darling animals, for the inert lump of shaggy fur that had been Sweetheart, and for Rollo and for Zizi, who could not possibly understand that anyone would wish to hurt them. She imagined Rollo returning to look for them, and being met with a soldier's bullet. She imagined Zizi's small brown body tumbling down from the trees to lie cold and still in the grass. She imagined the soldiers laughing and joking as they dragged Sweetheart's body over the gravel. It seemed so cruel, so pitiless. Emilia could only weep silently, unable to even gasp or sob because of the gag binding her mouth. She wiped her face on her sleeve and stared at Coldham's thick shape, for the first time in her life feeling real hatred.

On and on they staggered, the hard stone of the highway hurting Emilia's bare feet. Rain lashed their faces. Thunder muttered constantly. Every now and again, lightning flickered along the rim of the sky. It had grown bitterly cold.

A spark of anger lit in her. *I will not let him win*, she thought to herself. *I must not let him win.*

The sky was torn apart by lightning. In the sudden illumination – so bright it hurt the eye – Emilia saw the township lying in the dip of the valley. The river was wild with whitecaps, trees bent from the waist as if dancing a drunken reel. She saw Luka's face, down-turned, his eyes cavernous with misery.

Seconds later all was darkness again. Coloured dashes sizzled against her eyelids, the aftershock of the lightning flash. Emilia clenched her fingers about the rope, trying to ease its spiteful bite into her skin. *I won't let him win, I won't, I won't.*

Into the town they stumbled, bent against the driving rain. An overturned bucket rolled, clanking, along the road. Suddenly it was dragged up into the air, and sent spinning into a wall. Thatch was torn away from a roof and blown away in a shower of broken stalks. A chicken went tumbling overhead, claw over beak in a ruffle of feathers, squawking in terror. In a second it was gone, whirled away into the night. Emilia's wet hair whipped about her face. Her skirts were blown sideways, flapping wildly. Coldham's mare tossed her head nervously, and the thief-taker dragged hard on the bit, forcing her forward.

What can I do? Emilia thought in despair. *I'm bound and gagged and tied to that man's stirrup. Another minute, and we'll be at the gaol. Another minute and our last chance is gone.*

She could not touch her charms with her hands bound. She imagined them in her mind's eye, imagined holding them to the light, imagined touching their familiar shapes with her fingertips. Lovingly she stroked them, thinking of what the charms meant to her. Strength. Intuition. Compassion. Courage. The power to change. Emilia looked again at Coldham, hunched on his horse like the picture of Death in her grandmother's tarot cards, and felt pity pierce her.

They turned the corner and saw the Hand and Mace Inn, where her family was imprisoned along with the rest of the town's prisoners. A low, rickety building with a steep thatched roof and tiny mullioned windows, it had a single door on to the street with a lantern hung above it, swinging crazily in the wind.

Lightning zigzagged. The mare reared in terror. Luka darted forward, dragging at the rope tied to Coldham's stirrups. The girth broke, and the big man lurched sideways, lost his balance and crashed to the ground. The mare reared again, then took off, bolting into the darkness, the saddle flying off her back and bouncing on the cobblestones. Luka yanked away the gag, trying desperately to free his hands. Coldham was almost as quick. He staggered up, shouting in fury, and swung his fist at Luka's head.

Emilia flung out her bound hands. *No!* she screamed silently. *I won't let you hurt anyone ever again!*

Lightning flashed down from the thunderous sky. It struck Coldham on his steel gauntlet. For a second he stood sheathed in an eerie blue light that sizzled between ground and sky. It only lasted a moment. Then the lightning recoiled. Coldham was flung away, smashing against the far wall.

Emilia swallowed painfully. Her legs trembled, and her heart thundered. She took a few steps towards the thief-taker. Smoke was creeping out of his boots, and out of his hair. His gauntlet lay some twenty feet away, smoking. His eyes were wide open, staring at her blankly.

"Is he dead?" Luka whispered. Tom caught his breath in horror.

Emilia shook her head helplessly, shivers running all over her. She had cursed Coldham at Horsmonden. *With fire you fought, and so with fire shall you be struck down,* she had cried. Never had she thought it would come so dramatically true. Shakily she put up one hand and pulled down the gag, taking great gulps of blustery air.

Suddenly Coldham laughed.

The three children jumped as if stuck with a pin. They clung together.

Coldham laughed again, and lurched to his feet. The children cringed back, but he paid them no heed. He was looking up at the sky, lifting his arms up, crying aloud.

Lightning flashed again, over Kingston Hill. Luka and Emilia flinched, but Coldham turned his face towards it, his eyes and mouth wide open, gulping mouthfuls of the thunder-charged air. He flung away his pistol and his dagger, dragged off his helmet and his dark red coat and threw them away from him, ripped away his shirt. Half-naked, he began to run. One leg seemed stiff, half-paralysed. He lurched and stumbled and weaved from side to side, but did not stop, chasing after the lightning that flamed along the horizon.

Emilia watched him go, shivering with cold and uncontrollable terror.

"What . . . what just happened?" Tom asked.

"I don't know," Luka said. "But it means we're free now. Cold-Pig's gone! Come on, let's get out of this rain!" He drew Emilia under the eaves of the inn's roof, then ran back out into the tempestuous rain and scooped up Coldham's helmet and coat, his weapons and the steel glove. "Could come in useful!" he said with a flash of his old grin.

Awkwardly he cut their bound hands with Coldham's knife, then put his hand under Emilia's elbow and guided her down the passageway. She was as ungainly as a wooden puppet.

A clatter behind them. The children spun around, nerves shrilling. A huge hunched shadow leapt towards them. The crazily swinging lantern caught the eerie green glow of two sets of eyes. Emilia shrieked. The very next moment the two-headed monster was upon them, whining and wriggling and leaping with joy. Two huge, muddy paws thumped on Emilia's chest, and her face was washed thoroughly by a large, slobbery tongue, while a skinny little creature leapt for Luka, arms outstretched. He received her rapturously. "Zizi!"

"Rollo! Stop it! Yuck!"

"You found us! Clever monkey-girl!" Zizi cuddled into Luka's neck, crooning and whimpering and patting his face.

"Rollo must've followed our scent," Tom said. "What a clever dog."

"The best, the cleverest dog in the world!" Emilia hugged Rollo close.

Gladly the three children ran down the passageway, Rollo bounding ahead of them, tail wagging. Emilia was almost giddy with relief. She had dreaded having to tell Noah that his dog had been shot.

The stable was a low, rickety building behind the inn. Every board rattled, and the thatch rustled as if it were alive with rats. Shoved in one corner of the stable was a single gypsy caravan. The other had been chopped up for firewood. All that was left were a few carved panels, a broken wheel, and a pile of gaudily painted tinder. There was no sign of the family's big cart-horses either, and Luka guessed they had been sold to pay for their family's incarceration. It made him angrier than ever at the injustice of the justice system.

Luka kindled their lantern and the three children huddled into Maggie's caravan, wrapping patchwork quilts around them. Tom was white and sick-looking, and blood stained his white shirt. Emilia did what she could to staunch the wound, and wished she could kindle a fire and make him some hot tea. It was too dangerous, though, so she contented herself with crumbling some willow leaves into cold water and giving him that, and binding his wound with cobwebs.

With Zizi cuddled in his lap, Luka turned the pack out on to the table and arranged their loot in neat rows. There was the sheaf of papers with Oliver Cromwell's own signature on it. There was the bottle of powdered fish berries. There were the copies of Coldham's keys and the lock pick Old Man Smith had made them. There were Coldham's handcuffs, his clothes and helmet, his steel gauntlet, and his weapons. Luka was most pleased by these, and spent some time examining the pistol, and trying to determine how it worked. It made Emilia sick and nervous, seeing the long-muzzled gun in her cousin's hands, but eventually he laid it down.

"We're going to have to rescue Dado and everyone by ourselves, tonight," Luka said, looking inside Coldham's cartridge pouch. "We dare not risk being caught again, and besides, it's the perfect night for it; it's raining cats and dogs and no one will be around to see us."

Rollo looked up at the word *dog* and beat his tail against the floor. Giving him a quick pat, Emilia nodded.

"The best plan would be to get into the inn, and drug the ale, and hope that it knocks all the guards out cold. Then we could just creep in, and let everyone out, and get away without anyone being the wiser." He busied himself pouring the powder into the barrel of the gun, as he had seen Coldham do earlier, then shoved the musket ball in with the little ramrod.

"I doubt that it'll be that easy, though, and besides, it doesn't solve the problem of stopping the constables from chasing after us once they realize everyone's gone. I'm thinking I'd better dress up in Coldham's clothes and pretend to be a soldier. I'll say I've brought pardons from the Lord Protector."

"But won't they read the pardons?" The plan, Emilia thought, was as full as holes as her petticoat. "They'll see they're not for our family."

"I'm hoping the night guards won't be able to read too well." Luka tapped a small amount of powder into the priming pan, and then half-cocked the lock. "It'll be late, hopefully they're already half-befuddled with ale, and if we're lucky, we'll have got some of the sleeping drug into them. Besides, look at all the words on these things! Some of them are so long they take up half the line. No one but a pettifogger could possibly know what they mean."

"But what if they ask Old Ironsides why he freed everyone?" Tom asked.

"Cromwell's going to die, maybe even this very night," Luka said. "Emilia's seen it and you know she sees true. Once he's dead, there'll be no one around to know whether he pardoned our families or not. Besides, once he dies, everything's going to be in such turmoil no one's going to worry about a few poor gypsies."

"No, of course not," Emilia said. She yawned widely.

"I'm so tired. Do you think they'll be suspicious of you turning up on their doorstep at this time of night?"

"It was the storm, sir," Luka said, dramatically wiping his brow. "Trees falling down all over the place, rivers breaking their banks and flooding the road, branches falling on my head. I'm lucky to have made it here alive!"

"What if they guess it's all a trick?"

Luka handed her the pistol. "Then you'll have to come in and rescue me!"

The Mace and Hand Inn

Kingston-upon-Thames, England
31 August 1658

It was long past midnight. Luka and Emilia crouched outside the small window by the back door, rain lashing their backs. They had left Tom to rest in the caravan, though he swore he would come after them if they were more than half an hour.

"We'll just have to risk it," Luka whispered. He drew out his lock pick and deftly unlocked the door, opening it just a crack to let Emilia slip through.

The flagstones were cold and smooth under her feet. Emilia crept along, and found herself in the doorway to the public bar. Two men were sitting at a table before a roaring fire, drinking tankards of ale and playing cards. The one facing Emilia was quite the largest and ugliest man she had ever seen. He looked as if he made a living wrestling bears. His nose had long ago been smashed to a pulp, and his brown, leathery hands were so huge, the cards looked absurdly dainty in them, as if they belonged to a doll. He was dressed in a rough sort of uniform, and a cudgel leant against his leg.

The other man had his shirt-sleeves rolled up to his elbow, and a big ring of keys hung from his belt. Emilia guessed he was the warden.

"At this rate, Maloney, you're going to clean me out." The warden's words all ran together, as if he had been drinking for quite some time. "You've got the Devil's own luck tonight."

"You're not concentrating, sir," Maloney said. "You'd never have thrown out that six usually, Warden Riley."

"I keep expecting that sour-faced crow to come creeping up behind me," Riley said morosely. "It's a sad day when I can't even play cards in my own inn!"

"He'll be busy writing letters, like usual," Maloney replied. "You got to wonder who he's writing to, all the time."

"Writing reports on us all, no doubt, and sending it to that spymaster fellow, what's his name?" The warden's voice was so slurred this came out like "wassissname". He drained dry his tankard and banged it down on the table. "They say he's got spies everywhere, that man, and you can't drink a toast in your own home without him wanting to know why."

While they spoke, Emilia was examining the two men and the room closely. She saw a jug of ale on the table, and a small barrel with a cork bung on top of the scarred wooden bar. This was where the jug would be refilled, she guessed. The bar was about six paces away from where she crouched. She took a deep breath and crept across the open space, slow as a cat stalking a bird. It was quick, jerky movements that attracted the eye, she knew. At last she slid into the shadows behind the bar, and allowed her tense muscles to relax.

Once she was sure she had not been seen, Emilia got to her feet and risked a quick glance over the top of the bar. Both men were staring at the cards in their hands. She slowly prised up the lid of the cask and tipped in the bottle of powdered fish berries. She had to give the lid a hard tap to close it, and crouched down hurriedly, her pulse hammering so hard in her ears it made her feel sick.

"What was that noise?" the warden said.

"Prob'ly just a shutter banging somewhere," Maloney said. "Listen to that wind! It's howling out there. I bet you this is one night our gypsy friends are glad to be indoors."

"Can't understand them," Riley mumbled. "Why do they travel round the country like that, instead of settling down in one place like normal folks? It's not natural."

"Guess they have their own ways," Maloney answered. "You sure you want to throw out that ace, Mister Riley, sir?"

"Whoops! Guess not. Here, give it back. Thirsty, man? I'll get us some more ale."

Emilia heard a chair being pushed back, the sound of unsteady footsteps crossing the floor, then the pop as the bung was removed, followed by a low gurgle. Then Riley pushed the cork back in and carried his jug back to the table, pouring more ale into the tankards. The two men drank and talked, while the wind shrieked and drummed on the roof like a giant having a tantrum. Emilia rested her head on her arms and waited.

It took about a quarter of an hour – and a few more tankards of ale – for Riley to pass out. He snored loudly, his head pillowed on his arms. Emilia waited for Maloney to grow drowsy too, but either he had not drunk as much of the drugged ale as the warden, or he was simply too large a man to be much affected. He arranged a blanket over Riley's shoulders, then sat by the fire carving a little toy from a piece of wood.

Emilia was growing stiff and cold in her draughty hiding spot. She wondered how much longer Luka would wait before coming to the door. She wished she had some way to warn him that one of the guards was still alert. It would have been so much easier if they were both drowsy and confused.

An imperious *rat-a-tat-tat* sounded on the front door. Emilia jumped. She listened to the sound of Maloney opening the door, then heard Luka's voice, demanding to be let in.

"I have come from London, from the Lord Protector himself, with pardons for all who lie in Kingston Gaol tonight," he declaimed grandly. "I insist that you set free the prisoners at once!"

Emilia smiled to herself. She recognized the confident

tone, that note of command. Luka was mimicking the Marquis of Ormonde. She crept round the side of the bar so she could see him, and smiled again as she recognized the straight back, the lifted chin. He had his cloak flung back from his shoulder in exactly the marquis' way, one gauntleted hand on his belt, the other holding out the sheaf of rolled parchments.

Maloney seemed to take the sudden appearance of a damp and demanding young soldier at his door in his stride. He let Luka in, along with a great gust of icy rain, and shut the door hurriedly.

"Yes, sir, right away, sir," he said in a low voice. "Come on up. I'll unlock the cells straightaway and then record it in the ledgers. We don't want any questions asked on the morrow."

Luka frowned. "Certainly not," he said, maintaining his imperious tone.

"Wha-a-at? Wha-a-aat's going on?" a slurred voice asked. The warden lifted his head from the table.

"Nothing, sir. A soldier from London, about the prisoners. I can look after it."

"From London? About the prisoners? What does he want?"

"It's naught to worry about, sir," Maloney began, but Luka lifted high his scrolls and said, "I have here pardons from the Lord Protector. I insist that the prisoners be released at once."

"Pardons? From Old Ironsides! For a lot of dirty gyps?" The warden snorted in derision. "Let me see!"

Reluctantly Luka passed the scrolls to the warden, who peered at them through first one eye, then the other. "Criminy, that there is Old Ironsides' signature! Well, I'll be damned." He began to laugh. "Isn't that going to get the pastor's goat? What a joke! He'll be livid."

"I'll go up and make sure all is in order, sir. No need for you to rouse yourself," Maloney said.

"You must be joking. I want to see the old crow's face. Come on, man, let's go show him." The warden heaved himself to his feet, still clutching the pardons in his fist.

Luka fell back a pace, his face showing the same alarm that Emilia felt. The pastor! Here at the gaol? But it was well past midnight! What was Pastor Spurgeon doing here at this time of night?

Maloney said meaningfully, "You don't want to upset the pastor, sir. Friends in high places, you know. How about you have another cup of ale, and we'll get this business done nice and quiet, eh, sir?"

He poured the warden another cup of ale, which he drank greedily, and before Luka had taken three steps, had fallen asleep again and was snoring like an arthritic spaniel. Maloney winked at Luka, who straightened his helmet and tried to look soldierly.

They climbed the narrow stairs, and went through a passageway lined with heavy iron-barred doors. The stink and the darkness made Luka's muscles clench in dread, and sweat sprang up on his palms. He wiped them on his trousers nervously.

Maloney brought out the thick ledger. "I'll just make

a note of the pardons, sir," he said in a low voice. "Here, why don't you unlock the cells for me, sir, it's getting late and I'm sure you're keen to go on your way."

Luka nodded eagerly, caught the keys he tossed deftly and went at once to the door to the women's cell. Behind him, Maloney wrote laboriously, the tip of his tongue sticking out of one corner of his mouth, the quill looking like a down feather in his huge hand.

"Maloney, what is all this about?" The pastor's voice sent a chill down Luka's spine. He stiffened, his key turned halfway.

"A soldier's come from the Lord Protector, sir, with a pardon, sir, for the prisoners." Maloney spoke with great reluctance, shuffling his boots on the floor.

"What? The Lord Protector has pardoned the prisoners? Impossible! He has no such right. Besides, why would he? It is his agent who has been gathering information against the prisoners, evidence of treason to add to those of vagrancy and murder."

"Maybe they've got friends in high places," Maloney offered.

"A tribe of filthy gypsies? Don't be a fool!"

"Well, then, maybe this gypsy tribe's been working for Cromwell all this time," Maloney said. "You know, travelling around, gathering information. I've heard the Lord Protector has spies in the most unlikely places. Maybe that's why he's pardoned them."

"I do not believe it. It's a trick. Let me look at those pardons!"

Maloney held them tightly in his hand. "Well, sir, I'm not sure you have the authority to look over official documents such as these. Not being a magistrate yourself, you know. Mister Riley's seen the pardons and says that they're all right and tight. It's just my job now to record the judgement in the ledger and let the prisoners go."

"Absolutely not. Those pardons are obviously a forgery."

"They've got the Lord Protector's own signature on them and his seal too," Maloney said. "No reason to think they're fake. Besides, how could anyone get hold of a forged document like that?"

"Give me those papers!" The pastor could barely speak, he was so angry.

Maloney shook his head unhappily. "I would need Mister Riley's permission to do that, sir, and I'm afraid he's a trifle indisposed tonight."

"Where is the soldier that brought them? Let me interrogate him." The pastor made an angry movement, as if to push past Maloney, but found his way barred by the massive figure of the night guard. "What are you doing? Let me past!"

"Just doing my duty, sir," Maloney said stolidly. "You are, after all, not an officer of the court."

"How dare you disobey me!" Pastor Spurgeon shrieked. "Who do you think you are? I'll teach you to defy me!" He whirled about, seized a whip from the wall and lashed out cruelly.

Maloney shrank back, covering his head with his hands. The pastor raised the whip high, laughing. Just then, Emilia ran forward from the stairwell and hit the pastor hard on the back of the head with the butt of the pistol. He crumpled to the ground, unconscious.

"Thanks, miss," Maloney said, wiping the blood away from a cut above his eye.

"I was trying to get up the courage to shoot him. I'm glad he came close enough that I could hit him instead."

"Wouldn't want to have to arrest you for murder," Maloney said.

Emilia grinned. "What should we do with him now?" she wondered, bending over the pastor in concern.

"Don't you dare find him a soft cushion for his head," Beatrice cried, limping from the cell. Luka stood behind her, his arm about Mimi's thin shoulders, grinning broadly.

"Beatrice!" Emilia sprang across the room and into her arms.

Half-laughing, half-crying, the sisters hugged each other close.

"I cannot believe you're here! It's a miracle," Beatrice whispered, her voice rough. "How on earth did you manage it?"

"It's a long story," Emilia replied with a crooked smile.

The Stink of The Prison

"I know what to do with old Fish-Face," Luka said. He seized the pastor by the heels and dragged him into the cell, where he manacled him to the wall with Coldham's handcuffs. "He won't be too happy when he wakes up," he grinned.

Maggie was sitting on the ground still, her back hunched like a buzzard.

"Baba!" Emilia fell on her knees before her grandmother, frightened by her frailty.

"Milly, darling girl, you came," Maggie murmured in Romany. "Is all well?"

"Aye, all is well. Look, Baba, we found all the charms." She showed her grandmother the bracelet, gleaming at her wrist.

"Good, good," Maggie said. "Is the tale true? Do the charms have power?"

"Aye. They brought us luck many times. Believe me,

we needed it!"

"You are safe, you are well, all is good. Come, you will need to help me. I cannot get up."

Emilia and Beatrice tried to help their grandmother to her feet, but her bones were locked in place. Luka was just hurrying to help them when Maloney stepped forward. "Ma'am, can't you stand? Here, let me help you." He bent and lifted the old woman into his arms as if she were a little child. "We'll have you tucked up in your own bed before you know it."

"Thank you, Maloney, you've been a true friend," Maggie murmured. "I don't know how we would have survived these past few weeks without you."

"Aw, it was nothing." The guard turned red as a beetroot.

"The caravans are in the stable still," Luka said to his mother. "They've sold one of the horses, I'm afraid, but there's some horses there we can borrow."

"We don't want to be nabbed again for horse-stealing," Silvia said, trying to smile. Once a pink-cheeked, plump woman, she was now gaunt and sallow, the long black hair she had been so proud of hanging in lank rat's tails.

"You can borrow my horse," Maloney said over his shoulder. "He's sturdy enough to pull the caravan, as long as it's not too far."

"We'll go to Richmond Park; we have friends waiting for us there," Luka said. Maloney nodded and disappeared down the stairs, Maggie trying to hold herself upright in his arms, not at all pleased to be carried. Silvia stumbled after them, Mimi clinging tightly to her hands, dark eyes wide and fearful.

"Where's Noah?" Emilia asked, looking around.

"He's in the next cell," Beatrice said. "He's not been well. We heard him coughing all the time, but they would not let me go to him. It's all been so dreadful."

Luka had already hurried to the other cell and was unlocking it swiftly. He was almost bowled over by the press of men trying to get out. Apart from Luka's father, Jacob, there was a man with ink-stained fingers, a one-armed soldier, several thin, shabby men with desperate eyes, and a number of filthy hedge-birds with wild matted beards and stinking rags. Most of them barged past and ran down the stairs, almost trampling each other in their desire to get out, but the gentleman with ink-stained fingers bowed and nodded and said, "I thank you. I will not forget this service tonight."

"Don't thank me, thank Old Ironsides!" Luka said irrepressibly, waving the pardons.

"I'll thank providence," the gentleman replied, and left Luka to rush into his father's arms.

"Luka!" Jacob cried. "I thought I heard your voice. I could hardly believe it's true. Let me look at you. Why, you've grown. Look how tall you are! But so thin."

"I need to get some of Baba's stew into me," Luka grinned. He hugged his father fiercely.

Emilia had run straight past her uncle to kneel beside

her brother, who lay on a pile of damp straw. The little boy was a ghastly shade of blue, with purple shadows under his eyes and colourless lips. His eyes were shut.

"He's very ill," Jacob said. "We've done what we could for him."

Beatrice and Emilia both knelt beside their brother, murmuring endearments, patting and stroking him. He did not stir.

"We need to get him away from here," Emilia cried. Tears were hot in her eyes. Jacob nodded and bent to pick up the little boy, carrying him gently out of the cell. His head lolled sideways, and his arm hung limply. Beatrice and Emilia hurried after him.

Luka smiled to see the pastor lying alone in the filthy straw. He carefully shut and locked the cell door.

Hopefully he'll sleep all day, he thought, *and by then we'll be far, far away!*

Outside, the rain drummed down, turning the yard to mud. In the few scant seconds it took to run across the yard, Emilia and Beatrice were drenched through. The rain seemed to have woken Noah, for his eyes were open and he was turning his face from side to side. Jacob laid him down gently in the bunk.

"You're safe now, darling boy," Emilia wept, hugging him close. "We'll have you well again in no time! Don't you worry about a thing now."

"Milly?" Noah whispered. "Where am I? What's happened? Are you real?"

"Of course I'm real," Emilia said. "You're here in your own little bed."

"But . . . we were in the cell . . . I can smell it still. . ."

He groped out with one skeletal hand, his face turning anxiously from side to side.

"It's your clothes you smell," Emilia said. "Here, let me take them off you. There's some other clothes here in the chest."

As she turned away, Rollo pushed past her, whining and wagging his tail so hard his whole body wriggled. He jumped up and put his paws on the bunk, licking Noah on the face.

Noah smiled. "Why, it's Rollo," he whispered. "You've come back."

"Aye, darling, we're all back, we're all safe," Emilia said, gently undressing the little boy. "Everything is fine now."

She and Beatrice together sponged away the worst of the filth with rain-water, dressed Noah in a clean shirt and tucked him up warmly. Rollo whuffed with joy and leapt up on to the bunk, curling up in the crook of Noah's knees, his nose pressed into the little boy's hand. Noah, smiling, closed his eyes and let himself drift away into sleep.

Emilia smiled and sniffed, wiping her nose with the back of her hand. She turned to tend to her grandmother, sitting hunched in her rocking-chair. The big guard was waiting quietly on the step, and Emilia's heart lurched in sudden terror. But he smiled kindly at her, and ducked his head inside the caravan to nod at Maggie.

"Goodbye, ma'am," he said. "Thank you."

"Thank *you*," Maggie answered.

The caravan swayed and rocked under his weight as he stepped down, and Noah sighed and murmured in his sleep.

Emilia gazed at her grandmother, thinking that the old woman never failed to surprise her. Maggie, without opening her eyes, said, "Go help the men harness up the horses. I want to feel the road under our wheels again."

"Aye, Baba," Emilia said and jumped down the steps.

The men were all busy getting the caravans ready to go, even though Maloney was begging them to wait for the storm to blow over.

"What's a little rain?" Jacob scoffed. "It'll wash away the prison stink."

Luka was helping eagerly, his monkey back on his shoulder, her little paws gripped tight around his throat.

"So where's my Sweetheart, then?" Jacob asked. "She back at the camp?"

Luka and Emilia looked at each other. Slowly they shook their heads.

"I'm sorry," Emilia said.

"They shot her about a hundred times. There was nothing we could do."

"She saved us," Emilia said. "More than once."

Jacob stared at them, grim-faced, then bowed his head and went on with his work.

Slowly Emilia and Luka plodded along the muddy road, the cold wind plucking at their hair and clothes, carrying gusts of icy rain. Tom stumbled just behind, just as wet and bedraggled as the two gypsy children, for he had insisted on giving up his bunk in the caravan for Maggie and little Mimi. The other members of the Finch family trudged along before and behind, barely finding the strength to lift one foot after another.

It was almost dawn. The thin grey light showed a scene of utter devastation. Trees were uprooted, roofs had been torn off houses, and fallen branches lay across smashed walls.

"This has been the longest night ever," Luka said.

"It feels like it's been years," Emilia said and yawned so widely her jaw cracked.

"My legs don't want to walk any more."

"Mine either."

But they trudged on.

"Will they be there, I wonder?" Luka asked.

"Of course they will," Emilia answered, smiling across at her sister, who tried to smooth back her matted hair with one hand.

Hooves hammered the road ahead. Tense with fright, the children looked up. It was not Coldham riding towards them, though, or a troupe of soldiers. It was Felipe and Sebastien and Lord Harry, waving their hats and hullaballoing.

"Here they are!" Lord Harry shouted, drawing up his horse beside them. "We rode out to look for you, afraid you may have been hurt in the storm, but look at you!

Hale and hearty and with friends, no less!"

"This is our family," Emilia said.

"We rescued them ourselves!" Luka cried.

There was a glad hubbub, as quick greetings and explanations flew back and forth.

"We were worried when we did not find you at Gallows Pond," Sebastien said. "So, is all well? You broke your family out of gaol yourself?"

His eyes scanned the crowd and found Beatrice, turning away, her shawl drawn up, ashamed of her dirt and dark bruises. Sebastien dismounted and strode quickly to meet her, calling her name in delight. A bloom rose in Beatrice's cheeks, banishing the tense whiteness of a moment before. Sebastien seized her hand, then said, "Come, let me put you up on my horse. You look worn out! We'll soon have you warm and dry by the fire, eating some good stew."

"Thank you," Beatrice whispered, allowing him to lift her on to the horse's back. In a moment, the others were mounted too, Luka up behind his mother, and Emilia clinging to Tom's waist. The horses strode out smoothly, and Emilia sighed and let herself lay her cheek on Tom's shoulder and relax.

Soon the travellers reached a gate standing askew. The caravan turned through the gate, bouncing wildly on the rutted road. Although rain still fell in grey veils upon the horizons, the clouds had parted over their heads and a broad ray of sunlight broke through to shine upon the meadow. A herd of deer lifted their heads to stare at the caravans. Rollo's ears pricked when he saw a family of rabbits frisking about. Before Emilia could grab him, he was darting first this way, then that way, as the rabbits fled to their burrows.

"He never catches one; I don't know why he tries," Emilia said.

"I wish he would. I'm starving!" Luka said. "Do you realize we've only had a bit of bread since yesterday?"

"Oh, I realize. I was trying not to think about it."

The road curved down into a small wood, where a thin ribbon of smoke curled up from beside a gleam of water. Drawn up around a campfire were the familiar caravans of the Hearne family. Emilia smiled and waved as she recognized face after face. Cosmo and Gypsy Joe, smoking pipes by the fire; Old Janka, scolding the younger girls as they washed their clothes in the pond; Sebastien's mother, Julisa, cooking a mess of eggs and bacon over the fire; Fairnette and Van, jumping up and down in excitement, their huge brother Stevo close by.

Emilia's legs trembled as she slid to the ground. "Everyone's come, everyone," she said wonderingly.

"Though in the end we didn't need any of you!" Luka grinned cheekily. "We rescued our families all by ourselves. Look, here they are!"

"Come and be welcome," Julisa said. "What a night! We thought the end was nigh. Come sit by the fire, warm yourselves."

As the Finch family wearily settled down on the ground, looking about shyly, Julisa came and pinched

Emilia's and Luka's cheeks. "As for you, my weans, look at you! You're skinnier than ever! Fading away to nothing. Come and eat!"

"We can't afford to feed them; Emilia's horse has been eating its head off for weeks." Felipe smiled at them lazily.

"Alida! Where is she?"

"Over there, my wean, fat and well," he answered.

Emilia ran through the crowd, her skirts bunched up in her hands. A loud whinny greeted her as Alida cantered out from under the trees, tail held high. Emilia flung her arms about her mare's neck, then seized a handful of mane and vaulted on to her back. "Come on, Alida, let's run like the wind!"

The grey mare leapt forward. Emilia leant low over her back, hallooing in joy. Round the campfire they raced, leaping over logs and bundles, veering round groups of laughing gypsies, hooves drumming on the ground. The chain about Emilia's wrist caught the sun, flashing golden. She turned Alida's head towards the hill, and they galloped up the sunlit slope. When Alida soared over the crest, Emilia felt as if they could truly fly.

The Last Charm

Norwood, Surrey, England
13 September 1658

The warm rays of the setting sun slanted through the trees, turning the leaves to the colour of old coins. The air had a new bite in it, the whetted edge of a year turning towards its end.

Emilia sat back against her grandmother's knees, enjoying the gentle touch of Baba's gnarled fingers in her hair as she plaited the wild mass of curls into smooth plaits, bound with vivid ribbons.

"So our Beatrice is to be married tonight," Maggie said. "I will miss her pretty face about the place."

"Me too," Emilia said in a constricted voice. She thought she would never get used to the way joy and misery could be twined in the heart, like blond and black hair braided together. "But we'll see them. Maybe now we can travel about again now. We'll go to Kent for the hop harvest and visit Fairnette and Van, and go to the horse fair and see Bea. . ."

"Aye, I think we could do that now Old Ironsides is dead." Maggie spoke about the pipe clamped in the corner of her mouth. "So, you saw true, my little *drabardi*. The Lord Protector died before the week was out, just as you predicted. . ."

"Aye. But nothing else has come true. . ."

"Yet," Maggie said.

Emilia smiled wistfully. "Will I still see true, now that I've given back the charms?"

"It is your eyes that see true, darling girl," Maggie said.

"And will it bring us bad luck, breaking the chain again? I had to do it, Baba. I could not take their lucky charms away."

Maggie looked round the camp, where all their friends and family were laughing and working. A rare smile warmed her lined old face. "It's a chain of blood as well as gold," she said. "And that's been mended now."

"The charms did bring us luck, Baba," Emilia said. "But when I think about that storm I conjured . . . and that lightning bolt. . ." She shuddered.

Maggie went on binding her hair, not replying. Emilia thought about the tempest. It was the worst England had seen in hundreds of years, uprooting ancient oaks, demolishing houses, hurling cows high into the air, flooding rivers and streams.

And three days later the Lord Protector had died, on the seventh anniversary of his greatest victory against the king. The whole land was stricken with superstitious

403

fear. Surely such a storm was a warning from God? Everyone stayed in their houses, their doors locked, in case of riots or uprisings, while in London the chancellors hurriedly crowned Cromwell's third son, Richard, the new Lord Protector, even though he was said to be a mild, nervous man who much preferred pottering in the garden to ordering about armies and parliaments.

Emilia sighed. She knew how he felt. She had no desire to raise hurricanes and cast curses. All she really wanted was to wander through the forest, calling squirrels down to her hand and tiddling a trout out of the stream for their supper.

"I cannot help feeling sorry, about Cromwell, I mean. His family must be so upset, losing him so close after his daughter died, and his grandson too. I didn't like him at all, of course, but it's still sad. . ."

"Aye. Any death diminishes us," Maggie said.

"Everything will change now, won't it?"

Maggie nodded. After a while, she said, "Life is all about change, my darling girl. Seasons come, seasons go; we love, and then we lose. We cannot have one without the other, I'm afraid."

Emilia looked down at the golden coin hanging from her bracelet, thinking about all they had won and lost. Luck, magic, providence, faith – Emilia did not know its true name. She had seen it manifest in the lives of those around her, though, and she had seen what happened when it was lost. She did not want to take their luck away from those she loved. So, one by one, Emilia had given the charms back to those who had trusted her.

Meanwhile, the gypsies and their friends made surreptitious enquiries about Pastor Spurgeon, afraid he would continue to hunt them down. No one knew what had happened to him after the night of the storm.

"He was probably so embarrassed at being found locked up in his own cell that he felt he had to flee the country," Emilia cried.

Beatrice, for once, had no compassion. "Serves him right, the slimy snake," she said.

That had left only Coldham the thief-taker to haunt their nightmares. Yet his fate was the most strange of all. It seemed he had joined a pious group of peace-loving religious dissidents in London called the Society of Friends. Others called them the Quakers, for they were so shaken by their experience with the Inner Light that they often quivered and quaked all over. It seemed Coldham had become an inspiration to those who gathered in their meetings, seeming to be touched by God.

The thought of this filled Emilia with wonder. She rubbed her thumb over the golden coin. *Light, luck and magic. . .*

"Baba, are you sure?" she burst out. "That I can keep your charm, I mean? You really don't want it back?"

Her grandmother shook her head. "It's yours now, Milly," she said. "I think you've earned it, don't you?"

Emilia could only smile joyfully, and give her grandmother a hug and a kiss.

She went on to the campfire, where Beatrice was getting ready for her wedding, attended by the Romni. Old Janka was binding back her long hair with a red scarf, and Julisa was tying up the sash of her long, embroidered skirts. Fairnette sat peeling potatoes nearby, with Noah curled up on a rug beside her, drinking a posset of herbs and honey she had made for him. The little boy was still thin and pale, but he was so happy to be back in the forest, with soft grass beneath his questing feet and Rollo by his side again, that a smile was never far from his face. Gypsy Joe was busy with Father Plummer and Lord Harry, setting up the barrels of wine for the night's festivities, while Mimi was being taught how to stuff cabbage leaves with rice and herbs. Other women were plucking pheasants, skinning rabbits or slicing vegetables. The feast promised to be the best they had ever had!

A whole lamb was roasting over the fire, given to the gypsies by Sir Hugh Whitehorse in gratitude to Luka and Emilia for their help in rescuing the Marquis of Ormonde and saving Tom's life. He had also brought down a sack of potatoes, and a whole barrel of fine wine, which the men had already broached and declared an excellent drop.

Rather to the Finch family's discomfort, Sir Hugh had offered them a rundown cottage in the village to live in, and regular employment on the manor farm. They had not wanted to offend him, when he had always been kind enough to let them camp out in the forest, but

Jacob shook his head, and said, "Thank you kindly, sir, but I think we'll stay where we are."

"But why?" Tom said, obviously disappointed. "Your caravans are so small, so dark. They leak when it rains. You're hungry more often than not. Why would you not take a house when it's offered to you?"

"We're Rom," Luka explained.

"I don't understand it," Tom said.

"I don't understand why you would stay shut up in a stuffy old house when you could be travelling where the wind takes you," Luka flashed back.

"Well, when you put it like that. . ." Tom laughed.

"We're wanderers on this earth. Our hearts are full of wonder, and our souls are deep with dreams," Emilia said softly, translating the words that had been engraved upon her heart since she was a baby.

Tom gazed at her in surprise. She grinned at him. "You wouldn't like it, Tom. Well, not in winter, anyway."

"No, that's for sure," he replied. "Well, Father says to tell you that you and your family are always welcome on our land."

"Could he put it in writing for us?" Luka asked, completely in earnest despite his flashing grin.

"Absolutely," Tom replied solemnly. "And I'll get him to put you in the parish records too. No more getting arrested for vagrancy!"

The sun had set, and a pleasing smell of roast lamb filled the clearing. Once the moon had risen, the wedding would begin. Sebastien and Beatrice would eat bread dribbled with their own blood and swear to live by the three laws of the Rom. Only then would the feasting and music and dancing begin. Emilia could hardly wait.

Lord Harry had brought gifts – a fine silken quilt for the married couple, embroidered in France; and for Luka, a new violin from Italy, sweet and curved and golden.

"Milly told me how you gave away your old one to Joe's nephew, who hadn't spoken a word since his father died," Lord Harry said with his crooked grin. "That was a good thing to do."

Luka, speechless, clutched the violin to him, stroking its svelte shape, then lifted it to his chin, drew the bow over its strings, and began to play. Never had he played so beautifully, a tune that made you want to weep and smile at once. Everyone fell silent, spell-bound. There was only the firelight dancing in the leaves, the moonlight gleaming upon the water, the circle of rapt faces, listening, as the music lilted and swayed and danced. Emilia swallowed a lump in her throat. She thought again of her mother and her father, wishing they could be here to see Beatrice, so beautiful in her happiness. She felt a small hand grope for hers. It was Noah, tears bright in his sightless eyes.

A new music wove its silver cadences into the violin's cavatina, a long fall of warbling notes, then a high whistling crescendo. A nightingale had flown down out of the darkness and was perched on a branch above Luka's head. Small and plain and brown, its throat swelled with the largeness of its song. Luka's eyes were shining, his face full of joy, as he and his violin wrought their own kind of magic.

"When your father, Amberline, played, the birds flew down out of the trees to listen," Maggie said softly.

"I thought that was just a story," Emilia whispered back.

"There is often more truth in stories than you know, darling girl," her grandmother replied.

"I know," Emilia answered, and smiled.

The Facts Behind The Fiction

Most of the places that Luka and Emilia go to on their adventures are real places that you can go to also, if you wish. Similarly, many of the people that they encounter are real people who once lived and breathed and acted out their destinies on the pages of history.

Maggie Finch, the Queen of the Gypsies, was a famous fortune-teller who lived in Norwood, Surrey, which was then partly owned by the Whitehorse family. We know about her because Samuel Pepys wrote about her in his diary, and his wife travelled to see her and have her fortune told. I do not know the names of her children and grandchildren – Emilia and Luka are entirely imaginary, as is the chain of charms.

There were many Romanichal, as the English Gypsies are known, in the seventeenth century. They first arrived in England in the early 1500s, and were at first tolerated, if not exactly welcomed. The first anti-gypsy act in England was passed in 1530 by Henry the Eighth, twenty-five years after their arrival. The act's intention was to rid the country of all gypsies by forcing them to leave, or suffer execution.

England was not alone in passing such laws. In seventeenth-century Denmark, "gypsy hunts" were organized by the king. One hunter listed, amongst the animals he'd shot that year, "a Gypsy woman and a suckling child". Other punishments throughout Europe included flogging, torture, branding, mutilation, hanging and shooting. Under Oliver Cromwell's rule, gypsies suffered greatly. The last known execution of gypsies in England happened during his rule, in Suffolk. Many others were shipped to America to work as slaves.

In the Romany language, the word "Rom" means one of the Traveller folk, and this is the word that most people use today, as "gypsy" is considered an insult. However, in seventeenth-century England, the term "gypsy" was widely used, even by the Rom themselves. They were also called Egyptians (because they were believed to have come from Egypt), "tinkers" or "travellers".

The Rom are a race of nomads. The gypsies of seventeenth-century England travelled about the countryside, carrying their belongings in hand-carts and canvas-covered wagons, and pitching tents wherever they stopped. A few had wooden caravans, though these did not become widespread until the nineteenth century.

For the Rom, travelling is not merely for fun, but is a way of life. Rom who settled down in one place were scorned, and thought to have joined the *gorgios*, which is the Romani term for non-gypsies. They believed this wanderlust was born into them, part of their blood.

In seventeenth-century England, the Rom primarily made their living by hawking (selling small home-made goods) and tinkering (repairing pots and pans). Seasonal work harvesting fruit and vegetables was also an important source of income. Some families were known as animal trainers, especially of bears and horses. Others were known as musicians and entertainers, while others were renowned for their metal-working ability.

However, fortune-telling is the talent for which the Rom are best known. Fortune-telling was exclusively a woman's occupation, and many times kept the family from starving. Called a *drabardi*, a fortune-teller would read tea leaves or tarot cards, look into a crystal ball, and read palms. While there were undoubtedly imposters, most women of the Rom firmly believed in their abilities to see into the future. The Rom are also well-known for their belief in magical talismans or charms. The charms that Emilia and Luka search for are based on ones that were commonly prized by the gypsies.

A Note on Gypsy Names

English gypsies have a double nomenclature, each tribe or family having a public and a private name, one by which they are known to the *gorgios*, and another to themselves alone. Their public names are quite English, and are often chosen in an attempt to translate their private names from Romani.

For example, the gypsy family the Smiths have a private name of *Petulengro*. In Romani, *petali* or *petala* signifies a horseshoe; the affix *engro* is derived from the Sanscrit *kara*, "to make", so that *Petulengro* may be translated as a horseshoe-maker.

Many other gypsy families chose aristocratic names, such as Marshall, for themselves. Gypsy scholars believe that the different tribes may have sought the protection of certain grand, powerful families on their first arrival in England, and were permitted by them to stay in their heaths and woodlands, and so the families adopted the names of their patrons, as a way of explaining where they belonged.

The names of the Rom families in *The Gypsy Crown* are the names of real seventeenth-century gypsy families, all except for the name of the Graylings, which is based on a real family, the Grays. The Finch tribe of Norwood, Surrey were famous for their fortune-telling. The Wood family were wood-carvers and wagon-builders, and are said to have introduced the fiddle into Wales in the late 1600s. The Hearne or Herne family may have chosen their name for its similarity to either "heron" or "hairy" – gypsy scholars are not sure. I, however, was struck by its similarity to Herne the Hunter, and since the Hearne family were famous for their horse-dealings, I like to think that is where they got their name.

There are many more than five gypsy families in England.

Part 1: The Gypsy Crown

Oliver Cromwell was a leading figure in the bitter and bloody wars that tore England apart between 1642 and 1649, resulting in the execution of King Charles I on 30 January 1649. For the next eleven years, a period usually called the Commonwealth, the land was in great turmoil as the leaders of Parliament tried to find an alternative method of government.

In 1655, Cromwell dismissed Parliament and divided England up into eleven areas, which were each governed by a Major-General that Cromwell trusted. The Major-Generals were so strict that they were very unpopular. Fifteen months later, Cromwell was forced to dismiss them. Soon after, Parliament offered Cromwell the chance to be king, but in the end he refused it. So they offered him the same powers, but omitted the word "king". Cromwell accepted their offer, and in 1657, was invested as Lord Protector in Westminster Abbey. He wore purple velvet and ermine, just like a king.

Colonel Pride was one of Cromwell's generals, and best known as the instigator of "Pride's Purge". With his regiment, he took part in the military occupation of London in December 1648, which was the first step towards bringing King Charles I to trial. The next step was the expulsion of the Royalists from the House of Commons. He arrested about a hundred members, leaving the minority of eighty to bring the king to trial. Pride was one of the judges of the king and signed his death-warrant.

He died at Nonsuch Palace, in Surrey, in 1658. After the Restoration of 1660, his body was ordered to be dug up and suspended on the gallows at Tyburn, along with those of Cromwell, and other key instigators of the regicide. Nonsuch was later demolished by one of Charles II's mistresses. Only a few stones remain.

Part 2: The Silver Horse

Horse-racing has occurred on the North Downs for centuries. James I (1566–1625) used to attend races on the Downs near Epsom while staying at the palace at Nonsuch, and both he and his son, Charles I, were very interested in breeding horses for racing. Along with many other popular pastimes, horse-racing was banned during the Commonwealth. Many instances of soldiers being sent out to break up illegal horse-races are recorded.

Edward Hyde, the Earl of Clarendon, wrote in his famous histories that, in 1658, a meeting of Royalists was held at Banstead Downs, as Epsom Downs were then called, under the pretence of a horse-race.

In 1658, one of the king's men, **James Butler, the Marquis of Ormonde,** dyed his famously fair hair black and travelled through England in disguise, trying to raise support for a rebellion to restore Charles II to his throne. It is highly likely that he was present at the secret meeting on Epsom Downs.

Part 3: The Herb of Grace

Rue has long been considered one of the foremost protective herbs, especially against black magic and the evil eye. In southern Europe, faith in the protective qualities of rue is so great that a special charm, the Cimaruta, or "Sprig of Rue", is worn as a pendant or lucky charm. It is sometimes called "the witch's amulet", for it was apparently worn by hereditary witches as an emblem of their power. An old Cimaruta can be seen in the museum of Bologna.

The New Forest has long been considered the haunt of gypsies and witches, including the famous white witch, Sybil Leek, who lived in Burley in the 1950s and claimed to have gained her knowledge and powers from a long line of witches in her family.

Witches in Wiltshire in the seventeenth century were not so lucky. An old woman called Anne Bodenham, who wore a live toad in a green bag about her neck, was condemned and hanged in Salisbury as a witch in 1653. Before she was executed, Anne had the presence of mind to drink a beer, spit on a priest, and wish a pox on her executioner.

There is no evidence that she was a gypsy, but the wearing of a toad in a bag about the neck is indeed a gypsy charm. Toads are key animals in Rom folklore, and many tales are told about them, including one that a tame toad may assist a fortune-teller in her craft.

Part 4: The Lightning Bolt

You can go to Horsmonden, if you want, and have lunch at the Gun Inn and visit the hammer pond where the iron foundry used to be. There's nothing else left of it but stones, just as Emilia predicted. Apart from its guns and hops, Horsmonden is also known for the gypsy horse fair, which has been held there on the second Sunday in September since the twelfth century.

Part 6: The Butterfly in Amber

There was indeed a great hurricane on 30 August 1658, and many writers interpreted it as a harbinger for Cromwell's death. Samuel Butler wrote:

"Tossed in a furious hurricane,
Did Oliver give up his reign."

No one ever wondered aloud what had caused the death of the Lord Protector. Yet at the time Cromwell's sickness caused a great deal of puzzlement, for even though he was known to suffer from English malaria (called "ague" at the time) this was not a fatal illness, and many of his symptoms – especially the agonizing pains and vomiting – were not consistent with ague. Many people were suspicious, and a few suggested that he had been the victim of witchcraft or poison. Certainly it was not the first time Cromwell had faced the danger of assassination. Cromwell's doctor, George Bate, wrote how he "never was at ease" and was "suspicious of all Strangers, especially if they seemed joyful". Cromwell wore armour under his clothes at all times, was accompanied everywhere by bodyguards, and never travelled the same route.

Dr Bate had been King Charles I's physician, and after the death of Oliver Cromwell and the Restoration, became Charles II's doctor too. He was given a large sum of money by the restored king, and his family were rewarded with important jobs. A few years later a friend recorded in his diary that "Dr Bate died in London of the French pox and confessed on his death bed that he poisoned Oliver Cromwell . . . and his majestie was privi to it".

Many people discount this alleged confession as a mere rumour, or perhaps spiteful gossip, but mystery still hangs around Cromwell's death, and over the years many people have come up with different explanations for it, such as kidney failure. The truth is none of us will ever be sure – but I have always found the mysterious death of Oliver Cromwell, and the story of the ignored deathbed confession, intriguing. If Oliver Cromwell was to be assassinated, to clear the way for the return of the king, who better to administer the fatal dose but his own doctor? And certainly any unease over the death of the great dictator would be discouraged by those who benefited most from his death, the king and his exiled court.

After Cromwell's death, his son Richard ruled for a short while, but so badly he was eventually hustled away, giving birth to the expression "Tumbledown Dick".

King Charles II was playing tennis when he heard the news of Cromwell's death. Twenty months later – on 29 May 1660, the day of his thirtieth birthday – he rode back into London through cheering crowds, his throne and his crown restored.

King Charles arrested the men who had put his father on trial and signed his execution order. Many of them died the terrible traitor's death, hanged, drawn and quartered. A few escaped to Europe or to America, and most were then hunted down by vengeful Royalists and murdered. Only a few of the fifty-nine regicides managed to escape.

King Charles II did indeed have the bodies of Cromwell and his right-hand men dug up, hanged in chains at Tyburn Hill, then hacked into quarters. It took the axe-man eight blows to sever Cromwell's mummified head from his body. It was set on a pole upon the roof of the palace at Whitehall, gazing at the spot where King Charles I had been beheaded nine years earlier.

Two years later Cromwell's head mysteriously disappeared. No one quite knows the truth, but one story says it fell off in a storm and then was used as a football by some street urchins. It reappeared some years later as a curiosity in a circus show (but failed to make money) and was eventually sold. In the 1800s, a parson bought Cromwell's head for the princely sum of £200 (just to give you an idea of its value, one could have bought a house for about £50 at that time).

There was some argument that the purchased head could not really be Cromwell's, but it was ruled genuine, as it had a wart above the right eye just as Cromwell did (Cromwell had famously demanded that he be painted "warts and all", unlike most court portraits, which flattered the subject). Some generations later, in the 1930s, the descendant of the pastor who had bought the head allowed extensive scientific examination of it, which confirmed it was indeed the mummified head of Oliver Cromwell. It was subsequently given to Sidney Sussex College, Cambridge, where it was buried in a secret location on 25 March 1960 – almost exactly three hundred years after the Lord Protector was first dug up.

Q&A With Kate Forsyth

What was your favourite book when you were a child?
The first book I ever read all by myself was *The Lion, the Witch and The Wardrobe* by C. S. Lewis, when I was five. It's always had a magical aura for me as a result. I also loved *The Hobbit* by J. R. R. Tolkien, *The Glass Slipper* by Eleanor Farjeon, *The Little White Horse* by Elizabeth Goudge, *The Wolves of Willoughby Chase* by Joan Aiken and any of the *Famous Five* books by Enid Blyton. As I got older, my favourite writers were Susan Cooper, Lloyd Alexander, Ursula le Guin and Diana Wynne Jones. I also liked mystery stories, like the Nancy Drew books.

If you could be any character from a book, who would you be and why?
I'd like to be any of the heroines in my books, because they all get to do the things I've always wanted to do – talk to animals, change shape into birds and lions and dragons, have amazing adventures. . .

Can you tell us a secret about yourself? Something that readers might be surprised to learn?

I spent most of my childhood daydreaming, much to the despair of my parents and teachers, and when I wasn't daydreaming I was reading books. I used to have to hide books all round the house because I was meant to be doing my homework or my chores or outside playing in the fresh air. My mother's way of punishing me was not to say, "Go to your room!" because she knew I'd just curl up with a book, so she used to say, "Kate, you've been very naughty. Go outside and play!"

Lots of readers love writing and aspire to be authors when they're older. Please could you suggest a first line (or a title) for them to turn into a story?

"I know most people think it's very strange to have a ghost as a best friend. . ."

What inspired you to become a writer?

I've always wanted to be a writer. I think I was born knowing what I was destined to be. All through my childhood I wrote novels and poems and stories, and as I grew into an adult I began to get them published. I feel very lucky that I can spend my days making up stories and be paid for it!

If you weren't a writer, what job would you like to have?

I can't imagine a life where I wasn't writing, but it would have to be something to do with books.

Who is your favourite character in *The Gypsy Crown*?

Well, I love cheeky Luka and tender-hearted Emilia, of course, but after that I think I love Sweetheart the dancing bear the most.

What inspired you to write *The Gypsy Crown*?

When I was a little girl, my mother inherited a very old and valuable charm bracelet that had been handed down for generations. My great-aunt had always worn it, and used to tell me the stories behind the charms. The very first charm on the bracelet had been picked up off the shore of the River Thames by my great-great-great-great-great-grandmother the night before she left England for ever to travel to Australia, which was then a newly discovered country filled with dangers. I loved the idea of a charm bracelet with a story – an adventure – behind it, and always thought it was a good idea for a novel. I have lots of ideas for novels – I keep a big, fat notebook full of them – but usually I find you need three really good ideas before it actually triggers a novel. So the idea of the charm bracelet was transferred from notebook to notebook for quite a few years, until suddenly I got my next idea.

It was all because of my niece Emily. I was writing a series of Magical Misadventures for younger readers, and I asked her, "What are the five things you most like in a book?' She answered, "Princesses, fairies, mermaids, ponies and tropical islands." I was a little disappointed, because it seemed to me that there were a thousand books for kids about princesses, fairies, mermaids, etc. I wanted to do something that no one had ever done before. So I wondered to myself, what did I love reading about or playing when I was a kid that no one seems to have done to death? And at once, I thought, "Gypsies!"

I had been fascinated by the Rom ever since I was a kid, probably because my father was an adventurer who went off travelling all the time (usually in a boat, not a caravan). I had collected books on them for years, with fascinating titles like *Gypsy Magic and Witchcraft* and *Secrets of Gypsy Fortune-Telling*. And I knew from my reading that no one had ever written a children's book where the Rom were the heroes. So at once I was tremendously excited. I knew I could write the sort of book I most loved, one full of mystery and adventure and magic. I sat down that very minute, and begin to pour out ideas for the book. I knew at once that this was the idea that my charm bracelet story had been waiting for, and I just needed to think of the where and the when and the how. By the end of the day I had most of the book mapped out in my brain and I began writing it the very next day!

Have you ever visited any of the places in the book?
I have indeed. Some of my ancestors came from Kent, and my great-great-great-great-great-grandmother, who collected the first charm on the bracelet, actually lived in Richmond. So I had travelled to the UK when I was a young woman, and went to see where my ancestors had lived and where so many of my favourite books had been set. Then I had to do a lot of research while I was writing *The Gypsy Crown* to make sure I got everything right. I packed up my three children, who were then aged two, five and a half, and seven, and we travelled all the way to the UK so we could travel in the footsteps of my gypsy children. I had already worked out their route, and had written a rough draft of most of their adventures, and so I was able to go exactly where they would have gone, see what they would have seen, and smell the air they would have breathed.

What are you working on next?
I am now writing a novel about a girl who discovers that her family was cursed many hundreds of years earlier, and decides that she must break the curse. To do this, she and her friends need to go back in time to find the four loops of a puzzle ring, which was broken during the turbulent reign of the tragic Mary, Queen of Scots. . .

Would you like to live in the time of Cromwell?

I am so glad I don't live in the time of Oliver Cromwell! It was a very dark and dangerous time. Punishments were very cruel, and rules very strict. No dancing or feasting were allowed (two things I love to do!), you could be accused of treason simply for raising a glass to absent friends, and no one was allowed to think or believe or wonder anything new or different.

How did you find out what life was like for the Finch family?

You can find out anything you want to know in books! Luckily I love to research, and so would spend hours curled up happily reading books with titles like *The History of Torture*, *The Tudor Housewife*, *Fireside Tales of the Traveller Children* and *Reformation and Revolution*. Then, of course, there is the Internet. What a marvellous, wondrous, endlessly fascinating tool! It's incredible the things I was able to find out. I was even able to see what hillsides and river-banks on the other side of the world look like, using satellite technology, and I could search the court records of the Old Bailey and find out about trials of people who died three hundred years ago. What a gift to a writer!

Are any of the characters based on real people?

Usually I answer "no" to this question, as my characters are born from my imagination. But in *The Gypsy Crown*, I based the character of Luka – cheeky, talkative, always on the move – on my son Ben and the character of Emilia – gentle and warm-hearted – on my niece Emily. Ben and Emily were born only three weeks apart and are best friends, just like Luka and Emilia; Ben loves music, just like Luka, and Emily loves to dance and has always wanted her own pony, just like Emilia.

Quick Quiz

Dogs or cats? Both! I have a slim, elegant black cat called Shadow who is mute. She slinks around the house, never making a sound, so that you are never quite sure where she is. I rescued her from an amazing run-down old house like a castle when she was only a kitten. I also have a very large, boisterous Rhodesian ridgeback, red as desert sand, who races round the house knocking over ornaments with her tail, chewing up the kids' toys and imprinting muddy paw prints on the couch. She is the granddaughter of the dog my father had when I was a kid. I love them both!

Chocolate or sweets? Chocolates.

Pizza or burger? Lobster with caviar and champagne!

Favourite websites? Anything to do with books.

Text or call? A lot of calling, a little texting.

Favourite lesson at school? Creative writing.

Worst lesson at school? Maths.

Favourite colour? Blue.

Favourite film? I can't possibly choose. I love going to the movies!

City or country? My perfect life would be a big country house with a big garden by the sea, with a city apartment within walking distance of the theatres and shops. I'd spend most of my time in the country house, and go to the city regularly to see plays and music and the ballet, and have lunch with my friends, and go shopping. Perfect!